ALSO BY PETER BLAUNER

Slow Motion Riot

Casino Moon

THE
INTRUDER

A NOVEL

PETER
BLAUNER

Simon & Schuster

New York   London   Toronto   Sydney   Tokyo   Singapore

SIMON & SCHUSTER
Rockefeller Center
1230 Avenue of the Americas
New York, NY 10020

SIMON & SCHUSTER and colophon are registered trademarks
of Simon & Schuster Inc.

Manufactured in the United States of America

1   3   5   7   9   10   8   6   4   2

Library of Congress Cataloging-in-Publication Data
Blauner, Peter.
The intruder : a novel / Peter Blauner.
p. cm.
1. Homeless persons—New York (N.Y.)—Fiction.
2. Lawyers—New York (N.Y.)—Fiction.
3. Family—New York (N.Y.)—Fiction.
I. Title.   PS3552.L3936I57   1996
813'.54—dc20   96-759   CIP
ISBN 1-416-59357-8   ISBN 978-1-416-59357-7

I would like to give special thanks to Larry Schoenbach, Lee Stringer, and Myrna Rasmussen for their time, their patience and their insights. Any mistakes that remain in the book are there despite their best efforts.

I would also like to thank David Singleton, Terry Williams, Kathy Grunes, Sam Bender, Mark Stamey, Janet Allon, George McDonald, Michael Hinton, Michael Daly, Melissa Farley, Marcus Devilla, Lt. Wayne Costello, Howard Taylor, Ellis Henican, Ellen Bender, Kevin McGowan, Catherine Woodard, Harriet Karr-McDonald, La Rose Paris, Ivan Gallego, Judy Clain, Rose Marie Berger, Marty Markowitz, Peter Guber, Terri Seligman, Adrienne Halpern, Joanne Gruber, Todd Black, Adam Platnick, Sam Szurek, Arthur Levitt, Denis Woychuk, Ray Davies, Michael Siegel, Arthur Umar, Richard Pine, Arthur Pine, Lori Andiman, Sarah Piel, Casandra M. Jones, Dominick Anfuso, Chuck Antony, James B. Harris, and Spider.

To my family

Peggy, Mac, Mose, Sheila, Steven, and Andrew

LAWYER ARRESTED

OCTOBER 14   A prominent Manhattan lawyer was arrested yesterday and charged with killing a homeless man on the Upper West Side. Jacob Schiff, 44, a white-collar criminal defense specialist with the firm of Bracken, Williams & Sayon, is accused in the beating death of a vagrant who had allegedly been harassing his family. In state Supreme Court, Mr. Schiff, who was charged with second-degree murder, entered a plea of not guilty. He was released on bail after he put up his $1,000,000 town house as collateral.

A spokesman for the Manhattan district attorney would not rule out the possibility that prosecutors would seek the death penalty.

Mr. Schiff could not be reached for comment.

SPRING

1

At first, there's only darkness. Then a slight stirring breeze and a dot of light from somewhere deep in the tunnel. The dot turns into a beam and the beam widens as the train approaches the station. The man in the Yankees cap and the MTA jacket stands near the edge of the platform, watching, considering. The growing metallic roar almost matches the scream in his head. The light washes over the tiled walls and focuses into a pair of headlights aimed up the tracks. The train will arrive in fifteen seconds. In five seconds, it will be too late for the driver to throw the emergency brake. The man in the Yankees cap moves closer to the edge, waiting for the sound to catch up to the light. Trying to decide if the right moment is coming.

In the Dispatch Office of the 241st Street station in the Bronx, the red light has stopped moving across the black model board. Somewhere between East Tremont Avenue and 174th Street, a train has stalled.

A husky supervisor named Mel Green puts a soft thick finger up to the red light and shakes his head. "I bet it's another flat-liner," he says.

"A flat-liner?" A bald-headed conductor from Trinidad named Ernest Bayard looks up from his poppy-seed bagel and his Shoppe-at-Home catalogue.

"You know, a twelve-nine, man under, one of them guys jumps in front of a moving train," says Mel, who has a squared-off haircut and wears a purple T-shirt that says IMPROVE YOUR IMAGE— BE SEEN WITH ME. "We been having a lot of those lately."

"Why's that?"

"I don't know. Don't they say April is the cruel month?"

Ernest shrugs and goes back to looking at the hibachi ads in the catalogue. A number 3 train passes like an apartment house sliding by sideways. New York faces in a blur. The dingy beige room rumbles. Two conductors play chess under a clock that says it's five after eight in the morning.

"Ray Burnham was telling me a story the other day," says Mel, adjusting the brown Everlast weight belt around his middle. "Big fat guy was sitting on the tracks at the Union Square station. Four train passes over him. Transit cop comes down and says, 'How you doing?' Guy looks up, says, 'Tell you the truth, I'm kinda nervous. It's only the third or fourth time I've done this.' "

"Man, that's a lotta bullshit, that's what that is." Ernest laughs and flips to the patio furniture ads as John Gates walks in, wearing his Yankees cap and MTA jacket.

The dust particles in the air suddenly seem to move a little faster and the scrambled eggs in the office microwave glow a little brighter. Another departing train shakes the room.

"Hey, John G.!" says Ernest. "No way nohow you sit in front of a four train and live, right?"

John G. stares at him blankly and says nothing. His left eye twitches.

"Well maybe he was lying down," Mel Green mutters.

"All I know is if I had one of those, I'd just pull the brake and close my eyes." Ernest turns halfway around in his seat and puts his hands in front of his face. "I don't need to see that shit in my dreams."

"Yo, Johnny, you all right?" Mel watches him.

John G. has raccoon circles around his eyes and a chin dusky with three days' beard. He's a pale skinny Irish guy in his mid-thirties with a gauntly handsome face and discreet tattoos on both arms. In another era, he might have been said to have the look of a merchant seaman. Now he just seems like someone who's spent too many nights hanging out on street corners.

"Yeah, I'm all right," he says.

Everyone's noticed him acting a little buggy lately. Staring into space, mumbling to himself in the motorman's cabin. There've even been some nervous jokes about him maybe going postal: showing up for duty with a Tec-9 machine gun. But no one wants to say anything to headquarters on Jay Street just yet. John G.'s always been a solid dude; he's made employee of the month three times in the last five years. Besides, the man's been broken. Give him some space.

"You sure you all don't want Ray Burnham to take the shift for you?" Mel asks. "You worked Kwanza for him, right?"

"Nah, it's okay . . ." John G. stares at the general orders on the bulletin board like a man in a trance.

"Hey, John, you had two, didn't you?" Ernest the conductor looks over his shoulder.

"Two what?" John G.'s mouth goes slack. He still hasn't taken off his hat or his jacket.

"Two twelve-nines. You know. Track pizzas." Mel's throwing him a lifeline, trying to drag him into the conversation. "Guys you ran over."

The clock on the wall makes a loud clicking sound. The two conductors stop playing chess and look over.

"Yeah, I think I had two." John G. swats absently at a stream of dust passing under a desk lamp. "I don't really remember . . ."

Another train goes by.

"One was, like, three years ago," says Mel, trying to be helpful, "and the other was . . ." His hand hangs in the air, waiting for his mouth to complete the thought.

An awkward silence fills the room as it dawns on everyone that this may not be a fit topic for discussion.

"And the other was just before the thing with your little girl," Mel says quickly, trying to finish the thought and move on to something else.

John G. stares at him for a long time without speaking. His eyes are like lightbulbs with the filaments burned out.

"I didn't go looking for them, Mel," he says quietly. "They jumped in front of my train."

"Hey." Mel throws up his hands. "No one said it was your fault, G."

John G. carries his radio along the outdoor platform, heading for his train. The sky opens up above him like God's eyelid. Everything is strange now. The world is different, but all the people keep going on as if nothing has changed. The maintenance workers in orange-and-yellow vests clean out the garbage bins. A man with his body cut in half pulls himself along on a dolly with wheels. A young black guy in a business suit gets on board with a briefcase and a copy of the *Haiti Observateur*. Two pale white guys wearing Sikh turbans follow him. John G. is having trouble putting it all together in his mind. Less than a half hour ago, he was ready to jump in front of a train himself. But something inside him won't let him cross that threshold just yet.

By eight-fifteen, he's in the motorman's cabin, a space as dank and narrow as an old phone booth. He takes out the picture of his wife and daughter that he carries in his wallet and sets it on the ledge in front of him. Ernest, the conductor, gives the all-clear signal; he's about to close the doors. John G. pushes down on the metal handle, letting air into the brakes, and the train lurches forward, beginning the long trip through the heart of the city.

There's relief in the ritual and routine. Seeing the same faces, making the same stops. He's getting through life minute by minute these days—scrounging for reasons to keep going.

Most of the ride through the Bronx is aboveground, taking him over the rough topography of his childhood. Tar roofs. Wide streets. Spanish churches, gas stations, and lots filled with garbage and old tires. Some days it's like a roller-coaster ride. The rise up to Gun Hill Road, the steep drop before Pelham Parkway, the wild curve into Bronx Park East.

But just before the Third Avenue–149th Street station, the train suddenly plunges down and darkness swallows it like a mouth. He's in the long tunnel. Cheap fun-house lights flash by on the left. A baby cries in the car behind him. Though he's been making this trip every weekday for two years, that fast descent always fills him with dread.

As he snakes past Grand Concourse and then 135th Street, his worst impulses begin to crowd him. Go ahead, the voice in his head says. Hop off at 125th Street. Go smoke some crack on Lenox Avenue. Let the passengers fend for themselves. This train is out of service.

But it's not so easy to quit. As he pulls up to the next platform, he sees a tall, exhausted-looking Hispanic woman, done up in a red-and-white striped dress and lacquered hair, cradling a sickly child in her arms. A working mother bringing her daughter to the doctor or day care. Maybe a secretary on Wall Street or a receptionist.

He pictures her in a cramped Morningside Heights apartment, trying to put her makeup on with the baby screaming in the next room. Botanica candles on the windowsill, slipcovers on the couch, framed baby pictures on the bedroom dresser. The bathroom so clean and white you could go blind turning on the light in the middle of the night. If she's got a husband, he's probably off doing the early shift at the garage or the loading dock, with the pork sandwich she made for him in his lunch box. Not rich people, but not poor either. Just clinging to one another and dragging themselves into the future. And a life he should have had.

Grinding the train to a halt, John G. feels obliged to get her wherever she wants to go.

Pressure, pressure. Stay on schedule. His eyes are tired and his head is starting to ache. Just outside the Times Square station, he gets a red signal and a call from the master control tower. "You got a twelve-seven. You're being held because of a sick passenger in the train up ahead."

"How long's it going to be?"

"When we hear, you'll hear."

It's as useless talking to supervisors as trying to probe the mind of God.

God. For some reason, he finds himself thinking a lot about God this morning. Why does God do things? Why does God make trains stop? Why does God take the life of a child?

There's an angry pounding on the door of his cabin.

"Come on, boy! Give us some speed!"

He tries to radio back to the control tower, but all he gets is a blizzard of voices and static. No answers.

There's too little air in the cabin. He throws open the door, just so he can breathe. A car full of riders stares back at him. Men in dark suits. Women in running shoes and silk blouses. Young people on their way in the world, determining the value of the dollar, the price of doing business, the cost of living.

"Why is it like this every goddamn morning?" says one of them, a weak-chinned white guy in tortoise-shell rimmed glasses and a khaki poplin suit. He stands under the ad for Dr. Tusch, hemorrhoid M.D.

What does it say in the procedure book? John G. tries to remember. BE CAREFUL NOT TO IGNORE YOUR PASSENGERS. WHEN YOU IGNORE THEM, EVEN FOR A LITTLE WHILE, THEY THINK THAT YOU HAVE FORGOTTEN THEM. AND IF THEY THINK THAT YOU HAVE FORGOTTEN THEM, THAT IS WHEN THEY ARE GOING TO CAUSE YOU AND THE SYSTEM A PROBLEM.

"I'm sorry, sir," says John G. "It's beyond my control."

The weak-chinned guy turns to a friend of his, a young man with a face as pink and round as a baby's bottom. "See? They only get idiots to do these jobs."

John G. stands there with his eyelids throbbing. Should he take a swing at the guy? After all, he's got nothing left to lose. On the other hand, this job is the only thing between him and the abyss. Everything else that marked his place in the world is gone.

He struggles to decide for a few seconds and then goes back to the motorman's cabin.

Beyond my control. He looks at the picture of his family on the cabin ledge.

By the time he gets the train rolling again, it's seven minutes behind schedule. More pressure. His head feels as if it's filling up with helium. Pillars flash by like tiger stripes before his eyes. He forgets where he is for a few seconds and when he comes to again, the tracks are curving and Ernest, the conductor, is announcing the next stop is Fourteenth Street. John doesn't remember Thirty-fourth.

He looks down and sees the speedometer reading fifty-three, fifty-four, fifty-five. Brake shoes scream on rusty corroded tracks. The car rocks dangerously from side to side. Ghost stations, local stops, graffiti swirls, work crews. They all go rocketing by. His eyes barely have time to register them. There's too much going on. Some 120 yards outside the Fourteenth Street station, he sees the yellow signal. Then the green over yellow indicating the tracks are about to switch the train over to the local side. But something's wrong.

There's someone on the tracks beyond the switch.

He blows his horn but the figure doesn't move. A man waving his arms. Beckoning. Come on. Do it. Run me over. One part of John G.'s brain is denying it, telling him this isn't happening. He blinks and the man is gone. But when he blinks again, the man is back, waving him on with both arms. Blood rushes out of John G.'s heart and runs straight into his head. Stop. You're about to do it again.

The train comes hammering around the bend at sixty miles an hour, spraying the air with steel dust. There's no time to decide which of the visions is real: the beckoning man on the local tracks or the empty space. He just has to act. His eyes jiggle in his skull. Instead of slowing down to wait for the switch, he keeps going at maximum power onto the express side.

But then the darkness breaks and he sees he's made a terrible mistake. Another train is sitting directly in front of him at the station. The white-on-red number 3 on the last car grows like a bloodshot eye. He reaches for the emergency brake but it's too late. He's going to crash. A screech like a buzz saw cuts through his ears. Lights go out in the car behind him. Bodies whiplash against the sides. Voices cry out. In the nearing distance, he sees people backing away from the edge of the platform.

They're thinking subway crash. They're thinking bits of twisted metal, torn concrete, and body parts found among the debris. They're thinking last moments before life slips away amid terror and confusion.

But at the last possible second, he throws the brake and the mechanical track arm hits the trip cock on the undercarriage. Instead of stopping short, the train slows and bumps hard against the back of the number 3.

There's a jolt and the whole train shudders. John G. looks up and sees a shrunken old Asian woman staring at him from the back window of the 3 train. She looks less scared than sad, as if she somehow understands what's driven him to this point. The radio bleats.

"What the fuck happened there?!" asks the voice from the master control tower.

"There was someone down on the tracks," he says.

There's a pause and then static. In the car behind him, he hears people straightening themselves up and weeping in relief, trying to adjust to life at an angle. The voice on the radio comes back again.

"Eight-one-five, there's no report of anyone on the tracks," it says. "You been seeing things?"

John G. says nothing. He tries to picture the figure he saw on the local side, but there's no afterimage in his mind. Only black space. He knows now he can no longer control himself.

"Eight-one-five, you just missed killing about two thousand people," says the voice on the radio. "I hope you're happy."

He stumbles numb out of the cabin and looks around. The scene in the car is a low-budget disaster movie. No one looks seriously hurt, but some people are still on the floor crying. Others are trying to clamber back into their seats with bloody noses and disheveled clothes. The guy with the weak chin stands by the door with his glasses knocked sideways, ready to get off and go about his business. John G. stares hard at him and then ducks back into the cabin. He finds the picture of his wife and daughter on the floor. He puts it back in his wallet and walks the length of the train back to where the Hispanic lady in the striped dress is sitting with her daughter. They're cowering in the last car under an ad for Audrey Cohen College. It says: *It's never too late to become what you might have been.*

He kneels before them and looks into the child's eyes. "I'm sorry," he says.

The woman cannot speak. The child tries to bury her head under her mother's arm. John G. rises and opens the back door. And without another word, he drops down onto the tracks and disappears into the darkness beyond.

2

You're losing them, Jake thinks. Absolutely losing them. Especially the lady in the front row of the jury box. With the frizzy blond hair, the Chanel scarf, and the Upper East Side address. Barbara something. She doesn't want to hear some fat probation supervisor explain the reporting system. That's not how you're going to win her over, Jake tells himself. She wants that human touch. She wants drama. She wants someone she can root for. You're thinking *Court TV.* She's thinking *L.A. Law* and *As The World Turns.*

So Jacob Schiff for the defense plants his feet by the balustrade on the left side of the courtroom and tries to find a way to psych himself back into this trial.

The witness, a coagulated puddle of a man named Jack Pirone, has just blown a hole through the middle of Jake's case.

"So according to your records, Mr. Pirone, my client showed up for his appointment as scheduled, December thirteenth. Is that correct?"

"I have the date right here," says Pirone, chewing hard even though he doesn't appear to have anything in his mouth.

There goes the alibi, thinks Jake. He'd just put a girl named Shante on the stand to say she was with his client that day in Virginia; therefore Hakeem Turner, potential NBA rookie of the year, could not have been the one firing the shots from a red

Jeep Wagoneer that killed a young drug dealer on East 129th Street.

"A moment, please, Judge."

Jake circles back to counsel's table, looking for something.

"He lying," mutters Hakeem, who somehow looks even larger and more threatening in a green Italian suit than he does in shorts on a basketball court. "He's a lying motherfucker. Kill 'im. Tear his heart out."

Jake puts a hand on Hakeem's thick shoulder. Cool it. Something hard moves under his palm. Jake picks up the yellow legal pad covered in red scrawl about Pirone's grand jury testimony.

"Rip his throat out," Hakeem murmurs.

Jake tries to smile reassuringly as he returns to the podium. Remember: chin down, mouth relaxed. When you smile, you're a handsome dog, his wife tells him. When you frown, you look like a pit bull.

"Now, Mr. Pirone," he says, setting his feet as if he's about to try a three-point shot himself. "It's true, is it not, that as a supervisor you don't actually see the clients who come into your office, do you?"

Pirone, who must weigh at least 280 pounds, shifts the fedora and files on his lap. "I know what's going on in my own office, Counselor," he says. "I been with this agency almost twenty years."

"Well, then you're aware that my client had a special exemption allowing him to go out of town. Like on days when his team was playing in other states. Right?"

"Yeah, but this wasn't one of those days." Pirone's jaw keeps working. "Not according to my records."

"And your records are always correct. Is that right?"

"Far as I know." The left side of Pirone's mouth turns up.

This is a crucial moment in the case. So far the state is way ahead on points. The prosecutors have been able to establish that Hakeem not only knew the victim, a nasty punk named Soledad Nelson, but also had a reason to want to kill him, since Soledad allegedly threw Hakeem's cousin Ruthie out a window when she told him she was pregnant, causing her subsequent death at Columbia-Presbyterian Hospital.

Now, with Pirone on the stand rebutting Jake's witness, the prosecutors are inches away from proving that Hakeem had ample opportunity since he was in the city that day. This is Jake's last chance to introduce an element of doubt and save his alibi defense.

"So you trust your officers to always tell you the truth about report days, right?" Jake says. "You never think anybody would take part of an afternoon to go to the bank or go to the doctor and say they were there anyway?"

"Never happens." Pirone shakes his jowly head. "It's all on computers now."

"And the computers are infallible, right?"

"Just like the pope, Counselor. They don't make mistakes."

Jake glances over at Barbara again, in the first row of the jury box. She's not going to be a problem. The problem is the guy next to her. The ex-marine in the electrician's union. Jimmy Sullivan. With the red face and buzz-cut white hair. He was brought up to follow orders. If the state says this kid is guilty, lock 'im up and melt the key.

"Another moment, Your Honor."

Jake goes back to the defense table and picks up his own Day-Timer appointment book. Then he double-checks the computer printout with the probation schedules. Hakeem looks up, puzzled.

"Now, Mr. Pirone," Jake says, on returning to the podium. "I notice my client's previous appointment with one of your officers was on November twenty-ninth. Is that right?"

"That's what it says here. So it must be."

Jake looks down at the appointment book. "Are you aware the twenty-ninth was a Saturday?"

Pirone's piggy little eyes widen. He never saw the shot coming. A minor silence settles over the courtroom. And Barbara in the first row of the jury box is leaning forward, as if he's finally got her attention.

"Objection."

Francis X. O'Connell, the bright young guy from the DA's office, is on his feet. Francis with his ruddy cheeks and his blue rep tie. He looks about twelve with his Beatlemania haircut. Yeah, yeah, yeah. But make no mistake, Francis is a comer. Especially in this case, where the judge, Jeffrey Steinman, was his law professor at Fordham.

"Your Honor," says Francis. "Mr. Schiff is clearly going beyond the scope of this case with his questions. In pretrial conferences, we agreed to stay within a specific time frame. Now he's trying to take us on a fishing expedition so we'll lose sight of the issues."

Steinman waves with his two short flipperlike arms for both sides to join him at the bench. Jabba the judge.

"What about it, Counselor?" he asks Jake. "You driving somewhere or just taking us for a ride?"

"The witness opened up the whole can of worms. He's the one who said they never make a mistake with their schedules."

"Is it important?" From the saturnine look on his face, the judge is clearly hoping the answer will be no.

"Your Honor, my client is twenty-two years old and he's looking at twenty-five to life here." Jake puts his hands in the pockets of his brown Hugo Boss suit jacket. "Everything is important."

"I'll give you just a little bit of rhythm here," says Steinman. "But don't make me regret it."

Jake goes back to the podium and catches Hakeem's eye. Twenty-two years old. He thinks about that for a second and in his mind's eye, Hakeem metamorphoses into his own son, Alex, who's just six years younger. Alex, the shining star on his horizon, the repository for his hopes and dreams. His heart. He imagines his son talking to him through a smudged pane of Plexiglas in a Rikers Island visiting room, while various motherfuckers, child molesters, and machete murderers await him on the other side. So there's inspiration. Jake decides he will go down in flames if he has to during this cross-examination, and he will take Pirone with him.

"Now Mr. Pirone, we've established that Saturday the twenty-ninth appears in my client's record as a date when he was at your office. Can you tell us why that is?"

"Our office is often open on Saturdays," says Pirone, who's used the time to collect his thoughts.

"I see. And you're telling me that you'd use that time to see clients, instead of taking care of paperwork that's built up?"

Pirone blinks twice. "We would sometimes."

Now Jake is sure he's lying. But how to get at him? Jimmy Sullivan, the ex-marine, is sitting with his arms folded across his chest in the jury box: Prove it, he seems to be saying. Jake flashes on being back in the courtyard outside John Dewey High School in Bensonhurst. Buddy Borsalino bouncing his head off the asphalt. A group of kids jeering at him. How's he going to get up?

He flips back a few pages in the Day-Timer, looking for something. Jurors stir impatiently. Any more delays and they'll start to blame him and take it out on his client. But then Jake turns back one page and finds what he needs. It's like looking up at Buddy Borsalino and seeing just enough daylight between them to get a good punch in.

"Mr. Pirone," he says, gripping the podium with both hands. "I'd like to direct your attention to my client's previous appointment."

"The twenty-ninth?"

"No, the one before that."

"Okay."

"I see the date listed is November eleventh. Is that correct?"

"If I say it then it's so, Counselor." Pirone tries to cross his right leg over his left knee, but he can't quite get it over the railing.

The judge raises his eyes slowly, fed up and about to cut Jake off. Even Hakeem at the defense table seems restless with this line of questioning.

Jake closes the appointment book and fixes Pirone with a level stare. "Did you know, Mr. Pirone, that November eleventh was Veterans' Day?"

Pirone says nothing. But a small gagging sound escapes from his throat and his eyes move from side to side.

"So do you mean to tell me, sir, that your office was open on Veterans' Day?" Jake continues.

Now Sullivan, the ex-marine in the jury box, is looking at the witness with his arms folded across his chest. Obviously not appreciating civilian personnel who don't know when his holiday is. Things are turning around.

"Maybe a mistake was made," says Pirone, struggling to recover. "It's the computers. They make errors."

"I suppose that's true." Jake unbuttons his jacket, signaling to the jury that he's ready to relax and start enjoying himself. "Especially since you also have my client stopping by to drop off papers on Lincoln's Birthday."

He slams the Day-Timer down on the defense table for emphasis. Hakeem is smiling. Barbara is crossing her black-stockinged legs and rubbing her lips, as if she's suddenly finding all of this very stimulating. Even the court officers are nodding with mulish glee.

"Objection." Francis rises automatically, like a man at the end of a seesaw. But his heart isn't in it. "I don't see what relevance any of this has."

The judge calls him up to the bench with Jake.

"The relevance is he just took a sledgehammer to your witness," he says with a special hint of admonishment a once proud teacher reserves for a student who's disappointed him. "I'd say Mr. Schiff's alibi witness just started looking a lot better."

It's one of those subtle but unmistakable junctures when the momentum of a trial shifts. Defense counsel suddenly seems much more witty and interesting to the jurors. The defendant younger and more sympathetic. And everything the prosecutor says is subject to a new cold scrutiny. In some unconscious way, the case has already been decided.

Jake returns to the podium, feeling very much in his element. He's hitting his stride now, like an athlete in his prime. Botta boom, botta bing. Here's a guy who knows his way around the courtroom.

"So, Mr. Pirone," he says, turning back for the coup de grâce. "Is there any reason to believe these records of yours are accurate?"

"They usually are." Pirone chews his lower lip as if he'd love to get Jake alone in the John Dewey schoolyard with a crowbar.

"Thank you. That will be all."

The judge calls a recess for lunch and as Jake returns to the defense table, Hakeem rises to his full seven feet and gets ready to chest-butt him as if Jake just executed a triple-reverse chocolate thunder slam dunk. Jake touches his arm and accepts a handshake instead.

"Good going, Counselor," murmurs Francis, the prosecutor, as they walk out into the hall together. "Next time tell your client not to do it."

"He didn't do it, Francis."

"Norman's not gonna be happy if we lose this one."

The district attorney, Norman McCarthy, has despised Jake for years without being able to pin so much as an unpaid parking ticket on him.

"Norman's never happy." Jake starts to head into the bathroom, leaving Francis at the elevators. "At his age, I'd suggest Metamucil and tango lessons."

"I don't know, Jake. He hates losing these high-profile cases."

"I care," says Jake. "But not that much."

Francis glances back at the half dozen reporters staggering out of the courtroom, scribbling frantically in their notebooks. "Listen, you make him look like an asshole for bringing this to trial, he's going to make somebody pay," he says quietly.

"Ah, he'll get over it." Jake shrugs it off and pushes the bathroom door open. "You get over almost everything."

SUMMER

3

I lost my way. I lost my way. I was in a dark wood and I lost my way.

The words keep repeating themselves in John G.'s mind as he pushes a baby stroller full of soda cans across the Sheep Meadow in Central Park. The stars and clouds look like dots and splatters of white paint thrown carelessly against the dark sky. The apartment houses and skyscrapers along Central Park South and Fifth Avenue rise up in the mist.

These last three months have been a long, inexorable slide. He's still not exactly sure how he became homeless. He just knows it happened a step at a time. Everything only makes sense in light of what came just before it.

The job went first. Right after the near collision, there were ten days of administrative hearings, overnight psychiatric evaluations, and drug tests before the MTA finally got around to firing him.

He was divided by the news. A side of him was angry and defiant, not ready to give up. But another part was secretly grateful and relieved.

The next morning, he sat on his bed with the shades drawn and the day stretching out before him like a long road without signposts.

What was he going to do with the rest of his life? Everything looked the same. His wife's makeup compact was still in the bathroom medicine cabinet; her herbal teas were still in the kitchen cupboard. But he felt utterly alone and confused. Cookie Monster lay on the blue carpet in the middle of his daughter's empty room, like he'd been cast adrift on a cold sea. The Little Mermaid toys and the wooden railroad tracks John bought for her were heaped in a corner.

When he closed his eyes, he pictured her waving to him from across the street. The light turns red.

I lost my way. I've lost my way. I was in a dark wood and I lost my way.

He should have gone downtown and applied for unemployment right then. But he wasn't ready to face the long lines and the questions about failing his drug test.

Instead, he turned on the television and watched *Regis and Kathie Lee* awhile. He had to get on top of his situation. Find a way to deal with the stress.

He still had the Haldol prescription they gave him after his overnights at Psych Services. Six months' worth. But if he took one of the pills, he knew it would give him a stiff neck and a clear mind. Two things he didn't want at the moment.

The other option was to go around the corner, buy two bottles of crack, and get outside himself a little.

He looked at Kathie Lee until her pink outfit hurt his eyes. Then he decided to get high. Just for the morning.

I lost my way. Hey, hey, hey.

The next day he got up a little later and went out to buy crack a bit earlier. He wasn't falling into a real habit, he told himself. Just biding his time and saving his strength. He had about $1200 in the bank. There was still plenty of time to go out and look for work.

. . .

By the next week, though, he'd arranged most of his daily schedule around getting high. Instead of spending $10 a day on crack, he was spending $50, $60, and then $70. He was falling into a pattern: wake up, watch the Channel 2 *News at Noon* with Michele Marsh, buy a jumbo of ten vials, spend the afternoon smoking it in his apartment as the traffic went by on Bailey Avenue.

For hours, he'd sit there, staring out the window at the exact spot where she'd been standing. As if she might reappear at any minute.

In the night, questions would come. What had he done? Why was he being punished? Why does God tempt us with a vision of heaven in the perfection of a child's face and then condemn us to a lonely wretched existence?

At the beginning of the next month, Mrs. Gordy, the landlady, sent up Curtis, the handyman.

"You gonna make the May rent?"

"No problem." John opened the door only halfway, so Curtis wouldn't see he'd already sold his TV and microwave to pay for drugs. "I got a few things lined up already. The worm is about to turn."

Curtis looked doubtful. He was a tired man with skin as brown and veiny as an old autumn leaf. "Then I guess she'll be hearing from you."

But John knew he wouldn't come through. He was in the throes of some psychotic need to fuck up. He missed his face-to-face appointment with his caseworker and fell off the Medicaid rolls.

When he tried to call back his caseworker the next day, he was told she didn't work for the city anymore; he would have to reapply at a Staten Island office.

I was in a dark wood.

A week later, Curtis, the handyman, stood in the doorway, surveying the barren apartment. The May rent still hadn't been paid and it was almost June. There was $133 left in the checking account. All the living room and bedroom furniture had been sold. The refrigerator was next.

A part of John G. was standing back and wondering how far he'd let himself go. At some point he had to hit bottom.

"Maybe I oughta start looking for another place," he told Curtis.

The next day, he called the city social services office from a pay phone to ask about getting his benefits back. They put him on hold for forty-five minutes and then told him his case had been transferred out to Queens.

His mind went back and forth. Sometimes he thought this was just a temporary slipping-down period. Other times he wondered if it was all part of a plan. God was punishing him for a reason.

In the meantime, he needed another place. But most of his relatives were either dead, living far away, or fed up with him.

So his old conductor, Ernest Bayard, offered to let him sleep on the red vinyl couch in his apartment for five dollars a night. Just for a couple of weeks until John got his feet on the ground. But they started getting on each other's nerves almost immediately. Ernest liked to stay home at night watching religious programs and treacly family sitcoms. John hid in the bathroom, puffing on his crack pipe and blowing smoke out into the air shaft.

One hot morning he woke up headachy and paranoid from smoking a whole jumbo in one night and accused Ernest of stealing his shoes.

By the afternoon, it was time to move on again.

The night before Independence Day, he found himself wandering through Central Park, carrying a duffel bag with a few clothes in it and $1.50 in his pants pocket.

The murderous humidity of June had finally lifted and he took his first deep breath in weeks. In the back of his mind, he had a tingling feeling that things were about to change once more.

He stopped by the Sheep Meadow, where he'd gone to buy drugs a hundred times before, and found a group of a dozen homeless men lying like beat-up pieces of luggage on the crescent of benches along the periphery. Human wreckage. The seventh semicircle of hell. Two or three of them had clear plastic bags filled with empty soda cans. Diet Coke. Pepsi. Slice. Fresca. They still made Fresca? He remembered bums getting on his train with bags like these and bragging about how they were going to redeem them for five cents a pop at some Gristede's on the Upper West Side or a Times Square movie theater that'd been converted into a massive recycling center. Pathetic, he used to think, struggling with a sack full of a hundred cans on your back for a lousy $5. How could a man get so desperate?

But suddenly those $5 had an altered value. Five dollars was dinner at Burger King or a vial of crack. He was tempted to ask one of the guys where he went to return the cans, but he hesitated. He hadn't fallen that far yet, had he? He hadn't turned into one of the people he used to step over on the street. He had a skill. He drove a train, goddamn it. He could've been making $50,000 in a couple of years.

On the other hand, the night air was cooling and the benches looked comfortable. It didn't mean he was turning into a bum. It was just a place to stay awhile. Until the weather changed and motivated him to find something more permanent.

He threw his bag on an empty bench and stretched out. A great oak tree bent over him and shivered its leaves.

This wasn't really his life, he told himself.

Or maybe it was. This might be his penance, he thought. To end his days here. Maybe this was where he was supposed to finally die.

All right, so now he's a bum. For the first few weeks, it doesn't seem so awful. All right. So he's stopped shaving. Okay, okay, he's using bathroom sinks instead of showers to clean up. He's still alive, isn't he? He even renews his 'script and takes his Haldol when he isn't smoking crack.

In a way, he feels more alive now, being out here, exposed to the elements. Every moment counts. A bum has to be thinking all the time, searching for shelter, figuring out how to eat.

The best thing is never knowing what's going to happen next. The worst thing is never knowing what's going to happen next.

Over the second half of July, he learns how to sleep during the day and prowl at night, hustling soda cans. The other guys from the park benches tell him which uptown supermarkets stay open until midnight for recycling. So he gets an abandoned baby stroller out of a Dumpster to transport the cans and starts scavenging.

He promises himself that he won't resort to begging, though. Instead, he finds out which restaurants leave relatively fresh food in their Dumpsters. The ones on Forty-sixth Street have the best produce, but some of the local Dunkin' Donuts managers are evil; they sprinkle coffee grounds on perfectly good donuts in the garbage just to keep the bums out of their trash.

The whole month, he has only one bad dream, about being in a rotting, oarless dinghy floating away from a rich, green breast of land.

"Yo, Fonz, what's up?"

A voice snaps him out of thought and into the present moment. He's back in the Sheep Meadow. He looks up and finds himself surrounded. A group of belligerent teenagers seem to have materialized out of nowhere. Four boys and two girls in loose jeans and big shirts, all gangsta pose and slouchy bad attitude. At first he asks himself if he's imagining them, the way he imagined the man on the tracks all those weeks back.

"Yo, Fonz, give us a quarter," says their leader, a lanky boy wearing a Chicago Blackhawks jersey and gold caps over his front teeth.

John G. tilts his head to the side. He doesn't want any trouble.

"Yo, Fonz, this ain't no *Happy Days* rerun. I asked you something." The kid takes a step closer.

"I'm sorry, sir. I wasn't listening."

"Who you calling sir?" The kid pokes his tongue against the side of his mouth and the other guys in his crew giggle. "I look like a sir? Do I look like a old man to you?"

"No, no, I mean, I just meant it as a sign of respect."

"But how can you respect me if you don't know me?"

"I don't know," John G. mumbles. "Just the way you carry yourself."

"Just the way I carry myself. Is that why you respect me? Or are you just frontin' 'cause I'm down with the crew?"

"Well, ah, ah, ah . . ."

A boy with a pacifier in his mouth imitates John G. in a Gomer Pylish voice. The others crack up, slapping hands and bumping shoulders. Individually, they'd each barely have the nerve to stare a man down across a subway car. But together, they're a vicious little army.

It hurts John's heart, knowing they can treat him so badly. Has he let himself fall that far?

"Say, what's the matter with you, bitch?" asks the leader. "You got a stutter? You like a retard?"

"No, I'm just a little nervous."

"Why, 'cause you got so much respect for me? Let's get back to that, man. Why you got so much respect? You all afraid we're gonna fuck you up?"

"No, no, you seem like reasonable guys. We're all reasonable people."

"Well, what if I did decide we would fuck you up? You got a problem with that?"

"I don't think you really want to do that," says John G., trying not to sound weak.

"What're you, a mind reader? You know what's going on in my mind?"

"I don't even know what's going on in my own mind."

"You know what, man?" The kid in the Blackhawks jersey shares a smile with a girl sporting a cathedral of cornrowed hair and gold-painted fingernails. "I really don't think you're sincere. I don't think you know what it means, having respect, after all."

"Well, I, uh . . ."

"Man, you know what you are?" the kid says. "You are unclean. You know that? White man smelling all bad and bummy. People like you oughta be exterminated."

Get to zero, John G. tells himself. Offer zero resistance. Don't make them feel they have to prove something by beating you up.

"I guess you're entitled to your opinion," he says.

The leader takes a blue Bic lighter out of his jeans pocket and moves toward him.

"And what if my opinion is I should set your ass on fire?" he asks, reaching out and knocking the Yankees cap off John G.'s head.

Is this what's meant to be? Is this the punishment he's deserved all along? It doesn't feel right.

Don't come any closer. John finds himself trying to send the kid a mental message. Don't come any closer or I can't promise what will happen. Fight or flight.

"Would you still respect me if I did that?" The lighter in the kid's right hand flares like a firefly.

The guys in the crew laugh hysterically. The girls look impatient.

Fight or flight. Don't come any closer. John's right hand goes into his pants pocket and feels the razor-edged box cutter he keeps there.

"What? Are you gonna beg now?" the leader says.

Fight or flight. The kid's moving out of flight range and into fight range. He flicks the lighter right under John G.'s nose, so the hairs curl up inside. There's no longer any choice. John G.'s hand tightens around the box cutter and pushes out the blade.

"Come on, bitch, let me hear you beg. I want to hear you say how much you respect me."

The kid in the Blackhawks jersey thrusts out his left hand.

John takes the box cutter out of his pocket. The kid's mouth falls open. John lunges at him, slashing wildly at the kid's hand, nicking the side. The boy gives a girlish yelp and jumps back. He

40

puts the hand up to his mouth a second and then lowers it to his waist to look at it, as if it's not part of his body anymore.

"Man, why'd you have to do that?!" he says in a high-pitched whine. "We was just fucking with you."

All of a sudden, the boy seems smaller, younger. His posture is less threatening. The other kids in his group move away from him, as though he's disgusted them by the very act of getting hurt.

"Just get away from me before I cut your fucking eyes out," John hears himself say.

The kid in the Blackhawks jersey stares at John and tries to make a fist with his cut hand, but his crew has already started to disperse. One by one, they move across the Sheep Meadow and disappear into the fog like ghosts. Finally it's just John G. and the kid in the middle of the great field.

"Later for this shit," the kid says, scampering after his friends. "Hey, Charlie Ray! Blood! Wait up!"

Then John is alone again. He looks around and sees someone has kicked over his baby stroller. The empty soda cans look like silver fish lying in the moonlit grass. He starts to gather them up. All this time, he's been thinking he probably wanted to die. But the fierceness of his own resistance tonight has surprised him. Maybe it's not his time yet. It's enough, he tells himself. He's fallen far enough.

He finishes putting the cans back in the stroller and starts pushing it across the field, feeling dwarfed by the black starless sky above him. Maybe this isn't what was intended. Perhaps the problem is that he's just lost his way and God can't see him right now. But somehow, he knows, he must get back in his line of sight again.

4

The psych ER is in an uproar.

A stout and surly nurse named Beverly Watkins, who's always minding everyone else's business, went into the meds closet with a glass of water and accidentally drank a cup of methadone. They need two gurneys to get her over to the regular emergency room.

Dana Gerrity Schiff, Jake's wife, watches her getting wheeled down the hall and past the sign that says BE CAREFUL WHEN OPENING DOORS, RISK OF ELOPEMENT.

She remembers when elopement meant something romantic. Before she started working here. She turns back to her patient, Mrs. Lee, a tiny birdlike woman from the Philippines, perched on a hard plastic chair.

"I was wondering if you could tell me how long you've been depressed," says Dana, who is fair, blonde, and thirty-nine.

"Kay?" Mrs. Lee flashes a bright eager smile.

"How long have you been sad?"

"Kay?"

Dana scans the case file but finds no mention of the fact that the patient may not speak English. Just some information about how Mrs. Lee took an overdose of an herb containing speed and a line confirming that her husband, a glowering brute of a maintenance engineer, has the proper insurance to cover her.

"Why did you take too much of that herb?" Dana says slowly. What language do they speak in the Philippines anyway? Filipino?

"Kay?"

The phone rings.

"Dr. Shift?" A Midwestern voice with a lot of air around it.

"Yes?" No point in correcting either one of the mistakes. She's not a doctor, she's a psychiatric social worker.

"This is Katherine Baldridge from United Health in Atlanta. We had a few more questions about the forms you submitted for a Christopher Domindez."

"Dominguez, yes." Dana tries to give Mrs. Lee an assuring look —this won't take long—but Mrs. Lee is smiling on obliviously as if she's enjoying a sunny day in the park.

"Well, Doctor, we just don't see any need for an extended hospitalization for this customer," says Mrs. Baldridge from Atlanta.

"He has a severe bipolar disorder. He locked himself in a room for two weeks and took a hundred and fifty Bufferin."

"We feel he can be treated on an outpatient basis with medication," says Mrs. Baldridge.

Dana stares at a pale green wall and wonders what qualifies someone in a corporate office tower in Georgia to make that decision.

"Listen," says Dana, starting to search through the mountains of paper on her desk for the Dominguez file. "If we don't treat this young man here, his family is going to take him back to the Dominican Republic, where last I heard, their theories about treatment are about seventy-five years behind ours. They'll perform a lobotomy on him with a hammer and an ice pick."

"Be that as it may," says Mrs. Baldridge primly, "his coverage does not provide for thirty-day hospital stays."

Dana looks over and sees Mrs. Lee has somehow gotten up on the windowsill and is standing there grinning like an aging Broadway starlet on the verge of a triumphant comeback.

"Excuse me, I'm going to have to call you back," Dana says into the phone.

She hits the panic button under her desk, calling in security. Then she gently approaches Mrs. Lee the way she'd approach a wounded sparrow on a porch railing.

"Mrs. Lee, please come down from there," she says softly.

"Kay!" says Mrs. Lee cheerily, somehow breaking the word into two syllables.

She turns toward the window and squints at the sun, basking in its warmth. The light catches a purplish bruise under her right ear.

"Mrs. Lee, I'm afraid you're going to hurt yourself."

By now, Eduardo, the nervous young hospital cop from the front desk, has come in accompanied by Mr. Lee, a bristle-haired bull in a pink Lacoste polo shirt.

"Kay, lo-kay," says Mrs. Lee, as if she's happy to see both of them.

Mr. Lee mutters something short and harsh and his wife steps down from the sill, daintily taking his hand. The bowling ball and the pin, Dana thinks when she sees them standing together. He must knock her down twice a day.

"We go now," he says, starting to lead his wife out.

"I really don't think that's wise." Dana follows them out into the waiting area. "There are things we need to discuss."

A homeless man in a Yankees cap and an MTA shirt sits there watching them, with an empty baby stroller at his side. A woman from Honduras, in four-point restraints on a bed down the hall, is cursing out the nurses in Spanish. Mrs. Lee whispers something in her husband's ear and her hands flutter like pieces of paper caught in a sudden updraft.

"She say she wasn't going to jump," Mr. Lee tells Dana. "She was looking at the view."

They are on the first floor and there are bars over the windows.

Dana asks the couple to wait so one of the unit psychiatrists can talk to them, but she knows Mrs. Lee will probably just end up getting discharged because she's there on a voluntary basis. She starts to leave a message for Dr. Miller, and for the 147th time in the 147 days she's been working in the ER, she asks herself if she's really helping anyone this way.

"Excuse me."

The homeless man with the baby carriage is staring at her as she puts the pink slip in Miller's box.

"Yes?"

"I was wondering if you had a minute."

She checks the in box at the nurse's station to see if there are any other patients waiting. The one face sheet is for a John Gates. A momentary lull. The only other people in the waiting area are a Muslim woman in a white headdress and black basketball shoes and a Puerto Rican man whose lips are still blackened from the charcoal they pumped into his stomach to absorb an overdose. One way or another they've been taken care of.

"You're Mr. Gates?" Dana looks at the homeless man and tucks a couple of stray hairs into the bun behind her head.

"Yeah, uh, well. Last I checked." He smiles ambiguously within his beard.

She shows him into her office. He stands in the doorway for a moment, studying the bare walls and the anonymous furniture, as if he's looking for clues.

"I'm Ms. Schiff," she says. "Have a seat."

He takes off his cap and starts to sit. But then he suddenly stops, stands up straight, and slowly lowers himself into the chair. With his left foot, he carefully pulls the baby stroller close and puts his right hand on the back, like he expects someone to try stealing it.

"So what brings you to the emergency room?"

He looks at her for a long time.

"Some kids tried to set me on fire the other night."

She's not sure whether to believe him. In the five months she's been on the unit, she's talked to dozens of homeless people with hundreds of problems. Not that many were white, though. She wants to be careful here. Not just because she's heard white homeless people tend to be crazier than the others, but because she doesn't want to make a leap of empathy based just on skin color.

"So somebody tried to set you on fire," she says. "Why didn't you call the police? What makes you think you want to talk to someone here?"

He lowers his eyes and stares at the empty baby carriage. "Up until that happened, I think I kinda wanted to die," he says. "Now I'm not sure."

He hums and rocks the stroller with his foot. Though he smells and his clothes are dirty like other homeless people's, there's something a little different about him.

"You're not sure you want to die."

"I think I want more life."

"All right." She sighs and rubs the space between her eyebrows. Here comes another one. "I guess I need to get a little more pedigree information from you." She looks over the face sheet and swivels in her chair to get a twenty-page yellow form off her desk. "What was your last address?"

"Central Park."

"I see."

She notices the way his chin seems to be drawn down to his chest, as if by magnetic force.

"Are you currently taking any medication?"

"Haldol, five milligrams," he says in a deep, froggy voice.

"Anything else?"

"Well, I guess you wanna know about the crack . . ."

"How much?"

"Ten, twelve bottles a day. It offsets the Haldol."

"Well, that's honest."

"I never lie." He licks his ragged lips and starts tapping his foot. "The nuns taught me that in Catholic school. It makes things easier to remember."

She looks down to complete the first page of the form. He's definitely beginning to interest her. So many people who come in are disorganized and have no real hope of recovery. Maybe it's just the blue Transit Authority shirt he wears over his other layers of clothes. But she has the feeling that he was once connected to something in the real world and now he wants it back.

She's aware of him shifting his weight in the plastic seat as she runs through some of the other standard questions. But then he interrupts.

"Look, can I say something to you?" He stops her with a bold stare and she notices he actually has beautiful green eyes.

"Of course."

He pauses to take time with his words, like a man trying to figure out how to lift a grand piano by himself.

"I know you're gonna ask me all these questions on your form about previous employment and other treatment I've had. But none of that really matters. Okay?"

"Why not?"

"Because," he says, squeezing his hands between his knees, "none of it can ever make up for the death of a child."

Silence. He hunches over, looking at the empty baby stroller again. His face seems older. The net of lines around his eyes tightens.

"Is that something you'd like to talk about?" Dana asks, putting down the form.

He releases his hands and sits back. She hopes her voice hasn't betrayed too much. Countertransference. She's been warned about it since grad school: don't identify too much with your client's problems.

"No," he says quietly. "I don't think so. Not right now anyway."

He wraps his arms around himself and begins to pulsate in his seat.

"So are you thinking you might like to be admitted to this hospital?"

He shakes his head *no* vigorously without looking at her. She peeks out the door and sees patients are stacking up in the waiting area like planes on a runway.

"Then I'm afraid I still don't understand why you came here today," she says. "You don't want to talk about your problems. You don't want to be admitted. What is it that you do want?"

"Things have come apart," he says, crossing his legs and examining the sole of his left shoe. "They need to be put back together."

She watches him a few moments, trying to decide how to describe him in a write-up. White male in his mid-thirties. Once married, according to the information sheet. Reasonably sequential in thought process. Diagnosis unknown.

"I'm still not quite getting the picture," she says.

The gnarled scabby fingers of his right hand begin to play across the top of his knee like it's a piano. Index finger, thumb, pinky, ring finger, middle finger. "See, being out on the street like I am, it's changing me." The fingers start to play faster. Thumb, pinky, index. "There are things in my mind that shouldn't be there."

"What kinds of things?"

"I don't know." He half smiles shyly: if only you knew.

"Well, are you hearing voices?"

"Just yours and mine." He looks at the hand lying on his lap. Ring finger, index, pinky, thumb.

"And are you still worried you might hurt yourself?"

"I'm worried that no one is taking responsibility." The fingers stop moving.

"What do you mean?"

"I mean, I know I am not in complete control of my faculties." The fingers close into a fist. "Being out on the street like I am . . . It's like every day I wake up and I'm afraid of what I'm going to do." He stops and gives a little shiver. "And I don't think God meant for me to end up this way."

The mention of God is usually enough to make her scalp prickle. In this office, people attribute all kinds of things to God's will. God wanted me to cover my body in peanut butter. God wanted me to go to Atlantic City with the union pension fund. God wanted me to stand in line at D'Agostino's without any clothes on. But John Gates seems perfectly sober and serious mentioning the Lord even as his left knee does the crackhead jiggle.

"So you mentioned the idea of responsibility before," she says, turning to the evaluation page. "Who are you suggesting take on all this responsibility?"

"You."

"I beg your pardon?"

The air becomes very still between them.

"You." He leans forward on his elbows and looks up with his lost-little-boy green eyes. "You seem like a nice person. I can talk to you. I'd like you to be my regular doctor."

She looks at the empty extra-strength Tylenol bottle on her desk and wonders why she didn't get a new one this morning.

"But I'm not a doctor," she says. "I'm a social worker. And this is an emergency room. Nobody sees regular patients here."

From down the hall, she can hear Mrs. Berkowitz in the waiting area. That demented old lady from Cherry Street who always shows up waving the empty prescription bottles her late husband was given in 1951. He must have died a happy man.

"See, that's the problem with the whole system!" he says loudly and then catches himself. "No one takes any responsibility," he says, trying to modulate his voice. "Everyone's giving me the run-around. Every time I get a new caseworker they either get transferred or they lose my file. And somebody's going to get hurt!"

She looks at him. Eyes clear, left knee still trembling. He's not completely paranoid or delusional. At least not yet. He's a man on the cusp.

"So you want to get your life back in synch?" she says, testing his resolve.

"Yes."

"And you want to get off drugs?"

"Yes, I do."

"And you want to get off the street?"

"Yeah, and I'd like to get another apartment."

"Well this isn't a real estate office." She rubs her eyes. "Do you have any insurance?"

A slow mournful headshake. "I lost all my benefits with the TA, 'cause I failed the drug test. And then I fell off the rolls because I missed my face-to-face."

"You're going to have to reapply," she says, taking out a card and writing down some numbers on the back. "You need to start at the Emergency Assistance Unit office."

At least he once had a job. From the room next door, the Honduran patient in restraints is shouting. "I want *puta* music! *Puta* music!"

Dana notices John Gates staring past her, looking at something in the hallway. "Hey, what's that mean?" he says. *"Be careful when opening doors; risk of elopement."*

"It means they want to be careful about patients escaping."

"Oh. I thought maybe they were worried about patients and doctors eloping."

"No. I don't think that happens very often."

"Well you never know." He starts to smile.

Dana feels her chin sag and her ears get hot as she looks through the rest of her papers. The rumble of voices has grown louder in the waiting room and the mix of accents has become more dense. There must be a half dozen of them out there by now. Just the thought makes her tired. She's going to have to move him out soon.

"Look, give me a call in a couple of days," she says in a frazzled voice, adding her office number on the back of the card and giving it to him. "Maybe we can work something out so I can see you at the Mental Health Clinic at the hospital. I'll talk to my supervisor."

A major headache, to be sure. She can already see the sullen, heavy-lidded look on Rod Walker's face when she brings it up at the next staff meeting. "If you do this, you'll be setting a bad precedent for everyone else . . ." She hopes John Gates will be worth the effort.

He gets up and starts to push the stroller out the door. But then he stops and takes her hand, an almost courtly gesture. "Thanks, Ms. Schiff. You're good people. I knew I was right about you."

His fingers feel like sandpaper blocks as they brush hers. She takes her hand back and sucks in her cheeks. She wonders what she said to make him feel so trusting. Maybe it was just the look on her face when he mentioned the death of the child.

Probably she has to learn to put up a colder front, as Jake's been telling her. Or learn not to care.

5

"Who was the . . ." Dana's fork pauses in midair.

". . . the guy." Jake finishes the sentence for her.

"Yes, your old client. The one who . . ." Her face pushes up, straining.

"The one who threw his mother out the window? Al V. Strang?"

"Right. Didn't he . . ."

". . . cut off his penis and try to take a bite out of the patrol car when the police came to arrest him?"

"Well." Dana lowers her fork. "*He* was a hopeless case, wasn't he?"

Jake looks at his wife, curiously. "Yeah, I'd say so."

"So the one I saw today wasn't like that," says Dana. "This John Gates."

"Mom, pass the broccoli, will you?" says their son, Alex, who has long red-streaked hair and wears a blue-and-white checked flannel shirt.

When people ask Jake if he's married, he usually says "real married." Here he is in the dining room of his new Upper West Side town house with his boy and the most beautiful woman who'd ever agreed to have dinner with him. It's just recently that he's been able to slow down enough at work and enjoy the life they have together. If he hasn't quite arrived, he's just a station or two away.

"They say once someone's been out on the street six months, you might as well forget them," Dana goes on. "But this guy Gates has only been out a few weeks."

All right, what's up here? Jake wonders. There's definitely an agenda. He looks at the empty fourth chair at the far end of the table and listens to the sigh of traffic on Riverside Drive.

"Dana, why are we talking about this?"

"Because I think I can help this man," says Dana, who wears a white T-shirt and gray sweatpants. "But Rod and the other supervisors are bitching up a storm about me seeing him at the clinic."

"Well, can I offer my advice in this area, which is probably worth nothing?"

Jake can see from the vertical line on his wife's forehead that she's already made up her mind. It's the same look she had when she announced she was going to go to grad school instead of continuing to try and have another child.

"All right, let's hear it."

He rubs his hands together like a wrestler about to step out on the mat. "What I think is that people who've been out on the street—whether it's a week or a year—are not like you and me," he says. "I represented a lot of these hard-luck guys at Legal Aid and let me tell you, almost every single one was a complete scumbag. If someone's been at the bottom of the pile long enough, he doesn't care about playing fair. He just wants to get his hooks into you."

He sees his little speech has only deepened the line between Dana's eyes. Oh well.

"Jake, I want to ask you something," she says. "Why was it okay for you to start off your career working with people like that, but it's not all right for me?"

"Because you don't have to work with scum. You can afford to pick and choose. We have a little bit of money now, remember?"

"Yes, we do. But it's not money I made."

Aha. Now we're zeroing in, Jake thinks.

"Jake, you remember how much time you spent on the securities fraud case last year and how you were so jazzed you couldn't go to sleep most nights?"

"Yeah, sure." It was one of the few times a corporate case was as exciting as criminal defense work.

"Well that's what I want." Dana leans toward him with her chin on her fist and her lips slightly parted. The same expression she has when she's hungry or horny.

"You wanna lose sleep?"

"No." She sits back and pours herself a glass of Australian chardonnay. "I want to feel that way about my job. I want to work two nights a week at the clinic."

Bingo. So that's the subtext here. They're not talking about some crazy homeless guy. They're talking about changing the terms of their marriage.

"Can I be excused?" asks Alex, who's been sitting across the table, eating broccoli and yogurt while flicking hair out of his eyes.

"Yeah, sure. . . . No, wait." Jake stares at him. "What's that you got in your nose?"

Flick, flick. "It's a ring."

"What are you, kidding?"

"No, it's a nose ring." Two index fingers part the streaked hair.

Jake drops the piece of fish he had raised to his lips. "You telling me you got your nose pierced?"

The kid already wears a gold stud in his left ear.

"I went with Paul Goldman to a place on St. Marks this afternoon."

Jake looks over at Dana, wondering why this is the first he's heard of it. "What are you gonna do if you have to blow your nose? It'll come out three ways."

"Lisa likes it."

"You gonna wear it to school?"

"I can take it out." Alex starts to demonstrate, but his father waves him off.

"Jesus, you get another one of these things, we'll start calling you Tackle Box."

"Cool," says Alex.

"Remind me to talk to you later."

The boy starts to go upstairs.

"Hey, wait a second, you're forgetting something," Jake says.

Alex stops and returns to the table. His father puts his arms around him and gives him a hug.

"You're still my guy, all right?"

"All right." The boy looks both embarrassed and pleased when Jake half-stands to kiss him on the cheek.

"Love ya."

As Alex leaves the room, Jake puts his hands up to the sides of his head and pretends to scream.

"Twenty years I busted my ass to get out of Gravesend and go to law school, and here my son pierces his nose and my wife wants to bring bums into the house."

"I don't want to bring him into the house," Dana says. "I want to see people like him at the clinic."

"Yeah, I know, I know." Jake fumbles with the air as if he's trying to pull words out of it. "It's just, I'm feeling like we're finally getting things the way we want them after we've worked so hard. I just don't want to upset anything."

"So who's upsetting anything?" She looks around like somebody's tapped her on the shoulder. "I'm just talking about spending a couple of late nights at work, like you do. I'm not really helping people during regular hours. Face it. Alex is grown up and he doesn't need me the way he used to. The house is basically coming together. And it's not like we have another child around keeping us busy."

Jake looks down. Sometimes that empty fourth seat at the dinner table seems like a broken promise between them.

"I'm sorry about that, babe," he mutters. "I think about it all the time."

"Well, don't blame yourself."

"The thing is, I do blame myself." He studies the side of his fist. "Maybe if I hadn't been working so hard, we could've started trying for another kid earlier."

Then perhaps they wouldn't have gone through the ectopic pregnancy and the series of miscarriages that made the doctors tell them to stop trying.

"We still could adopt," she reminds him.

"Ah, neither of us . . ."

". . . has the heart for that. All right, fine," she says. "I never complained."

"Sometimes you complained."

"Well I never complained as much as I felt like complaining," she says, finishing one glass of wine and pouring another. "At any rate, it's fine now. I'm working."

"So what do your supervisors say about you seeing more people at the clinic?"

"They went apeshit, as you would say." Dana rubs the back of her own neck as if she's still tense from the argument. "They were saying it would set the wrong precedent for all the other social workers on the ward. 'Bad juju' is the phrase they kept using."

Jake sighs. "Why can't you set up a private practice and start seeing people with nice middle-class problems? You know? Like frigidity or fear of commitment. The worried well. I even heard about a partner at a white-shoe firm the other day who's got a bran addiction. He can't stop eating bread . . ."

"Look, Jake." A thin smile plays on her rosebud lips and she puts her bare feet up on the table. "You're good at fighting and defending people. I'm good at taking care of them. I took care of my mom when she had cancer. Then I took care of my father and my brothers after she died. And when Alex had encephalitis, I took care of him too. That's my calling."

"I know. I just hate to see you stick your neck out for a bunch of . . ."

". . . skells." She frowns. "Are you saying you don't want me to do this kind of serious work?"

There's that other look of hers. The one that says: If we're going to have an argument, I'm going to outlast you.

Jake reaches over and massages the bottom of her left foot. "No, that's not what I'm saying."

If anything, her work has given them something to talk about at a time when other marriages run out of gas.

"It's just, you know, it's New York City, hon," he says. "I hate to think about you coming home late at night."

"We didn't have to buy this house," she says, batting a stray hair out of her face like an intrusive thought. "Five hundred thousand dollars down would've bought us a lot of land in Rowayton and we wouldn't have had a mortgage hanging over our heads the rest of our lives."

"Yeah, and then I'd get bitten by a tick the first weekend and come down with Lyme disease." He squints at a plume of soot over the fireplace—just what he needs, another contractor to deal with. "There's no safety anywhere."

He's long since accepted the fact that he's addicted to the rude shuck-and-jive of the city. New York is where he's triumphed. Where else could a poor Jew from a housing project end up borrowing enough money to buy a million-dollar town house with an $8,000 chandelier over the dining room table? The nicest light fixture in his parents' two-room apartment at the Marlboro Houses was a cracked bowl with three dead flies in it.

"This is where I want to be," he says.

"All right, so I've accepted that." Dana flexes her left foot three times. "And now I'm asking you to accept this is what I want to do for a living."

He leans over and kisses her on the lips. "I love you."

Upstairs, Alex is blasting an old Jimi Hendrix tape and playing along on his 1959 Fender Stratocaster electric guitar. The long sustained notes and feedback swells sound like loud tears coming through the concrete.

In a perverse way, the volume is thrilling. It pleases Jake that his son has a room bigger than the apartment he grew up in, with more than $5,000 worth of audio and computer equipment. Though there are still money struggles ahead, he loves giving Alex things he never had. Spending cash, love, and a kind of ease that comes from not being worried all the time. It makes Jake feel that something's been accomplished in this life.

"So you've already made up your mind about this thing with the clinic, huh?" he says, turning back to Dana.

"I'm going to start off seeing John Gates and a couple of other people twice a week on a volunteer basis. I wouldn't back down to Rod and the rest of them."

Jake looks bemused. "And did you just want to hear yourself talk about it?"

"Yes, I suppose I did."

He throws up his hands. "I guess that's one of the three basic differences between men and women. Women like to talk out their problems without necessarily hearing a solution."

"Interesting." She finishes what's left of her wine. "What's the second difference?"

"Women have more shoes."

"And the third?"

"You come upstairs, you might find out."

They start to make love.

Jake rubs Dana's back for a few minutes, and then pulls off her T-shirt from behind. They stand, front to back, as he eases off her sweatpants and panties and then removes his own clothes, so he can lose himself in the smoothness of her body.

In the mirror on the open closet door, he sees a stocky, hairy Jew nuzzling this beautiful blonde woman and wonders what that guy did to deserve such luck.

"Let's take a bath," Dana murmurs.

She goes into the bathroom and starts the water. He follows her in and she stops him at the door a moment, listening for the sound of Alex on the phone upstairs with Lisa. That ought to keep him occupied for an hour.

When the tub is half full, they get in together, watching the water level rise dangerously. They are face-to-face and Dana climbs onto his lap, straddling him. He starts to move into her.

"Is this all right?"

"I think I can manage," she says, guiding him in deeper.

She begins to moan. The inside of her is like a warm bath within the bath. She throws back her head and arches her back, as droplets of water slide down her breasts. Twenty years of marriage and he still wants her as much as he did that first night he saw her at a college party. He's never been seriously interested in another woman. Other partners at the firm would complain about what happened to their wives' bodies after childbirth or would acquire younger, trophy wives after the first models reached a certain age, but Dana has only grown more sexually attractive to Jake with the passing years. His desire for her hasn't diminished; it's deepened and developed character and contours. Maybe it's his familiarity with her body. Her velvety skin, her long legs, the dimples just above her buttocks, the sound she makes when he licks her nipples.

Or maybe it's just that they've been through so much together. Every small wrinkle and strand of gray hair can be traced back to a memory he shares with her.

Twenty years of marriage. It began for both of them as a refuge from an unhappy childhood. But over the years it evolved into something infinitely more intense and mundane. They'd survived major and minor resentments, periods of neglect, meaningless flirtations, and near breakups. They'd sustained themselves with small mercies, selective memories, and hard-won tolerance. And after two decades, they were both amazed to find there was no one else they'd rather sit next to on the bed, watching television and paying bills. It was love, but it was also more than love; it was a life.

He thrusts into her again and she folds herself around him, arms and legs across his back. A perfect fit. Why would he want anything else?

"The bed," she says, standing and drying off. "I'm getting pruny. Let's finish on the bed."

He picks her up and carries her unsteadily out of the bath and into the bedroom. He drops her onto the white down comforter and they finish making love in a wild improvisational frenzy, with Dana flipping her husband over and riding astride him, arms out, eyes closed, hair whipping around like lashing rain and then finally pouring down the front of her face like a waterfall.

She sighs and shudders and rolls off him. Jake looks over at the mirror on the open closet door.

The image is not altogether familiar. In the past, he's seen himself as a fighter, an outsider, the Jewish kid trying to get by in a tough Italian neighborhood, a lonely boy shooting baskets by himself, the object of his father's rage and his mother's comfort, the despised Legal Aid lawyer, the struggling Brooklyn son striving to make his way through the brutal city. But now the angle has changed and he sees himself slightly differently. For a fleeting moment, he sees a man who is happy.

6

John G. is standing outside the Bedford Avenue homeless shelter in Brooklyn, a huge medieval-looking fortress in a neighborhood full of churches and auto body shops.

A hard rain is starting to fall and a line of angry, confused men stretches out before him. But somehow his heart is full of hope. He checks the back pocket of his jeans and makes sure he still has the card Ms. Schiff gave him. He studies the curved zeros and soft twos in her writing, and wonders how long it's been since he touched something made by a woman. He savors the moment when he stood next to her in the doorway. Tomorrow he will seize control of his destiny and reapply for his benefits. It's time to live again.

The line moves and he nearly runs into the young man ahead of him, who wears a black sweatshirt with the hood up.

"Next time you say, 'Excuse me,' a-right?" The young guy barely bothers to turn around. The threat in his voice doesn't need a look to back it up.

John glances down and sees the kid has a knife in his back pocket. Not a little Swiss Army number with a can opener, but a big hungry serrated blade with a wood-grain handle.

As the young guy walks through the metal detector, there's a high-pitched beep. John takes a bite out of the bologna sandwich he got at the assessment center and braces himself for the inevitable hassle with the security guards. It's a good thing he gave away that box cutter he was carrying.

But instead of stopping the kid, the guard, who looks about fourteen, laughs and waves him through.

"My man Larry Loud's in the house," he says, slapping hands with the young guy.

"G-Love, 'sup?"

"Yo, yo, that shit was fly, man. That shit was phat. I'm goin' have a talk with you. Five dollah you owe me."

Larry Loud screws up the right side of his face, as if to say such matters are beneath him. John G. starts to walk through the metal detector.

"I'm sorry, sir, you can't bring that in here," the guard says.

"What?"

"That sandwich. You're not allowed to bring food in."

John G. looks startled. "You're kidding me, right?"

"Those is the rules. You don't like them, get the hell on out."

"I just saw you let in a guy with a knife," John says.

He's suddenly aware that people have stopped talking in the line behind him. Then he turns and sees Larry Loud with his hood still up, waiting for him on the other side of the metal detector.

"You a troublemaker, man?" says Larry, leaning against the metal detector's wooden frame and ignoring the beeping it sets off.

"I just want to finish my sandwich," John G. steps up to the threshold and faces him.

He knows he should be backing down. But something won't let him. Maybe it's Ms. Schiff's card in his back pocket.

Larry Loud's face goes slack and his hands drop to his sides. No knife. "You want a piece of me, white boy?"

White boy? John G.'s never thought of himself as particularly white. He's been around black people most of his life. Grew up and went to school with them in the Bronx. Worked with them at the TA. Learned to walk like them, talk like them, even do the same drugs as them.

So why are so many of them staring at him now? The guard. Larry Loud. The other homeless guys in line behind him. All waiting to see if he'll hand over the sandwich and succumb to the Rikers Island laws of survival: give up your shit once and assume permanent punk status.

He looks at Larry and tries to gauge the risk of standing his ground. All he sees is a scared kid. This is not the day he will die, he decides. After all, if he could handle that wolf pack in the park, he can handle one punk.

He walks through the metal detector with his chin held high and steps right up to Larry. The security guard stands a yard away, shaking his head.

"You and me later, we've got a date," Larry mumbles. But he doesn't sound like he means it.

"Excuse me." John G. moves past him. "I'd like to find my bed. I've had a very long day."

A half hour later, he is sitting on a cot in the middle of a vast concrete drill floor, surrounded by three hundred other beds. A thick hazy scrim of funk hangs about twenty feet off the floor, like an atmospheric condition created by the dozens of aimless men wandering around. John can almost hear the distant admonition in their murmuring voices: this is where you go if you go wrong.

"Say, man, you might want to hide those shoes you're wearing," says a heavyset black man on his right who has Asian eyes and a beatific smile that immediately makes John think he's out of his mind. He smells from urine and old Chinese food.

"Where?"

The fat man points to his own battle-scarred Adidas, impaled under two steel legs of his cot.

"That way you'll feel it if anybody tries to steal 'em," the fat man explains.

"Think they'd steal your shoes in here?"

"Motherfuckers'll kill you for the salt in your shaker."

"Yeah? So this is a dangerous place?"

"The worst." The fat man smiles and hums. "I only wish I was living back in that tunnel under Riverside Park. At least I knew I was safe there."

When the lights go down a few minutes later, John feels as if he's being left overnight in a zoo cage. The knocking and grumbling noises seem louder, the odors seem more pungent. Someone gives out a loud whoop from across the drill floor and a lit match goes flying over his head.

He tries to lie back and relax on the cot, but he keeps thinking about Larry Loud and his knife. Maybe he shouldn't have been so bold with him. What if Larry does intend to come looking for him? It's a long shot Larry would find him among so many people in the dark, but still he wonders, Would anyone care if he got hurt?

He thinks about his wife and his daughter, feels their absence like missing limbs. Somehow he hasn't felt complete since they've been gone. All the drugs in the world can't change that. What he remembers most is the small things. Happy Meals at Mickey D.'s. Stroller rides through Van Cortlandt Park. Sunlight through the trees. The memory of love. When he dwells on it too much, he feels himself coming apart inside. So he moves on.

He begins thinking about his own childhood. Growing up in Patchogue. Crabbing at the marina. Swimming in the mill pond. The smell of vanilla and fresh-cut lumber from the old converted lace mill nearby. His mother pushing him in a shopping cart through the Bohack's on Main Street. Happy days. The scrappy little fake carriage house on South Ocean Avenue with the horse and coach on the screen door. He remembers lying on a patch of brown grass in the backyard, watching clouds as thick and slow as cotton floating in water. Sitting on the porch next to his mother in the days before she got sick and started having her moods. Laughing Mary. That's what everyone called her. Always laughing too loud, drinking too much, bringing home too many men. She was a lunatic: she put pizza crust in the goldfish tank and fried hamburgers in $12 olive oil. He can still smell the smoke in her hair and the patchouli on her neck where she'd let him nuzzle her. Before she started hiding in the bathroom and telling him to just let her be.

He remembers the long drive up to the Bronx where they were going to live with her old Aunt Rose from Donegal. How his mother was supposed to pick him up from P.S. 156 one day and never showed up. He walked for blocks and blocks looking for her, passing under the shadow of the el and Yankee Stadium, until he wound up at the precinct, a frightened eight-year-old sucking his thumb while a grumpy old patrol sergeant pounded out a report on a manual typewriter.

He remembers crying for her before bed that night in Aunt Rose's apartment in the Webster Houses. But all he got was Rose without her dentures and a warm glass of milk with hair in it. He can still see those car shadows on the ceiling and feel that yearning for the way things used to be. The memory starts to carry him away, though he wonders now whether Mary really did love him. His eyelids grow heavy and his breathing slows down. From across the drill floor he hears someone singing an old song:

"I can't stop loving you, I've made up my mind, To live in memories, Of a lonesome time."

And just as he's finally about to fall into a restful sleep, he feels the sting of cold metal against his throat.

"Yo, excuse me, man," whispers a voice. "Remember me?"

Hot breath forces its way into his ear. He realizes he must have rolled onto his stomach when he fell asleep. Now the serrated blade is against his larynx.

"You best just lie back, relax, and enjoy the show," Larry Loud says in a low voice. " 'Cause I'm gonna cut your fuckin' throat if you make a sound."

He starts moving on top of John G., shifting things around. John tries to resist, but the knife tightens on his Adam's apple.

"Come on, bitch, I ain't gonna hurt you none."

The knife pulls back against John G.'s carotid artery like a bit in a horse's mouth.

"See, they think I got the virus," Larry says softly. "You know how I'm saying? Like I might be what they call HIV-positive."

John tells himself that the kid is lying and just trying to frighten him, but then he remembers the fear he saw in Larry's eyes downstairs.

"So I don't give a fuck," Larry says, trying to pull down John's pants and force his way in. "I'm gonna die anyway. So now I'm gonna put my virus right into you."

John rocks from side to side, trying to throw him off. Every cell and muscle in his body is crying out, protesting what's about to happen. Everything that he is depends on keeping himself intact. Until tonight, he'd thought he had no pride left. But just as he realizes there's still something there, he loses it.

"Lord have mercy on the faggots," Larry says afterward. "If I got the virus now, so do you. It's just like that Clint Eastwood movie, man: the question you gotta ask yourself is, Do I feel lucky?"

He laughs to himself as he gets up and walks away.

And for the next few minutes, the only thing John G. hears is the sound of his own mind breaking.

Watch the closing doors. The train goes plunging down.

7

The table in the conference room of Bracken, Williams & Sayon is made from wood that's over ten thousand years old, Todd Bracken III once told Jake. The original tree hailed from a Tasmanian mountainside, where Jake supposed a brontosaurus might have once taken a leak on it. It had survived fire, termites, atmospheric changes, and the death of most surrounding vegetation before it was shipped to the States, bleached blond, and sold by a custom retail outlet in Delaware for $50,000. Jake taps it twice waiting for Todd to come to the next point in the partners' meeting.

"The partnership retreat," says Todd, wiping a swatch of thinning blond hair off his broad forehead. "I was thinking Miami this year. Boca Raton was so . . ."

He draws back his lips, trying to find the right word, and slips his tongue over his tiny teeth. He crosses his legs, letting an English leather shoe sole hang lazily above the tabletop.

"So . . ."

Mike Sayon, eating walnuts with his plump fingers, and Charlie Dorian, the high-strung head of the litigation department, lean forward, ready to laugh at anything the founding partner's son might say.

"So . . . " Todd's long, manicured hands stroke the air. "So . . . I don't know . . . suntan oil and Judith Krantz. So Five Towns . . ."

Mike Sayon and Charlie Dorian chuckle appreciatively.

"So parvenu," Mike adds helpfully, struggling with a silver nut-cracker.

Spoken like a true self-hating Jew, thinks Jake.

"Exactly," says Todd with a bonded smile. "Exactly."

"I was thinking we should talk about making Kelly Lager a partner," Jake interrupts.

A silence falls over the room. It's as if he's just belched loudly.

Charlie Dorian, gray haired, red faced, and constantly plucking at his left eyebrow, picks up the ball.

"I thought we weren't going to be discussing candidates for another three weeks."

"I wanted to put him on the morning line now," Jake insists. "The guy's probably the best technical lawyer we have at the firm. He's forgotten more case law than any of us will ever know. And he writes a brief so sharp you could cut your hands on it."

Todd Bracken gets up and walks over to the window, watching the midtown Manhattan buildings glisten like glazed fingers reaching for the sun. As everyone in the room knows, Kelly Lager, a thirty-seven-year-old diabetic with psoriasis and four lovely children, has been doing most of Todd's paperwork since Todd's father died and left him in charge in the eighties.

"He's been turned down three years in a row and I think he belongs in the winner's circle," Jake goes on. "Besides, the guy's got a name like a beer company. What else do you want from him?"

Mike breaks open a nut, and bits of shell fall down the front of his jacket. "It's just a matter of simple economics, Jake," he says. "We can't justify making more partners at our current level of growth. We're down twenty-three percent from this quarter last year."

Jake casts a skeptical eye at the Milton Avery painting on the wall. "That twenty-three percent was from the Wyatt-Campbell litigation last year," he says. "That was my case. So let's not kid ourselves. Your associates make partner every other year. Why not Kelly?"

Charlie starts tearing more furiously at his eyebrow. Mike goes to work on breaking open another walnut and the cracking shell makes a sound like tiny firecrackers going off. And Todd Bracken remains over by the window, arms crossed like a petulant tennis star disputing a line judge's call.

"I think," says Todd, "what we're talking about is a matter of style."

"And what's that supposed to mean?" Jake asks.

Todd shoots a look that goes from Mike to Charlie before ending in a smirk. "I don't think Kelly has ever been what we'd consider a Bracken, Williams lawyer."

Of course, that never stopped Todd from signing his name on Kelly's briefs.

"So what's your problem with him, Todd?"

"Well, frankly . . . " Todd glances over his shoulder, as if a window washer might be listening. "The man smells."

"What?"

"I mean, he actually has a foul odor. Haven't you ever noticed that?"

For a moment, Jake is so stunned that he can't think of anything to say.

"My secretary and I call him the Stench." Todd lifts his chin slightly, offering a glimpse of the arrogant little boy who probably once staked a claim on other children's toys in the sandbox.

"You're telling me you're going to deny him partner because you don't like the way he smells?" Jake puts his hands on top of his head. "Put a fragrance tree around his neck, for Chrissake. What's the big deal?"

Todd makes a small tutting sound, as if he's despairing of ever teaching Jake the secret language the rest of them understand by instinct. "It's not just the way he smells. It's his entire presentation. Part of being a good lawyer has to do with intangibles. Good judgment. Useful contacts. Ask yourself. Is this someone you want to spend the next few years with? Honestly. Do you want Kelly meeting with clients? Coming to your house for dinner?"

"Why not?" asks Jake, growing testy.

"Because he doesn't fit in."

"Fit in what?" Jake feels his eyeballs start to roll back and his knuckles begin to itch. "Is there some mold the rest of us ought to know about?"

" 'If you have to be told, don't ask,' " says Mike, putting down the nutcracker and mimicking what old man Bracken used to say.

But Todd's father was a sententious old hypocrite who would lecture junior associates about ethics while screwing his secretaries and playing golf with judges.

"All right, Jake, let's lay it on the line," says Todd. "I hadn't wanted to bring it up so early but you've probably heard the rumors that we've been discussing a merger with Greer, Allan."

"I've heard."

Greer, Allan. The *über*-Wasps. Every one of their lawyers looks like he walked out of a Land's End catalog. And hardly one of them could find the jury box in a courtroom. Still their revenues were above $100 million last year.

"Well, the rumors are true," says Todd.

Of course, all rumors are true.

"They already have over two hundred lawyers at their firm and fifty-five of them are partners." Todd rubs the fingers of his right hand together. "The last thing we ought to be doing when they're about to go over our books is adding another partner. Especially one who doesn't fit the mold."

"So do I fit the mold?" asks Jake, his voice sharpening with the rise toward conflict. After all, he's the only lawyer in the room who went to Hofstra, not Harvard.

"Well, truthfully, Jake, the last time I walked past your office I felt like I was going through a subway station," says Todd.

"What're you talking about? The music?" Jake wonders if Todd's complaining because he likes to blast Mott the Hoople and the MC 5 while he's writing briefs.

"No, I meant the people sitting outside. They looked like a couple of common criminal defendants."

"They are common defendants. The Ramirez brothers. They have a combined IQ of about seventy. They like to rob the same restaurants they eat in. They figure if the food's good enough, there'll be money in the register."

"So you're representing a couple of stickup men?"

"Actually, they're up on a double homicide at the moment. It's a bullshit case. I sent everybody a memo on it."

Taking them on is a gesture of fond remembrance for Jake's old days at Legal Aid. He loved the rough-and-tumble of criminal defense work. He had no stomach for being a prosecutor: one summer internship with the Queens DA was enough to convince him he wasn't cut out to be a white knight. He liked getting down in the gutter, at least at first: toughing it out with judges, going toe-to-toe with the ADAs, and yes, even mixing it up with the clients. Shootings, stabbings, senseless acts of passion. Every day was a soap opera. Jake used to jump out of bed in the morning. But the need to make a living and support his family beckoned, and then there was the case of Enrique, the vicious moronic crack dealer who beat his two-year-old son to death because he wouldn't stop crying. Jake made him take twenty-five to life upstate, and then quit Legal Aid. Everyone had the right to competent defense counsel, he reasoned, but it didn't always have to be him.

So after a cup of coffee with a small midtown outfit, he became the first former Legal Aid lawyer ever to join this stiff-necked firm. He started representing white-collar criminals: tax dodgers, inside traders, insurance company defrauders, and various cold-blooded bankers and corporate accountants who never had to listen to their victims scream. To his surprise, he found he was good at it. Clients liked his smarts and street-fighter attitude. He began to diversify, handling contracts and real estate deals. After a couple of years, *New York* magazine called, wanting to include him in a cover story about the ten toughest lawyers in the city. Fifteen months later, the *Times* gave him a profile of his own in the D section. Soon he was making enough money to go into debt; he borrowed cash to buy the town house so he could sock away a few thousand a year in zero-coupon bonds for Alex's college education fund. Without meaning to, he'd become a kind of rising star.

But he keeps the MC 5 and the Ramirez brothers around just to assure himself he hasn't completely sold out.

"Well, I don't appreciate you ramming these people down our throats," Todd says with a click of phlegm.

"And I don't appreciate you not discussing this merger with any of us," Jake snaps back.

"The Greer, Allan people are very sensitive about who they represent."

"Listen, Todd." Jake feels something like a diving bell slowly lowering itself into the pit of his stomach. "Out of seventy lawyers here, I've brought in five percent of this firm's business last year. Including the Anderson real estate group, ABT cable systems, and Bob Berger over at BBH. Hakeem Turner alone paid us a quarter of a million dollars to defend him in all his cases. So don't tell me who I can represent."

"Most of the clients you just mentioned probably would've come over because of the firm's reputation before you arrived." Todd comes back to his seat as if he's rushing the net to return a backhand. "And they'd probably stay with us if you decided to leave."

"You want to put that theory to the test?" Jake says, loosening up his shoulders like he's getting ready for a brawl.

Mike Sayon, his jacket almost completely covered in broken walnut shell, looks at Charlie Dorian. Charlie looks at Todd. Todd looks back at Mike with a smile like a tight belt on a fat man's waist. And all at once, Jake realizes he's never felt comfortable around these men. For ten years, he's been laughing at their vaguely anti-Semitic jokes. Emulating their pretentious faux-English style of dressing with the Savile Row shirts and the bench-made shoes. Enduring their loud, frustrated wives at those endless, boring $500-a-plate charity balls to support the historic preservation of some damp footpath in New Canaan, Connecticut. Putting up with their practice of billing some destitute old widow seven or eight times what she owes to settle her late husband's estate while some tax-evading corporate client haggles over every cup of coffee and phone call on the expense account.

And doing all of it fourteen to eighteen hours a day, seven days a week, while his son was growing up and his wife was struggling to raise the boy and start a career of her own.

The voice in Jake's head says quietly but firmly: No more.

But before he can say the words out loud, the intercom box on the table buzzes.

"Mr. Schiff," says a secretary's voice. "Your wife is on line four. She says a strange man has been following her and she needs to speak to you immediately."

Jake looks up at Todd and nods. "To be continued."

"My breath is bated," says Todd.

8

Three hours earlier.

A playground on the corner of Seventy-seventh Street and Amsterdam Avenue. Broken pieces of sun in the tree branches. A boy and a girl on a seesaw. A redheaded child in denim overalls climbing a pyramid of logs. John G. stands behind the brick bathroom house, smoking crack from a glass pipette. The rock goes snap, crackle, pop in the bowl and a dragon of smoke rises toward the sky.

The past is the present and the present is the past.

He's stopped taking his Haldol since that night at the shelter. For the past week, he's been out on the street 24-7, scavenging for crack money wherever he can find it. Things have changed. His beard is getting mangy and there's lice in his hair. His skin is rough and scabby. The purplish bruise on his right elbow won't heal. And the fence in his mind that used to keep his thoughts ordered and separate has come down. Now ideas and memories are jumping back and forth like frolicsome sheep.

The past is the present and the present is the past. I was in a dark wood and I lost my way.

From behind the bathroom house, he watches a group of children crawl into a tunnel made of tires, and all of a sudden, he's back on the floor of his daughter's room, playing with the trains he gave her for her sixth birthday.

• • •

Who's God? Shar asks, pushing Thomas the Tank Engine along a wooden track.

God made everything, he tells her.

God took my mother from me.

God made me suffer. God made me lonely. God made me cry. God made me put needles in my arm.

Then God gave me you, to make up for it.

Having Shar in his life was like holding a sunbeam in his hand. Somehow he knew it couldn't last. The love he felt for the child was unbearable. He knew he wasn't meant to be this happy. Sometimes he thanked God for her, other times he cursed him because he knew he would lose her. Six years old. She was like an angel sent to earth, to make sense of his senseless life.

Did God make the trains? she asks.

I guess he did.

Did God make you a conductor?

I'm a motorman, sweetie.

Oh right. Did he make you a motorman?

I suppose he did.

Why?

I don't know.

I know. She throws her warm little arms around him. Everybody has to do something, Daddy.

When she was taken from him, it was like the sun was blotted out.

Then he's back in the playground. A small girl in a green jumper runs up to him, stops, and raises her huge liquid brown eyes to him.

"Hello, baby. Where you been?"

He stoops to pick her up. His heart is so full that it hurts. His little girl has come back. Forgive me, daughter, I have sinned. He starts to put his arms around her.

But then he sees this isn't Shar. This is a stranger's little girl. She doesn't even have blond hair. Her nanny, a hard-faced Irish number in stonewashed jeans and Nikes, pushes him aside and scoops her up. Looks over her shoulder. Shame on you, ya filthy bum. Trying to touch the children. Shame. Shame. Shame.

He backs away, wondering who has stolen his life. He wants to lash out and hurt someone the way he's been hurt. But who? Who's responsible?

In his mind's eye, he's back in the hospital corridor, with the cops waiting to talk to him. He sees the poster on the wall: BABIES ARE GOD'S WAY OF EXPRESSING HIS OPINION THAT THE WORLD SHOULD GO ON. But why should the world go on? They know it's his fault.

The doctor comes out and looks at him with baggy eyes.

I'm sorry, Mr. Gates, we lost her.

He cries out in pain. God is punishing him.

His scream echoes across the asphalt playground and stops the children's playing. Soon a cop car arrives.

What's the problem here?

No problem, officer. I'm just enjoying the sun.

All right then, just move along. You're making the children nervous.

Keep moving. Keep moving. The pain and guilt are more than he can handle alone. Someone else must be responsible.

He leaves the playground and starts to cross Amsterdam Avenue against the light. A blue Gran Fury comes hurtling toward him and for a second he thinks about stepping into its path. Come on. Kill me.

But then he looks up and sees Shar waving to him from across the street. The pale little hands. The flapping blond hair. That helpless toothless smile. This time he will save her.

Wait for me, baby. I don't want to lose you.

As he steps off the curb, the car goes sweeping by and she's gone again. Like the wind of Christ. Stations of the cross—stations of the IRT. Watch the closing doors. Forgive me, daughter. I do heartily detest my sins and fear the loss of heaven.

Sunlight fades from the trees.

And then he sees someone who still has what he's lost. It could be two hours later, it could be ten minutes. He's lost track of time. She's in the jackpot of people rushing out of the Seventy-second Street subway station and flowing past the Fairway market on Broadway. Blond hair running over her shoulders and a crochet bag bouncing on her slender hip. The other people on the street just seem to fade to gray.

There's a reason he's seeing her again. There's a connection.

"John," she says, looking surprised. "How are you?"

Who is she? He's trying to place her but it's hard with all the neurons firing back and forth in his brain. Molecules pushing molecules.

One side of his mind says this is the lady he talked to at the hospital, Ms. Schiff. The other says this is someone he used to be married to. A woman he loved. It's nothing about the way she looks that jibes with his memory. It's more a feeling he has. That this is someone who once cared about him.

"If you care about me so much how could you let another man put his dick in my ass?" he says abruptly.

"What?" She looks flustered. "Wait a second, Mr. Gates. I thought you were going to come by the clinic and see me again."

Oh now she's pretending to be somebody else. It makes him mad. An old soul song starts running through his head. Some people are made of plastic. Some people are made of wood.

"What happened to you?" she says. "You look terrible."

Like she doesn't know what happened. Some people are made of plastic.

"You know," he says. "You know about those probes they did on me. Parasites."

Though he can hardly bear to think about it himself. The virus. The bruise that won't heal. The disease spreading through his body. Some people are made of wood.

"I think you need to come back to the clinic and talk about this," she says. "We can help you there."

"But why can't you help me here?"

A half hour later, Jake is on the phone in his office, trying to calm Dana down.

"I told him the sidewalk wasn't the appropriate place for a

consultation, but he kept following me," she says, talking at twice her normal speed.

"Was he abusive?"

"No, not at all. Just very insistent. He seems to think there's some connection between us. I don't know what happened. He wasn't like this before."

"So where's he now?" asks Jake, trying to picture the scene as he stands at his window.

New York spreads out before him. The clouds like cartoon thought balloons over Wall Street. Jersey on the right, Queens on the left. The old bridges linking the land masses together like long intricate bracelets. And the hundreds of taxicabs crawling along the grids in between like yellow ladybugs. It all seems so controlled and peaceful from up here that it's hard to imagine disorder anywhere in the city.

"He's outside."

"Outside where?"

"He's outside our house, Jake." She makes it plain for him. "He's on our front steps. He followed me all the way home."

9

At around quarter past six, Jake gets out of a cab and finds John Gates standing in front of his town house, holding a plywood board with a rusty nail sticking out of it.

"How's it going?"

"Can't find my keys," Gates says calmly, patting the pockets of his blue MTA jacket with his free hand.

It's close to eighty degrees and the sun is still up, casting long shadows over the front steps and the Romanesque archway. Jake sees Dana peeking out from behind the curtains in one of the bay windows.

"You live here or something?" he asks Gates, who's now using the free hand to scratch himself like a dog with fleas.

"One-three-five-five Bailey Avenue. That's my address."

Jake glances at the numbers painted in gold over his front door. "That says five-three-five West Seventy-sixth Street."

Gates squints at the numbers and stops scratching. "Somebody must have changed it."

Oh boy, thinks Jake. Mr. Crazy Rambling Smelly Homeless Guy. At least he's not menacing anybody with his two-by-four. Yet.

"That's my doctor in there," Gates points the board at Dana in the window. "I have some papers I have to give her."

"Oh yeah?"

"And she has my little girl in there," Gates says, his face hawkish and creased in concern.

A white Project Return van pulls up to the curb. Two outreach workers climb out and stand around like actors on a movie set without any lines.

"Who farted?" John G. says.

The guys stare at each other. Dana comes out of the house wearing a blue sleeveless dress with large white dots on it. John G. puts his arms out like Christ on the cross. The whole scene would be funny if it weren't so embarrassing. Neighbors are leaning out of their windows to gawk. The stocky light-haired guy who's been renovating apartments across the street stands by his red Dodge van, watching.

"What's up, guy?" asks one of the outreach workers, a young man with a hoodlum's short haircut and the sound of Bay Ridge in his voice.

"That man stole my wife," says John G., pointing the board at Jake. "He took her away. Now he's living with her. Doing the nasty in my bed."

Dana takes her husband's arm. The two outreach workers look at them, like they're wondering if this could be true.

"I was the one who called," Dana says. "I think this gentleman needs help."

"Yeah, come on, buddy." The one from Bay Ridge points at the board in John G.'s right hand. "You wanna go to the hospital?"

John G. holds the board between his legs and starts pushing his ears forward like Dumbo the elephant, muttering, "Kiss me! Kiss me!"

"No, really," says Bay Ridge. "I think you'd be comfortable. You'd like it there."

"Kiss my ears!"

The outreach workers look at each other again.

"So what emergency room are you going to take him to?" Jake asks the second worker, a bulky guy with a weightlifter's body and a tiny head.

"Parkside."

"Why don't you take him downtown to where my wife works?"

The bulky guy stares right through Jake. "Parkside needs the money. They're looking to keep their beds filled."

"I'm not going to any goddamn hospital," John G. interrupts.

The bulky one sighs. "All right, let's just take him to the shelter then," he tells Bay Ridge.

John G. suddenly takes the board from between his legs and holds it up defensively. "I'm not going to a city shelter!"

"Why not?" asks Bay Ridge.

"Because I've been in a city shelter!" John G. hits the sidewalk with the board and the nail. "I've slept in a city shelter! I have had a bad experience with the city shelter system! They've deprived me of my definition of what it means to be a man!"

His voice echoes down the block and out into Riverside Park.

The Bay Ridge guy turns to Jake. "Well, we can't force him to go anywhere, you know."

"What about getting a mental health removal order?"

John G. abruptly drops the board and lets it clatter to the sidewalk.

Bay Ridge shrugs. "Well now he's not really bothering anybody."

"It's for his own good."

"Mr. Defense Lawyer." Dana lets go of her husband's arm.

As she moves away, Jake stares at the space where she was just standing, wondering what he did wrong.

She moves toward John G. cautiously. "John, are you all right?"

Gates looks at the dots on her dress as if he's hypnotized. Jake feels a knot of tension in his gut. It's not just the potential for danger here; it's like watching his wife dance with someone else.

"You know, I'm really very worried about you," she says to John in a warm calming voice. "I really think you need to be in the hospital. It's not safe for you out here."

"You're damn straight it's not safe," John G. says, his cracked-out eyes shifting back and forth. "They got all kinds of shit going on. Parasites. Radio signals jamming everything. They got you all confused about who you are. They even got me messed up. Every time I try to think about how it was with us, I keep hearing, 'Pass de dutchie on de left-hand side, pass de dutchie on de left-hand side.' " He swivels his hips as he sings in a Jamaican accent.

Jake looks across the street and sees the stocky guy by the red Dodge van shaking his head in disgust. As if he's wondering why none of the guys are taking charge of the situation. Goaded, Jake starts to move between Dana and Gates, but his wife waves him away.

"Look." Jake turns back to the outreach workers. "Isn't there any way we can just get him out of here?"

"Yeah, come on, guy," says the bulky one, flexing his arms and moving toward Gates as if he's about to heave him across his shoulder. "You're bein' a nuisance to these nice people."

"Okay-okay-okay, I'm going." John G. throws up his hands. "But I just wanna say one more thing to her."

He stares at Dana like he's looking at the sun. "You can't get rid of me just like that. A-right?"

"Okay, that's enough." Jake finally succeeds in getting between them.

"I'm serious." John G. keeps looking over Jake's shoulder at Dana, still trying to reach her. "We're all connected, you know. Just like New York Telephone."

The two outreach workers come over to stand on either side of him, just in case he needs to be restrained.

"Just gimme one more second!" John G. tries to wave them off. "It's random displacement of molecules. What you do has an effect on me."

He points a righteous finger at Dana. Jake tries to push it away.

"I'm telling you." John G. drops the finger, but he stands his ground. "I know it's true. Like I know Horace Clarke struck out that time because I opened a window, just like I know a little girl got hit by a truck because maybe you sneezed." He looks around wildly, grinding his teeth. "And you know what connects us? It's the memory of love. All right?"

The two outreach workers have now joined Jake in standing between John G. and Dana. They're like a sandlot football team making a goal-line stand.

"You can fuck me in the ass and you can put electrodes in my brain and parasites in my body!" John G. shouts. "But you can't kill the memory of love. That's the most powerful virus in the world, girl." He turns and starts to storm off toward the park. "And they haven't invented the vaccine that can wipe it out yet!"

10

Two days later, Jake finds himself deep in enemy territory. He is deposing a man named Noel Wolf in a book-lined conference room at the Greer, Allan law offices on Wall Street. Intimations of Waspdom surround him. Plush red leather furniture; portraits of the founding partners staring down like angry gods; a replica of the Bill of Rights on the wall, as if the original document had been signed at this very address.

"Before the break, we were starting to discuss the board's vote to sell Starrett-Smith Communications," he says, organizing his papers.

"Yes, that's right," says Wolf's lawyer, a Greer, Allan preppie named Russell Sloan, who looks ever so slightly like young John F. Kennedy. "Except you had all the facts wrong."

"Russell, I don't need you to correct me, I know where I am."

Just a little jab to straighten him out. The good thing about these depositions is that there usually isn't a judge present. It's like having the teacher out of the classroom.

Jake turns back to Noel Wolf, a sixtyish investment banker with fleecy white hair and the face of a lion made soft and feminine by the pampered life.

"Sir, did you in fact tell my client, Mr. Berger, the vote was coming up imminently before he went away?"

"All the board members were sent letters," says Wolf, letting his left arm hang limp while keeping his right arm crooked and his fist closed.

"Yes or no, sir."

"Yes I did. I sent him a letter."

"Bullshit," mutters Jake's client, Bob Berger, sitting beside him. "Absolute fuckin' bullshit."

Battling Bob. The roughest-spoken real estate developer in New York and Jake's first major client with Bracken, Williams. He's a low-down kind of father figure to Jake, encouraging him to cut corners and knock heads. Today, he's shown up without a tie just to piss off prissy old Noel Wolf, who stands accused of going behind Bob's back to convince the other board members to sell Starrett-Smith, a large television and publishing outfit with seven thousand employees on both coasts. Hence, Bob is suing Noel for breach of contract.

"Mr. Schiff, please admonish your client to keep his invective to himself," says Russell Sloan, who's clearly a little out of his depth in this type of case. He's just a hardworking securities litigator. The kind who stays up all night doing paperwork and then endears himself to the senior partners by falling down a flight of stairs in exhaustion.

Jake ignores him. "So why is it, if you sent out letters, that you can't produce a copy of the one you sent my client?"

"Don't answer that," Russell Sloan tells Wolf.

"Well, what's the problem? You had a secretary type up the letters on a computer at the office. Right?"

Not even a cautious nod from Wolf. Just a sidelong glance at his lawyer. He's lying.

Jake laces his knuckles together over his right knee. "So most computer systems keep a record of what time and date something was entered." He pauses to let that sink in. "Therefore you ought to have a record."

Something in Russell Sloan's smooth pale face flinches, and Jake knows he may have just given the young lawyer his first real wrinkle.

"Don't answer that either," he tells Wolf, who sits there batting his eyes. "Interoffice communication is privileged."

"No, it's not," says Jake, hearing Bob Berger grunt with approval near his ear. "You don't know the rules of evidence, but I'll get back to that. First I'd like to know who authorized you to begin discussions about selling the company to Leonard-Stanley."

Before his lawyer can shut him up again, Noel Wolf uncrooks his right arm and starts holding forth as if he's regaling a table full of guests at his country house.

"I don't need authorization to talk to Jim Leonard, he's one of my oldest friends," he says. "We have dinner together all the time with our wives."

"How nice. But how is it that you ended up talking to·him about selling Starrett-Smith?"

"The iron was hot. Starrett was coming off its best year ever. Two of the television shows they produced were in the top ten and the magazine group was showing a profit for the first time in nine years. Now was the time to sell."

Jake presses forward like a boxer seeing an opponent drop his guard. "But Mr. Leonard has never run a successful business of his own. All he does is buy other companies, break them up, and sell off the assets. Did you consider the fact that you'd be putting more than seven thousand people out of work?"

Noel Wolf raises his chin like a hunting rifle. "It's called the pursuit of happiness, Mr. Schiff. Not the grant of happiness or the right to happiness. Life is a race and it goes to the swift. If any of those people who used to work for Starrett-Smith have a problem, let them go start their own companies. My responsibility is to my shareholders."

"And lining your own pockets, you gonif," Bob Berger snorts.

"I move to have that remark stricken from the record," says Russell, flaring his nostrils at the female court reporter present. "You have absolutely no evidence to support that accusation."

Though Jake would bet it's true.

"Whatever," he says. "I'm more interested in hearing what qualifies Mr. Wolf to make a decision about who to sell the company to without including my client in his discussions with the board."

"I've run an investment firm on this street for more than forty years," Wolf says, drawing himself up indignantly.

"And been unsuccessful for the last twelve of them," says Jake, glancing down at his papers. "You've put two businesses into Chapter Eleven and you've been losing investors steadily since the eighties." He turns a page. "You've also had operating losses of more than three million dollars for the last two years running."

"Fuckin' guy couldn't run a whorehouse in Tijuana at a profit." Bob Berger leans forward and a little puff of white chest hair shows through the open buttons of his shirt.

Russell Sloan sits bolt upright. "This is outrageous."

Noel Wolf's face starts to turn bright red, contrasting against the burnished maroon spines of the law books on the Greer, Allan shelves.

Jake keeps coming. "Isn't it true, Mr. Wolf, that you've only been able to maintain your position on the board because of social connections and previous relationships?"

"I don't know what you mean by that."

"I mean, you went to school with half the directors and your wife plays tennis with the wives of the other half." Jake glances over at Bob Berger, who nods.

Ah, yes. The secret is out. Noel Wolf is a member of the lucky sperm club. All his life he's been coasting: going to the right schools, marrying the right woman, playing golf at the right clubs. Now in the autumn of his years, he sits there, having accomplished little in his tweedy clothes.

"I don't have to listen to this crap," he tells his lawyer, whose lips are curling back into his mouth.

"I guess the race is to the swift if you start next to the finish line," Jake says.

"All right, that's it." Russell stands up abruptly. "We're out of here."

"Where you going?" asks Jake. "This is your office."

Russell looks around as if he's confused. Then he tells Wolf to wait outside. The stenographer sits, with her long red nails poised hesitantly over the machine, spider's legs ready to drop.

"I thought we were going to be able to work together, Jake," says Russell, turning white with fury.

"You represent your client, Russell, and I'll represent mine."

"And I'll let Todd Bracken know that some of us are going to have a very serious problem working with you if our firms merge," Russell warns him.

"Ah, lighten up." Jake tries to touch him on the arm. "In this business, you get a sharp elbow or two, it's not the end of the world."

Hell, it's conceivable the two of them might be friends in a couple of months. But right now Russell isn't having any of it.

He draws away as if he's just stepped in raw sewage. "You just watch yourself, Jake," he says stiffly. "Things can change around here in a hurry. No one's ever a hundred percent secure."

11

This one I like. She more like a motherly type of figure."

Dana is back at the psych ER. The patient is showing her a picture of a hefty naked woman spreading her labia with two fingers, which formed an upside-down Nixon V-sign. Dana bites her lip and tries to keep her eyes glued to her clipboard.

"Now this next one is more like my sister," says the patient, turning the page of his magazine. He's a stumpy, roundheaded man who claims his name is Dwight Eisenhower. "She was a dear, sweet woman. Even though the only use she ever had for a black man was to give her a little dick and then get the hell on out of her bed . . ."

There is a knock at the door and Dana's supervisor, Rod Walker, sticks his head in. "You got a minute?"

Dana sets aside her clipboard and excuses herself. Dwight Eisenhower barely glances up from his pictures.

Out in the corridor, Rod is waiting, fluorescent light reflecting off a pink scalp that looks as if it's been buffed with a shoe-shine rag.

"Your friend came by the clinic yesterday," he says in a pinched nasal voice.

"Who?"

"I think his name is Gaines. Gates. Something like that." Rod's nostrils quiver. "He was looking for you. He said you might not recognize him. The shape of his head has changed."

"Uh-oh." Her right hand goes up to her chin.

Rod fingers the buttons of the navy blazer his mother bought him. Forty-six years old and still living with his parents in Rego Park. It's true, Dana thinks, some people in psychiatry need as much work as the patients.

"He was very insistent about seeing you," Rod says. "He said he had some papers for you. And something he wanted to say about random displacement. Apparently he made quite a fuss. He even threw a chair at one point."

"He threw a chair?"

"Well, maybe he just knocked it over." He takes a few strands of hair from the left side of his head and tries to pull them over to the right to cover his bald spot. "In any event, it was very disruptive for everybody there. Several patients needed their dosage adjusted."

"I'm sorry."

Rod's eyes get closer together. Dana instantly regrets having said anything. The words "I'm sorry" are like blood in the water to a career bureaucrat like Rod.

"This was your responsibility, Dana," he says like the class tattletale. "No one asked you to take on this patient. You practically begged me for permission."

"I really think you're overreacting," says Dana. "No one's talking about Mr. Gates being seriously violent. He's not even an inpatient."

He can't be dangerous, she tells herself. It's too frightening to consider. He knows where we live.

"I'm just telling you, Dana," he says, his voice honing in like a dentist's drill, "it's your name on his file."

The secretaries at reception stop fixing each other's hair, aware they're witnessing a ceremony as solemn as the unveiling of a statue: the covering of a bureaucrat's ass.

"Well, did anyone ask if he wanted to be admitted?" Dana says. "Or if he wanted his medication changed? I mean, he must have come in here looking for help."

"He came here because he said you're his wife," Rod corrects her.

Her stomach sinks and the corners of her mouth follow. Over at the nurses' station, a squat unshaven Polish man is trying to get one of the staff psychiatrists to give him back his harpoon.

"No one else wanted to take him on," Rod says. "They have enough clients of their own. And he has no insurance. Remember?"

"I remember," says Dana, wiggling her right knee nervously.

"And bear in mind, we're still cleaning up after your last patient." Rod shakes his head as if he's almost too mad to speak.

"Who's this?"

"Mrs. Lee," he tells her. "They found her on the sidewalk."

Dana stares at a smudge on the wall, feeling dizzy, as if her blood pressure just dropped.

"Oh my God, what happened?"

"She took a dry dive from the tenth floor."

Only someone who still lives with his parents could afford to be so callous.

"Jesus, when was this?"

"The day before yesterday," says Rod. "The police may be by to ask you some questions."

Dana keeps staring at the smudge as if it's a Rorschach test. In her office, Dwight Eisenhower is still looking at pictures of fat naked women. She wonders what she's accomplishing here. Her patients are throwing themselves out windows and showing up at her house.

Why is this happening? All she's ever wanted out of life is to be the good girl. To take care of people. Somehow she always assumed she'd get rewarded along the way. For all those times she drove her mother down to Sloan-Kettering and hid her liquor bottles after chemotherapy. For staying home being the good wife and the good mother while Jake was out beating the world. But now she sees there's no reward for goodness. There are just complications.

"I don't understand," she says to Rod. "I had her talking to one of the staff psychiatrists and I thought he prescribed Prozac for her. She didn't seem like she was imminently suicidal."

Though if Mrs. Lee is capable of going ahead and throwing herself out a window, she shudders to think what John Gates could do.

"She didn't jump," Rod says.

"What?"

"She was pushed. That moron husband she brought in here. He tossed her out through the glass. Maybe he's the one you should have admitted."

Before Dana can respond, Rod turns and stalks away like one of the early mammals marching back into the sea.

12

John G. sits at a table in a gourmet Korean deli in Times Square. A neon ad for a Japanese camera company blinks on and off across the street.

He keeps trying to stab at the moment and pin it down to reality. But his thoughts are coming in like tides, each one overpowering the one that came before it.

The memory of love. Sunlight through the trees. Shar waving to him from across the street. Everything he's had and loved, he's lost. Like the sun.

He remembers the day after his mother left.

He messed his pants at school. A fourth-grade field trip to the Museum of Natural History. Two weeks before Christmas. His snot frozen on the sleeve of a thin windbreaker and his fingers red and chapped because his aunt didn't give him mittens. He'd been looking at the apes exhibit in the glass display case when it happened. Something about seeing the mother gorilla with her children. He just forgot himself for a moment and lost control.

No one would sit with him on the ride back. Stinky John! The cheese sits alone! For months afterwards, he'd sit by himself in the back, taking comfort in the warmth and the feeling of the wheel moving under him.

I don't want to lose you again. Oh forgive me, my daughter.

He finds himself thinking about what his life would be like if Shar were still alive. Maybe if the molecules had gone in just a slightly different direction. A phone would have rung. Rain might have fallen. The light would have stayed green a second longer. Everything could have turned out all right. He sees himself years in the future, sitting by the door, waiting for Shar to come home from a date. The TV and the fireplace going. Margo fixing him a late supper in the kitchen. The life he should've had. Somehow it's slipped through his fingers. Who's responsible? Who made the molecules go the wrong way?

Shar waving from across the street. The screech of brakes. Random displacement. He should've been there for her.

Outside, it's getting dark and the neon camera ad is glowing brighter. Green and then white. White, then green. Little chaser lights around the letters. Like molecules pushing one another around.

He's tired. Soon he'll have to find a place to sleep. Anxiety presses down on him like the hot breath of an animal. Where can he go? The shelters are out of the question. And so are the parks and hospitals. He doesn't want to be wandering around some ward, ballooned on Thorazine, eyes blank, chin tucked into his chest, with another young predator like Larry Loud stalking him. No. He has to keep moving. He has the virus.

His stomach hisses and pops. He starts to think about going home, but then he reminds himself that he no longer has a home. All he has is the virus.

I'm worried about you, John. It's not safe out here. He hears that lady's soft voice from a few days ago. Maybe she can give him a place.

• • •

The light from the neon ad turns white. But she's only a social worker at the hospital, he tells himself.

The light turns green. She wants him to come back. She knows he belongs in that home. She loves him. He wants her.

"No sleep in here."

Mr. Slit-Eye-TV-Shaped-Head, who'd been wiping off the salad bar, is staring down at him. "No can sleep here."

"I wasn't sleeping." John G. feels the lethargy in his limbs and realizes that actually he might have been asleep for a second or two. "I was going to order coffee."

"No coffee. Now go."

He looks around, confused. Green light splashes in through the window. Night. He's still a little bit high from the last jumbo he smoked.

"What's the matter with you, man? My money's no good here?" He reaches into his pockets for some change but all he can find is his Haldol prescription bottle and the new boxcutter he picked up the other night to replace the one he gave away.

"No money. Go." The man slaps the table. *"Go."* Another worker drops his broom and comes over from beside the beer refrigerator.

"No money. *Go.* No money. Go," John G. mimics him. "This is America. Why don't you learn to speak fucking English?"

Mr. TV-Head pulls the chair out from under him. His friend, who'd had the broom, is squaring off in a fighter's stance. "Now you leave," Mr. TV-Head says, leading with his left shoulder to set up a right cross.

"You can't do this to me!" John G. wobbles on his feet. "I'm a white man in America. I got my rights."

Two Puerto Rican kids in striped shirts and chains are laughing at a nearby table. The boy opens his mouth and shows the girl the half-eaten shrimp roll on his tongue. Seafood? The girl peeks at John G. through the pickets of her long green-and-brown painted fingernails. The combination of utter exhaustion and humiliation makes him feel like crying.

"I'll sue you, man," he tells the Koreans. "I'll sue your fuckin' ass."

"Gai na pa na." Mr. TV-Head pushes him toward the door. "Yeah, yeah, sue me, sue me."

"Don't touch me! Don't you even try to touch me, you fucking parasites!" John G. warns him as he shuffles along. "I'm not just some bum. I have a house on the West Side."

The guy who'd had the broom has gone back to start spraying John G.'s seat with Lysol disinfectant.

"I'm going and I'm never coming back here again!" On his way out, John G. slams his fist against the door frame in frustration.

Before he can even feel the pain in his hand, Mr. TV-Head gives him a good kick that sends him flying out onto the sidewalk.

"And stay out, ya fuckin' asshole," says Mr. TV-Head in perfect Brooklyn-accented English.

He lands on his right arm and more pain shoots up to his shoulder. He slowly rolls up his sleeve and looks at the elbow. That purple bruise still isn't healing. If anything, it's getting worse. The virus. It's going to kill him. He tries to stand, but his knees won't cooperate. He just lies on his back, looking up. Everything he sees reminds him of death. Cigarette ads on billboards. Car exhaust fumes. A gun jouncing on a policeman's hip. And here he is, in the middle of the filthiest city in the world, with his immune defenses down.

He closes his eyes and sees Shar again. Still waving from across the street. Wanting him to come get her. Hunks of metal flying between them. Molecules pushing molecules. The light turns green. The light turns red. Why can't he reach her?

A cab hurtles by, spraying gutter grit in his face.

He wants so much right now that he can't keep it all straight in his mind. He wants a place to stay. He wants more life. He wants the life he once had. He wants his baby back. He wants release from the past. He wants to get high and stay high until the moment he dies. And he still wants to hurt someone as badly as he's been hurt.

But he can't even stand up.

He thinks of a commercial he once saw—an old woman lying at the foot of her stairs, talking into the little microphone tied around her neck: 'Help me, I've fallen and I can't get up.'

All of a sudden, it strikes him as funny. Help me, I've fallen and I can't get up.

He starts cackling to himself and when no one notices, the cackle turns into a loud chuckle. Then the chuckle becomes a gale-force roar. Soon hordes of people are stepping around him like streams diverging around a rock as they head to Port Authority. Help me, I've fallen. Help me. Help me. Help me.

But then the camera-ad light turns green and he hears that lady's nice voice again. "I'm very worried about you, John." She cares about him. She wants him to come back. He heaves himself up to his feet and starts staggering toward the bright lights uptown.

13

Jake and Dana's son, Alex, is walking home with his best friend, Paul Goldman, just before twelve-thirty that night. They are both dressed slightly grunge, in black Nikes, oversized flannel shirts, and jeans as baggy as potato sacks.

"So what'd your father say about the nose ring?" Paul asks.

"He was cool about it."

"Ah, that's cool. Your father's cool."

"Yeah, he's all right." Alex puts his hands in his pockets and sighs as if he's feeling every one of his sixteen years. "But I think I'm going to stop wearing it soon. What if I get a cold and have to blow my nose? It'll come out three ways."

Paul can't think of an answer, so he keeps walking. "I think I'm gonna shave my head," he says after a while.

"Cool."

They are on the west side of Broadway, going past a drugstore full of white light and a newsstand where a frail Pakistani man arranges stacks of gay pornographic magazines.

"If I shaved my head, would you shave yours?"

"No way," says Alex, flicking hair out of his face.

They keep walking. Paul bows his head and rocks from side to side, mumbling the words to a hip-hop song. "Insane in the membrane, insane in the brain." Alex has his mother's straight back but his father's slightly pugnacious bearing, so that he always seems to be leaning forward on the balls of his feet.

Paul flips a Turkish cigarette into his mouth as they round the corner and head toward West End. "Can I copy your paper from English?"

"What? The whole paper? Dude! Didn't you read the book?"

"Dude!" says Paul. "I didn't even know what book it was."

"We're up to the *Odyssey*."

"Huh." Paul lights his cigarette and immediately starts coughing. "What's it about?"

"Dude! That's so bogus! We spent the last two classes talking about it. What's the point of going to summer school if you don't pay attention?"

"I was spacing, dude."

Alex flaps his arms. "It's about a guy trying to get back to his family after he's been away twenty years."

"Cool," says Paul.

They cross West End Avenue, heading toward Alex's house. The street is dark and lined with parked cars. Right before they get to the front steps, they hear a grunt and look over to see a skinny bearded white man in a Yankees cap and an MTA shirt, taking a leak in the gutter and singing in a cranky wayward voice.

"I been in the wrong place but it musta been the right time . . ."

"Yo, the Night Tripper, what's up?" Paul calls out from twelve feet away. "That's a golden oldie, bro. My father listens to that shit."

The man looks up, dazed and slightly offended. "Ha?"

"You gotta pardon my friend," Alex intercedes. "He acts kinda retarded sometimes."

Paul punches Alex on the arm.

But the man doesn't seem to notice. He trips coming out of the gutter and glares at the boys as if it's their fault.

"Where you guys going?" he asks.

"I live here," says Alex. "This is my house."

In the light of the street lamp, the man's eyes go up and then suddenly move over to the right. It's as if he's picking up some frequency no one else can hear.

"Is one of you here to see my daughter?" he asks.

"No," says Alex.

"Like, we don't even know your daughter," Paul adds, bopping in place.

Somehow their words don't make it across the eight feet of sidewalk that separate them from the homeless man. He's hearing something else entirely.

"Well, I don't think that's right, a girl her age going out with anybody," he says, completing the non sequitur. "She's too young. I'm gonna have to talk to my wife in there."

"Mister, you don't live here. I do."

The homeless man seems thrown by that answer. It's as if someone has just changed the channels in his mind. He looks confused and then upset as he tries to regain his bearings on the street.

"Where am I?"

"You're on the Upper West Side."

"Then gimme some money," he says.

"Paul, go up and ring the buzzer," Alex tells his friend. "Wake my parents."

"Don't go in there! Don't go anywhere!"

The man's switched channels again. He suddenly seems angry and feral. He even crouches a little, like an animal sniffing the sidewalk between them. Getting ready to pounce.

"You come to take her away. Right?! Well that ain't gonna happen."

He reaches into his pants pocket and pulls out a boxcutter with the edge exposed.

"You touch my daughter or my wife, I'll cut your fuckin' balls off," he says, grinding his teeth and advancing on the boys. "Fuckin' little parasites."

His blade catches a glint from the streetlight as he holds it above his right ear.

"Hey, Paul, forget the bell. Let's get out of here," says Alex, backing up slowly.

But Paul is frozen. He's too scared to take his eyes off the boxcutter. The homeless man's grinding teeth begin to make a cracking noise.

"What, you think I'd do a thing like that to my own daughter?!'' he yowls, as if he's indignant at some invisible interrogator. "How could you think a thing like that?"

Without warning, he turns on Alex and the blade slices the air a foot or two from the end of the boy's nose. It makes a sickening whoosh as it goes by and Alex feels his scrotum seize up like someone just grabbed it.

"How could you think that?!"

The man takes another step and kicks a green Heineken bottle that was lying on the sidewalk. It shatters and sprays glass on the front steps. He's now less than a yard away from Alex. He smells so terrible that the air seems to die around him. Flies wouldn't get near him. Oh shit, Alex thinks. He's going to kill me. I'm gonna die without ever getting laid.

He catches sight of Paul whimpering and cowering by the wrought-iron courtyard gate, and it occurs to him that this might be the last thing he'll ever see.

"What do you think I am? A fuckin' animal?" the man shouts.

Just then there's a loud squeak and a wash of bright light from the top of the steps. Alex looks up and sees his father standing at the front door. For the first time in years, he allows himself to feel a full rush of love for the old man.

"I thought I told you to get out of here." Jake comes pounding down the steps, fists clenched.

The man in the Yankees cap doesn't pause to face him or pocket his boxcutter. He just turns and runs off toward the park, knocking over a plastic garbage can on the way.

"You all right?" Jake says, coming down the rest of the stairs and putting an arm around his son.

"Yeah, fine, Dad." Alex squirms and shoots a sidelong glance at Paul. "Don't make a big thing of it."

14

How's your boy doing?"

The man coming up the front steps looks familiar, but Jake can't quite place him. A stocky guy about his age—maybe a year or two older—with wheat-colored hair, a middleweight's physique, and a drinking buddy's face.

"He's all right, I guess," says Jake, sweeping some more of the broken glass off the stairs. "Pretty shook up, at first. He's never had anybody stick a knife in his face before."

The man exhales and shakes his head. "They're taking over, aren't they?" He looks beyond Jake's shoulder at the exploded star of broken glass in the front-door window.

It's just after ten in the morning. Fragments of green glass sparkle in the sunlight. Jake sweeps them into a yellow dustpan and dumps them into a garbage bag. He still hasn't figured out how the glass in the door got broken. Maybe John G. threw a rock at it before the boys came along.

"Philip Cardi," says the stocky man sticking out his left hand. "I'm doing some work rehabbing a couple of my man Thomas's apartments across the street."

He points to a red Dodge van parked outside the town house on the south side. Jake remembers the buzz-sawing and the hammering he's heard the last couple of mornings and everything starts to fall into place. He even recalls some vague discussion he had with Thomas, the pale, squinty-eyed landlord, about the legal complexities of converting his building into a small co-op.

"Forgive me for intruding," says Philip Cardi, running a hand through his close-cropped hair. "But when I heard about what happened to your boy and his friend last night, I had to come over." He shields his eyes from the sun. "What are the police gonna do?"

"I don't know." Jake sets the broom against the black iron rail for a moment. "We were up until three in the morning, waiting for a cop to show up and take a report. And then they say they'll only take the complaint over the phone because they don't have enough people on the shift to send one around. So now I'm going to have to go to the station myself and make sure they're going to follow up and investigate."

"Ah, they don't care." Philip mops his brow with a red bandanna.

"Yeah. Well. You didn't see anything last night, did you?" Jake notices a particularly jagged shard near his feet. "I don't suppose you live around here."

"Nah, I didn't see anything. And neither did the people I was talking to. I'm from out on the Island. I got a place, Massapequa. Beautiful out there, you know. I got a pool in the back and I can barbecue every night in the summer. It kills me to see what they've done to the city. You know? I used to love it here. But now with all the dirt and the crime . . . It's starting to be like I get a headache every time I get on the LIE to drive in."

"I know what you mean." Jake shakes his head. "I'm beginning to think I should've done the suburban thing too. For my kid, you know."

"Hey, children, they're the most valuable things we've got." Philip throws out his right arm and winces slightly. At first it looks like an aggressive gesture, but then Jake realizes it's just an involuntary reflex.

"I got two of them," Philip says. "A boy that's five and a girl who's eight. And I swear if anyone ever laid a hand on either of them the way that bum tried to lay a hand on your son, I'd be right after him with a baseball bat and a crowbar. Botta beep, botta bing. His brains are on the sidewalk and that's the end of your social problem."

"Botta beep, botta bing." Jake laughs. "Hey, where you from anyway?"

"Sixty-fourth Street in Bensonhurst."

"No shit. I grew up on Avenue X. Marlboro Houses."

"Hey . . ."

They shake hands again, with a different feeling this time. It's not the exact same neighborhood, but who cares?

"Sixty-fourth Street, huh?"

"Yeah, and Twentieth Avenue," says Philip. "Right above the surgical supply store. You remember it?"

"Sure. With the prosthetic arms and legs in the window."

"Where'd you go to school?" asks Philip Cardi.

"John Dewey."

"Lafayette, Class of seventy. You hang around Eighteenth Avenue?"

"I was down at Sweet Tooth's about once a week," says Jake, hearing himself slip into his old neighborhood attitude without feeling self-conscious about it for once.

"My place was the Milano sports club on Seventy-third Street. Associazione Italiana. You ever go there?"

Jake remembers the hard-eyed old men in their straw hats sitting in the lawn chairs out front, listening to soccer games from Italy on the radio. Through the front window, you could see the plaster saints and the local knock-around guys standing by the pool tables, brandishing their cues like Revolutionary War soldiers' muskets. Not a place for a nice Jewish boy.

"Eighty-sixth Street was more my turf," says Jake.

He finds himself hoping this doesn't cost him any status. Twenty-five years later and he's still worrying what people in the neighborhood think of him.

"Hey, Brooklyn is Brooklyn," says Philip Cardi, letting him off the hook.

"Brooklyn is Brooklyn."

"And we wouldn't let the neighborhood go all to hell like they have up here. Am I right?"

Jake nods, though he can't help noticing this stretch of the Upper West Side still looks pristine, while Bensonhurst was full of vacant lots and graffiti-smudged walls the last time he drove through. No wonder he's never taken Dana for a visit.

"So your boy's going to be okay?" Philip asks. "He need somebody to walk him to school this morning?"

"Ah, he's fine. He's a stand-up kid."

Listen to this, Jake thinks. A stand-up kid. As if he's suddenly inducted Alex into the Bensonhurst tribe.

"Well, all the guy that did this to him needs is a little attitude adjustment," Philip says, with a smile like a grimace. "You let me know if you want me to go with you, have a talk with him."

"A little attitude adjustment," says Jake.

Botta bing. He remembers Nunzi the Knuckle catching a beating outside a candy store on Twentieth Avenue because he'd been propositioning little boys in the bathroom. From then on, Nunzi wore a head bandage and kept his eyes to himself when you stood next to him at the urinal.

"I'll have to get back to you about that," says Jake, with a deferential look. "I'm a lawyer, you know."

Philip throws up his hands as if he's just touched a hot porcupine. "Forgive me. I didn't mean to suggest anything outta line. It just upsets me when I see the way our children have to grow up now."

A Ford Explorer jeep pulls up at the West End Avenue stoplight. Hardcore hip-hop blasts from its speakers, rattling the windows and shaking the tailpipes.

An involuntary snarl forms on Philip's lips. "What'd I tell you? They're taking over. You can't even walk down the street without having your ears assaulted. Makes me wonder why we fought a war overseas."

The light changes. The jeep pulls away. The sound of sparrows singing fades in.

"You in Vietnam?" Philip raises his right hand, like he's ready to give Jake a high five and bond with him at another level.

"Ah, I had a deferment," Jake mumbles. "I was in school, you know."

The hand hangs in the air, turns, and then goes back down to Philip's side, as if it's no big deal. Hey. Brooklyn is Brooklyn.

"Do me a favor, will you?" says Jake, changing the subject. "Let me know if you talk to anybody who saw what happened last night. I came out a little late. And my boy and his friend, I don't know if they could pick the guy out of a lineup."

"I'll give you a holler if I hear anything," says Philip. "By the way, you need a hand replacing that glass in your door?"

"How much do you charge?"

"It's on the house." Philip lifts his shoulders and drops them. "Hey. You're from the old neighborhood. You got any other problems?"

"Well we may be having some trouble with our chimney. I noticed soot coming out of the fireplace the other day."

"That could be serious." Philip bites his top lip and cocks his head to the left. "You oughta let me have a look at it."

"You do chimney work too?"

"I do everything."

Jake opens his hands. "Whenever you have time."

"You got it, buddy." Philip starts to walk down the steps.

Jake picks up his broom again. The stoop is mostly clean, except for five or six fragments that glint like mica. He thinks about Vietnam and wonders how he would have done in combat. There's always been a little stab of guilt about not going. Just as he starts to wince, Philip Cardi calls out to him from the bottom of the steps.

"Mr. Schiff," he says. "Think about what I told you. About having a talk with the guy. I'd go with you. Whoever he is."

"I'll think about it." Jake lifts his broom. "Whoever he is." Though even in the dim light, Jake is almost sure he recognized John G.

"I'm not an educated man like you are," Philip says, "but I remember something I heard in high school. I think it was from an English philosopher. He said all that evil needs to succeed is for good men to do nothing."

"Okay."

"So don't do nothing."

15

The sergeant has hair the color of Orange Crush and a complexion like a strawberry.

"I want to follow up on a complaint," Jake says.

"Yeah, yeah." The desk sergeant, who is named Lategano, moves some papers and puts his head down, so he's looking up at Jake from the tops of his eyes. "What's *your* problem?"

"I made a call to the precinct last night because my son and his friend got attacked. I'm still waiting to hear back from someone about investigating."

The sergeant rolls up his mouth in boredom as Jake goes over the details of the incident one more time.

"So you called in a report last night?" the sergeant interrupts, drumming his fingers on a beat-up math textbook near his phone.

"Yes, that's what I just said."

"So what do you want us to do now? It's been reported."

Jake feels himself starting to flush. He's a lawyer. He ought to know his way around the system better than other people. He's taken cops like this Lategano apart on the witness stand a thousand times. So why is the sergeant talking to him as if he's mildly retarded?

"I just want to see if anything is being done," Jake says. "Talk to people in the neighborhood. Maybe somebody saw something and can help make a positive I.D."

The sergeant picks his left ear like he's never heard anything so stupid in his life. With great reluctance, he writes down Jake's criminal complaint number and picks up a telephone receiver, which suddenly seems to weigh at least seventy-five pounds.

"Yeah, gimme eight-three-eight-nine," he mumbles into the phone. He flicks his eyes over at Jake. "You got a minute, right?"

He turns away without waiting for an answer.

Jake studies the community policing charts and the robbery beat maps on the green tiled walls. Again, he's reminded that a precinct is not a place to relax or take your station in life for granted. A bull-necked detective wearing a crewcut and a yellow polo shirt leads a young black kid in a Bart Simpson T-shirt and handcuffs through the room. The kid is looking around, a little scared and a little curious. A newcomer to the system, Jake thinks. Over the next few years, he'll learn to swagger and lie that he likes being in jail.

Sergeant Lategano is still muttering into the phone and letting his eyes wander over the book on his desk.

"Yeah . . . yeah . . . Really?" He looks over at Jake with new interest. "I didn't know that."

Jake finds himself sitting up straight. As if he's going to impress this timeserver.

"What, were you falling asleep in class? The answer's the Pythagorian theorem," the sergeant says into the phone, looking down at the math textbook. "Do your own homework from now on. Good-bye."

He hangs up abruptly and gives Jake a bitter look. "Night school," he says. "So the report says this might have been one of your wife's patients who was bothering your kid. Is that right?"

"We think so."

"Well, there's nothing we can do about it," the sergeant says.

"What're you talking about? A guy comes at my son with a razor and you're not going to do anything about it?"

"It's simple harrassment," the sergeant explains. "That's only a violation. The lowest form of criminal complaint. It'd barely be worth giving the guy a desk appearance ticket if we could find him."

"What about the razor?" Jake says. "That should raise it to menacing. That's a misdemeanor."

"What're you, a lawyer or something?"

"Yeah," says Jake reluctantly, knowing his chances of getting any cooperation have just dropped off sharply.

"So the report we have says it was a box cutter. You ought to know that isn't classified as one of the eight deadly weapons."

"So what? He's still waving it around like a weapon."

"Did he ask your son for money?"

"No."

"Did he cut him?"

"No."

"So it's not robbery and it's not assault and battery." The sergeant leans back with his legs crossed and his pant cuff riding up his pale white calf. Case closed. "If this were your client, Counselor, and we were talking about arresting him, you'd be squealing like a stuck pig."

Jake works the muscles in his jaw, knowing it's true. "What about disorderly conduct?"

"For what?" the sergeant asks. "Taking a leak in the street? Come on. We'd have to lock up half the Borough Command every Saturday night."

"You mean to tell me this guy can stand outside our home threatening our child, and you're not going to do anything about it?"

The look of winter crosses the sergeant's face, even as the window fans battle the humidity of August.

"Mr. Schiff, you've studied the Constitution, right?"

"Yeah, sure."

"Well, so now I'm going to Fordham at night and I'm studying it—because you gotta have a degree or an African mother in this department now—and you know what I figured out?" The sergeant rocks back and folds his hands on top of his stomach. "That the laws were made by a bunch of lawyers trying to protect their own property. And then when they stole enough property, they began feeling guilty and started granting rights to the so-called disadvantaged. Which left it to your working stiffs in the militias and the police departments to keep those mopes in their place, so they wouldn't rise up and try to reclaim some of those lawyers' property. So you know what I think you ought to do, Mr. Schiff? I think you oughta get together with some of your lawyer friends and some of your wife's psychiatrist friends and put the law back the way it was. Make it less confusing for everybody."

"Oh for crying out loud!" Jake erupts. "I'm supposed to wait around until this guy hurts someone? Jesus. What would you do if this was happening to you?"

"Hey." The sergeant draws back his head and a roll of stubbly fat appears under his chin. "I live out in Rockland County. I don't have to worry about this shit."

16

Stay high 'til you die. Die 'til you're high. High 'til you die.

Life without the crack buzz has become almost intolerable to John G. When he'd first hit the street, he'd promised himself he wouldn't mug anybody to support his habit. But the money from collecting cans and panhandling just isn't enough anymore. He needs a massive infusion.

He's scared out of his mind as he walks up Broadway at night looking for a victim. His eye sockets feel raw and his throat is dry. It's been years since he even thought about doing crime and he's not sure if he's up to any kind of confrontation. Plus, there's still a small voice in the back of his mind telling him this is wrong, that everything he's doing is wrong, and he ought to go back to that nice lady and ask for help.

The street is full of distractions. Taxi headlights. Models flashing their tits on magazine covers at the newsstands. Steam rising from a hole in the road. He can't screen any of it out.

Finally, while he's waiting for a light to change on the corner of Seventy-ninth Street, he turns and sees a man in black clothing closing the front door of a hulking gray building. He moves up behind him quickly and closes his right hand around the box cutter in his pocket.

That mental voice is still trying to warn him off, telling him it's not too late. But the part of him that wants to get high is stronger, and he reaches up and wraps his arm around the victim's throat.

"Give it up," he says.

"The wallet's in my left pocket," the vic says, bending back, not struggling. "Just take it."

John G. sticks his hand in, pulls out the wallet and a set of rosary beads.

"What the fuck's this?"

"I'm a priest."

The victim turns around and the white square in his collar hits John G. right between the eyes.

"Oh fuck!" John looks up and sees they're on the steps of a Roman Catholic church.

"Is something the matter?" the priest asks, as if he's accustomed to dealing with a more professional class of mugger.

"Oh shit!" John G. drops the beads and the box cutter. "God fucking damn it. I'm so fucking sorry, Father."

"It's all right."

"No, really. I'm all fucked up. I don't know what I'm doing here."

He scoops up the beads and hands them back to the priest. The box cutter goes back in his pocket. His brain frequencies are scrambling. All of a sudden, he's not sure what to do with his hands or where to put his eyes. And he's not even that high at the moment.

"You want to come in awhile?" asks the priest, seeing his confusion. "We could talk."

He looks a little like Father Drobney from Aunt Rose's parish up in the Bronx. He has the same kind of dark tonsure of hair around a bald pate and a similar moon-pale face. John G.'s body sways as if it's ready to follow him into the church, but his feet stay anchored to the sidewalk.

"I don't know what I could say to you, Father. I'm so mixed up. It's been about twenty years since my last confession."

"That's okay."

The priest goes fishing into his other pocket for keys. But John G. isn't moving. He jiggles in place, looking at the traffic lights across the street and the stars overhead.

"Is there something you want to tell me out here?" says the priest, sensing resistance.

"I'm in turmoil, Father. I can't control myself. I'm afraid I'm going to hurt somebody."

"I see." The priest visibly tenses and three ridges appear on his forehead like steps to the top of his skull. "And how are you going to do that?"

"There's these people, Father." The jiggling becomes more frantic and he starts grinding his teeth again. "They live like right around the corner from here."

"And they're the ones you think you're going to hurt?"

"I can't leave them alone. You know? There's just something about them. I have these feelings for the lady in the family. You know what I'm saying?"

The priest wipes his brow with a handkerchief. "Feelings."

"Yeah, I have these feelings because she's just like my wife. I'm very attracted to her."

"I see." The priest moves his mouth around, trying to accommodate John and appear empathetic.

"So now she's with this other guy and it's like he has the life I was supposed to have. See? He even has a kid like I used to. It's like he stole my life by moving the molecules around. Do you think that's possible?"

"Well it sounds a little unusual," the priest says, trying to sound reasonable about it.

"Yeah, I know it!" John stomps his right foot. "I know it! And I know what I'm doing's wrong, but I can't help myself. There's this part of me that says I have to get rid of this guy she's with before the molecules can go back in the right place and I can get back what I used to have."

"I think you have to fight that impulse. Have you sought counseling?"

"I've sought everything!" John G. says loudly, looking furtively from side to side. "I been trying to work it out with science! I been trying to work it out with God. And I'm not getting any answers!"

"Well, what's the question?" The priest fingers his beads.

"The question is why would God give me everything and then

take it all away? Why would he kill my daughter and end my marriage? I mean, I start off telling myself it's all my fault. I mean, I was standing there when it happened. I could have saved her. But then it's too much. I fuckin' trip out. So then I get high and all hell breaks loose.''

He wrings his hands and mashes his teeth together, as if he's suddenly in great pain.

"So what do you think, Father? You think my daughter's dead because of what I did? There's gotta be a connection, right?''

The priest moves his hands around, as if he's trying to conjure comfort out of the night.

"I don't know,'' he says finally.

"Well sometimes that's what I think. That he's punishing me. By giving me the virus. But then other times I think it's somebody else who's responsible and I just want to hurt them. So what do you think?''

"I think you need to talk to someone and then I think you need to look inside yourself and ask God to forgive you.''

John G. turns his head and looks back at the steam rising like a white exclamation point from the hole in the street. He thinks about what can build up underground.

"You're telling me God's inside me?'' he says. "I gotta go someplace and . . . think about this.''

In other words, if he doesn't get high within the next five minutes, he'll start tearing his own skin off.

"I don't suppose I could borrow some money,'' he asks the priest. "I'm good for it. I swear.''

"You've still got my wallet.''

"Oh yeah.'' John looks down at the black billfold in his hand and takes out fifteen dollars. "That all right?''

"I can handle it. But do me a favor, will you?''

"What?''

The priest reaches out with smooth, marble white fingers. "Stop by and see me sometime. Okay? I think we might have a lot to talk about. I'm very interested in this business about the molecules.''

"Oh yeah, sure thing.'' John returns the wallet and starts walking away backward, as if trying to escape the watchful eye of God. "And thanks, Father. You're a lifesaver. I'll come by and pay you first thing next week."

The priest gives out a heavy dubious sigh, like an exhausted steam engine. "Go in peace," he says.

17

Bob . . . Bob . . . It's not that kind of thing, Bob. They want you
to serve on the School Construction Board. It's a dollar-a-year
job. If it's money you want, go join some corporate board with
Kissinger and have your meetings in Vail. This is goddamn public
service.''

Jake is on the cellular phone with his old friend and client Bob
Berger. Dana sits on the edge of their bed, brushing out her hair
and watching the news.

All of a sudden, a voice shouts from the street below. "Repent,
you sinner! Damnation awaits you!''

"What the hell is that?'' says Bob Berger, who's calling from
Pound Ridge. "It sounds like you got the Red Army outside your
window.''

Jake goes over and pulls back the drapes. John G. stands in the
middle of the street, arms akimbo and face contorted.

"Jesus is angry!'' he cries out. "The army of Christ is
marching.''

Jake drops back the drapes and starts pacing around the room,
his mouth tight with fury. "Ah, it's just some bum.''

"Now I know why I moved.''

"Take the job. And give my love to Scotty and Brenda.''

The line goes dead, but as soon as Jake puts the phone down it
purrs again. Dana's friends Rick and Marjorie Baumgarten want-

ing to know if they're still on for dinner at the Gotham Bar and Grill on Friday.

"Fine," says Jake.

"YOU WILL NEVER REACH THE KINGDOM OF HEAV-ENNNN!!" John G. shouts up from the street. "JESUS WON'T FORGIVE YOU FOR LAYING WITH THE WIFE OF ANOTHER MAN!"

"That's it," says Jake.

He puts the phone down and goes to get his sneakers from the closet. "I'm gonna go down there and fuckin' kill him right now."

"Jacob, sit down," his wife says. "Are you out of your mind?"

"Well, what am I supposed to do, Dana? Call the police again? He'll be gone by the time they send a car and back an hour after they leave."

There's bashing and rattling downstairs. Jake goes over to the window and sees John G. trying to lug a shopping cart up the front steps of the town house.

"HEY, get away from there, you sonovabitch!" he yells down.

"Stop that. What's the matter with you? He can't get in. You sound like a nut shouting at him."

Jake turns on her. "Doesn't it bother you that this bum attacked our son?"

"Of course it does." She suddenly looks like a solemn school-girl. "It makes me furious. It makes me want to kill him too. But what would that accomplish?"

"Let me tell you something, Dana, sometimes a little force goes a long way." He bends down to tie his sneakers. "My old man used to beat my mother into a hospital bed twice a year and then complain about the bills. But after I got a little forceful with him there weren't any more trips to the hospital. Understand?"

"You know I hate it when you talk like that." Dana leans over and props her head up on her right hand. "It makes me think you're still this angry violent guy inside."

A long silence begins. A vein pulses near his left temple. For years, he was an unguided missile looking for a target. But being married to Dana has changed him. Somehow she's helped him make peace with the world, at least for a while. Still there are moments when the distance between them seems as great as the distance between her parents' house in Stamford and the streets of Gravesend. The moments always pass, but she can never really know what it was like growing up in a housing project.

"It's just talk, babe," he says quietly, standing up.

"I know, but he's sick. You can't get so pissed off that it poisons you."

"I still have to protect my family."

"Of course, but you're not trying to fight your way out of Gravesend anymore. You don't have to settle everything with your fists. He's going to go away eventually. Don't make the repair worse than the problem. Our life is good now."

He puts his head against her chest, listening to her heartbeat. Long ago, he discovered he couldn't really sleep unless she was next to him, so he could hear the rhythm of her breathing. The bond of love.

"Our life *is* good," he says. "That's why I don't want anything to happen to it."

"I know."

"THE VIRGIN IS CRYING!!!" John G. calls up from the street. "SHE KNOWS YOU'VE STOLEN A LIFE!!"

On the floor above, Sonic Youth is making dirty, skronky music in Alex's room.

"Maybe I could try talking to my supervisors again," Dana says. "Maybe they can talk to somebody at Bellevue about having him brought in for forty-eight hours' evaluation."

"And what if they let him go after that?"

"Then we'll have to think of the next thing."

A story comes on the news about a deranged homeless man slashing a woman and her dog in Central Park with a pair of scissors.

"And meanwhile we just wait until somebody seriously gets hurt?"

There's a loud clang on the gate downstairs. Jake goes to the window and sees John G. on the front stoop, his right arm cocked back like a baseball pitcher's.

"Oh shit, he's trying to break in," says Jake.

"Don't worry. The gate's locked."

"What about the inside door?"

Dana looks stricken. "I thought you locked it."

"I thought you did."

Wearing only shorts and a T-shirt, Jake bolts from the bedroom and goes rushing down the stairs. As he reaches the bottom, he sees the front door has been pushed open and the only thing between him and John G. is the locked wrought-iron gate. Fifteen feet away, John G. appears divided into sections by the bars like a figure in a cubist painting.

He reaches into the shopping cart, pulls out a piece of rotten fruit, and hurls it through the bars at Jake.

"Body of Christ," he says.

WHAPP! A half-eaten plum whizzes past Jake's face and smashes into the framed Picasso print at the end of the hall.

Jake ducks and bangs his head on the wall. Dana calls to him from upstairs, asking what's going on. John G. throws an old pear at Jake.

"Body of Christ."

The pear hits Jake on the temple and juice dribbles down into his ear. It's like some new postmodern humiliation ritual: getting pelted by rotten fruit in your million-dollar town house. The only way he can stop John G. is if he moves out into the open part of the hallway and lunges to close the front door.

"Blood of Christ!"

A peach hits him straight on the chin as soon as he steps out.

"Goddamn it," he mutters, putting his hand up to his face to inspect the damage.

John G. howls and punches the bars with his fists, oblivious to the damage he's doing to his knuckles. Even if the police were to come and arrest him right now, Jake thinks, the charge would only be a misdemeanor for vandalism.

"Baby, please come back! I can still make you happy!"

With one more lunge, Jake manages to reach the oak door and slam it shut. His shirt and shorts are completely soaked in putrid fruit juices. One way or another, this must stop.

From outside, John G. roars one last time.

"BABY, PLEASE DON'T SLEEP WITH ANOTHER MAN!"

18

This time when the cops come for John G. they give him a choice: Rikers or Bellevue. Rikers is thirty days, minimum. He pictures a thousand Larry Louds in cages next to him. Yo, yo, I think I got the virus, man. Bellevue is two or three days on the mental ward, max.

"Take me to Bellevue, you motherfuckers. I'm not responsible."

He's brought in the morning after the fruit-throwing incident and immediately sedated. For the first few hours, his mind drifts. He keeps seeing parts of his life playing over and over like scenes from an old movie.

He sees himself as a Patchogue boy growing up in the Bronx. The crumbling tenements and apartment houses gray and frightening as old elephants. The dusty churches and stale Communion wafers. Yankee Stadium and the el tracks. Just about the only white boy in the bleachers on Westinghouse Take an Underprivileged Kid to the Ballpark Day. The kid next to him saying Danny Cater could figure out his batting average by the time he ran down the first baseline. The smell of lavender in Aunt Rose's living room and overheated plastic slipcovers on the furniture. Instead of his mother's patchouli and cigarettes. The memory of love.

He remembers when he first started running away. Right after the time he messed his pants at the museum. He became the Hooky Kid. His truant officer must've carried his picture around in his wallet. Let the nuns slap somebody else for a change. There he was. Playing tag at the auto graveyard near Highbridge Park. Sneaking into afternoon games. Riding the subways all day. The A train was the best. The tracks ran right over Broad Channel going out to Far Rockaway and on rainy days water pelted the windows and threatened to wash the cars away.

By high school, he was hardly showing up at all; the only book he read all the way through was Dante's *Inferno*. Nuns, football players, algebra nerds, the rough gang hanging out at lunchtime. He couldn't identify with any of them, couldn't relate to any of the symbols of success or failure. Perhaps the capacity for homelessness had always been within him. "I wash my hands of you," said Aunt Rose. "You're as bad as your father." Whoever that was. She shipped him off to the foster homes. Long silences and leftovers for dinner. He hunkered down inside himself and learned never to show how scared and lonely he was. It was only later he realized that the families took him in because they got extra money from the state for each foster child who lived with them.

It didn't matter, though. He was a full-time runaway by then. Spending all his time at the second-run movie houses on Forty-second Street. Continuous showings of *Alien* and *Death Wish 2*.

Sometimes he'd fall asleep and the movies and his dreams would blend together.

He reached twenty with a good-sized heroin habit. A guy he knew from the movie theaters introduced him to the clubs downtown. Elgin, he called himself. An educated middle-aged white guy with an accent from somewhere in the middle of the Atlantic. All he ever wanted was a hand job in the balcony. In return he took Johnny G. to the Mudd Club and Tier 3. And introduced him to the kind of people he'd never met before. People who thought it was romantic that he had a heroin habit. They were older and they had money. He was poor and an addict, but who cared? He was riding through the drugs on a burst of youth.

Looking back, he remembers the music better than the people. "Too Many Creeps." "Love Will Tear Us Apart." "All your life, all your life, you've been a loser all your life." Everyone had a habit there. Within a month, he was standing in a line behind a tenement on Eldridge Street with a bunch of other skinny scraggly white guys. Waiting for a black dealer with a medicine-ball-sized belly to give him his package so he could shoot up. A hundred dollars a day. In the afternoons, he'd shoplift from grocery stores and mug the occasional old lady for the money. Felt bad about it too, a hangover from the early years in Catholic school. At night, he'd dance and try to forget it at the clubs. Until finally, he realized no one else was shooting up and he was the only one left dancing.

He got busted on Delancey Street for possession and did thirty days on Rikers. It was enough to sober him up. Sharing cells with old scags and Maytags. He went back to his aunt at the Webster Houses on his hands and knees. Age had softened her heart. Through the cousin of a friend she helped him get a job with the maintenance crew at the Transit Authority. When the drug arrest didn't show up on the computer search, he told himself there was a God.

A whole new world opened up to him. Work. Earning money. Having something to show at the end of the day. He discovered his own capacity for pulling himself together. He started studying the real estate ads, looking for an apartment to rent. And he met Margo.

Of course, she was too good for him. She wore muslin pants and peasant blouses and took classes at Hunter. And had a cupboard full of herbal teas with names he couldn't pronounce. She was working at the DMV but studying to be a nurse. A good-hearted Irish Catholic girl from a Sunnyside family. He met her dancing in front of a jukebox at a bar called the Dispatch in Kingsbridge, where transit workers used to hang out. Ernest the conductor had been trying to pick her up for months without any success. But she gave John a smile she'd been keeping to herself for years. No one in her family could figure out what she was doing with a lowlife like him—though her da was a drunk and her sister was a junkie, mind you. They made each other happy for a while. Especially in bed. She'd offer her perfect peach of an ass and let him take her from behind. The ride of his life. Better than the A train even.

They honeymooned in Atlantic City. Checked into the Marriott in Absecon and realized by dinnertime that they were outclassed. Surrounded by shipping executives with golf clubs. They checked out by nine and went to stay at the Econo-Lodge near the board-walk. By Saturday morning, they'd spent all their money at the slots and blackjack tables and were heading back to the Bronx. By six o'clock, they were holding hands and drinking Jack Daniel's at the Dispatch. All they'd ever wanted was to be together anyway.

They had Shar six months after they were married and the walls of his chest moved back to make room for his enlarged heart. From just looking at her in the incubator he could tell she'd inherited her mother's restless spirit and generous soul. He began to see himself in a different way. As a family man. With dreams of moving out of their cramped apartment on Bailey Avenue and buying a house in Woodlawn. He began moving up the ladder at the MTA. From cleaner to clerk to conductor to motorman within five years. Double shifts and no drugs. Except for the odd amphetamine to stay awake and the occasional joint to cool down after work. This is the Allerton Avenue station. Watch the closing doors. Every weekend in Van Cortlandt Park with Shar and Margo. Pushing her in the stroller and later teach-ing her how to catch the ball like Danny Cater. She looked like a fairy princess and wrestled like a Seminole alligator. She liked trains, so he bought her a set of Brio train tracks. Sunlight through the trees. The memory of love.

• • •

God made everything.

God took my mother.

God made me suffer. God made me lonely.

Then God gave me you, to make up for it.

The molecules shift. She waves to him from across the street. The light turns red. The screech of brakes. He tries to reach her.

She died in his arms.

He knew it couldn't last. It was all a dream. The rest of his life was the harsh reality. After Shar was gone, everything fell apart. Even his marriage to Margo. They couldn't bear to be together anymore because they reminded each other of what they'd lost. He kept working for a year but he was empty and broken inside. It was just a matter of time until he ended up back out on the street. He was living in a house without foundations.

They give him Ativan and he sleeps for a while. Soon the images begin to slow down. Birth, school, work, death. He awakes to the hum of fluorescent lights. By the time he moves on to his first dose of Haldol, the world starts to make a dreary sort of sense again. A kind of pressure builds up with sobriety. It nags and then threatens to overwhelm him. He's alone, he tells himself, and utterly bereft in the hash he's made of his life. Waiting to die from the disease spreading inside him.

The hospital is intolerable. Too many rules, too much order, too much time to recognize the world for what it is. As soon as he gets out, he decides, he must get high and stay high until his vital functions give out.

After forty-eight hours, the lawyer from Mental Hygiene Legal Services comes to see him in the dayroom. A rerun of *Bewitched* is on the TV.

"You can stay here or I can help you get out," says the lawyer.

"Help me get out."

19

"What's the matter, don't you have a cleaning girl?"

Philip Cardi's face appears through the bars of the front gate.

It's three days after the fruit-throwing incident and Jake is still finding little pieces of peach and plum tucked into the corners of the hallway. He puts down the mop and opens the gate.

"Our friend, the bum," he says with a sheepish smile. "He got a little wild the other night."

Philip looks at the bucket and Jake's yellow rubber gloves. "Every time I see you, you're cleaning up after him."

"Seems that way, doesn't it?"

Jake's going to have to fire the cleaning lady, Esmeralda. She sits around all day, watching the Weather Channel and Pay-Per-View movies. He gives Philip a check for fixing the glass in the front door.

"What's this?" says Philip. "I told you I'd do it for free."

"I insist." Jake nudges him.

"You sure?"

"Yeah. Come on, let me give you a tour."

He leads Philip down the hall past the living room and into the dining room. It feels good, showing somebody from the old neighborhood his beautiful house. Not in an *ain't-I-hot-shit* kind of way. More like: *Hey, look, one of us regular shmucks off the street made it.*

But instead of following him right into the dining room, Philip hangs back in the doorway, checking out the oak table, the Louis XIV chairs, and the chandelier. Jake hesitates, wondering if maybe he has been acting a little too much like an ostentatious fuckhead.

"What is that?" says Philip, pointing at the chandelier. "Cut glass?"

"Yeah." Jake looks surprised. "You into antiques?"

"I like to look once in a while. That must've cost, what, ten thousand?"

"Something like that."

Philip whistles, impressed. His eyes settle on the white mantel over the fireplace. He goes over to give it a closer look.

"So I haven't seen him for a couple of days."

"Who?"

"Your guy. The bum." He glances back at Jake with a tough mouth and eyes as clear as marbles.

"Yeah, my wife, she made a call. They've got him locked up at Bellevue."

"Hey, that's great," says Philip. But something flat and cold in his voice tells Jake he's either skeptical or disappointed. "I hope they keep him there. I think the fuckin' guy stole a hammer from my truck last week."

"Yeah, well, he's asked for a hearing tomorrow to get out. So I'm gonna go see if I can lend a hand by offering my alleged *expertise.*" Jake smiles self-effacingly.

"Good luck getting the system to work for you."

Again there's that look that's hard to read. Eyes downcast, mouth slightly puckered. Jake wonders if he's fallen in Philip's estimation by letting a woman get involved.

"Hey, is that Bob Berger?" Philip asks, turning his attention to a framed picture of Jake and Bob in tuxes on the mantel.

"Yeah, you know him?"

"A friend of mine did some contracting work for him a few years ago. Seemed like a good guy. He paid for the dry-wall, at any rate."

"Bob's a piece of work."

Philip reaches up and touches the soot smear over the picture. "Yeah, you definitely got carbon leaking," he says, switching gears.

"So what's it gonna take to fix it?"

"I don't know." Philip shrugs. "Could be something or it could be nothing. You might have a bird's nest in your chimney or a problem with your boiler."

"Does this mean we're going to have to start chopping into our walls?" Jake asks.

Five thousand dollars. Six thousand dollars. He tries to remember how much money they have in the checking account. But it's not so much the amount; it's the principle of spending more money on this place, instead of salting it away for Alex's college fund.

Jake knew the house wasn't perfect when they bought it, but he didn't mean for it to be a full-time fixer-upper. He could imagine Bob Berger saying, "Tell that Jew to put the soldering iron down before he hurts himself." Jake can handle the minor home repairs himself, but when it comes to major improvements, he's a lawyer, not a carpenter.

"You're going to have to keep an eye on this," says Philip. "The one thing you want to be sure of is that the repair isn't worse than the problem. You have a nice house. You don't want to fuck it up just to get rid of a minor obstruction."

A minor obstruction, thinks Jake. That's a good way to describe this John G. It's the same thing Dana was trying to tell him about yelling out the window. Don't make the repair worse than the problem.

"So you know anybody who could handle the job?" he asks Philip.

"I could give it a shot."

"You sure?" Jake feels a ripple of envy; he wishes he could do more things with his hands.

"Yeah," says Philip, checking his watch. A Rolex, Jake notices. Pretty ritzy for a regular contractor. Maybe just a knockoff. "I don't have time right now, but would there be somebody around to let me in early next week?"

Jake considers the options. Esmeralda, the cleaning lady, will be history by Monday. That means he'll either have to hang around the house himself to let Philip in, when he's due in court all week, or have to arrange for Alex to do it—a dubious bit of responsibility for a teenager. Besides, he shudders to think what Philip would say if he saw the boy's nose ring. What the hell. Philip already did a good job fixing the glass in the door; the handyman over on Broadway charges $25 an hour and does squat. Jake feels that he can really trust this guy. Hey, he's from the old neighborhood.

"I'll get you a set of keys," he tells Philip.

20

Jake is just settling into the witness box the next afternoon when John G.'s lawyer rises and points to him.

"Your Honor, I object to this man's presence," says Steve Baum, a young former probation officer with a discolored patch of skin on his left cheek.

Jake has to stifle the urge to answer. He's never been in a Mental Hygiene hearing before. The hospital courtroom looks about the same: the judge sits up on a bench flanked by the American flag and a sleeping court officer. But there are subtle differences. For one thing, all the lawyers and the defendant sit at the same long table before the judge. For another, Jake is the one testifying today, instead of cracking the whip as an attorney.

He looks over at John G., ten feet away, resting his head on his arms. A thrift shop tweed jacket is draped over his shoulders and a skinny tie is wrapped around his neck.

"Your Honor," says the lawyer for the hospital, Robin Hamilton Jr., the son of a famous TV and movie comic. "We feel Mr. Schiff is uniquely qualified to give testimony today. Not only is he a member of the bar and a part of the community, he's the one Mr. Gates has been harassing."

"So what?" says Baum, thrusting his hands deep into his jacket pockets. "He has no standing in this courtroom."

Judge Eugene DeLeon, who's been distracted writing a note to himself, looks up and fixes Baum with a beaky stare. "You wanna disqualify this witness?"

"What he has to say has no relevance." Baum stands. "He's not a doctor. He's not in any position to judge whether my client is an imminent danger to himself or to anybody else."

"All right, all right, let's get a couple of things straight," says DeLeon, a cantankerous former prosecutor with a face like a paper bag that's been crumpled up and smoothed out again. "Mr. Schiff is known to the court as an officer in good standing."

He nods, silently acknowledging that Jake kicked his ass righteously the last two times they were in state court.

"However, I have to agree with you, Mr. Baum, that what he has to say in this context is of limited value."

"But—"

"Sorry, partner." He casts his rheumy eyes over at Jake. "You're gonna have to step down off that horse."

The back of Jake's neck starts to hurt. He wants to stay and argue. In hundreds of his own cases, he's accepted the jocular give-and-take between judges and lawyers; you win some, lose some. It's a different feeling, though, with the safety of his own home and his family on the line.

As he leaves the stand, he glances over and sees a *New York Post* opened to the horoscope page on the judge's table. One of the entries is circled in red and the word "Good!" is written next to it.

Jake's butt does not rest easily in the spectator section.

Dana is called in next. She comes in through a side door, wearing an olive skirt and a beige linen jacket. She smiles briefly at Jake before she takes the stand and gets sworn in. John G. stares up at her intently, as if she were his opponent in a child custody fight.

Robin Hamilton Jr., who has his father's bulging eyes and pronounced Adam's apple, runs through his questions quickly and perfunctorily. Jake wonders if this is his first case. Dana still manages to make a strong argument for Gates staying in the hospital.

"He obviously has a substance abuse problem," she says, "but we haven't really had a chance to assess the rest of his needs.

He's not doing well on the street. He's seriously decompensating. Maybe with the right medication—"

"Objection," says Steve Baum. "The witness is not a doctor. Why's she testifying as an expert?"

Hey, that's my wife, Jake thinks. On the other hand, he's right. As a psychiatric social worker, Dana is not qualified to prescribe drugs.

"Well do you think Mr. Gates belongs out on the street?"

"I think he'd benefit from an extended hospital stay," says Dana.

"Okay, I haven't got any other questions." Hamilton sits down. The man was born to throw in the towel, Jake thinks.

Baum rises slowly for the cross-examination, studying the loose-leaf binder in his hands. He doesn't seem like a young man, Jake notices. He moves with too much gravity. There's an air of bitter preoccupation about him, as if he's constantly reexamining old wounds and arguments.

"Ms. Schiff," he says. "I gather from your notes here that Mr. Gates was your client. Is that correct?"

"After I saw him in the ER, I agreed to see him at the outpatient clinic," Dana answers in a composed voice.

Before she can go on, Baum is on to the next question. "Isn't that unusual?"

"Well . . ."

"Do you see any of your other patients from the emergency room at the clinic?" A singed left eyebrow goes up. The patch on his face is a skin graft, Jake now realizes.

"No, but—"

Baum cuts her off again. A lawyer's trick that Jake's used a hundred thousand times himself. Get them to dance to your rhythm.

"Well, so you agreed to see Mr. Gates on an outpatient basis because his prognosis for recovery seemed so good." Baum waves the book at her. "At least that's the story according to your hand-written notes. Right?"

Dana starts to blush and stammer a little. "Well, well, that was before—"

" 'The patient has a positive attitude and a willingness to adapt.' " Baum paces back and forth, reading from the three-ring binder as if it were scripture. " 'He's lucid and able to make decisions.' Isn't that what you wrote?"

"Well . . ."

"Yes or no? Is that what you wrote?"

"Yes, but that was before he went out on the street and started getting high again," Dana blurts out.

Jake has to smile. That's his girl. Trying to steal home plate while no one's looking. Baum isn't having any of it, though.

"I move that the last remark be stricken as nonresponsive," he says, getting a nod from the judge.

He turns his back to Dana, giving her his hard-boiled side. "Isn't it true, Ms. Schiff, that in your experience with Mr. Gates he responds well to the drug called Haldol?"

"He seems to function well when he's taking his Haldol, but when he stops taking it and starts smoking crack, he shows signs of psychosis."

"Are you qualified to give that diagnosis?"

"No, but . . ."

Jake finds himself staring at the back of Hamilton's head. Stand up, you asshole. Object. Can't you see my wife's being attacked? But Hamilton remains stubbornly seated. Probably too busy thinking about the grosses of his father's last movie.

"In fact, did you make any attempt to ascertain the source of my client's problems?" Baum asks with a slight Queens accent. "Were you even aware that he'd recently suffered the loss of his wife and his child?"

Jake's stomach feels caught up in thorns and string. He wants to help Dana, but he's powerless here in the spectator's seat. It's as if she's trapped behind a wall of thick glass and he can't get to her.

"I was aware of his loss," Dana says, balancing her words as precariously as books on her head. "But I never really had a chance to talk to him about it."

"I see," Baum says, with a twitch of sarcasm. "You don't know much about my client, do you, Ms. Schiff?"

"I'm aware that he needs to be hospitalized."

Baum smiles thinly and swings back to the defense table, dropping one file and picking up another. He pauses to put a hand on John G.'s back, but Gates doesn't move. He just sits there with his head bowed in abject sorrow. For a fleeting moment, Jake catches a glimpse of the human being beneath all the raving and screaming. He wonders how he could have felt threatened by this shabby diminished little man.

In the meantime, Baum is making another run at Dana. "Are you aware, Ms. Schiff, that a staff psychiatrist who's interviewed Mr. Gates within the last twelve hours found that he's not an imminent danger to himself?"

"He hasn't seen Mr. Gates when he's high," Dana shoots back.

"That's not the question." The judge wags a gnarled finger at her. "Mr. Baum asked if he was an 'imminent' danger. We're not talking about what he might do tomorrow or the next day. We're talking about how he is right now."

Dana looks over at Gates slumped down in his seat. Then she stares out at Jake, but he can't think of any way to signal her. "I guess he's all right at this particular moment."

Baum starts to ask another question, but the judge is on a roll. "Young lady," he says. "Let me give you a little history lesson."

He's been waiting all afternoon to give someone a lecture. And in Dana, he has a captive audience.

"Back when I was a young prosecutor, before the Civil War"— he flashes a roguish smile—"I had occasion to investigate some of the more infamous mental hospitals in our area. I saw people forced to wallow in their own excrement and a man chained down naked, being force-fed through a tube. Such things did happen! But thanks to miraculous drugs, we no longer have to keep these unfortunate individuals in these filthy hellholes. We can return people to their communities."

It really is true, Jake thinks. In most jobs, they make you retire once you get too old and stupid to function. Whereas that can be your beginning as a judge.

"No further questions," says Baum.

Dana steps down, looking dizzy. The judge takes a few minutes to review his papers and confer with his clerk. In the meantime, doctors, lawyers, and patients involved in the next few cases file into the back of the courtroom. Jake spends a few seconds trying to tell them apart.

"I must say, Mr. Baum," the judge says, finally clearing his throat. "I'm in complete agreement that there would be no point in keeping your client in the hospital against his will."

A phone rings twice in the background and then stops. DeLeon looks disappointed about missing the call. "As far as his current activity on the street is concerned, I'd remind Mr. Hamilton and Mr. Schiff that most of the old loitering laws have been thrown out recently, except where they apply toward drug dealers and prostitutes soliciting business."

Of course, as half the New York bar knows, the judge roams the West Side Highway like a Texas ranger on Friday nights, searching for working girls in his Lincoln Town Car.

"I'm going to ask that your client stay away from the Schiffs and start taking his medication," the judge tells Baum. "I leave it to Mr. Gates and his doctors to work out whether he wants to stay on at the hospital."

"Then he'll get out right away," Hamilton Jr. protests.

A Criminal Court judge has already given Gates time served on the vandalism and resisting arrest charges.

"Then so be it," says the judge. "I'm suggesting Mr. Gates find himself a treatment program within the next thirty days. Otherwise, you'll be back before me, Mr. Baum, and I won't be so lenient."

The gavel comes down. Baum offers his hand, but John G. doesn't shake it. He just looks dazed, as if he hasn't been present for most of the hearing.

Dana comes over looking forlorn and Jake hugs her. He's furious with himself. It's not losing an argument before a judge. It's the feeling that he's let his family down at his chosen profession.

"Let's get outta here," he says. "This place is starting to depress me."

21

You know," says Dana, "the whole time we were in court today I was thinking about—"

"Connecticut." Jake finishes the thought.

The Schiffs are making their way down Broadway after dinner. It's the kind of languorous summer night that slows the step, makes the air stand still, and engulfs the lit buildings in a buttery haze. Even the long-legged high school girls seem to drift instead of zip by on their Rollerblades. In the distance, the old Ansonia Hotel looks like a cloud made of concrete.

"We'd probably lose a third of our investment in the house," she says in a tense voice. "I'm not blind to that. But we'd still be able to afford a place in Westchester or Connecticut. Maybe not Scarsdale or Greenwich. But Tarrytown, for sure. I looked in the *Times*. They were selling an imitation colonial for four-fifty . . ."

"Dana . . ."

"You could still practice here and we could live somewhere else."

Alex begins to slouch, as if he's trying to shove his entire upper body into his pants pockets.

"Dana . . ." Jake starts shaking his head. "Dana, will you listen to me for one second?"

"What?"

"Look over there," he says. He points to a run-down old coffee shop across the street that's somehow held its ground between the lacy boutiques and pretentious condominiums. "You know who works behind the counter?"

"No, I don't."

"The ex-president of Liberia."

"I thought they ate the ex-president."

"That was the other one. I'm talking about the guy before him. I helped him get his green card. On his employment application, he put down, 'Former sovereign ruler of developing African nation. Commanded army of three thousand.' "

"No way," says Alex.

"It's true." Jake turns toward a Korean deli on the far corner. "I met the guy who owns that place twelve years ago, when he was sitting on a milk crate outside snapping green beans for the salad bar. Now he just bought an apartment house in Queens and he's got half his family from Seoul living over there."

"So?" says Dana.

"So that's the Ansonia," says Jake, as the old hotel's rococo facade comes into focus. "That's where Saul Bellow wrote *Seize the Day*. Stravinsky and Flo Ziegfeld lived there too. Before your time, Alex, they had Plato's Retreat in the cellar."

"What's Plato's Retreat?"

"It's where I met your mother."

"It's not." Dana draws back her fist. "So what's your point, Jake?"

"My point is, this is still the greatest city in the world. This is where we raised our son. And I'm not going to let some screwball stampede me off the reservation."

"Can we get some ice cream?" asks Alex, as Dana starts to sigh in exasperation.

They stop and watch their son bound into the nearest red Häagen-Dazs parlor with the most animation he's shown all evening. He's reached the age where his parents are a constant source of bother and humiliation. Again, Jake finds himself wishing there were a second child in the space between them, a little one who would actually enjoy still having his mother and father around.

"You know, I think the city you're talking about doesn't exist anymore," Dana says. "Sometimes I wonder if it ever existed."

"It existed, all right. And I'll tell you something else. A hundred years ago, things were just as bad as they are now. They had the Plug Uglies and draft riots. Half the population was squeezed into lower Manhattan and dying of typhus. But you know, no matter what happens, the city always keep going."

"I'm beginning to wonder if that's such a good thing."

"Please help me get something to eat . . . Please help me get something to eat . . ."

John G. is shaking his cup to a rhythm no one else can hear and chanting the Upper West Side beggar's mantra.

As soon as he got out of the hospital, he headed right up to this part of town and smoked himself a jumbo. But after a couple of days of being clean, he finds it's requiring greater and greater quantities to truly get off. Instead of that familiar buzz, he just feels angry.

Angry at the doctors who wanted him to stay at the hospital. Angry at the people who put him away in the first place. The Schiffs. The Shits. And angry at the ice cream customers who won't give a man a quarter to get high on a nice summer night.

"Please help me get something to eat, you goddamn motherfuckers . . . Please help me . . ."

Why should he bother being polite? Now that he's getting back down in that nasty dank little crack groove, he doesn't see the point of being nice to anybody.

And then he sees them. It's almost as if he'd summoned them. The people who tried to put him away. The Shits. The Schiffs. What's the difference?

"Hey, you motherfuckers!"

The lady grabs her husband's arm. Their kid walks out of the ice cream parlor holding a vanilla cone. John G. tells himself it can't be them. It's his mind playing tricks on him again. But then he remembers they live right around the corner from this place. In the house they stole from him.

• • •

At first, Jake can't believe they've run into John G. again so quickly. But then he looks around. A hot summer night with a long line of guilty liberals outside an ice cream parlor on the Upper West Side. Where else would you go if you were a panhandler?

"I said, hey, you motherfuckers!"

Alex comes out with an ice cream cone.

"Gimme some of that, you little motherfucker. I'm hungry." John G. tries to grab it from him.

All the teenage bravado instantly disappears. The boy huddles by his father's side.

"What are you afraid of?" says John G. "You're not in any 'imminent danger,' are you?"

"Come on, let's go." Jake puts one arm around his wife and one arm around his son and starts walking downtown.

"'Imminent' means right now." John G. starts to follow them. "Not tomorrow or yesterday. Right now!"

He knocks over a garbage can on the corner. Jake feels his wife's shoulder shaking and sees the ice cream cone trembling in his son's hand.

"Gimme some of that ice cream, you little motherfucker. I'm your father. Do you wanna see your father starve?!"

The Schiff family starts to move more quickly. Past hardware stores, Tex-Mex restaurants, and sidewalk vendors with blankets full of Dumpster goods and antique lamp shades.

"What are you all running for?" John G. shouts as he lurches after them. "Don't you know what 'imminent' means? 'Imminent' doesn't mean I'm gonna kill you right now. 'Imminent' means I'm gonna kill you in a minute."

Finally Alex can't take it anymore. Perhaps it's the memory of the box cutter being waved in his face. He drops his ice cream cone and sprints right into the traffic going both ways on Seventy-ninth Street. From the corner of his eye, Jake sees a taxi turning west on Broadway and a pair of headlights coming straight toward his son.

Some primal instinct takes over. He jumps off the sidewalk and comes running at Alex. His heart is banging against his ribs. He reaches the boy at the yellow center median and pushes him out of the way with both hands.

Alex goes stumbling toward the safety of a bus shelter on the south side of the street. Jake turns, just in time to see a pair of headlights come rushing at him. His body stiffens and his breath freezes. There's no time to get out of the way. The brakes screech and light moves across the windshield.

But the cab stops less than two feet in front of Jake. He looks down at the scratched yellow hood and breathes a sigh of relief.

And then a bike messenger in purple Lycra shorts and goggles plows into him going the other way.

22

A seagull crying. A motor starting.

John G. forces his eyes open and finds himself on a park bench along the Hudson River promenade. Tall white houseboats float beside old gray docks. Caribbean women with music in their voices push small white babies in well-appointed strollers. A merciless sun stares down hard.

He's not high anymore. But in his mind, he keeps hearing the screech of brakes from last night and seeing the cab rushing at Mr. Schiff. The lady standing next to him screams and then her voice melds with the one in his head. And when he looks again, the headlights are rushing toward a child.

The shifting molecules. She waves to him from across the street. The light turns red.

Her last words were, "I love you, Daddy."

He shuts his eyes and covers his face with his hands.

"You all right?"

A wiry old white man in a black Speedo bathing suit is staring at him.

"Yeah. No. Yeah."

"You sure? You don't look all right."

John G. blinks three times, trying to pull reality together. "You know what time it is?"

" 'Bout quarter after three," the old man says, shaking his head and going back to his tai chi exercises.

Five more hours until evening. John G. doesn't trust himself to be outside anymore. He's done too much damage already.

He goes to the railing and looks out at the river. He feels sick at heart. An oil-black duck swims amid the driftwood. John G. wishes he could at least be around someone or something from the old days. But all he sees when he looks ahead is New Jersey.

Another homeless guy comes trundling along in a battered straw hat, pulling a shopping cart full of soda cans.

"Say, bro," John G. calls out. "There any safe place to sleep around here?"

The guy turns; his face is like an eroded beach and his beard is like a piece of seaweed stuck to his chin. "I been staying in the tunnels."

A train's horn blares in the background and John G. starts to vaguely remember something one of the guys said at the shelter. The one with the big belly, who smelled from Chinese food and urine. He said he'd rather be back in the tunnels under the park.

"It's all right down there?" John G. asks.

"It ain't the Hilton." The man in the straw hat moves on, as if pushed by a strong breeze.

The horn blows again in the distance. Big train heading south. Probably the Amtrak Albany-to-Washington line. It gets John thinking about how he once had a train of his own. Eight hundred thousand pounds of flesh and steel harnessed by the handle in his hand.

The memory brings him to his feet and he begins to follow the sound through the park, all the way to the Seventy-second Street entrance. He sees another homeless guy in a big gray coat disappearing through an opening in the iron fence under the West Side Highway. The entrance to the tunnel. He goes over and sticks his head between the bars. There's just a yawning void ahead.

Part of him doesn't have the heart for this. But the other part remembers the screaming brakes and Larry Loud's breath on the back of his neck. It can't hurt to look.

He squeezes the rest of his body through the fence and starts to edge along a jagged concrete ledge to the left. But then some of the stone crumbles and he falls six feet straight down.

His body screams from all the outrages he's perpetrated on it the last few months, but then the pain subsides. Slowly his eyes begin to adjust to the darkness. What he sees is a long gray tunnel, stretching out for miles and miles to the north. Only a stark shaft of light slanting through an overhead grating hints that there might still be a world outside.

On the right, some twenty-five yards away, a stubby white man missing an arm stomps Rumpelstiltskin-style around an oil drum full of fire, daring John G. to pass.

The frightened part of his mind is telling him to turn back. But the other part is going Doris Day on him. *Que sera, sera.* Whatever will be, will be. Maybe he does belong here. He's either reached the end of something or the beginning.

To the left, there's a kind of underground man's neighborhood behind a low stone wall. Five identical cardboard boxes, side by side, like homes in the suburbs. He comes over and looks inside one of them. In the darkness, he can make out a GE toaster oven, an old Zenith black-and-white TV with rabbit-ears antenna, a Waring blender, pots and pans. Just like Aunt Rose's place. Except all the electric equipment is hooked up by extension cords to the streetlights through the grating twenty feet overhead.

A hoarse voice calls out. " 'Scuse me, mister, you lose something?''

Lose something? It's like a question he'd ask himself. Only now somebody else is asking it. He takes his head out of the cardboard home and backs away.

Rumpelstiltskin. The one-armed man who'd been stomping around the fire is staring at him. From a distance of ten feet, his reddish brown hair looks like it's been scalped back off his forehead, and ugly purple blotches are visible all over his face.

"No," John G. says, patting his pockets and feeling discombobulated. "I didn't lose anything here."

"Then get the fuck out!"

The one-armed man picks up a black cast-iron skillet and throws it at John G.'s head. "WHHAAAAAAA!!!"

It crashes into a wall a full foot away and snaps him into a new state of alertness.

"Get the fuck out of here!!"

But before John can move, a red brick catches him flat on the chest and sends him staggering back against the wall. Booosshhh. The air goes out of him. His lungs feel bruised and his head feels light. He can't seem to catch his breath.

Rumpelstiltskin is advancing on him with a rusty tire iron and an avid look, as if he can't quite believe he's finally found someone he can dominate.

"I SAID GET THE FUCK OUTTA HERE!"

John G. can't stand. Now he's going to die. He's sure of it. In a way, it's a relief. This is what he's deserved all along. He hears traffic shifting the heavy steel road plates above and he closes his eyes, awaiting the final blow. He smells wood smoke and tries to come up with a mental picture of his wife and child to hold on to at the end.

But the picture doesn't come and neither does the blow.

After a few seconds, he opens his eyes and sees a husky black man with dreadlocks talking to the one-armed man and poking him in the chest with a sharp index finger.

"He was a spy," Rumpelstiltskin is arguing meekly.

"Don't you be trippin' on me, James. You hear? We don't need no Amtrak police down here. My God is the God of Abraham and I am the head nigger in charge. So you gonna bug out, go do it somewhere else."

The one-armed man drops the tire iron and slinks away, his jeans drooping off his ass in discouragement. The man with dreadlocks turns to John G.

"The hell you look at, man? Get the fuck up. What are you? A animal lying there?"

John G. rubs his eyes, not sure whether the whole incident has been another hallucination.

As if to answer the question, the big guy comes over and gives him a hand standing up. His grip is strong and sure, and his eyes are calm. But a long scar runs from the right side of his nose over to his ear. It's impossible to tell how old he is.

"You looking for a place to hide out awhile?" he asks.

"What makes you think I'm hiding?"

"Ain't nobody comes down here after they won the lottery, man."

He goes over to a shopping cart full of aerosol cans and old Jergens bottles and starts pushing it up the tracks, as if he just expects John G. to follow.

"I'm Abraham," he says, barely glancing back.

John G. jogs alongside him and introduces himself, but Abraham doesn't shake his hand.

"Man, you gotta get yourself situated," he says. "Look at you. You a mess. You got those drugs running rampant in your system. They wreaking havoc on you, man."

"How do you know?"

"Man, I been there. I put shit in my veins that would peel the paint off your car."

John G. stands there, trying to figure out how he got from where he was to where he is now.

"Well, come on, chief. You coming or what?"

He leads John G. around a slight bend toward a small white abandoned construction trailer. Two pit bulls tied to the front steps bark furiously. John G. notices that the shack next door has been burned to the ground. Charred pieces of wood and clothing fragments are strewn in the gravel.

"Get on in here a second, man," says Abraham, going up the steps. "We gotta get you orientated."

He fiddles with the padlock on the front door. "Fuckin' white people," he mutters. "You all ain't used to living like niggers. You hit the street and you all lose your fuckin' minds."

A stout brown rat runs across John G.'s path and he gives out a little yelp of panic.

"Yeah, I used to hate rats too," Abraham says, smiling and stepping into the trailer. "But I got over it."

John G. goes in after him. He smells incense and sees a small room lit by hundreds of Hanukkah candles in dozens of ragtag brass menorahs. Margo had a Jewish friend once. Mindy Feirstein, from City College. She used to tell Margo, "Don't marry that guy John, he'll never amount to anything." She never knew how right she was.

A mattress sits in the corner with hunks of foam spilling out. In the other corner, there's a burgeoning mountain of empty Sprite and Diet Coke cans in clear plastic bags and a bunch of old car parts.

"See, I had an unusual experience with a rat when I was over in Vietnam," Abraham says, pointing to a U.S. Army helmet at the foot of the mattress. "A rat saved my life."

"Yeah, how was that?"

"We was sleeping in a graveyard right outside of Mytho, when this huge, tremendous rat bit me right on the tip of the nose. So I jumped up screaming and this mortar shell came in and hit right on the tombstone where I'd been."

John G. laughs. "If you ever have a son, you oughta name him after that rat."

"Well, for a long time, I didn't see it that way," Abraham says solemnly. "See, I had to take twenty-one shots in the abdomen because of the way that rat bit me. So I had this hatred for rats. I used to put cheese down and throw gasoline on them when they came along. Light a match. Watch 'em go, EEEEEEewwwww!!"

He shakes his hands in front of him and makes a high-pitched squealing sound. John G. just stares.

"So I guess you could say I got some complicated feelings about rats," Abraham tells him.

John takes another look around the place as Abraham reaches into a torn purple Jansport bookbag and hands him a ham-and-American-cheese sandwich on Wonder Bread wrapped in cellophane.

"It's from the Saint Stephen's soup kitchen," he says, putting a hand on John's shoulder. "Whatever I have is yours. You can sleep here if you want for a few nights. We can share some of the food. All I ask is that if you're gonna bug out, you go do it somewhere else."

John G. notices he's standing next to a stack of scratched-up old Paul Anka records and a pile of CDs by a rap group called the Wu-Tang Clan. The past is the present and the present is the past.

"What's all this mess?"

Abraham takes a serrated steak knife out of his pocket. "I'm trying to combine the sounds of the old with the sounds of the new," he says, pointing between the two stacks. "If I could put 'em together, I know I could have me some hits."

John G. nods. For some reason, this makes sense to him.

He casts his eyes over at the mountain of cans in the corner. This is not quite hitting bottom. It's a ledge. A place to rest a while. *Que sera, sera.*

"So you taking medication, man?" Abraham asks.

John G. shows him the amber Haldol bottle. About a dozen pills left.

"Well, you wanna stay with me, you start taking them again," says Abraham. "You hear? I don't go for no lunaticking screamin' homicide down in my tunnel."

"What if I don't feel like taking them? What if I don't see any point in taking them?"

"There's always a point. The scriptures say the head of every man is Christ, and the head of every woman is the man, and the head of Christ is God. You got to be aware of who you are, man. God put us here for a reason. You may not get better all at once. You may not even stop falling down. You just may not fall quite as far each time."

What the fuck, John G. thinks. It's a place to hide out awhile. He'll start taking the damn pills again.

A train goes rushing by. The cans and bottles clatter. The dogs howl. Even Abraham looks perplexed, though it's a sound he must hear several times a day.

"There's something else I gotta tell you," says John G. "I'm gonna die."

"Dag, man." Abraham pulls his lips back from his teeth. "How long was you planning to stay?"

23

How's the leg?" asks Philip Cardi, watching Jake hobble across the roof.

"It's all right." Jake touches his left knee gingerly. "Just feels like a charley horse. Fucking bike messengers. Guy plowed into me and started bitching he was gonna sue."

They are up on the roof of the town house. Philip takes a fifty-pound sash weight with a long rope tied around the end and drops it down the chimney. He waits until it hits something about fifteen feet down and then hauls it up again.

"Yeah, you definitely got an obstruction," he says, taking a break to wipe the sweat off his brow. "Something's in the flue line."

He lets the weight drop once more.

"You think you can just knock it out?" asks Jake.

"I'm gonna try." Philip lets the weight crash into the obstruction before he pulls the line again, like an urban fisherman.

It's nine-thirty on a Saturday morning. The streets below are empty and quiet, except for John G. trailing a blue plastic bag full of soda cans and talking loudly to himself.

"We still haven't gotten rid of him, huh?" Philip asks.

"We still haven't got rid of him." Jake looks down over the ledge, clenching his fists in frustration. "He disappeared for a couple of days after the accident, like he was lying low or something, making sure the cops weren't going to arrest him."

"So why don't they lock him up?"

"He still hasn't broken the law technically. Alex ran out into traffic and I ran out after him. All Gates did was threaten us verbally."

"Minchia." A frown wrinkles Philip's tanned face. "It's the lunatics running the asylum."

"The thing is, I'm starting to think he knows the law better than I do. He keeps just coming right up to the line without actually crossing it."

"Sneaky fuck," Philip mumbles, peering down into the chimney with a flashlight.

"Yeah, well, pretty soon I'm going to be the one walking down the street talking to myself."

John G. stops in front of Jake's house, matter-of-factly opens the gate to the front courtyard, and starts going through the garbage cans as if he's the owner of this home.

"Get the fuck away from there!" Jake calls down. "How many times do I have to tell you?"

John G. squints up at him, smiles, and goes about the business of looking through all three aluminum cans. When he's done, he deliberately knocks each one over with a loud crash. Then he bows like an arrogant Flemish fop and leaves the courtyard without closing the gate.

"Did I tell you I've been missing some more tools from the van since the weekend?" Philip asks.

"No." Jake is still shaking with outrage. "What'd he take this time?"

"A tack gun and a Black & Decker power saw. How many vials of crack you think you could buy with those?"

John G. crosses the street and starts menacing an old lady with a walker. He blocks her on the left, blocks her on the right, and then starts walking directly behind her, like a malevolent suitor.

"I swear sometimes I'd like to kill him," Jake says, wincing as he puts weight on the bad leg.

Philip moves up close behind him. "Forgive me, but have you thought about what I said before?"

"What's that?"

"About you and me paying him a visit with a baseball bat."

Jake just looks at him. Everything seems very still. The Broadway traffic noises have faded away. Even the birds seem to have stopped singing. The only sounds are John G.'s distant cursing and the dull thud of Philip's sash weight hitting the obstruction.

"I'm a lawyer," Jake says quietly.

"I know you're a lawyer."

"So I can't go around whacking people just because I have a problem with them."

"Who said anything about whacking anybody? I'm just saying we should have a talk with the guy."

"A talk." Jake turns his head and looks sideways at the sky.

"Yeah." Philip shrugs *fuhgedabout it*-style, shoulders back, palms up, as if all they're talking about is a paint job. "I mean, he can't be that crazy, he keeps coming right up to the line without crossing it. I say we go over to where he lives, try to talk some sense into him." He wraps the rope around his knuckles. "You know where to find him, right?"

"He's out every night by seven-thirty, begging for crack money on Broadway. By ten o'clock, he's hollering under our window."

"*Minchia,* if they could get somebody to run the subway that regular, it'd still be a beautiful city."

Jake decides to let that go.

"Look, what are your options?" asks Philip, pulling up his sash weight and mopping his brow. "You already been to the police and you been to the doctors, and basically no one else gives a shit. What are you gonna do? Sit back and wait 'til this miserable fuck kills someone?"

"So you're suggesting we go seek him out for the purpose of intimidating him?" Jake's head wags from side to side.

"Listen, if you don't want to do it, you don't wanna do it," Philip says, putting a brotherly hand on Jake's shoulder. "To me, it's no big deal. I was over in Nam. I know how to handle myself. I'd bring my cousin Ronnie and we'd have a talk with the guy. Not busting heads. Just letting him know we don't appreciate the way he's acting. But if that's too . . . I don't know, heavy, for you, then forgive me for saying it. I just know that where I come from, a man can't go too far to protect his own family."

Jake stands quietly for a moment. He thinks about his wife

staring out the window and his son standing by the door, hesitating before going out in the morning. He thinks about the long silences at the dinner table and the ways their lives have gotten smaller and smaller, hemmed in by apprehension. And he thinks about the pair of headlights coming right at him on Seventy-ninth Street.

"Supposing I decide to go along with this, up to a point," he says to Philip. "What if I got a bad feeling along the way? Would you be willing to pull back?"

"It's your call, Counselor. I'm just here to help." Philip gets ready to drop the weight again. "But let me tell you, you gotta draw the line somewhere. The guy stole my tools, not once but twice. If you're not in with this, maybe me and Ronnie will handle it on our own."

The sash weight goes down and Jake hears something breaking in the chimney. He sees another six feet of rope get swallowed up. Then the weight stops again.

"Ah shit," says Philip.

"What's the matter?"

"You got another obstruction."

"Is that bad?"

"There's only two ways you deal with a blockage." Philip gives him a hard, serious look. "You try to destroy it from the top, and if that doesn't work, you have to reline the whole chimney, chop into the walls on every floor of your house, and break the mantels over the fireplaces. And then you live with a terrible scar on every floor."

"What happens if you just leave it there and don't do anything?"

"The exhaust from your boiler backs up and you can slowly choke to death on the carbon monoxide."

24

At quarter to eleven two nights later, a man with a Burmese mountain dog walks past the baseball diamond at the south end of Riverside Park. Sodium vapor lights cast an eerie glow over the batting cage. Philip Cardi and Jake stand in the shallow part of the outfield, staring at the hole in the fence they just saw John G. go through.

After a couple of minutes, Philip's cousin Ronnie, a swarthy Italian kid in enormous black shorts and a Snoop Doggy Dogg T-shirt, comes down the hill carrying a couple of aluminum baseball bats.

"Were they in the trunk like I said?" Philip grabs one from him and takes a practice swing.

"In the back."

"Hey, what do we need these for?" asks Jake nervously.

"We need them so we don't have to use them," says Philip, resting the bat on his shoulder. "You understand what I'm saying? Where we're going, we don't want anybody to get the wrong idea about messing with us."

For the last couple of hours, they've been following John G. from a discreet distance. Stopping at a coffee shop while he rummaged through cans in front of Gristede's. Watching from a corner bodega while he tried unsuccessfully to buy crack on Amsterdam. But now that he's disappeared into the mouth of the tunnel, they're hesitating.

"So we're really gonna do this, huh?" says Jake, looking back at the hole in the fence some fifty yards away.

"Why, you got a problem with that?"

Philip turns slowly. Jake can feel the potential for disappointment coming up like a wall between them.

"I'm just starting to wonder if this is still such a good idea."

Ronnie windmills his bat like a charter plane's propeller. Jake notices his black sneakers have blinking red lights in the back.

"So where's all this coming from?" Philip says. "We're not breaking any law here."

"I know we're not breaking the law. It's just, you know, I have a bad feeling about it." Jake looks away. It's like he's punking out of a street fight in front of Sweet Tooth's.

"A bad feeling? What're you, afraid of a railroad tunnel?" Philip takes another swing. "Forget about it. I was on one of the crews that helped clear out the tracks a few years ago. I know my way around there better than most of the bums. We had kids coming down there all the time, trying to ride in our geometry cars. We hadda shoot them with salt pellets, make 'em go away."

"But what if something goes wrong? How would I explain it to my family?"

Ronnie and Philip look at each other. Then Philip spits on the grass and hands Jake the bat he was swinging.

"Here, hold this a minute."

He bends down to tie his shoe.

"Jake," he says, "you and me, we're men of the world. Am I right?"

"I guess." Jake feels his palms and fingers sweating on the taped bat handle.

"I mean, we've both been around—even if you weren't in Vietnam. We see how things operate."

Philip stands up and Jake gives the bat back to him. "You could say that."

Philip smacks the ground with the bat. "So one thing we understand that women and children don't understand—that most *people* don't understand—is that nothing important in life is ever accomplished without risk. Okay? There's always a chance somebody's going to get hurt."

Jake stares hard at him, knowing it's true and wondering how Philip can know him so well. For every significant achievement in his life, there's been an underlying threat of emotional or physical violence: standing up to his father, destroying his best friend, Joe Loehman, during moot court in law school, regularly eviscerating witnesses on the stand. His guilty secret, which he's never admitted to anyone, including his wife, is that success has always come at the end of a dagger pointed at someone else's heart.

And now he sees that in order to protect his family he has to be willing to do it again.

"So all right already, where's the opening to this goddamn tunnel?" he asks Philip. "I don't want to stand here all night."

"Good man."

Philip pats him on the back and they cross the outfield toward the wrought-iron fence. Philip's flashlight quickly finds the opening they saw John G. go through and the three of them squeeze between the bars. They make their way along the ledge and then drop down, one by one, onto the tracks.

The first thing that strikes Jake as he struggles to get his flashlight working is that it's the darkest place he's ever been. Even by shutting his eyes, he's never experienced such blackness. Philip's flashlight illuminates a foot or two of track before them and Ronnie's sneaker lights blink faintly behind them, but otherwise there's nothing. Not even vague shapes or nuances. This must be what it's like inside a coffin.

There's a shivering sound, like an electric current snaking through the tracks.

Jake takes his first steps carefully, trying to figure out where the third rail might be. His left leg still hurts a little from the bicycle accident and he has the uneasy feeling that people are watching him.

"Freaky deaky," Ronnie mumbles.

But Philip's flashlight is already pushing on ahead, challenging them to follow. Something passes lightly over Jake's left foot, and a second later, he realizes that it might have been a rat. Every nerve in his body is straining, telling him to go back home, fix himself a drink, and snuggle up in bed with Dana. But if he leaves now, he's a coward. Not just in Philip's eyes, but in his own. He finally gets the flashlight working and moves to catch up with Philip.

The tracks begin to curve around to the left and Jake smells leaves burning in the distance. The smells of September. After a few seconds, he catches a glimpse of fire.

Philip's beam moves toward it quickly, lighting up sections of track, old hubcaps, and stray garbage along the path. The flame is about forty yards away, under a rounded stone archway. A wild orange light throws shadows of crude housing against the walls.

"Welcome back to Planet of the Apes," says Ronnie.

The sound of rolling tin approaches. Closing in from the right.

"Stop your mouth," says Philip.

He swings his flashlight beam toward the noise, splashing Jake's face with light before he finds a short one-armed man with a shopping cart full of cans. He's like some kind of drugged-out troll with his ripped clothes and burnt-looking scalp.

"Ow, my eyes. What're you doing, man?"

"Where's the other guy?" Philip says.

The man shields his face with the one arm. "Who?"

"We're looking for John Gates," Jake speaks up. "The white guy who wears the MTA shirt."

"John G.?" says the troll, making the name sound like a curse. "He lives over in the suburbs with Rat Man."

He points to the fire under the archway on the left. "Hey, Abaham!" he calls out. "Company! Man wants to talk to John G."

A black man's voice answers from somewhere under the archway, but the words are lost in the rumble of West Side Highway traffic overhead.

Philip's flashlight beam moves toward the sound but finds only a flaming oil drum.

"Abraham, come the fuck out, man!" the troll yells. "These people came to see youse guys."

More rats scurrying. The shivering sound again. Jake glances behind him and sees that the lights at the south end of the tunnel are gone. There's no easy way to turn back.

"Who's that calling out my name?" Abraham shouts.

Jake raises his flashlight and sees a tall black guy in a baseball cap stepping from behind the fire. As he comes toward them, dreadlocks swing like a ragged curtain around his head.

"Yo, get that shit outta my eyes," he says. "You tryin' to blind me?"

Jake moves the beam away from his face and sees a second shadowy figure emerge from behind the fire. Bony hips, lopsided walk. There's no mistaking John G.'s silhouette.

"Yo, whatchoo you looking for, man?" says Abraham, moving out of the light's beam as he approaches. "This is my tunnel. Who invited you down here?"

As Philip moves past him to confront Abraham, Jake catches a sour tart odor with a sting on the end of it. House scotch. It takes a couple of seconds to fully register that his new friend has been drinking. He suddenly has a vision of himself tied to a huge rock rolling down a steep hill.

"We're not interested in you," Philip says to Abraham. "It's your friend we wanna talk to."

"Well, he's with me," says Abraham. "You wanna talk to him, you talk to me."

Jake hears the tap of metal on metal to his right. Ronnie touching one of the rails with his aluminum bat; he better watch it, or he'll catch six hundred volts. A train horn blares.

Philip raises his flashlight again and shines it in Abraham's eyes.

"Whaddya, deaf, asshole? I just said I don't wanna talk to you. I wanna talk to your friend."

"Yo, what'd I tell you, man, about keeping that light outta my eyes?"

Jake moves his flashlight beam around until he finds John G. standing a little bit behind Abraham, wobbling and squinting as if he's just waking up from general anesthetic.

Again, he seems so vulnerable. Jake has to remind himself that Gates almost caused him to get hit by a car the other night.

The train horn sounds again, getting closer. The Albany-to-Washington. The red lights in Ronnie's sneakers blink.

"I just want you to leave my family alone," Jake tells John G., trying to wrap things up so they can all go home. "We don't want any more problems with you."

"Yo, you're the one with the problem," Abraham interrupts. "Get the fuck outta my tunnel."

Ronnie hits the rail two more times with his bat, as if he's starting to tap out a warning signal. The lights in his sneakers go on and off a little faster.

"Just stay away from my family," Jake tells John G.

"Yo, this is my family down here." Abraham breaks in again. "You stay away!"

The five of them are converging on the tracks, with the third rail somewhere in between. Ronnie keeps hitting the steel with his baseball bat. Gates seems to be shrinking before Jake's flashlight beam. The one-armed man is pulling away with his shopping cart, as if he senses something bad is about to happen.

Philip keeps a steady beam shining in Abraham's face. Now that Jake knows he's been drinking, the scotch stench is overwhelming.

"All right, guys, let's get outta here." Jake shines his light toward the south end of the tunnel, showing the way out. "I think we've made our point."

The southbound train is almost visible. A hard tiny circle of light appears at the north end of the tunnel coming toward them.

But Philip and Abraham have moved closer and are now face-to-face in the middle of the tracks, with Philip blinking the flashlight on and off in the taller man's eyes. They're like a couple of ferocious Dobermans refusing to back away from each other on the street.

"Take that fuckin' flashlight outta my face before I shove it up your ass," Abraham says in a measured voice.

"Try it." Philip flashes the light three more times and tightens the grip on the bat in his right hand.

"Philip, gimme that." Jake steps between them and tries to grab the bat from him.

But Philip looks right through him and holds the bat aloft. "Get outta my way, Jake."

A cloud of belched-up alcohol passes between them and Jake

suddenly realizes what a terrible mistake he's made in trusting this man. He can hear the train's wheels chugging down the tracks.

"Come on, Philip, give it up."

He starts to reach for the bat again, but before he can get it, Ronnie blindsides him like a nose tackle. Jake stumbles forward and falls to one knee between two slats in the tracks. A bell rings in his head and a light flashes behind him. He turns and sees the Albany train bearing down on him less than a hundred yards away. Its light replaces the flashlight Philip has dropped.

Jake looks over to his left just in time to see Philip swinging the bat at Abraham's head. Both hands on the grip. The air slithers and sighs. Metal hits bone. There's a hollow sickening pop and then Jake feels a light splatter of blood on his right cheek.

For a moment, no one moves. The train light fills the tunnel and the sound of the wheels is almost deafening. Then Philip steps off the tracks. Abraham starts to crumble, grasping for air with his hands as if he's falling off the side of a building.

He lands on one of the rails and then rolls away as a tiny spark goes off.

Jake struggles to his feet and jumps off to the left of the tracks just as the train goes by.

In the flickering light from the passenger cars, he sees John G., also on this side, backing away and waving his arms in panic. Philip and Ronnie are after him like herky-jerky figures in an old nickelodeon movie with frames missing. Philip cracks Gates across the left temple with his bat and Ronnie catches him clean in the midsection with a level swing. John G. doubles up and Jake comes stumbling over, trying to break it up.

But before he can get there, a sharp blow to the back of his head reduces everything to black again.

When Jake comes to, Philip and Ronnie each have him by an arm and they're dragging him down the track, back toward the open south end of the tunnel.

"Yo, you see that shit?" says Ronnie.

"What?" asks Philip.

"The spark. You know. The spark from the track just before the train came. You fried that nigger."

"I didn't see any spark."

"You must've dropped him on the third rail, cuz."

"Ah, that's terrible," says Philip. "They're supposed to have those things covered. Somebody could get hurt down here."

They both start laughing.

"What did you do?" says Jake, only now realizing Philip hit him from behind.

"Ha?" says Philip, sounding irritated.

"What the fuck did you do? You fucking killed a man. You may have killed two men. Are you fucking crazy?"

"Jake, it hadda be," says Philip.

"But we can't just leave the scene of a crime." Jake drags his heels, trying to force them to stop and turn back.

"Look, I'm not gonna stand here and argue with you." Philip almost jerks Jake's right arm out of its socket. "What's done is done."

Again, Jake is aware that dozens of eyes are watching them from the tunnel's dark corners and recesses.

"We should call the police," he says.

"You do and you'll go to jail with us. You know what the law is, Counselor. You're an accessory to murder."

Jake's stomach feels like a bloody abattoir. "But I didn't know things were going to turn out this way."

"Like hell, you didn't. You wanted to get rid of him. This is what it takes."

This is what it takes. Philip touches Jake on the arm with the baseball bat. "Look, this is gonna have to be our secret," he says, hurrying Jake along. "We can't tell anybody what happened here tonight."

"We're gonna have to stick together," says Ronnie, pulling hard on Jake's left arm.

"Yeah, like family," says Philip.

It's another couple of minutes before they reach the ledge and climb back through the opening in the fence. The park is deserted. Dozens of pigeons sit on top of the batting cage. Across the river, the lights of New Jersey glitter like a thousand accusing eyes.

Jake finally tears himself out of Philip's grip and goes to stand at the edge of the outfield, trying to catch his breath. The whole time he was underground, he'd been praying for the moment when he could surface again and rejoin the world of the living. But now that he's back, he feels as if he doesn't quite belong here anymore. Even the cool September air feels wrong in his lungs.

His life has just been divided into two halves: everything that happened before tonight and everything that will happen afterward.

25

John G.'s ribs feel broken. His face is sticky with blood and his legs are weak. His head is a bell full of pain. He keeps waiting to go into shock, so that he won't be able to feel anything. He wants to be numb. But numbness doesn't come. He still feels too much.

Keep moving. Keep moving. The men with the bats could be along any minute to finish him off. It's not just the Haldol that's been kicking in again lately. Fear has shot a hot wire into his brain and brought him to rapt attention. Every detail of what's just happened is now tattooed on his memory: the flashlights, the train approaching, the baseball bats, Mr. Schiff's voice calling out, telling them to stop.

He keeps limping along the tracks, dragging himself from the scene. He's too scared to go back and see about Abraham. All he's about at the moment is hurting and moving. Through the dark, past the grate by the boat basin garage, around the bend at Seventy-ninth Street, beyond the yellowing burlap tent with the light flickering inside.

For a brief second, he's back in Father Tortora Park in Patchogue. Playing cowboys and Indians. I'm a good guy. I'm a bad guy. Come get me. Bang, bang. Ka-chow. Hide behind the rock. You're dead. No, I'm not. You just think I'm dead. Come get me, sucker.

But then he remembers that Abraham is dead. It's no game.

That burly light-haired guy with Mr. Schiff beat his brains in with a baseball bat. Slaughtered him like an animal. He keeps seeing the spark off the third rail where he fell.

There's no time for mourning, though. The men with the bats could be along any second.

He goes staggering on, the pain in his head spreading down his spine and curling up through his stomach. With each step, he gives a little involuntary yelp. I'm a good guy. I'm a bad guy. He hears something scurrying along behind him and realizes it's just more rats. Gotta keep moving. An old Doors song is playing on a distant radio. "I tell you this, no eternal reward will forgive us now . . ."

What's the point? Why not give up? Why not stop and wait for them to catch up and finish him off? What's there left to live for? Back in Patchogue, he'd be standing up from behind the rock, throwing his hands in the air, shouting, I quit, I'm going home, I'm taking my guns and my hat with me. Expecting to find his mother with a drink by the stove as he walks in, seeing him and singing, "He's a root-tootin', high-falutin' Cowboy Joe."

But here in the tunnel, a slant of light beckons from a grating at Eighty-sixth Street. Though it's only street light, his shoulders hunch forward and his knees refuse to buckle.

It's as if his body still has the will to live, even after his mind has surrendered. Damn it. Against his heart's desire to lie down and die, he keeps moving toward the light. Left foot, right foot. I'm a good guy. I'm a bad guy.

26

Tired, sullen, bruised, and confused, Jake makes his way back to the comfort of his marriage bed. The steam from a hot shower is still rising from his body and his pores feel open but somehow not clean.

It's too late to call another lawyer about what's just happened. He's not even sure he should make a statement to the DA at this point.

He turns to spoon Dana from behind, wanting to feel nothing more than the assurance of her body heat and the rhythm of her breathing. Instead, she squirms away from him, as if even in slumber she senses something's wrong.

"Where were you?" she asks, still three-quarters asleep.

"Just doing some work."

She rolls onto her side, making little smacking noises with her mouth. "Todd Bracken called for you."

"What time?"

"I don't know. Ten-thirty."

He freezes for a moment, caught in the lie. Was Todd calling from the office? Does she know Jake wasn't there?

"I was out meeting a client," he says.

She's already on her stomach and asleep.

He lies on his back and stares up at the ceiling, wondering how he could've broken their bond of trust so easily. It's not that he's never lied to her before. It's just that he's never lied about anything that truly mattered. There've been no affairs, no hidden bank accounts, no deep family secrets. He's always told her about every case he's had, even when she wasn't particularly interested. The witnesses, the depositions, the judges, the motions. The only thing he's ever held back from her, he realizes, is the murder in his own heart.

Weird-shaped shadows stretch across the ceiling. Car windows, elongated tree branches, telephone wires. The street is absolutely silent, though. John G. is gone. Instead, there is dripping. Hardly discernible at first. But a steady tap-tap-tap over Jake's head.

From living in an apartment most of his life, he's grown used to sounds from other people's homes—babies crying, couples arguing, glasses breaking, water rushing. He remembers standing outside his own parents' bedroom and hearing the violence in his father's voice threatening to bring the walls down.

His father was the angriest man he'd ever known. Other immigrants found success and opportunity in the New World; Gregor Schafransky found only justification for his precious outrage. The rest of the family came over from Poland just before the war and flourished in the plumbing supply business. For a while, they tried to support Gregor by giving him a job as a salesman, but he had neither the aptitude nor the temperament. He retreated into drink and blamed everyone else for his problems. He clashed with the relatives repeatedly and wound up working behind the counter of a deli on Stillwell Avenue. His only true accomplishments were the beatings he doled out to his wife and his resented son.

He was the Joe DiMaggio of wife beaters, the Muhammad Ali of domestic abuse. He beat them with righteous fury and with blind drunken abandon. For insanely specific reasons and for general discontent. It wasn't that he was violent all the time; that would've been more manageable. There was no telling what would set him off. Too many bottles of ketchup in the cupboard, not enough beer in the refrigerator, newspapers on the bathroom floor, a pair of glasses lost. Once he brought home lamb chops from the deli and when Jake couldn't finish eating them, his father beat him until he vomited. Then he demanded the boy eat what was left on his plate.

But his masterpiece, the crowning achievement of his sacred inviolate outrage, was his wife's face. Her flesh was the clay he pounded with his fists. What he left was a sculpture of collapsed cheekbones, black eyes, and splintered teeth. A grim Russian girl, she'd been raised to believe a man would always take care of her. Sometimes she'd run into Jake's room and try to hide in his bed. But her husband would always come and drag her out, leaving Jake shivering like a coward under the covers, filled with shame for not being able to protect her.

One Friday morning the old man backhanded her across the kitchen for burning his eggs and she crashed into the stove, breaking her left wrist.

Instead of hiding in his room again, Jake, who was all of fifteen, stormed out of the house. He took the B train all the way into Manhattan and wound up wandering aimlessly through the Central Park Zoo. He found himself in front of the lion's cage, trying to summon up the courage to go home.

The lion was magnificent up on its perch. All coiled strength and dark glimmering eyes. Watching her, Jake felt the animal was trying to tell him something about how to survive in this life.

He took the train home just before nine and fished a broken bottle of Piel's Real Draft out of the garbage can on the corner. With a head that felt like it weighed a hundred pounds, he climbed the six floors to their apartment. His father was asleep on the couch, snoring with his mouth open and a Clark Gable submarine movie on the TV. Jake touched the soft spot at the base of his father's throat with the jagged glass and waited for the old man to open his eyes.

"Someday," he told his father, "I will kill you."

What did Philip say before? *A man cannot go too far to protect his own family.* Up until tonight, Jake believed that too. After all, his father beat only inanimate objects after the night of the Piel's bottle. But now Jake wonders. How has he gone so wrong?

Without waking Dana, he slips out from between the sheets and listens for that sound. Tap-tap-tap. He follows it out into the hallway and up the stairs. A dim light is on in Alex's room and Jake looks in on him. The boy is sprawled across his bed, asleep in plaid boxer shorts and a Pearl Jam T-shirt. Sixteen. He's all long gangly arms and hairy legs now. But when he's sleeping, he's still the little boy Jake pushed down the sidewalk on the tricycle. He leans over and kisses his son gently on the cheek.

What else can a man do except protect his family?

Tap-tap-tap. That sound in the hall again. Jake goes and stands out on the landing. Straining to hear what's wrong.

All his life, he's believed that if he had a house of his own he'd be able to keep his family safe and have peace of mind.

But now he has the house. The little piece of the city he insisted on owning when Dana wanted to stay in the apartment and save for a country house. But something feels wrong here. That tapping is beginning to sound more like creaking. Actually a low shuddering moan. Like plaster, steel, and wood grinding against one another. It could just be old pipes knocking. But the sound is too deep and resonant. Harsh even. Like the voice of God. He listens harder and thinks he hears little timbers snapping and bolts loosening. Maybe the foundations are shifting.

And he wonders if this house, his only true home, is subtly and slowly falling apart.

27

Uncle Carmine has slicked-back white hair and glasses so thick they make his eyes looked tilted. He always smells like a barber.

"I hear you had a situation get out of hand," he tells Philip.

"Says who?"

"Says Ronnie. He says you had to tune up some bums with a baseball bat."

"Ronnie's got two good ears. He oughta learn to use them and keep his fuckin' mouth shut."

"That's my boy you're talking about." Carmine rubs his hands together and Philip smells hair tonic.

They're sitting in the living room of Philip's mother's apartment, above the surgical supply store on Twentieth Avenue. A statue of Saint Anthony stares out from a glass-enclosed bookcase. There's a full 1957 *Encyclopaedia Britannica* but no other books. The carpet is plush red and there's gold leaf around the light switches. Philip's mother watches *The Song of Bernadette* on the TV down the hall.

"So what was this about, anyway?" says Carmine, who wears a pair of tan chinos and a blue short-sleeved shirt with a lacy pattern on the front.

"This Jew lawyer I was telling you about before. One with all the connections."

"What about him?" Carmine lifts a cup of espresso with a pinky extended.

"It's the same thing we always talk about. You want somebody to do something for you, you have to give him a reason to do it. You do him a favor and if that doesn't work out, you put him behind the eight ball. So that's what I did with this Jew. I put him behind the eight ball."

"So you went and killed a guy?"

"I didn't plan it that way, C. Life is full of conflict. Shit happens."

"Yeah, but now you got my son on the spot for murder." Lamplight flashes off Carmine's lenses.

Philip draws back into himself, trying to figure out how to deal with this subtle breach of mob etiquette. The problem isn't that Ronnie's now involved in a murder; it's that Ronnie's involved in a murder that doesn't directly benefit his father.

"Look, the lawyer's not gonna say anything, C. He's in it as much as we are."

"And now you think he's going to come through with these contracts?"

"Well he better come through with something, or I'll drop a fuckin' atom bomb on him, I will." Philip throws his right arm out.

"No, you better come through or I'll drop a bomb on *you.*" Carmine reaches over and squeezes Philip's knee.

"Why you getting a hard-on with me?"

"Because I'm getting tired of bailing you out, Phil. That's why. I paid for your house in Massapequa. I got you the job over at the Javits Center. I bailed you out when you had a problem with that girl in the warehouse. I talked to Angelo when half his crew wanted to whack you. When am I gonna see some return on my investment?"

Philip looks down at Carmine's hand on his leg. His manicured fingernails look as hard and shiny as little ice cubes. The gorge in Philip's throat starts to rise.

It's that hair tonic smell again.

Philip remembers that smell from when he was a boy. When

Carmine would stand over his bed. Carmine was always touching things. Money in bank vaults, stolen credit cards, dresses off the backs of trucks. After Philip's father died from a heroin OD in sixty-one, Carmine started touching Philip's mother too. And on nights when he was drinking, he'd sometimes slip into the bedroom and give Philip a little touch under the covers. Always leaving behind a trace of that hair tonic smell. Carmine understood that in order to possess something you had to be able to put your hand around it. To dominate it. That's how he'd gotten to be head of his own crew on Staten Island. Life was not about half measures or reasoning with people. It was about grinding them under your will. Humiliating them. Crushing their spirit. So you could touch them whenever you felt like it.

When Philip did that thing to the girl in the warehouse all those years ago, he made her feel the way Carmine had made him feel. And when he gave his wife a little smack once in a while, she felt that way too. In fact, sometimes it seemed like his whole life was dedicated to making other people feel the way Carmine made him feel.

"So I'll get the contracts, don't worry about it," he says, noticing that all the furniture in the room suddenly seems bigger, as if he's become a small boy again.

"Well it better be worth it. I don't want you getting my Ronnie involved in this nonsense without a good reason."

"It'll be worth it. We're talking the whole public school system."

Carmine looks up at Philip's face. There's still twenty-five years between them, but something in that face no longer interests him. He takes his hand off Philip's knee.

"Meantime, I got a piece of work for you," he tells Philip, his jowls corrugating below the jawline. "This fuckin' Polack Walt. Still owes me two G's and he's out at the Doll House the other night, stuffing twenties into the girls' G-strings. I think he needs a little thrift lesson. Bring Ronnie along and show him the ropes."

"Oh come on, C.!" Philip stands up and his brow wrinkles. "Don't make me do that. I'm not a goddamn leg breaker anymore. I'm an intelligent person. Let me have some dignity."

"I've given you dignity. If you weren't my flesh and blood, I woulda had you cut up and left in a fuckin' bird sanctuary."

"But I'm about to set things up so you're making a thousand dollars a day off every school in the city."

"Well, when you start getting those contracts, I'll start sending Ronnie and his friends out to do these jobs insteada you. Meanwhile you still work for me, and when I say 'frog,' you jump. Understand?"

Even after all these years, just the sound of Carmine's voice can make Philip's insides move around.

"But C. . . ."

"But nothing. Do like I say. If you're so smart, you'd be rich already. I tell you." Carmine starts muttering to himself. "You put a dwarf on top of a mountain, he's still a dwarf."

Philip blinks. He's noticed Carmine saying some strange things lately.

"Look," he tells his uncle, "let me talk to the Jew one more time before I see Walt."

"Well, don't take too goddamn long about it."

Carmine steps around Philip's mother's wheelchair and starts moving down the hall toward *The Song of Bernadette* in the back bedroom.

"It's a good thing I feel the way I do about family," he grumbles.

FALL

28

The day after the incident in the tunnels, the weather starts to turn. Brown leaves litter the gutters and a chill bites the air. On Fifth Avenue, women drop their hemlines an inch or two and horse carriage drivers throw extra blankets in the back.

Up in his office, Jake is trying to act as if nothing has changed. He returns phone calls, works on briefs, reads transcripts, but as he gets up from behind his heavy oak desk and starts pacing, he feels like an imposter. The guy in the framed *New York Times* article on the wall isn't him anymore. He's involved in murder.

For the third time this morning, he picks up the phone and calls his old friend Andy Botwin, the defense lawyer.

"He's still not back in," says Andy's secretary, Beth. "Can I leave a more detailed message?"

"Just tell him I need to see him in person right away. You think he has any time tomorrow morning?"

"I'm sure he'll make time for you, Mr. Schiff."

The other line buzzes. It's Deborah, Jake's secretary.

"Everything okay in there?"

"Yeah, why?"

"I hear you moving around a lot in there. You playing handball or something?" The voice like an old engine turning over.

Jake likes to say that if he's ever sick, he'd want Dana to take care of him. But if he's ever in another street fight, he wants Deborah on his side.

"No, I'm fine," he says. "Everything's fine."

"I just wanna remind you about your schedule for the morning. You got a ten-thirty with Todd and the other partners about the merger. And then you got lunch at the Four Seasons with Margaret Dunleavy."

Right, Margaret Dunleavy. The forty-four-year-old widow of a famous Truman-era diplomat and bank chairman, who's being sued by her seventyish stepchildren over the estate. He looks over at the teetering pile of bank documents on the left side of his desk and sees a yellow sticky note he wrote himself: "Check codicil."

"I also wanted to let you know there's someone waiting out in reception for you."

"Who's this?"

"Rico Carty," she says.

"Guy who used to play outfield for the Braves?"

Deborah sighs and riffles through some papers. Jake can picture her sitting there, legs crossed, plastic cigarette substitute between her painted fingernails, files precariously balanced on her nyloned knees. My guardian angel.

"Philip," she says. "That's the guy's name. Philip Cardi. He says he's done some contracting work for you. I told him no one gets in without an appointment. So he's still sitting there. You want me to call security?"

Jake feels as if a firm hand has just been placed over his throat. The rest of Deborah's words are lost in the riot in his mind.

". . . or do you want I should send him in?" he hears her asking.

All right, stay cool, he tells himself. What are the options? Call security and risk having a scene trying to get rid of Philip? Todd Bracken and the other partners would love that. Especially with the Greer, Allan people arriving any minute. Maybe it would be better to talk to him quickly and quietly, find out what's on his mind.

"All right, tell him I got a minute," he says to Deborah.

"You sure?" Knowing his schedule better than he does, she's aware he can't afford the time.

"Yeah, but buzz me if I go too long with him. I may need to be rescued."

Some twenty seconds later, Philip is standing in his doorway. Wearing a light blue sports jacket, a pink button-down shirt, dark slacks, and that same easygoing smile that made Jake let his guard down in the first place.

"Hey, buddy," Philip says, like they're two best friends meeting up Monday morning after a weekend of hard drinking. "How ya doin'?"

"What do you want?" Jake says.

"You mind if I sit down? Forgive me for interrupting."

Jake just stares at him. Philip pulls over one of the brown leather-backed chairs with copper studs around the sides.

He sits and turns his head for a moment to admire Jake's view of downtown. Ten million passengers and predators, moving past traffic lights and stop signs.

"You know, I've been reconsidering about your chimney," says Philip.

Jake doesn't respond. He imagines he can hear the distant rumble of the subway some fifty-seven stories below.

"I'm thinking maybe we don't have to reline the whole thing," says Philip, resting his right hand on the arm of the chair. "You know, it would be terrible to have to open up the walls on every floor. You'd have an unprecedented amount of soot pouring into your house. You'd never get it cleaned up."

Jake continues to glare at him. But nothing in Philip's voice or relaxed face begins to suggest the violence the man is capable of.

"So maybe we just open up one spot on the wall and take out the obstruction and keep the mess to a minimum. A little carpentry work, we set up an enclosure, and then we put the bricks back in and plaster it up. What do you think?"

"I think I don't know what you came here for," Jake says evenly.

Philip ignores him. "But then you might still have the problem of asbestos in your basement."

The word "asbestos" is somehow a signal that things have changed. It's not just that it has nothing to do with the chimney problem Philip's been blathering on about. It's the particular emphasis that he puts on the word. Like he's suddenly decided to raise the stakes.

"I bet you haven't thought much about asbestos," he says.

"It's all been removed," Jake tells him, wondering how long they can keep talking about one thing when they're both thinking about something else.

"Yeah, but maybe you only think it's all been removed. It's just like the carbon monoxide. You can't see it, you can't smell it, but once it's in the air, it can slowly poison you. You're dying and you don't even know it."

Jake feels his jaw lock in his face like a loaded cartridge sliding into a gun. Why is Philip playing with him? Is he going to bring up the murder? Jake has a slight spasm of panic, remembering a story he'd heard about old man Bracken bugging the partners' offices back in the days of the Nixon White House. But then who was supposed to be sitting around all day, listening to these excruciatingly boring tapes? Forget it. It's not true.

Just the same, he has to be careful about what's being said here. The Greer, Allan people are arriving any minute. He looks at his telephone, willing it to ring.

"Philip," he says slowly, "I'm really kind of busy here. Is this something we can talk about later?"

Philip studies the back of his right hand, seemingly oblivious to the rising tension in Jake's voice. "Did you know I do asbestos work too?" he asks.

"No, and I'm really not sure I have time to hear about it right now."

"That's too bad." Philip sinks deeper into the chair, making himself comfortable. "Because the school year is beginning and you know that out of the—whatever it is—six or seven hundred public schools in the city, at least thirty percent of them have some asbestos still in the physical plant."

"So?"

"So I was thinking your friend Bob Berger probably has the

final say over who gets the contract to remove all that material," says Philip, broadening his smile. "He's going to be with the School Construction Board, right? I was thinking you could put in a good word for your *paisan* from the old neighborhood. Tell 'im I'm his guy for the job."

All right, so there it is. Out in the open. An old-fashioned kick-'im-in-the-nuts shakedown. At least now he knows what Philip wants.

"What happens if I say no to you?"

Philip's smile disappears. "Well, that wouldn't be right."

"Why not?" Jake takes a blank sheet of yellow legal paper off one of the piles and begins to fold it into smaller and smaller sections.

"Because that would show a basic lack of gratitude, if you forgive me for saying so. That would be a situation in which I'd done a favor for you and you failed to reciprocate."

"Maybe I don't see it that way," says Jake, remembering the splatter of blood on his cheek.

Philip gets up and ambles over to the bookshelf where Jake keeps his law books and various presents from Dana and Alex.

"See, in the neighborhood I come from . . ." Philip stops and corrects himself. "In the neighborhood *we* come from, there's always been what I like to call the social contract. Am I right? That's what holds us together. One hand washes the other. You scratch my back, I'll scratch yours. You understand what I'm talking about, Jake? The idea that we can trust each other to fulfill the *obligations* we've made to each other."

He picks up the gold Tiffany clock Dana bought for Jake on their twelfth wedding anniversary and watches the movement of the hands. "So I got this theory," he says, deliberately pronouncing the word as "teary." "When that social contract breaks down, we break down. As a society."

He drops the clock on the red-and-beige carpet and puts his left foot over it, like he's about to crush it. "Oh, forgive me," he says. "How clumsy."

"Okay, I'd like you to leave now," says Jake.

But Philip has turned back to the bookcase and grabbed the maroon-and-gold Oriental vase Dana bought for him at a Westchester antiques fair. "I'd even go so far as to say, that's the cause of all our problems today. We're not teaching young people the right values. What do you think?"

He puts the vase down and cuts his finger on its chipped lip. Jake's been meaning to have it fixed.

"Ah shit," says Philip, looking at a trickle of blood on his thumb.

He puts his hand up to his mouth. Jake starts to rise and come toward him. But now Philip is holding a stumpy ceramic figure of the baseball pitcher Dwight Gooden. Alex molded and glazed it in fourth-grade art class.

"Forgive me if I misunderstood the terms of our contract," Philip says, examining the figure. "Forgive me if I mistook you for a man of honor, who kept his word. I didn't realize you were just another fucking lawyer."

He drops Dwight Gooden. The figure bangs a shelf on its way down and breaks into pieces on the carpet. Jake moves to his left a little. The distant subway rumble he thought he'd heard before is roaring between his ears now.

"So what are you gonna do, Counselor, take a swing at me?" Philip smiles.

Before Jake can answer, the door opens and Deborah sticks her massive dyed-blond head in the room.

"Hey," she says. "Todd and the other partners are waiting for you. They just had the whole horse-and-hound crowd pull in. Don't be fooling around in here."

"I'll be right with you," says Jake.

"Everything all right?" She looks from Jake to Philip, as if she's assessing her chances of taking both of them in hand-to-hand combat.

Jake starts to back away from Philip. The magnetic force that brought them together has been defused by the presence of a woman in the room. The confrontation is over, for the moment.

"Come on, Jake, shake a leg," Deborah says sternly.

It's not clear to Jake how much of the commotion she heard before she decided to interrupt, but he's reminded of the debt he owes her. *My guardian angel to the rescue again. Even Philip* seems a little intimidated. He drops his eyes to avoid looking at her and leaves a card on the edge of Jake's desk between two piles of legal papers.

"There," he mumbles. "In case you come to your senses."

He leaves. Deborah looks at the clock and the broken baseball player on the floor.

"You're paying this guy to be your contractor?" she asks.

"Something like that." Jake hunches his shoulders and goes back behind his desk.

"Why don't you call my cousin Georgie? He'll wreck your house for free."

29

John Gates," says the emergency room doctor named Wadhwa. "Do we have a John Gates?"

Slowly a pile of clothes begins to rise from the corner. A gray blanket, part of a blue official-looking shirt, ripped jeans, a matted beard. Haltingly the mass limps toward him.

Homeless man number three on the shift. It's been a wild night in the ER. There's a black man covered in white flour wearing bunny ears, who says he's Hitler and clearly should be at the psych ER but for the cut on his neck. A fat pink woman near him is squatting on the floor and grunting as if she's about to give birth, though she's obviously not pregnant. A little earlier in the evening, the cops brought in a deli guy who got his right hand caught in a meat grinder. The machine with the hand still in it arrives twenty minutes later.

"I'm John Gates," says the pile of clothes.

"This way please," says Dr. Wadhwa, a young resident from Bombay with a pudgy build and a clipped colonial school English accent.

He leads Gates into a room and has him sit down on an examining table. "What's wrong with you?"

"You see, this lawyer Mr. Schiff brought some people to the tunnels under Riverside Park and they attacked me with their baseball bats . . ."

The doctor nods absently, unimpressed. He's beginning to think the beggars of New York are no match for the ones back home when it comes to creative delusions.

"So what kind of injuries did you sustain?" asks the doctor, wondering if he should even bother inquiring whether the patient has any insurance.

Like a museum curator displaying an art exhibit, Gates lifts his shirt, revealing an ugly purplish yellow bruise on his ribs. Possibly several broken. He bows and gives the doctor a good look at a grapefruit-sized knot on the side of his head. When he glances up, Dr. Wadhwa sees Gates's nose has been broken and blood is caked into his beard.

No question: somebody has given this gentleman a good beating. Probably best to get a rib series and some film of the nose.

"So when did all this happen?"

"The night before last." Gates shudders. "I been trying to sleep it off and forget about it. But now I'm scared those guys with the bats are gonna come after me."

"I see . . ."

Gates coughs and the doctor makes him put on a mask that looks like an athletic supporter. It's getting to be like a TB ward in here. Gates winces when a strap touches his nose but otherwise seems too whipped to protest.

"There's something else I have to tell you," Gates says, his voice muffled.

"Yes?"

"I've got it."

"Got what?"

"The virus."

"I see." The doctor gets a pair of rubber gloves out of a cellophane package and puts them on. "Are you just HIV-positive or do you have full-blown AIDS?"

"Whatever. I got the virus."

"Well, have you been tested?" The doctor pauses and pulls on the long right middle finger of his glove.

"Why do I wanna get tested? I know what I got."

Across the room, there's a commotion. Two police officers and two doctors are trying to pry open the meat grinder and retrieve the deli guy's hand.

Dr. Wadhwa rests his fingers on the examining table next to Gates and then draws them back up quickly, as if he's been burned. A pinprick. He looks down nervously, searching for a needle that might have stuck him. He sees nothing, though, and there's no hole in his glove. It's just morbid imagination. But enough's enough. This man should get an AIDS test.

"So what'd you do?" he asks Gates. "Shoot up with somebody else's works? Have sex with somebody in a risk category?"

Gates's eyes linger on a doorway across the hall where a trauma team is working on a victim of a subway shooting.

"I was with somebody who had it," he says in a vacant absent voice.

"Did they tell you that afterwards?"

"During."

The doctor shakes his head. It takes all kinds in this country.

"I still think perhaps you should be tested. Otherwise you'll never know for sure."

Gates's jaw drops and swivels a little, as if it's trying to act independently from the rest of his face. The eyes remain cloudy and confused, though. "I know what's going on," he says. "I was exposed."

Amazing, thinks the doctor. The difference in attitudes about dying between here and India. This man has already made up his mind he wants to die. So why stop him? Too many people come through here begging and praying for a second chance. Small children, old women, young men in the prime of their lives. They're brought in talking, pleading with you to save their lives, scared out of their minds. One minute they seem okay, a couple of hours later they're dead from a bullet doctors can't get to in time. In some cases, they don't even know there's a chance they're going to die, which just makes the end that much more sad and horrible.

"Well you should at least get your T cell count," says Wadhwa, giving it one last try. "Then you can find out what kind of preventive medication you can take. There's different stages, you know.

One set of antibiotics fights off pneumonia. Another set's for eye problems . . .''

"Doesn't matter. I'm still gonna die."

"Well then you might as well be comfortable," the doctor says.

30

Jake takes the next morning off from work and goes to see his old friend Andrew Botwin, attorney-at-law.

In the ten years since they worked at Legal Aid together, Andy has flourished, even more lavishly than Jake. His practice has expanded to include hotel chain executives, television producers, CEOs with awkward divorces, and celebrities with a habit of punching out photographers. His face appears regularly on *Court TV* and the cover of *American Lawyer*. You don't go to Andy to win a case. You go to him to settle it. The consummate deal maker. People say that in the days of old, Andy could have gotten probation for the Salem witches.

"How the hell are you?" he says, rising from behind a clean desk with an inlaid leather top.

Jake's eyes slide over to the framed book jacket on the wall with Andy's smiling face in bright color. Then he looks back at Andy, holding the identical smile under his bushy eyebrows and moustache.

"I'm good, Andy. But probably not as good as you."

"You're kind to say that." He shakes Jake's hand warmly and gestures for him to sit down. "How's Dana and Alex?"

"Fine and fine."

"It's funny. I had a client in here the other day whose son has encephalitis, just like your boy did. I'm glad everything worked out."

Andy sits in his leather chair and tilts back so he appears to be looking at a corner of the ceiling, a familiar pose from the network panel shows. The thinker. The pontificator. Jake is having trouble separating his actual memories of Andy from the image he projects on television.

"So what brings you here today?" he asks Jake.

Where to begin? Jake hesitates and sees Andy's eyes narrow even as his smile remains in place. "I was wondering if you could make some inquiries for me," he says.

"About what?" The smile starts to thin.

"There was an incident in Riverside Park the other night. I was trying to find out where the police were with their investigation."

Andy looks confused, as if somebody had just switched his furniture around. The phone rings and he picks it up.

"Yeah?" The bushy eyebrows waggle. "ABC? Put 'em through."

He holds up one finger to tell Jake this will take only a minute. "Sandra, my love!" he exclaims into the receiver. "How the hell are you?"

His features move close together in concentration as Jake studies some of the other pictures on his wall. Andy with Geraldo Rivera. Andy in boxing gloves squaring off with the heavyweight champ. Andy with a bunch of shaggy-haired heavy-metal musicians gripping V-shaped electric guitars.

"Are we on or off the record now?" Andy is saying into the phone. "There's no way he's going to appear before the judge like that. All right? I don't care what the DA says."

He listens intently for a few more seconds, holding the finger up at Jake again.

"I'll tell you what," he says into the receiver. "Have a camera guy here by quarter to six. We can go live with him . . . Really, an exclusive . . . Love you too. Bye."

He hangs up. "So I don't get it," he says to Jake, not missing a beat from their previous conversation. "You need me to make inquiries to the police for you? About one of your clients?"

Jake clears his throat and lowers his eyes. One of his wing tips is untied and the black lace lies like a tiny snake on the white

Indian rug. "This might be something a little closer to home, Andy."

A long, lawyerly pause. They both know the proper etiquette here. Don't tell your lawyer anything until he asks.

"So," says Andy. "You don't feel comfortable talking to the DA about this yourself?"

"Well, you know, Norman and I don't have the best history."

Andy nods. The old story. A couple of years back, when Norman McCarthy, the current Manhattan district attorney, was the ambitious executive assistant, he'd had a mob stool called Vinnie the Razor making a case for him against one of Jake's clients, Ralph Ingelleria. It turned out Vinnie was addicted to tranquilizers. So true-blue, straight-arrow Norman McCarthy had his wife, an earnest young registered nurse, bring Valium and Percodan right into Vinnie's jail cell. Naturally, Jake put Norman's wife on the stand and forced her to testify about Vinnie's precarious mental state, and Norman, naturally, never forgave Jake.

"All right, so there's a lot of water under the bridge and there's a lot of water over the bridge," says Andy.

"There isn't any bridge at all." Jake wraps his knuckles around the claw at the end of the left armrest. "That's why I need you to make these inquiries for me."

"Well, can you narrow down what I'm asking about?"

"I believe there might have been a murder in the tunnel under the park two nights ago. In fact, there may have been two murders. I'd imagine the police are looking to talk to someone who knows something about them."

"And you might be that someone?" Andy's eyebrows rise and his chair tips back at an even more precipitous angle.

"Yes."

"And does anyone else know what happened?"

"Yeah, the guy who did the actual killing. He came by my office yesterday to pressure me."

"I see," says Andy, getting out a pad to take notes. "And is he likely to make a statement to the police on his own?"

"I wouldn't think so."

The phone rings again.

"Yes? CNN?" Andy cradles the receiver against the side of his neck as he puts down the notepad and takes an electronic appointment book out of his inside jacket pocket. He punches a few numbers. "Well if three o'clock doesn't work for them, tell them we can do the interview at four-thirty."

The phone goes back on the hook and the appointment book goes back in his pocket. Jake feels an uneasy fluttering in his gut.

"Look, Andy, if you don't have time for this, I completely understand . . ."

Andy brings the chair forward so suddenly that he almost bangs his elbows on the desk top. "Oh come on, Jake. You're like family. I wouldn't let this fall between the cracks."

Jake studies his old friend again and tries to remember what specific cases they worked on at Legal Aid together. None come to mind, but somehow he feels comforted in Andy's presence. It's not just media hype, he tells himself. Andy cares about him.

"So you're sure you don't mind checking this out for me? Do you want a retainer?"

"Oh please, Jake." Andy waves his right hand through the air like a dismissive butterfly. "Your money's no good here. Now tell me some more about what happened."

31

Hey asshole!"

Walt Matuszyk, a muscular guy with black hair extensions, looks up. Philip Cardi is getting out of a blue Honda Accord. His cousin Ronnie remains in the car with a guy called Faffy and a pale blonde girl in the backseat.

Philip climbs up onto the loading dock where Walt's been working, behind a supermarket in lower Manhattan.

"Nice-looking girl," Philip says, looking back at the car. "Be a shame to put her head under a truck's tire."

The girl looks sullen and bored in the back, like she's stuck in calculus class.

"Look, look, Phil, I'm sorry," says Walt. "Tell Carmine, I know I fucked up. I'll have him the rest of the money a week from Saturday."

"He's gettin' tired of hearing that." Philip squints up at the sun. "There someplace we can talk around here?"

"Why do we have to go anywhere?"

Philip nods and Ronnie gets out of the car to join them.

"Oh now," says Walt, the hair extensions hanging halfway down his back with colored beads on the ends. "We don't have to do it like this, do we Phil?"

"We do it like this, or we take her for a ride."

Walt looks over at his girl and gets nothing back.

"All right, let's go downstairs."

"Spoken like a true gentleman," says Philip.

They descend to the boiler room and Ronnie shuts the door.

"You're a fuckin' moron, Walt." Philip turns on him. "Carmine's given you every break. He used to like you, you know."

"I know, it's just, like, what can I say, Phil? I got rotten timing. Check that. I got no timing. A guy says he's gonna come through for me with half a kilo, he shows up with twelve pounds of marijuana. Kiddie dope. You know, who smokes marijuana? Bunch of fuckin' Deadheads and college students. They practically give away joints at the registrar's office. What do they need me for? So now I'm stuck. Give me another week, I'll unload the whole thing."

Philip kicks him hard between the legs and Walt crumples to the floor.

"So what's gonna happen in a week? You gonna go to five more topless places where you gonna go around stuffing twenties into girls? You think my uncle wasn't going to find out about that? Jesus Christ, you motherfucker. I oughta do that girl outside a favor right now and blow your fuckin' head off. Save her the heartache you're gonna cause her later."

Tears well up in Walt's eyes. "Please, Phil. I swear, things are gonna be different."

Philip sighs and Ronnie pulls hard on Walt's hair extensions, yanking him to his feet and then pinning his arms behind him.

"You know I hate it when things have to come to this," says Philip. "But experience has taught me that it's very hard for people to change. They need real incentive. Negative reinforcement, they call it. You ever hear of that, Walt?"

"Yes. No. I'm not sure."

"It means I think I'm gonna have to really hurt you to make sure my message gets across."

"Phil, no. Listen. You really don't have to—have a heart."

"Have a heart? Have a heart? You're asking me to have a heart? Fuck you! I was in the Green Berets in Vietnam, you motherfucker. I bayonetted old ladies and stuck grenades up people's asses. You think it bothers me that you're gonna cry?" He looks befuddled for a second and then reaches for his fly. "You wanna suck my dick? Is that what you'd like?"

Walt shakes his head vigorously.

"What? You don't wanna suck my dick? What? Is your mouth too good for me or something?"

Walt tries turning his head to beg Ronnie for mercy, but Ronnie just ignores him and bends back Walt's elbows, as if he's about to break both of them.

Philip takes his hand off his fly. "All right, now look, I want us all to be practical about this. I was thinking when I came over here. There's no point in breaking your legs, 'cause then that's just another excuse for you not to go to work. Then I considered crushing your balls, but that would make you even less of a man than you already are and I don't want to be party to that. Then I remembered how we once slit open a guy's eyelids during an interrogation in Vietnam, but that could mean optical surgery and I don't know what kind of insurance you have."

Walt is trembling so badly that foam is gathering at the right side of his mouth like the head of a beer.

"Are you listening to me, you motherfucker?" says Philip. "I'm trying to be nice to you."

"I hear you, I hear you."

"Good," says Philip, taking a switchblade out of his back pocket and nodding to Ronnie. "So I decided to do you a favor. See, I took this college extension course a few years ago and this science professor I knew, he had a very interesting theory about secondary sexual characteristics."

Walt tries to squirm out of Ronnie's grasp but he gets punched in the back of the head and kicked in the stomach by Philip. Then Ronnie hauls him back up to his feet, wraps duct tape across his mouth, and holds a knife to his throat. Philip uses his own switchblade to slit open the front buttons of Walt's shirt.

"Anyway," he says. "This professor, Professor DeLaszlo was his name, he started talking about the mammaries. You know."

He puts his free hand on Walt's hairy chest.

"Now everybody knows the purpose of a woman's breasts," he says. "Right? They produce milk and nourishment for small children. But why do men have nipples? Have you ever asked yourself that?"

Philip squeezes the left side of Walt's chest and Walt makes a muffled sound under the heavy silver tape.

"Well, the professor's theory was that it has to do with evolution," Philip goes on. "See, back in the old days primitive man was a hunter-gatherer. Just like all these other animals and primates running around. Except a lot of them were bigger and stronger than him. So this professor's theory was that man's nipples gave the illusion that he had enormous eyes in his chest. Especially if you were looking at him through the fucking jungle. Those nipples could intimidate you. But now that we've progressed out of the jungle, we don't need them anymore. Am I right?"

He grabs a fistful of flesh from the right side of Walt's chest and gets a buried yelp out of him.

"So you see, I'm actually being very nice to you," he says, bringing the blade in close. "I'm only taking something you don't need anymore. It's all part of evolution. Right? We don't have to live like animals."

32

For the past week, John G. has been out of the tunnels and back on the street. Eating from garbage cans and sleeping on grates again. But somehow the feeling's different this time. He keeps hearing the words "Friday three o'clock" in his mind. That's when the doctor will give him the results of his AIDS test.

He stares up at the clock on the Apple Bank building and sees it's quarter to two in the afternoon. An hour and fifteen minutes until his cause of death will be confirmed.

It's hard teaching himself to keep track of time again. For months, everything's just been a blur—day, then night, then day —and sometimes when he's been on a crack binge, just night, night, night. But now every moment matters again.

He hasn't been getting high lately. It's not a conscious effort at changing. He just hasn't felt like it since Abraham died and he took the test. It's time to say good-bye to the world and for once it seems appropriate to get his thoughts in order.

After he'd taken the AIDS test, he went back to the tunnel. The police had taken away Abraham's body and started breaking up some of the cardboard boxes and huts where their friends lived. John G. hid in an archway until they were gone. What was he supposed to say to them? He'd seen everything that happened that night, but he still couldn't put it together in his head. Mr. Schiff trying to get between Abraham and the stocky guy. Even with Haldol clearing his mind like fire clearing a forest, it still didn't make any sense to him.

John had waited until the police took the body away before he made a memorial to Abraham on the trailer's front steps, using dandelions from the park and the old Hanukkah candles from inside. He meant to say a novena for his friend, but couldn't think of the words. "Our Father . . ."—that was it.

He watches 1:46 turn into 1:47 on the Apple Bank clock. Then it says the temperature is seventy-six degrees. The sun feels good on the back of his neck. It makes the hair on his arms stand up and turn around. Across the street, in Needle Park, an old woman in a brown dress is sitting on a bench, throwing bread crumbs at pigeons. John imagines her sitting on this same bench, sixty years ago, with smooth legs and saddle shoes, putting on lipstick and waiting for some smart young man to come up out of the subway and walk her home, arm in arm. Another lifetime.

Now she sits on the bench alone and John G. waits to hear when he will die.

He arrives at the medical clinic fifteen minutes late, thinking he'll be made to wait anyway. But Dr. Wadhwa is already standing by the reception desk, looking impatient.

"I thought you weren't going to make it," he says.

"Man's got a right to be late to his own funeral, hasn't he?"

The doctor, a little man with thick wavy hair and a dark cherub's face, furrows his brow and leads him through a waiting room packed with angry pregnant women, sad stoned men, and joyous children unaware of what awaits them here. They remind John G. of exhausted passengers on a late afternoon train. Watch the closing doors. Why isn't he being made to wait with them? Poor bastards. One of them, a guy with a smear of greasy black-gray hair, has what looks like a massive purple hickey on the back of his neck. On closer inspection, it turns out to be a huge lesion. In fact, his face and neck are covered with lesions. Like he's being kissed to death. So why am I getting in before him? John G. wonders.

Wadhwa takes him into a bright narrow office with a desk and an examining table. Pictures of babies and reproductive systems on the walls and a little bit of blood on the floor. Birth, death.

"Pardon the mess," says the doctor. "We share space with an OB-GYN clinic."

"I'm not fussy."

The doctor sits down behind the desk, folds his hands, and smiles.

"You're fine," he says.

"What?"

"I said you're all right. At least for the moment."

The sun coming through the windows. A baby cries in the next room.

"What're you talking about?" says John G. "Is this some kind of fuckin' joke?"

"No, it's not a joke. Your tests came back negative." The doctor lowers his deep brown eyes to the file on his desk. "Your T cell count is normal. Your CD 4 is well above two hundred. There are no guarantees, of course, and you will want to get retested in a few months. But for now everything appears to be fine. I wanted to tell you personally. I thought you'd be pleased."

The shelter. The tunnel. The hospital. We have a few more questions before you go, Mr. Gates. You're being held at the station. Wait for the signal.

"I don't understand."

"Whoever told you they'd given you AIDS might not have had it themselves or perhaps didn't transmit it to you."

A voice calls Dr. Wadhwa's name over the public address system and he looks distracted. For some reason, John G. finds himself fixating on the way the doctor has his lab coat fastidiously buttoned up. Not like American-born doctors letting theirs flap open casually. This guy doesn't take one button for granted.

"So that's it?" says John G.

"Yes, that's it."

He feels angry. Cheated. A side of him won't accept this. He's been ready to welcome death with open arms. Everybody dies, Daddy. He hears Shar's voice so clearly she could be sitting on his lap. He should be dead now. He should be with her. He could have saved her when the light turned green. She died in his arms. The guilt of being alive is like a heavy stone on his chest.

The doctor rubs his forehead and checks his watch. "I must say, Mr. Gates. I'm somewhat surprised by your attitude. In the part of the world I come from, millions of people die of disease and hunger. Yet you've been given the gift of life and you don't seem the least bit moved by it."

John G. stares down at his hands. "I just need time to adjust, I guess."

"May I ask you something?" Wadhwa swivels in his chair.

"What?"

"Are you taking any medication for your . . . ?" He makes a vague circling motion next to his head.

John G. takes out the amber Haldol bottle and rattles it at him. Just two or three pills left. He didn't think he'd be needing much more.

The doctor takes the bottle and studies the prescription on the side. "You might want to stop upstairs and get this refilled."

He hands the bottle back and reaches into his pocket for a card. "I'd like to make one other suggestion."

"What's that?"

"I know that some of the homeless people we see at the clinic go on to a place called the Interfaith Volunteers Center on the Upper West Side. I thought I'd give you the address if you were interested." He hands over the card.

John G. takes it without looking at it. He's too busy staring at the pictures of the babies on the wall. Black ones, white ones, brown ones, yellow ones; some old enough to walk, others newly born. Right now, he feels like one of them. Reborn here in this grubby old hospital, surrounded by the sick and the dying, people who deserve a second chance far more than he does. But it isn't the pink-and-white cooing kind of birth. It's more like being wrenched from a warm, dark, comfortable place and forced out into a bright, frightening world where nothing is certain.

"Congratulations." The doctor stands and offers his hand. "You may have another thirty or forty years ahead of you."

"And what am I supposed to do with them?" says John G.

33

How you doing, Mrs. Schiff? My name's Philip Cardi. I've been doing some work for your husband."

It's eight-thirty at night. Jake is upstairs, making a phone call. Philip stands on the front stoop, grinning through the bars of the front gate.

"Oh yes, he's told me."

"Mind if I come in?"

Dana gets the key and lets him in.

Philip steps into the foyer and gives her a long once-over twice. She blushes slightly and leads him into the living room.

"So you're the psychiatrist, right?"

"Psychiatric social worker."

He gestures like he's taking off his hat to her. "It's wonderful your husband lets you work."

She crosses her arms. "Well, it's not so much that he lets me work," she says, shifting her weight from foot to foot. "It's that I choose to work."

"Yeah, I guess you can do that if you're not home raising children."

He takes a blue glass pitcher off the credenza and looks at the bottom of it. Why is he making her so uncomfortable? She wonders. It's not just the long rude stare. It's a certain arrogance, almost a sense of entitlement as he moves through their living room, picking things up and examining them.

"So why is it that you're coming by so late, Mr. Cardi?"

"Your husband and I, we have some unfinished business to discuss."

His smile feels like fingers on her face, probing into places where they don't belong. She doesn't want to be alone with him anymore.

"Jake!" She calls up the stairs. "You have a visitor!"

Philip puts down the pitcher and starts flipping through a coffee table book about African art. "You ever hear about the things these guys do to their women? How they cut them?" He makes a tut-tut sound as he turns the page. "Right in the privates, so they can't experience pleasure."

"Women have it tough all over," she says stiffly.

"It's sick. That's what it is. A bunch of savages mutilating each other."

Jake comes thumping down the stairs, wearing pinstriped trousers and a white shirt from work with the tie undone. When he sees Philip, his eyes become slits and his mouth hardens.

"Honey, can you give us a couple of minutes?"

"Sure," says Dana, looking uneasily from her husband to Philip. "Holler if you need anything."

She goes bounding up the stairs and Philip watches her gray sweat bottoms and bare feet disappear along the landing.

"She's a real piece of ass, your wife," he says. "I sure hope you know what to do with her, Jake."

"What the hell do you want?"

"I still want that school contract for the asbestos work. You thought any more about that?"

"I think I told you to go fuck yourself. Isn't that the way we left it?"

Philip whistles and puts the African art book down on the Mies van der Rohe glass coffee table. "Well, that's not a very lawyerly thing to say, is it?"

"You get out of my house."

"Hey, your wife invited me in. Maybe she saw something she liked."

The fraudulent neon smile again. How could Jake have allowed himself to be taken in so easily by this fake macho camaraderie? Hey, Brooklyn is Brooklyn. He realizes now the whole thing was some kind of setup. He should've known better. He's represented dozens of criminal defendants just like Philip. But this time he let himself be blinded. He's sometimes told himself he'd give up his own eyes to protect his family; now he's done it.

"I'm giving you a choice," he says to Philip, circling in close enough to smell his aftershave. "You can leave now or I'll call the police."

"Oh the police!" Philip throws up his hands and thrusts out his lower lip. "That would be something! I think I'd like to talk to the police. I might have some interesting stories for them about something that happened the other night under Riverside Park. I think they call that felony murder, what you did. They take your license for that, don't they?"

"I didn't do anything, Philip. You swung the bat."

"Yeah, who's your witnesses? The homeless guy from the subways? Gates? He's dead. Remember?"

"If it's your word against mine, I know who they're going to believe."

Philip's face reddens. "You try turning me in and I'll bring this whole fucking house down on your head."

Jake takes a quick glance up toward the top of the stairs to see if Dana or Alex have been standing there listening. But there's just a white plastic garbage bag waiting to be taken out.

He takes another step and goes chest-to-chest with Philip. "Now you listen to me," he says quietly. "I don't knuckle under to you or anybody else. Understand? My friendship with Bob Berger is not for sale and my wife's ass is not for your eyes."

"I think you're forgetting who you're talking to," says Philip, pulling his shoulders back and drawing himself up to his full height.

"No, I know who I'm talking to. I'm talking to a guy who committed the actual murders the other night. So before he starts talking about somebody else, he's going to have to talk about what he did and then go to jail. They don't do much plea bargaining with murder two cases."

Philip's pretense of a smile is gone. All Jake sees before him is a weak chin and a soft forehead. And in an instant, he knows he probably could have taken Philip in a fair fight. Again, he's flushed with guilt for not having done more to stop things the other night.

"You must figure you're a pretty good poker player, huh, Counselor?"

"You get out of my house and you stay away from my office."

"What if I call bullshit on you?"

"Try it," says Jake, remembering what Philip said to Abraham in the tunnel.

"Maybe I will." Philip smiles and bows, as if he's just received a bit of thoughtful advice. "Kiss your wife good-bye for me."

Once more, Jake has to hold himself back from throwing the first punch. Rage is bubbling up inside him like carbolic acid. Philip stops to look at the framed Ben Shahn PEACE poster on the wall and then moves toward the front door.

"It's all right, I'll let myself out," he says. "You gave me the keys. Remember?"

34

Back upstairs in his study, Jake closes the door and picks up the telephone.

"Andy, it's Jake again," he tells his lawyer's voice mail. "I'm going crazy here. You gotta let me know what's going on with this case or tell me to get another lawyer. My balls are in a vise, buddy."

That makes twelve calls in the last five days and he still hasn't heard back from Andy. There hasn't been anything in the newspapers either. Not bad news, but not necessarily good news either. He wonders if there's some problem with the police. Of course, he could just pick up the phone himself and volunteer to tell the cops what happened.

I was involved in a couple of homicides.

Oh really? Hope you got a good lawyer. Murder two in New York State can carry a sentence of twenty-five to life.

But you see, officer, I didn't know that's what was going to happen. I thought we were just going to throw a scare into a guy.

Oh yeah? Who'd you think you were going with, Mother Teresa? You were going to give these bums a civics lecture? Sure you were. Come on, Counselor, you're a shrewder judge of character than that. Aren't you?

He hangs up the phone and tries to lose himself, channel surfing with the TV remote control. MTV bodies writhing. Pesos plummeting on the business channel. A film clip of Hakeem Turner slam-dunking on some hapless Phoenix Sun player. A televangelist talking damnation. Then on Channel 16, a familiar fuzzy head and a set of bushy eyebrows against an artificial New York skyline backdrop. His lawyer Andy Botwin is holding forth on some cable call-in program.

"What I'm saying, Bill, is that my client cannot expect to get a fair trial because he's a succesful person living in America," he intones, waving a finger in the air. "He's being punished for playing the game too well . . ."

For a split second, Jake feels a surge of panic: is Andy discussing his case on national TV?

"There's too much prejudice in the air." Andy goes on, propping that thoughtful fist against his chin. "A jury of his peers should have at least one or two people familiar with the world of entertainment . . ."

Good. It's one of his other cases. Calm down, Jake tells himself. You haven't been charged with anything. Yet.

35

Philip is stuck in a line of cars outside the Midtown Tunnel. A matchstick-thin homeless guy with a mop of wild filthy hair stumbles up with a squeegee and offers to wash his windshield.

"Get the fuck away from me, ya hairy puke." Philip reaches for the aluminum bat still in the backseat.

The bum backs away, as if he'd somehow divined Philip's history just by looking at his face.

The light changes and Philip drives on fuming into the long tunnel under the river. Bums. Niggers. Spics. Faggots. Jews. Women. He truly hates this fucking city.

For a few minutes tonight, he thought he might finally be able to conquer it. If only he could have worked things out with this lawyer Schiff and the contracts, whole new vistas could have opened up. From the school asbestos deal, he could have moved on to bigger projects: more school construction, bridges, roads, civic centers, and then on into the private sector. He'd pictured himself subcontracting superstores for Bob Berger, hotels, skyscrapers. The day would come when he'd be able to stand on a rooftop, look out at the horizon, and calculate the amount of money he's owed for each building on the skyline. He would become . . . a player.

Instead of just being a meatball collecting debts for his ungrateful uncle.

Emerging from the tunnel and heading out onto the Long Island Expressway, he turns on the radio and starts punching through stations. He's meant for better things, he decides, but the odds in life have always been stacked against him. He's never gotten the respect he's deserved. Not from the college loan officers, giving all the breaks to the nigs and spics after he got his discharge from the army. Not from the guards and the other shit birds on his cell block when he went away. Not from Carmine, and especially not from his wife and kids.

"Make way for the homo superior!" a song on the radio bleats.

Philip punches in another station, still not exactly sure what he wants. He drives past the old World's Fair grounds and a plane from Kennedy roars overhead, a red streak through the night. Why has he always felt so trapped and held down? He's never been sure why he got married in the first place. The dirty little secret is that the first time he really felt turned on as a teenager was seeing Little Joe stripped to the waist and getting whipped over a wagon wheel on *Bonanza*.

That certainly didn't make him a faggot, but it could be that he's just one of those guys who never should have gotten hitched in the first place. Instead he let his uncle and his mother pressure him into marrying Nita, a mousy little girl from the old neighborhood with stringy hair and thick glasses. Of course, he could never really make it with her. In bed, it was like trying to put a wet noodle through a keyhole.

When she'd ask him what was the matter, it got him furious. What right did she have, implying there was something wrong with him? Yeah, he had to smack her around a little. He was the man in the house. It was his biological imperative. Of course, when he tried to exercise that imperative with other women he couldn't get hard most of the time either. But that was because of all the pressure he was under from his uncle and the rest of them. He had to think of Little Joe and the fucking wagon wheel just so he could get hard enough to get Nita pregnant the two times.

Kids. The truth was the kids were just background noise to him. Blurred reflections of a misconceived union. Two more things he couldn't control. That made him feel trapped. No wonder he felt happier sometimes beating people over the head with baseball bats and crowbars. At least then they'd do what you want. You had some control over them. It was his biological imperative. To dominate.

But now he has this divorce to think about. He couldn't believe it when Nita served him with papers five months ago and asked him to move out. The *infamia!* At least he's been able to keep Carmine from finding out about it so far, since Nita's covering for him. No one else in the family has ever even thought about getting a divorce. 'Til death do us part. Isn't that what it says? That means you stay together until you kill each other. But then Nita had the nerve to say, "I'm sorry, Philip. I just can't do this witchoo anymore. You need help."

He needs help? She's the one needs help. What the fuck was the matter with her? Didn't she understand she couldn't just leave him? It wasn't that he ever wanted to fuck her again. But she belonged to him. The kids too. No one else could have them. In fact, he'd just as soon see them all dead before he'd let another man move into the house and take his place.

He veers off the LIE and takes the Seaford–Oyster Bay Expressway south to Sunrise Highway. Barry Manilow breaks through static on the radio. "I Made It Through the Rain." Guilty pleasure floods Philip's bloodstream like pure sugar. His other dirty secret: unlike other guys in the crew, he prefers Manilow to Sinatra. Somehow Manilow understands what guys like Philip have been through. What it's like to be rained on.

He decides to go by the wife's house again and see what she's up to. Hell, it's just three, four miles from the Gateway Motor Lodge where he's been staying in Merrick and he has a right to know what's going on with her. More than a right: an imperative. He's not just some stalker. He was married to the bitch.

As he pulls in across the street on Andrews Lane, he barely takes notice of the red Caprice that's been following him for a couple of blocks. He's too busy looking at the strange car in the driveway.

A blue Chrysler. His blood begins to make noise. Has she let another man move in already? Philip can't believe it. He's already killed someone this week. Is he going to have to do it again? He reaches for the bat in the backseat.

36

Jake can't quite get comfortable in bed. He turns to the right, but there are three sharp creases under his side. He turns to the left, but the pillow is too hard.

His thoughts keep going around like clothes in a dryer. He's going to be implicated in a murder. Someone's going to find out. A man's dead because of his actions. Probably two men. He feels sickened. What could he have done differently? He flips onto his back and his stomach starts to growl.

These are the hours when a man adds things up and tries to justify the life that he's lived.

"What are you thinking about?"

He freezes. He hadn't even realized Dana was awake.

"Nothing."

"You're never thinking about nothing." She brushes his left temple with her fingertips. "Are you going to tell me what's going on or are you going to make me guess?"

He sits up and looks at her in the dark. She seems somehow smaller and more vulnerable, nestled in the sheets.

"I think I'm gonna get a beer," he says. "You want anything?"

She looks at him as if she knows something that he doesn't. She says nothing.

He gets up off the bed, wraps a towel around his middle, and starts to go downstairs. From the landing above, he hears Alex making a sound on his guitar like a monkey being strangled and smells incense burning. Incense. It makes him think of Earth Day in Central Park and old Iron Butterfly records. Has his sixteen-year-old son become a pothead on entering eleventh grade? The temptation is there to burst through the door and question him like a hostile witness. But what good would that do? If he finds nothing, Alex's wellspring of resentment will be replenished for years to come. My father, what an asshole. Better to move on right now, and find another way to come back to it.

He continues down the stairs to the first floor, some of the steps groaning and sinking suspiciously under his feet. The last thing he needs is another contractor to fix the treads.

He comes off the last step and turns left across the wide hallway with the newly finished parquet floors. From the kitchen ten feet away, he hears a sudden scuffling noise. He stops. Someone is there. Moving across the wood floor, brushing against the stove. Has Philip come back?

It doesn't seem fair. Jake's not ready for him. He should have called the locksmith. He backs up several feet to the antique brass umbrella stand by the front door. He feels around for a sturdy umbrella. Not one of those $3 Korean jobs you buy from Senegalese peddlers on Broadway. But a good solid $45 number from Saks with a maplewood handle. He grabs it and comes back toward the kitchen cautiously.

The sound becomes more and more distinct. Nails scratching the marble countertop near the sink. He stands in the doorway and flips on the light. A large black-brown rat is standing by the dishrack. He stares at Jake with dark beady eyes. His long yellow fangs are bared and his belly quivers. Daring Jake to enter. Like the kitchen is already his domain. He gives a razory little squeak and rears back on his hind legs. Jake feels the towel slipping off his middle and dinner rising in his esophagus. The umbrella isn't going to do him any good. He moves slowly to the right, toward the cabinets Dana recently had redone. Where they keep the pots and pans.

The rat creeps up to the edge of the counter, its forefeet pawing the air. Considering which part of Jake to sink its teeth into first. Just seven feet of kitchen floor separate them. Jake saw rats make much longer leaps at the Marlboro Houses. Mr. Colangelo from upstairs spent a week in the hospital with bites on his right ankle. Jake opens the cabinet door carefully and takes out a long-handled cast-iron skillet. The rat cocks its head to the left, as if it's curious about what's going to happen.

Alex's music curdles and squeals upstairs. A garbage truck rolls by outside. Four years of law school, ten years slugging it out in private practice, a lifetime trying to get out of Gravesend and trying to get Gravesend out of his mind, and still he has rats in the kitchen of his million-dollar town house. He suddenly lunges with the skillet. The rat backs up quickly and throws itself against the tiled wall, unable to find the hole it entered through. Jake brings the skillet down hard, smashing a primrose-bordered tea-cup, but the rat dances out of the way with an excited squeal. It hides behind a Williams-Sonoma dish like a sniper in a World War II movie. Then it peeks around the side, ready to jump at Jake.

There's no hesitation now. Jake swings the skillet again, smash-ing the plate and the rat. The rodent teeters to the right a bit, like its sense of balance is impaired. But Jake doesn't trust the injury. He attacks once more, slamming the rat with all his might, crushing its skull into the counter, so it will never threaten him and his family again. Three more shots just to be sure. Then he stands back to see what damage he's done. The rat lies flat, its paws outstretched, brackish dark blood oozing from its sides and its skull. The pink marble countertop around it is dented and chipped where Jake struck it with the skillet.

He turns and sees Dana standing behind him in the doorway. Staring at him as if he were the intruder. He lowers the skillet but before he can say anything, she turns and goes back upstairs.

37

Philip walks across the front lawn, limbering up his shoulders and taking practice swings with the baseball bat. Is he going to give Nita and her new boyfriend a beating first and then ask questions, or the other way around? He hasn't made up his mind. He just knows that if he finds another man there he won't be responsible for the carnage.

For some reason, the revolving sprinkler is going. Throwing ropes of water into the night air. Bitch.

Suddenly a light flashes behind him and a voice over a loud-speaker says his name.

He turns just as two Nassau County police officers come rushing at him and force him face-first down into the crabgrass. Soil and pesticides fill his nostrils. He looks up and sees he's surrounded by five cops. A malevolent surprise party. Two of the others wear NYPD uniform shirts. The fifth's in plain clothes. As big and round as a beach ball, he is. With a face as black as Flip Wilson's. A fucking *mulignan'*, for crying out loud. He sits down on Philip's stomach and shoves the gun right in his face. Now Philip knows affirmative action has gone too far.

"You're under arrest, asshole," says the cop. "You fuckin' move, I'll blow your damned head off."

Philip looks up and sees Nita and the kids watching him

through the living room window. Those same forlorn expressions: Our daddy's done it again.

He doesn't want them to see him like this, yet when Nita draws the curtains, he feels angry and abandoned. Fucking bitch. Just wait until he finally gets home.

38

The next morning John G. shows up at the Interfaith Volunteers Center, a crumbling old town house just off Broadway with chain-link gates over the windows.

Inside, the smells of urine and strong ammonia vie for supremacy. A tall black man with a long scar across his bald head meticulously mops the checkered linoleum floor in the hallway. He works in long straight streaks so that exactly half the floor is wet and half the floor is dry.

John G. studies his work cautiously before deciding to step on the dry side.

"Hey, goddamn it, what's the matter with you?" the man with the scar on his head snaps. "Can't you see I just got done with that side?"

John G. just stares at him with his mouth hanging open, not sure where to step next.

"Ah, just go on ahead," the man snarls in disgust. "Shit."

John G. edges past him and goes looking for the center's director, Elaine Greenglass. He finds her in a surprisingly clean office at the end of the hall. A short anxious woman behind a tall stack of files. She has fine Latinate features and billowing black curly hair, which she seems intent on pulling out one hair at a time with her left hand. Her right hand lies on her desk, having its nails painted red by a sallow girl with a silver ring through her left eyebrow.

"What's the matter?" Ms. Greenglass asks suddenly, not giving John G. a chance to introduce himself.

"Nothing."

She puts on a pair of horn-rimmed glasses. "I'm sorry," she says, all twitches and flutters. "I thought you were one of the regular residents. I was worried there might have been another stabbing."

Stabbing. Hospitals. Blood transfusions. John G. starts thinking this might not be the place for him.

"It wasn't a resident that got stabbed," says Ms. Greenglass quickly, seeing his hesitation. "It was two security guards who got in a fight and stabbed each other. We're looking for another company."

She stands up to welcome John G. into the room and the girl with the ring through her eyebrow departs.

"Are you one of the people who came in through our outreach program?" Ms. Greenglass asks tremulously.

"I have a card."

He searches his back pockets for the tattered and crumpled card Dr. Wadhwa gave him at the hospital.

But the card is no longer there. He looks down at the floor. Black-and-white linoleum squares. The pattern starts to give him trouble. He looks back at Ms. Greenglass.

"I need a place," he says.

"Okay!" She tugs on a clump of hair.

His eyes flick over to two small posters taped to a rusting green file cabinet. DON'T JUST DO SOMETHING, STAND THERE!" And ONE OF THESE DAYS I GOTTA GET MYSELF ORGANIZISIZED!! It's as if Ms. Greenglass is using the posters to admonish herself, and John G. feels like he's interrupted a personal conversation.

"Did the volunteer explain the rules?"

"I didn't see any volunteer."

"Well I can fill you in." She pulls out a form. "We're a not-for-profit organization specializing in helping the mentally ill and substance abusers."

"Then I'm your man," John says.

She twists another ringlet of hair around her left index finger.

"If you're accepted, you'll be expected to participate in five NA meetings a week and two encounter groups a day, including self-esteem sessions. Do you have a problem with that?"

"Uh, I guess it's okay." John G. feels himself break into a cold sweat. He hadn't realized there'd be this many rules.

"I also must warn you, some of the men don't do well in a structured setting." Ms. Greenglass takes her glasses off. "They start to decompensate when they stop using their regular drugs."

Part of him wants to turn on his heel and leave right now. But the other part reminds him he doesn't feel safe on the street anymore. Who knows if he'll run into the guys with the baseball bats again?

"So do you think you might be interested in being here?" Ms. Greenglass asks.

John G. notices she's wearing a pair of gold earrings shaped like ram's heads. Nothing ostentatious enough to get them torn off her earlobes on the subway, but tasteful and probably expensive in a quiet way. He wonders if she's another rich lady slumming it with volunteer work or if somehow she's making good money off this.

"I'd want to know if I can have my own room," he says suddenly.

"Well first you have to make it through the interview process." Ms. Greenglass grimaces in distaste, leaving lipstick stains on her upper row of teeth. "Generally speaking, we prefer to have the men bunk five or six to a room. We feel it gives them a chance to reinforce therapeutic values."

An elderly man with a whiskery nose and stubby fingers barges into the room, wearing a blue *Don't Ask Me 4 Shit* T-shirt.

"Do I know you?" he asks John G.

John G. stares back, but can't place him. The old man's face is as worn and woolly as an old Brillo pad. "Do I?"

"You were part of the old gang from Atlantic Beach."

"I'm from Patchogue."

"No, you're one of the Jews." The woolly man waves a scabby hand. "Arlene Finkelstein. Bennie Levine. What's his name, you know, Herbie Leonard, who ran the bar association. I remember they had me surrounded on the boardwalk outside Jackie Kannon's Rat Fink Club. They were working for Jack Warner. He was the head of the Jewish Mafia, you know. I had to shoot two of them. At the time, I was going with Miriam Sulzberg, you know. But I had to shoot her too, because I got interested in some other girl . . .''

"Yankel, is there something I can help you with?" Ms. Greenglass interrupts, sounding weary and impatient.

"Yes. I have a plan for getting rid of Eddie Fisher. So I can run off with Liz Taylor. Remind me to tell you later."

He walks out.

"Does he have his own room?" John G. asks.

"He has to." Ms. Greenglass purses her lips. "He can't get along with the other consumers. He's too erratic. He needs his own space."

"I see . . ." John G. scratches his ribs, considering the state of things.

Five guys in a room. Stink and sweat. In Catholic school, he once went on an overnight retreat and Daniel Fitzpatrick stole the outfielder's glove his mother bought him. Took it from right under his mattress, with the linseed oil still wet in the pocket. The last thing she ever gave him. He's not sharing any room.

"You know, it wouldn't be a bad idea for you to come here," Ms. Greenglass is saying. "We've seen a lot of men turn their lives around. I know you're concerned about sharing a room with other men, but something about that closeness can be very nurturing."

John G. stands up suddenly. "Fuck the Irish!" he says, amplifying the distortion in his mind so she can hear it. "Motherfucker cocksucker kill all the donkeys!"

"Hmm, perhaps you would do better on your own," says Ms. Greenglass.

39

The female ADA sits in her scuffed-up white office downtown at the Manhattan Criminal Court Building. She's reading the charges and rubbing the right side of her chest. On the corkboard behind her, there are pictures of her on horseback and a black-and-white portrait of the Civil War general William Tecumseh Sherman.

"Jesus," she says. "You cut off this guy's nipple. What kind of sick bastard are you anyway?"

Is that what this is about? Philip shrugs. *Minchia,* he thought it was something serious.

He stares at this little prosecutor. She can't be more than five feet tall. Ms. Fusco. She looks as if she hasn't had her First Communion yet, in her cream blouse and navy blazer. With her olive skin and long black hair, she reminds him of Mrs. Califano's daughters who used to work at the bakery across the street on Twentieth Avenue. Karen and Lisa—with the lips that looked like they could suck the chrome off a '65 Buick.

"How'd you think of something like that?" she asks.

"What?"

"Cutting off a guy's nipple."

"I don't know nothin' about it." Turning up the Bensonhurst in his voice, just in case she is from the neighborhood.

She looks over at the cop standing in the corner. Red-faced guy with silver hair and a waxed moustache. Fourth-generation mick detective, Philip figures. The Irish wooden Indian. There's one like him in every station house. They probably wheel him out to frighten first offenders. He's just supposed to stand there and look scary. Fact is, he's probably bombed by the middle of the afternoon and couldn't talk if he tried.

Ms. Fusco continues looking through her report. "We have sworn witness statements from the victim of the assault and from his girlfriend, who says you and your cousin Ronnie picked her up and drove her to the scene."

Rat bastards. Walt and his girlfriend. Now Carmine's going to have to send somebody out to put both their heads under tires until they withdraw their complaints.

"I don't have anything to say about this." Philip half turns in his seat. "I think I ought to call my lawyer."

Ms. Fusco keeps turning the pages in her file, a little bit of tongue sticking out of the left side of her mouth. "You know, he went into shock and almost died at Beekman," she says without looking up. "The charge against you is going to be attempted murder, not just aggravated assault . . ."

Philip suddenly feels his sphincter cramping. "No way."

He knows Ronnie has been arrested and is cooling his heels in an interrogation room down the hall. He hopes the kid can stand up to this pressure.

"Plus, I see this would actually be your third violent offense if you're convicted," Ms. Fusco goes on turning pages. "When you were eighteen, you assaulted a gay man on West Broadway and stuck a crowbar up his rectum. Right?"

"I was part of a group. It was a long time ago."

She turns another page and starts biting her nails. "And what about this?" she says.

"What about what?"

She doesn't answer for a moment. Her eyes move back and forth across the page.

All of a sudden, he's not just nervous; he's scared. They know about the girl in the warehouse. But how?

"What about *this*?" Ms. Fusco repeats, taking a page of hand-written notes out of the folder. "In nineteen seventy-four, you helped kidnap a businessman from Staten Island and put him in a hospital for a year."

Oh that. He almost smiles in relief. They don't know about the warehouse.

"Mike Torro? He was an asshole. He didn't pay his debts. And again, I was just part of a group."

"Well, you and your friends broke his jaw and collarbone. He lost most of his hearing in his right ear."

"Hey, you don't understand what my life was like," Philip says loudly, shooting out his right arm. "I'd just got back from Vietnam. I'd seen all kinds of shit over there and it messed with my mind. I was suffering from post-traumatic stress!"

"You're full of it." The red-faced detective steps forward, his waxed moustache twitching. The wooden Indian speaks. "I commanded a rifle company for a year and a half over there and none of my men ever got up to crap like that. I bet you're one of those assholes who goes around saying he went to Vietnam when he really washed out in boot camp."

Philip shrinks down in his seat a little, wondering if this mick has actually somehow seen his service record.

"The point is," says Ms. Fusco, "you're in a lot of trouble. If a judge sees your record, you're going for at least twenty to life with this case. With an emphasis on the upper range. Understand?"

Philip feels another wave of self-pity wash over him. What kind of world is this where a girl this age can threaten him? He wonders what Ronnie is telling them down the hall.

"So what do you want from me?" he asks.

"Your uncle." The Irish wooden Indian speaks again.

"Wha?"

Ms. Fusco leans forward on her brittle-looking elbows. "We want you to give up Carmine. We want everything. The whole criminal enterprise. Structure of the organization, list of all known associates, and a signed agreement to testify in any and all related cases. Plus you admit to all previous crimes you've committed. You leave out anything and the deal is off."

"We already have your cousin in custody," the detective says.

"If you don't start talking, he will. Train's pulling out now, Philly, better get on it."

Philip puts his head in his hands, thinking about things he's seen Carmine do to people for far lesser offenses. He keeps seeing bodies cut up in bathtubs and parts buried in the bird sanctuaries on Staten Island.

"What happens if I say no to you?" he asks Ms. Fusco.

"Then you're going back to prison." She lines up all the papers in the file so the edges are even. "And judging from your record, I see you don't do time very well."

Philip shivers a little and looks to the old mick detective for sympathy. At least they're both men—not like this little girl pulling the wings off a fly. But it's useless. The man's face has about as much give as a tree trunk.

"I think I gotta think about this," says Philip.

40

After a half-dozen intake interviews and encounter groups with the staff, John G. is sitting on fresh bedsheets in his own room at the Interfaith Volunteers Center.

In his locker, there's a special shampoo to kill the lice in his hair and the first set of washed clothes he's had in months. He never truly appreciated clean surfaces before; now he finds himself hanging around the laundry, just to enjoy the smell of detergent.

The room is not much bigger than a motorman's cab and the walls are filthy. And one of the previous occupants drew in Magic Marker on the window, marring the sunlight. But the space is his, for now.

41

Philip has been in custody for more than twenty-four hours, but he still hasn't called any of the crew's regular lawyers for fear they'll tell Carmine he's making some kind of deal. In his mind's eye, he sees a robin taking wing and flying skyward with part of his liver in its mouth. In the meantime, his bowels are backing up because he's afraid to use the DA's bathroom and catch some nasty skell's disease off the toilet seat.

"All right, I wanna ask you something," he says as Ms. Fusco and the mick detective come back in the room.

His wrists feel scraped and raw from the handcuffs and his mind feels scarred from worry.

"What is it?" Ms. Fusco takes a seat and smoothes her gray gabardine skirt. As if she's really a nice girl.

"What if I could give up somebody bigger than my uncle?"

She turns and looks at the red-faced detective, who's resumed his position, glowering in the corner. Philip wonders idly if there's something going on between them.

"Who do you have in mind?" she says.

"What if I could give up somebody legitimate? Somebody well known? Like a guy you've never been able to get anything on?"

"Look, Philip, don't play games with us. You fuck us and we'll fuck you."

Such a mouth on this one. If it was his daughter, he'd smack her right now.

He frowns. "You know who this Jacob Schiff is?"

"The defense lawyer?" Her eyebrows go up and she glances once more at the detective in the corner.

Now Philip's sure they're fucking. Disgusting. A man his age and a girl like her. It's like father and daughter.

"You got any favor bank going between him and the DA?" Philip asks. "Some kind of special relationship."

"No, he's just been defense counsel on a couple of cases where I was the assistant."

"So what if I could tell you something about him that would make you forget Carmine? At least for a little while."

"I'd say you were full of shit."

It doesn't sound right, a girl like her cursing. It bothers him. "No, you're full of shit. I'm trying to give you something of value and you're not listening."

She leans away from the table, getting ready to bluff him. "We already know about Mr. Schiff."

He sees right through her composed expression. "You don't know anything," he says. "I'm not talking about some crappy tax evasion case you're gonna have to turn over to the feds. I'm talking about a serious capital crime. And Ronnie will back me up on this."

Of course, Ronnie would sleep on thumbtacks if Philip told him to.

"We don't care about Ronnie," says the Irish detective. "He's your codefendant."

"Then I have other witnesses and physical evidence to go with him," says Philip.

All of a sudden, Ms. Fusco is the one fidgeting uncomfortably. Lawyers. If you were a regular citizen, they had no mercy. They'd rip your throat out, threaten your children, tell you that you'd never see the light of day again. But say something bad about one of their own and they get all wide eyed and worried. Professional courtesy. One shark to another.

"So what exactly are we discussing here?" she says, rising a little on her pert little butt and biting her nails again. "What kind of physical evidence do you have?"

Even her boyfriend seems a little more interested, pulling a notebook from the inside pocket of his brown NBO suit.

"Uh-uh," says Philip. "Before I say anything else here, I want to get a lawyer of my own and talk about what my exposure is. I'm not testifying without immunity. And neither will Ronnie."

"Well that would be something for the DA to decide. I'm not going to make any promises here."

She's trying to sound cool and professional, but clearly this whole turn in the conversation has caught her off-guard and left her unnerved. She knows she's in over her head.

"Yeah, you talk to Norman," he says. "And tell him I'm not interested in doing any more time upstate. I've had enough of institutional life."

42

The district attorney is tired. He has a thirty-four-year-old wife, a three-month-old baby who wakes up twice a night, and a black-tie fundraiser at the Sheraton Centre tonight, where he'll probably be trapped next to some bore like Chet Allan or Andy Botwin. He's feeling more like sixty-four than fifty.

"Listen," he says to his two assistants, Joan Fusco and Francis X. O'Connell. "I can't stand Jake Schiff, but are we doing the right thing here?"

It's almost seven o'clock and Norman McCarthy is sitting behind his desk, wearing a tux and shoes with bows on them.

"I think we have to get out in front of this," says Francis, raking his fingers through his Beatle mop. "We have a campaign coming up next year, so we have to stay on message. Are we going to tolerate vigilantism? Are we going to tell ourselves that we let a defendant slide because he's a lawyer and he has money?"

The DA closes his eyes for a second and his drawn lids look like the backs of polished spoons. What to do? Another thirteen months until the elections. Just the thought leaves him exhausted. The next year is going to be a blur of pollsters and media consultants telling him to smile during debates and comb his hair over his bald spot. Like it or not, he's going to have to delegate more responsibility to ADAs.

"So what about you?" he asks Joan Fusco. "Do you believe this guy Cardi?"

She crosses her legs and her skirt rides up an inch or two above her knee. "I think he's a good witness. Everything he's said checks out and he's pointing us in the direction of all the leads we'll need. Besides, if I can work on him a little bit, I might eventually get him to roll over on his uncle too."

"But what about this case? Do we have enough?"

"I think we have to go for it," she says, punching the air.

A real fighter, Joan Fusco. No wonder the head of her bureau awarded her the picture of General Sherman for her aggressiveness. The deal makers and backpedalers had McClellan on their walls.

"I'm not sure if I'm quite that gung ho." says Francis, putting an arm in front of Fusco as if he's trying to keep her from getting whiplash. "But I think it's developing into something. We need to track down this third witness, though, and get a set of Schiff's fingerprints to see if they match the ones on the weapon."

"So what are we going to do?" Ms. Fusco turns in her chair to look at him. "Invite him down to the station and ask him to give us a set?"

"Why not?" Norman McCarthy straightens his bow tie and stands up to go. "He's going to find out we're looking at him soon enough. Send a detective over and rattle his cage. Who knows what Jake will say?"

43

Mr. Schiff, Mr. Schiff. Slow down a sec. I been trying to get you on the phone."

It's three days since Philip stopped by the house. Jake is just leaving his office building on Fifth Avenue to meet Bob Berger for lunch when he runs into a burly detective with Velamints on his breath and Grecian Formula in his hair.

"Got a minute?" says the cop after flashing his badge and giving his name as Seifert.

"Probably not." Jake watches the revolving glass door, making sure none of the partners are coming out.

"I was wondering if you'd mind stopping by the station, seeing as it's lunchtime and all."

"That's nice. What would we talk about there?"

"Come on." Detective Seifert smiles just enough for Jake to see his caps look brownish and crooked. You'd think the PBA would have a better dental plan. "We both know what there is to talk about."

Jake starts to walk toward the corner. The detective follows him. It's an oyster gray noon sky, but the midtown streets are still jammed with the mad tramping hordes. No one seems to notice Jake and the cop. They're just two ants in an ant farm.

"I've got a lot of cases involving the police department," Jake says. "I'm not sure which one you want to discuss."

Seifert puts his hand on Jake's right shoulder. "Hey, listen," he says. "You know what I want to talk to you about. We know about what happened in that tunnel."

Jake can feel the grip of the detective's fingers go right through his shoulder and down into his heart.

They know. This is the beginning of the end.

Who could have said anything? He tries to figure it out but the wires won't connect. Philip couldn't say anything without incriminating himself. But who else could it be? All right, stay cool. Jake straightens his tie. Find out what's going on.

"So what do you know?" he asks the detective.

"Hey, I live in this city, just like you. I know what goes on with these bums in the street."

Seifert looks over at a legless man in a wheelchair on the corner, ostentatiously displaying his stumps at people walking by.

"If one of these pieces of shit got anywhere near my daughter, I'd beat his fuckin' brains in with a baseball bat too," says Seifert. "Seriously."

Right. Like we're just talking man-to-man, here. Don't worry about it. You can trust me. We're all regular guys here. Sure. Probably works great on sixteen-year-old chain snatchers at the precinct.

Jake draws away from him a little. "Detective, are you a fan of award shows?"

"How do you mean?"

"I mean, do you sit at home and watch the various award shows that are broadcast live on TV? You know. The Academy Awards, the Emmys, the Grammys, Country Music Awards, NAACP Image Awards. You watch some of those, right?"

"I guess." Seifert's eyes narrow, not sure where he's going with this.

"So are you aware of any award given for the stupidest attorney in Manhattan?"

"Okay, look—"

"Well, if you're not aware of any award like that, then I can't think of any reason why I should talk to you. 'Cause I'm not getting anything out of it otherwise."

"Hey, let me give you a little insight into your situation, Mr. Schiff." Seifert puffs out his chest and hitches up his belt as he gives Jake a crooked smile. "We have sworn statements from witnesses putting you at the scene of this crime. We have sworn statements from people indicating your predisposition for violence against homeless people. And we have physical evidence from the crime scene."

"Bullshit," says Jake.

"Well, if it's bullshit then you can accompany me to the precinct so we can get a set of prints off you and clear this up right away."

"All right," says Jake, not believing half of what he's just heard. "Let's not have any more of this ex parte communication. If you got something you want to ask me, you call my lawyer."

He takes out a small notebook, jots down Andy Botwin's number, and then tears out the page. Goddamn *Andy*. Why didn't he take care of this?

Seifert takes the number and looks at it almost sorrowfully, like a man handling his own bill of divorce. "You're making a big mistake."

"Am I under arrest, detective?"

"No, not yet."

"Then I don't think we have anything else to talk about."

Jake turns and walks away, losing himself in the battalions of fresh-faced young bankers and lawyers marching down Fifth Avenue, foot soldiers trying to take over a beleaguered city.

44

The next day, Francis O'Connell walks into the DA's office with a slightly yellowed newspaper clipping. He puts it on the desk before Norman McCarthy and stands back.

"What is this?" says the DA. "It's that goddamn article about Jake Schiff from three years ago. Do I have to read about him calling me a martinet again?"

"Look at the twelfth paragraph."

Norman McCarthy puts on a pair of half glasses and starts counting. He's been up since four this morning with the baby. God, he's too old for this.

"It's just a bunch of nonsense about how he worked for the Queens DA one summer and didn't like it." He frowns.

"There's our fingerprints," says Francis.

"What?"

"Everyone who works for the DA gets fingerprinted. So we already have Schiff's fingerprints on file. This case is coming together. All we have to find is that last witness."

45

A Detective Marinelli called the house this morning, wanting to talk to you,'' Dana says on Saturday afternoon, two days later. "Any idea what he wants?"

Jake shrugs, but his eyes look tired. "Probably some old case I haven't thought about in a year."

They're jogging around the reservoir in Central Park. It's the kind of brilliant autumn day that makes children and real estate people think they can possess all of New York. The grand old buildings look like a mountain range along the edge of the park. The Dakota. The Beresford. Ten-forty Fifth Avenue, where Jackie Onassis lived. Even Trump Tower looks pretty in the distance.

She feels the spring in her legs as she comes along the northern curve and catches sight of Belvedere Castle through the trees and foliage. This is the mythic city she dreamed about when she was a little girl. She still remembers her parents bringing her and her brothers in from Connecticut for the occasional Broadway musical when they were kids. She can still see the white tablecloths and smell the men at the next table smoking cigars at the fancy steak houses where they'd eat before the shows. Her father in an expansive mood, not even scolding her when she ordered the surf and turf and didn't take a bite of it. Her mother having a drink or two and feeling giddy, singing "The Impossible Dream" as the station wagon sped past the bright gaudy marquee lights and the mysterious silhouettes of street people.

The black gravel grinds under her sneakers as she thinks about how she found the city a cold and frightening place when she moved here a dozen years later to go to college. Every week, it seemed, there were stories in the newspapers about the horrible fate befalling some hopeful young girl like herself. There was the Harvard girl raped and stabbed to death on the rooftop by the super's son. The shopgirl gunned down inside a Columbus Avenue boutique by a junkie stickup man. The investment banker they'd found hacked up in a trunk.

She'd taken to staying home at night, studying and watching old movies on television, while her roommates partied the night away with obnoxious premeds at the uptown bars. She was already thinking about moving to some anonymous half city in the Midwest after graduation, where she could lead a secure if slightly dull life full of children and car pools and unacknowledged yearnings.

But then she met Jake. She'd let a friend talk her into going to a party at a broken-down prewar building on West 106th Street, and before she knew it some drunken jock named Larson had her cornered in the kitchen. She'd made the mistake of sleeping with him once before and he was after her again, not taking no for an answer and calling her a cunt when she tried to walk away. At one point he grabbed her by the shoulders and shook her a little. And then there was Jake, getting in the guy's face, telling him to back off, defending her honor without even knowing her.

"Weren't you scared?" she asked later.

"He's an Ivy League nose tackle," Jake said, brushing it off. "That's an oxymoron. It's like a compassionate dentist."

She wasn't quite sure what that meant, but she liked it. She liked him too. She liked his hardness, his brash attitude, his pugnacity, his lack of pretension about his working-class roots—neither hiding them nor making too much of them.

What she didn't expect was to fall in love with him. But in a strange way, she'd come to think about Jake the same way she thought about Central Park. As a sanctuary and oasis in the middle of a harsh, unforgiving city. As in the park, there were unexplored places of serenity and even beauty inside of him. He was a great father and a selfless, mature lover. He'd go around the corner to get a carton of milk and bring her back flowers. Lying next to him in bed sometimes was like lying in the middle of the Great Lawn on a quiet starry night, feeling the enormity of the city around them and the strength of his heartbeat within it.

She puts on a burst of speed and pulls alongside him as the Guggenheim Museum appears above the tree line to her right.

"So why'd he call the house instead of calling you at the office?" she asks Jake.

"Who?"

"The detective."

"I don't know," he says a little irritably, clutching two five-pound weights as he runs. "Maybe his shift is today."

She pauses, deciding to let it go at that.

"So I was thinking of going to the antiques show at the pier tomorrow morning," she says, breathing hard and feeling a little tightness in her chest. "Pick out an armoire for the bedroom. We can give Alex the one we have. Any interest?"

He keeps his head down, maintaining a steady determined stride. "Can't do it, babe." Bap, bap, bap. One foot after the other, like stakes driven into the dirt.

"Why not?"

Pausing to catch his breath. "Got a business meeting."

"Who wants to meet with you on a Sunday?"

Bap, bap, bap. The stakes going into the gravel a little harder and a little faster. Not quite running away from her, but no longer matching her stride.

"Ah, it's just some pain-in-the-ass thing. You don't wanna know." He turns his head slightly and the last syllables drift away in the passing breeze.

She's been noticing more and more moments like this lately. Tense silences, brooding looks, unexplained absences. It's impossible to ignore it anymore. Something is going on. Spaces are opening up between them.

Again, she gets ready to confront him and ask what's going on.

But when she looks up, Jake surges ahead of her on the track and disappears around the bend twenty yards away.

For some reason, she's reminded of the afternoon a dozen years ago when she made a wrong turn walking home through the park after dropping Alex off at nursery school. Somewhere beyond the Loeb Boathouse, she'd lost her way and found herself in an unfamiliar setting: a wild untended field surrounded by a grove of thick trees and hedges. There was a rustling of bushes and then a man stepped into the clearing. At least she thought it was a man, at first. He was like a Cro-Magnon. Naked except for a long mangy red beard and a mass of curly body hair. Another naked hairy man followed him out and she'd felt her heart stop. Obviously she'd interrupted some act of sexual congress, and they stared at her with animal loathing. For a moment, she was unable to move. Then one of the creatures grunted and she bolted, not allowing herself even a small scream until she'd run all the way home and poured herself a tall stiff vodka.

Now, as she puts her head down and races after her husband of twenty years, she wonders if parts of him, like parts of the park, are off-limits to her.

46

I wanted to see you," says Jake on Sunday afternoon, "because a couple of detectives from Midtown North have been trying to talk to me."

His eyes focus on a run in Susan Hoffman's stocking. Actually just a small hole right above the knee, revealing a quarter inch of pale flesh amidst the dark hose. It's visible just over the top of her cherry-wood desk when she crosses her legs. It bothers him that she doesn't seem to notice that hole. He hopes she isn't that sloppy when it comes to her clients.

On the other hand, Andy Botwin never forgets a child's birthday and he hasn't picked up the phone once since Jake came to see him.

"So why do you think they've been doing that?"

"Huh?" He catches himself wondering why she's wearing hose and a skirt on a Sunday anyway.

"Why do you think these detectives are seeking to question you?" asks Susan.

Right. Straighten up. You are the defendant here. Tell your potential new lawyer what she might need to know.

"Well, one of them told me he had sworn statements and physical evidence linking me to the scene of a homicide. Maybe two homicides."

He sits back and waits for the whistle or the sharp intake of breath. But after fifteen years prosecuting murderers and sex offenders at the Manhattan DA's office, Susan Hoffman doesn't rattle that easily. In 1940s movies, they would have called Susan a tough broad. But she looks less like Barbara Stanwyck than a debauched math teacher. A smoker's prematurely wrinkled face, small eyes, and a tight bitter mouth. She'd whipped Jake soundly twice in one year in state court. Once when he was at Legal Aid representing a Haitian marijuana dealer and then six months later after he'd gone into private practice, representing a petulant twenty-six-year-old stockbroker named Paul Martin III, who was running a cocaine business on the side. The cops lied blatantly in both cases, but each time the juries were out for less than half a day.

So when Susan bumped into Jake at Alison on Dominick earlier this year and said she was going into private practice, he told himself that if he was ever in trouble, she'd be his second choice to be his lawyer after Andy.

"Have you spoken to anyone else about this?" she asks.

"Well, Andy Botwin was supposed to be looking into it for me, but I guess he's a little preoccupied these days."

"Andy Botwin." She lights a cigarillo and snorts two jet streams of smoke out of her nose. "Was he too busy going on the Letterman show?"

"It was a disappointment. Particularly since it's a matter of some urgency."

Susan looks distracted for a moment. "You know, goddamn it, I've had this hole in my stocking since this morning and I haven't had a chance to change them."

"What are you all dressed up for anyway?"

"Ah, my niece's wedding tonight. Who ever heard of a wedding on a Sunday night? I have to meet Babs at six and go over to the temple."

From the offhand way she says "Babs," it's clear she's talking about a longtime girlfriend. Jake had never considered that Susan might be a lesbian before. Now he notices a certain butch cast to the decor: heavy brown furniture, thick navy curtains, and pictures of Susan mountain climbing next to her degrees on the wall. On reflection, it doesn't matter. He just wants a lawyer with six sets of teeth.

"All right, let's establish some ground rules," says Susan, snapping him back to attention. "I know you're a good lawyer and I do want your input, but in this office, you're the client. Understand?"

"Of course."

Her mouth turns into a skeptical squiggle. "I'm going to need information from you. If you can't tell me the truth, don't tell me anything. You got that? I don't want to hear the sky is green or the moon is made of Gorgonzola. Because that will only come back to haunt us in front of a jury, if God forbid this business ever comes to trial."

"Couldn't have said it better myself," Jake tells her.

"I'm sure you have." Her sharky little smile makes it clear that she hasn't forgotten some of their sharper exchanges. "Do you still have that detective's card?"

He takes it from the back pocket of his jeans and gives it to her, noticing his hand is shaking a little. Up until now, it's all been lawyerly bantering. But now that she's about to pick up the phone, he feels his guts revolting again, just as they did when he was talking to Detective Seifert on the sidewalk. This is not a joke. He's being investigated for murder.

She lifts the receiver and he has to fight the urge to ask her to put it down. Is it too late to turn back and return to the life he had before? He realizes that he must have had a few hundred clients who'd asked themselves the same question at this very moment.

She dials the number, holding the cigarillo between her middle and index fingers, and asks for Detective Marinelli in a voice used to giving orders. When the detective gets on the line, she introduces herself with a kind of stern familiarity. Jake wonders if she might have worked with this cop before. His heart lightens. Maybe there's a way to work this out without the investigation going any further. He's glad he came to this office.

"Detective, I understand you've been attempting to speak to Mr. Jacob Schiff," she says. "You mind telling me why that is?"

A pause. Susan drums her short wrinkled-up fingers idly over the hole in her stocking. She blows a line of smoke at the ceiling and her eyes rise dreamily to follow it.

"Look," she says abruptly. "This can be a short friendly conversation or we can make it difficult. What do you have?"

There's a series of short "uh-huhs" out of Susan and then a long grim look across her desk to Jake.

"Well, be advised that Mr. Schiff now has a new lawyer and you're not to try speaking to him unless I am present. You're not to try calling him directly or showing up at his house . . ." She frowns in concentration as she listens to the detective's reply. "Yes, of course, I understand it's a criminal investigation. Who do you think you're talking to?"

Jake's heart has turned into a bowling ball, slowly sinking down toward his stomach.

"And the same to you, I'm sure, sir," says Susan, slamming the phone down.

The rush of confrontation has brought a glow to her cheeks and warm life to her blue eyes. She puts her feet up on her desk and rubs her ankles together. Jake wonders if arguing is a turn-on for her.

"I'll send him a follow-up letter, repeating what I just said," she tells Jake. "I always find it's better to put these things in writing."

"Right," he says numbly.

"The detective says they want to talk to you in connection with the killing of a homeless man in Riverside Park."

"He only mentioned one?"

"He only mentioned one. My impression is a grand jury may have already been convened. Can you tell me anything about it?"

"Perhaps." Jake hesitates, not sure where to begin.

As a lawyer, he's had to browbeat his clients into learning a basic lesson: never discuss the details of a case directly, even with your attorney. Never say, "I killed the bitch." Always: "The police say I killed the bitch." Keep your lawyer out of ethical trouble and avoid committing perjury if you're called to testify. But Jake finds he just can't get comfortable on this side of the fence.

Sensing his uneasiness, Susan puts down her cigarillo. "Maybe before we get into any of the details, we should discuss the price of justice."

Jake looks up at her, like a dog facing a rolled-up newspaper. "How much?"

"My fee is fifty thousand dollars, plus twenty-five hundred a day if it goes to trial."

She holds his gaze for a few seconds before her composure begins to dissolve and an embarrassed smile begins to tug at the corners of her mouth.

"You know what?" says Jake, "I'll give you fifty. But it's worth more."

"You think so?"

"Yes. And you'll never be a top-ranked criminal attorney until you go home and practice saying, 'My fee is one hundred thousand dollars,' into the bathroom mirror without cracking up."

She begins to chuckle and for the first time he feels a human connection with her.

"So do I get a break for giving you good advice?" he asks.

Her smile fades. "Just write me a check for what you have right now. I understand if you need time to raise the rest." Her cigarillo smolders in the ashtray. "Now what else can you tell me about this case?"

47

Yo, what time is it?'' the man with the hard round gut asks.

"I don't know." John G. can't bear to look at him.

A jaundice-yellow sun over 145th Street. Hardly any traffic. Locked-up storefronts. Four gray men stand on the sidewalk, looking down at their feet.

The regular Narcotics Anonymous meeting was canceled at the Interfaith Volunteers Center, so John G. and three other homeless men have been sent to an uptown meeting. However, the people running it haven't arrived yet with the keys.

"You got to put jelly to jelly," says the man with the round gut, who calls himself Mao.

"So are they coming or not?" asks John, standing next to him and staring at the corrugated gate pulled over the front of the clinic. "They're supposed to be open at two-thirty."

Over these last few days, he's been struggling to replace the orderliness of the drug addict's life—scoring, smoking, bugging, chilling—with the orderliness of the recovery cycle. He keeps telling himself that every meeting, every clinic counts. If one gets canceled, he feels despondent and in danger of falling into bad old habits.

Stay clean. Easy does it. One day at a time. He's trying to keep all the NA slogans in his head.

The other three guys stamp their feet and sniffle quietly. A man walks by in a white Muslim skullcap, talking on a cellular phone. John G. wonders idly about the effect of all those radio waves going through the air.

"You got to put smelly to smelly," says Mao.

"Say, you wanna go get a beer?" says the man standing to the left of John, a stout coffee-colored man named Charles Harris, who claims he was once a cop in Nassau County.

"Nah, you know. I start drinking, the medication doesn't work as well." John shuffles his feet.

"Yo, come on, man. Let's just split a forty."

"Nah, they're gonna be open any minute."

He's beginning to wonder if he should spend so much time hanging around people like Charles, who are always trying to get him high.

Two women walk by with white Muslim scarves covering their heads and faces.

"You got to put belly to belly," says Mao, wiggling his big gut at them. "Say sisters! What time is it?"

"Yo, shut up, fool," says Charles Harris. "Their man hear you talk like that, he'll come on over here and stomp your head with them big old Muslim feet. They leave a treadmark on your face, just say *Property of Allah*."

The man on the far left, who's freakishly thin like a sideshow contortionist, opens his eyes for the first time in five minutes.

"I tell you what happened the other night?" he says. "I was hanging out behind Saks Fifth Avenue going through the Dumpsters, right? So this limo pulls up and this old white guy gets out, dressed real nice. Right? So he goes up to the Dumpster next to mine and starts going through it with his white gloves. And I'm like, 'What's up with that?' Right? He says, 'Fifty-seven years ago, I was living like a bum and I found two bags of cash in this garbage.' Two thousand dollars, man. Started his whole business. Launched his career. So now every Friday night, he comes back to see if they make the same mistake."

"So what's your point?" asks John G.

"Anything could happen on the street, you hang out long enough."

"Yo, what time is it?" asks Mao.

"Say, fuck this shit, man," Charles Harris interrupts, poking his tongue into the right side of his cheek and then the left. "Let's go get high. These people ain't coming. They probably got car trouble. They're stuck on the LIE. They don't care about us."

Another strong gust of wind blows down 145th Street, taking garbage and grit in its wake.

"I wanna hang out," John G. demurs. "They ought to be here any minute."

It's hard putting things back together. All the connections that seemed so obvious on drugs are no longer there. Random displacement. Molecules pushing molecules. It doesn't make quite as much sense anymore. He's going to have to put the world back together the hard way. He'd gotten used to living like a dog and rummaging through garbage cans. Getting high whenever the urge hit. Now there's all these rules to contend with. Having to shower every day, signing in for your bed, making meetings, taking your medication. Ms. Greenglass on your back all the time. No wonder you had so many guys bugging out from the stress.

"How's long's it been since you got high anyway?" asks Charles.

"I dunno. Two, three weeks."

Easy does it. One day at a time. Since he stopped taking drugs, his teeth have started falling out and he only takes a shit about once every three days.

"So that's long enough," says Charles. "You been good. So come the fuck on. I got my man Marcus selling me jumbos on consignment. You smoke every tenth bottle and sell the rest, you got a habit that pays for itself. It's a beautiful thing, man."

"Nah, nah, I'm really trying to stop," says John.

Charles pulls his face back, as if it's a camera lens going for a wide angle. "What? You wanna smoke some cheeba? Is that what you're trying to tell me? Don't be shy. I'm down with that."

"No, I'm trying to work on my steps, man."

"Your steps?"

"Yeah, you know the Twelve Steps."

Step Seven: We humbly asked God to remove our shortcomings.

"Yo, man, let's ride on," says Charles. "Let's the four of us go around the corner, share a bottle of Brass Monkey. I used to help my man at the liquor store with his security. He'd give us a bottle on credit."

"Yo, I asked what motherfuckin' time it was," says Mao with the big gut to no one in particular.

John's heard enough. He turns on Charles. "Why can't you just leave me the hell alone? Don't I have enough problems? Why do you want to see me get high so badly? Am I making you nervous or something?"

Even as he says this, though, his resolve is weakening. Step One: We admitted we were powerless over drugs and alcohol—that our lives had become unmanageable. So fucking what? What difference would it make if he went around the corner and smoked a joint with Charles? Who else would he be hurting?

On the other hand, maybe he's hurt enough people already. Step Eight: We made a list of all persons we harmed, and became willing to make amends to them.

He's been thinking lately he'd like to see Margo again. It's a good goal for him to concentrate on when he gets up in the morning. Instead of just figuring out how to waste the day getting high. He wants to stay focused on putting things back together. But he's not sure if he's ready to see her just yet. Maybe he has to build up to it.

"Hey, that's the lady," says Freakshow Slim on the left.

He points to a big blonde woman struggling to get out of a broken-down Town & Country station wagon with a blue food cooler. Sister Patrice, from Manhasset. She crosses the street, getting the keys out of her red barn jacket.

"You got to put deli to deli," says Mao.

"Shut up, fool." Charles is already backing away from the group. Weirded out by the sudden proximity to the meeting, where the fluorescent lights will be bright, the coffee will be lukewarm, and the expectations for him to stay clean will be serious. "I'm outta here. I'm gonna get high. Then I'm gonna go get some stinky on my hangy-down thang."

"You mean you're gonna get laid?" John asks.

"Yeah."

"I doubt that," says John, who wishes he were going with him anyway—women or no women.

Charles's face shrivels in the wind. "Yeah, me too."

He scoots across the street, leaving John to figure out the best way to say he's sorry.

48

Jake's secretary, Deborah, is home sick with a savage yeast infection, so he's having to field some of his own calls.

"Mr. Schiff?"

"Yeah."

"Please hold for J. Harrell Pearson."

Jake silently curses to himself. J. Harrell Pearson is the head of the fourth-largest motor oil company in the country. He is calling to scream. J. Harrell likes to scream. In fact, he likes screaming better than most people like eating. Sometimes he'll experience spontaneous nosebleeds while berating a boardroom full of junior executives. This time he is almost certainly calling to scream because Jake and the accountants he's brought in have only managed to put him in the second-lowest tax bracket possible, instead of the lowest. J. Harrell will be handing the government no larger a proportion of his income than a city bus driver, yet he will still shriek about having been raped.

Jake braces himself for the opening salvo as a buzzer goes off on his phone. There's a knock at the door. Someone is coming in. He tries to remember if he asked for coffee and a bagel this morning. If Deborah were here, she'd have it organized. Instead, somebody else's secretary is buzzing the delivery boy in, probably while keeping two clients on hold on the phone.

Jake half rises as his door opens and a man who looks like the Las Vegas singer Jerry Vale walks briskly into the room.

"Mr. Schiff, you're under arrest," he says, whipping out a black billfold and displaying a gold shield.

Jake's eyes flick over to the left and he sees two young uniform officers with well-defined bodies and unformed faces have followed the man with the shield into the room. Meanwhile, J. Harrell Pearson has gotten on the phone.

"Schiff, goddamn it, how could you do this to me?!" he squawks. "Have you no compassion?!"

It's a moment so surreal and disorienting that all Jake can think to ask himself is: Why is Jerry Vale trying to arrest me?

"Mr. Schiff, please put the phone down," says the man with the gold shield, who is clearly a detective.

"Harrell, I gotta go," Jake says into the phone.

"Don't hang up on me! I won't pay this bill . . ."

The phone goes back on the hook and Jake stands there, looking from the detective to the two uniform cops. For several days he's been telling himself this scene might take place, but now he finds himself totally unprepared, a diver without swimming lessons. Somehow, despite all his knowledge and experience, he'd been hoping Susan Hoffman could have made these charges go away.

"Mr. Schiff, my name is Marinelli. I'm from the Midtown North detective squad," says the detective, dropping the billfold and the shield back into a pocket of his brown suit. "Please stand against the desk and assume the position."

"Come on, guys." Jake holds up his hands. "We don't have to do it this way. We all know the drill here. You could've called my lawyer. I would've surrendered downtown."

"Assume the position," says the detective, hardening his voice and giving him no slack.

He turns to one of the uniformed cops, a pale pug-nosed kid who can't be more than five years older than Alex. "Go ahead, frisk him," he says.

Jake dutifully turns his back, spreads his legs, and puts both hands on the edge of his desk. They're really going to do this, he thinks. Unbelievable. They probably have a special routine worked out to punish defense lawyers.

The young cop starts out by slapping both of Jake's thighs, still a little sore from the run in the park with Dana last weekend. The kid brings his right hand up sharply as if he's about to grab Jake's balls and Jake starts to pull away a little.

"Easy there, pally," says the young cop.

"You know this isn't right," says Jake. "We could still work things out. I'll call my lawyer, we'll meet you down in Part Forty-seven."

"We do things by the book here," the detective says in his sour rhythmless voice. He turns to the other young cop, a strapping buck with puffy cheeks and a pencil-thin moustache. "Cuff him already. In the front."

Jake presents his wrists and the cop with the moustache puts the handcuffs on as tight as he can. His name tag says Pollo. Chicken. Jake tries to catch his eye and nod as if to say, It's okay, you're just doing your job. Anything. Just to stimulate a little human contact and make things easier further down the line. But the young cop steadfastly refuses to look at him. He's probably been coached beforehand, Jake realizes.

"All right, let's walk him," says Detective Marinelli.

"Look," says Jake. "I got a trench coat in my closet over there. Maybe you can just throw it over my hands, so everyone outside doesn't see the cuffs."

They all ignore him and Jake decides to keep his mouth shut. Every time he says something, it just encourages them to mistreat him. Clearly, the decision has been made somewhere up the chain of command to maximize embarrassment with this arrest.

The detective leads the way out the door with the two younger cops coming up behind Jake.

Word has spread quickly across the office and a crowd has gathered around Deborah's empty desk. If she'd been here, Jake thinks, the cops wouldn't have been able to get in without her giving him fair warning. Instead, the secretaries, paralegals, associates, and senior partners have all had a chance to stop what they are doing and come to watch his moment of ultimate humiliation.

"Ladies and gentlemen," says the detective, stopping to address the crowd, "this man is being arrested for the charge of murder. Officers from our precinct will be back in a few hours to recanvass this office. We would appreciate your cooperation. Thank you."

Jake sees Todd Bracken watching from the edge of the crowd with a look of surprised wonder. With his open mouth, he could be saying, *Why, I didn't know you sailed, Jake.*

Deeper in the pack, Mike Sayon and Charlie Dorian exchange grim huffy looks. What will this mean for the image of the firm? You can almost hear them telecommunicating like a couple of wizened old extraterrestrials in a Spielberg film. Next to them, Kenneth Daugherty looks as if he's enduring the suffering of the ages. Since Todd Bracken's father died, Kenneth has assumed the position of the firm's grand old man. Only a select few knew he was actually a doddering idiot who hid in his office all day playing Game Boy.

Jake hears the murmurs and sees attractive women who'd once given him appraising looks casting their eyes down. Just to complete the spectacle of shame, Detective Marinelli begins to recite his Miranda rights for the benefit of the crowd, stumbling a few times because he's clearly out of practice. Obviously, the crackheads and drunken miscreants he usually arrests don't get the full warning.

"You have the right to an attorney," says the detective, putting special emphasis on the words. "If you cannot afford an attorney, one will be provided for you."

Jake looks up at the room full of lawyers. A sea of gray flannel and cold eyes. He feels like a fish caught in the jaws of a larger predator while the rest of the natural order looks on impassively.

"Call my wife," he says as the cops start to take him away. "Somebody please call my wife."

There's some stirring in the crowd. Todd Bracken peels off to go back to his office. Mike Sayon claps a hand on Charlie Dorian's shoulder, as if he's the one in need of comfort. And old Kenneth Daugherty is busy staring down into a secretary's cleavage. Life in the office is already going back to normal. Bills will be sent, phone calls will be returned, motions will be answered. And after ten years at this firm, Jake realizes he doesn't have anyone who's enough of a friend to even call his family for him.

49

Mr. Cardi, will you please tell us why you decided to cooperate as a witness in the case against Mr. Schiff?"

"I felt it was my duty as a citizen," says Philip.

He's sitting in a book-lined conference room at the Manhattan DA's office, being questioned by Ms. Fusco again. His new lawyer, a sandy-haired, ruddy-faced guy named Jim Dunning, sits in a corner quietly, like he's dying for a cigarette. The lighting is less harsh and the coffee is a little stronger than in the other rooms he's been in here.

"Wouldn't it be more accurate to say that you were arrested on a different charge and decided to make a deal?" Ms. Fusco says, like a schoolteacher correcting a remedial student.

Philip twists in his chair. "That's one way of looking at it."

"And isn't it true, Mr. Cardi, that the other charge stemmed from an incident in which you cut off another man's nipple?"

Philip frowns, waits for his lawyer to interrupt, then raises his hand. "Forgive me, miss," he says. "But is it really necessary for us to reexamine all this bullshit? I mean, we're not Boy Scouts, right? We all know what I'm doing here."

Ms. Fusco stands up, making her hemline drop and ruining Philip's view of her knees.

"Listen, Philip. Mr. Schiff has just been taken into custody. This is a very important case to our office. If you're going to testify before a jury at trial, we have to establish your credibility and your motivation. So don't fuck around.''

"What are you worried about?'' His lawyer, Dunning, finally speaks up. "You've got Philip here, you've got his cousin Ronnie, you got Jake's prints on the bat. You even got one of the bums from the tunnel saying he saw Jake down there. When I was with the DA's office I made cases with a helluva lot less.''

"Well, it's not your case to try, is it?'' Ms. Fusco replies snippily. "We still don't know what that other homeless guy, Gates, would say if he showed up.''

"Ah, forget it,'' says Philip. "He's probably dead by now anyway.''

His lawyer gives him an uncomfortable look.

"We're not forgetting anything here,'' says Ms. Fusco. "The DA doesn't want to lose this case.''

Philip looks at the folder in her hand and notices for the first time that she's bitten her nails down to bloody nubs. The bitch is nervous. Really nervous. Really scared. He likes that. She must've gone to old Norm McCarthy and told him they had enough evidence to make a case before she was ready. Maybe even rubbed his arthritic knee a little to get his motor revved.

Now she's got her tit caught in a wringer. She needs help from her buddy Philip. He has leverage. Come to Papa.

"You know what I'm thinking?'' he says, throwing out his right arm. "I'm thinking I don't like it here so much. I'm thinking maybe I could help you a little more if I was out on the street. It might improve my memory some, being able to walk around.''

Her face darkens. "I doubt that's possible.''

"Why not?'' says Dunning, picking up on Philip's lead for once. "You let cooperating witnesses go all the time. You even pay some of them. I had a kid from out in Mill Basin who made seventy thousand dollars testifying against his father's gasoline bootlegging outfit last year.''

Philip feels an itching deep down in his ear canal. He's been looking for a way to get out of here for days now. Christ knows what Carmine thinks about him and Ronnie being locked up this long. He probably assumes they're making a deal to rat on his crew.

Ms. Fusco paces back and forth. "We'd have to see a lot more cooperation out of you if we were going to let you go," she says. "You might have to think about making some cases on your uncle somewhere down the line."

"All the more reason you should let me and Ronnie out to see him."

"You'd be willing to testify against Carmine?"

Whoa. Slow down. He doesn't want to get himself into anything he can't get out of. He leans over to whisper in his lawyer's ear.

"Put the brakes on this bitch before she runs me over."

"That's something we can talk about." Dunning leans back with a bright smile. "Maybe we could start off with Philip feeding you some bits and pieces. See what develops."

Philip starts to object but then he stops himself. It's actually a good idea to keep them on the line like that. Greg Scarpa, one of the Colombo guys, strung the FBI along for twenty years that way and never had to testify in open court.

"Yeah, yeah, yeah," Philip says. "You don't want to blow my cover right away."

"And what about your cousin?" asks Ms. Fusco. "Will he cooperate?"

Dunning looks at Philip questioningly. He doesn't know what the fuck is going on. What does he care anyway? He's getting his measly $40 an hour as a state-appointed lawyer.

"We'll see," Philip tells Ms. Fusco. "I'll have to feel him out."

She hugs the folder tight to her chest. "I'm going to have to take this up with my supervisors," she says. "It's going to be an awkward situation, letting you go so soon after Schiff's been arrested."

Philip stares deep into her dark brown eyes, imagining what it would be like to lift her navy attorney skirt, grab her bony shoulders, and have a go at her from behind. *Madonna!* He'd find out if she was a screamer then.

"You'll figure it out some way," he says. "I have faith in you."

50

For almost eight hours, Jake has been locked in the bowels of the system, getting a full doctorate in Advanced Motherfuckery and High Bullshittism.

First, his paperwork was lost at the precinct, which caused a two-hour wait in the holding pens. Then the arresting officer, Detective Marinelli, announced that one of his kids was sick with chicken pox and he had to go home. A half hour later, the new officer assigned the case decided it was time to go to lunch, and when he came back, he couldn't find the keys to the car to drive Jake over to Central Booking.

Now Jake finds himself in a massive beige-tiled holding cell under One Police Plaza. He's surrounded by a half dozen young Asian punks in leather jackets and rockabilly pompadours, two old drunks, and about twelve other assorted skells and low-lifes. It's like being back in the Legal Aid waiting room, except there's a more direct sense of menace in the air and a stink of sweat, piss, and undifferentiated body funk. His eyes begin to swell.

"Hey, come here a sec, will you?"

He looks up and sees one of the officers in charge of the area, beckoning to him from the cell door. Jake rises slowly, with the handcuffs biting into his wrists, and goes over to him.

"I could segregate you, you know," says the guard, a squat

young guy named Giambalvo, who has a receding hairline and wears a white TB mask over the lower half of his face.

"Why would you want to do that?"

"Hey, I know you're a lawyer and you're in a tough spot. You're not like the other guys back here."

Meaning: You're white.

The cop's eyes drop on to the lapels of Jake's suit jacket. "I got some holding cells in the back," says Giambalvo. "I could put you back there with just a couple of other guys."

It's a tempting idea. Jake looks over at the prisoner who'd been sitting next to him on the bench. He's now lying on his back with his legs and arms sticking straight up in the air, like a cow with anthrax. On the other hand, the "couple of other guys" in back might have just hacked up their landlord with a meat cleaver.

"Thanks," Jake says, holding up his cuffed hands. "But I think I'll take my chances here."

Giambalvo's eyes dance over his white mask. "Have it your way, tough guy."

Jake goes back to sit with his fellow prisoners and his misgivings. As soon as he reenters the cell, though, he realizes he's made another mistake. His eyes begin to itch and his nose clogs up. He's definitely allergic to something in here.

Meanwhile, an emaciated bearded black guy whose skin looks like it's been melted over his skeleton is holding forth about what he had to eat last night.

"I had me a mess of fried chicken, a chef's salad, and a side order of greens and fries. All right? You know, them fat juicy boys they cut right off the side of the potato. But I had 'em fry it up in this low-cholesterol shit that's good for your heart . . ."

"Like saffron oil," says a husky man with a gold earring. "What about dessert?"

"I had a sweet potato pie à la monde," says the bearded man. "All right? That means I ate the world."

Jake can almost feel his stomach pressing against his spine. It's about seven o'clock. In the eight hours he's been in the system, he's been given just one sandwich with blue bologna meat and processed cheese. By now Dana will be on her way to meet him at the restaurant downtown, unaware of what's happened. He hasn't been able to get a message to her all day. There's no callback number to leave on her beeper and she generally doesn't check the answering machine until she gets home. She doesn't even know the code. And Alex has had his own phone since he was thirteen and hasn't checked his parents' messages in years. Susan Hoffman's been out of reach too; her assistant says she's been tied up in court all afternoon.

He tries to tell himself he hasn't been forgotten and abandoned, even as he ignores the stares from across the cell and the sluggish movement of time. Remain detached and stoic. After all, the worst that can happen *is* happening and he's surviving it. Moment by moment. All he has to do is not allow the sense of shame and disgrace to overwhelm him.

"Say, man, did I hear the guard say you was a lawyer?" The skinny bearded guy sidles up next to him.

"I was when I got up this morning." Jake sneezes hard.

"I want to talk to you about my case. All right? Man, the DA's saying I'm a loan shark. They callin' me the kingpin of Lenox Ave. All right? They're saying I broke a man's legs because he didn't pay my vig."

The man has arms like a Biafran poster child, Jake notices. He looks like he'd barely have the strength to break a breadstick.

"So what kind of case do they have against you?"

"Man, it's bullshit. All right? Pure bullshit. They're telling me that if I take a plea to just the loan sharking, I can go home and have dinner in my own kitchen tonight." The man leans in on Jake; he smells like the back of a fastfood restaurant. "So what do you think I should do?"

"Sounds like they're kind of anxious to make a deal," says Jake, sneezing again and rubbing his eyes. "It might not be a bad idea for you to sit here a while and see what kind of evidence they have."

Though Jake could not sit here for one second longer than necessary himself. He feels raw and exposed, like he's just been shipwrecked on a hostile island. The cell door flies opens with a bang. Giambalvo the guard shoves in a new prisoner. A flyweight

Puerto Rican kid wearing a red do-rag on his head, skin-tight jeans, and a flannel shirt with a leather vest over it.

"Yo, man," he says. "I'm a career criminal. I just saw my moth-erfuckin' jacket. They be callin' me a career criminal now."

He struts around the perimeter of the cell like a little rooster, head high, chest out. Trying to show everybody how dangerous he is. Jake notices a bloody piece of gauze taped to his right ear. Uh-oh. The kid probably caught a little beating in the squad car on the way to the precinct. Now he has something to prove.

"Like I don't got youthful offender status no more, bro'," he says, clenching and unclenching his fists. "I'm seventeen now. The DT say I'm gonna do one and a third to four for this bid. So I don't give a fuck, mama."

Territorial pissing. Marking his plot. The other older prisoners move away from him a little. They don't want any trouble. They just want to do their thirty days on Rikers and get back out on the street.

At just that moment, Jake's allergies reach a new peak. His eyes begin to water and a maelstrom of dust kicks up in his sinuses. Before he can stop himself, he sneezes all over the boy walking by.

"Yyyo!" The boy's voice goes up and he looks appalled. He begins wiping frantically at the front of his shirt. "What's up with that shit?!"

"Sorry."

"What the fuck's the matter with you, man, you blowin' all your stuff on me?"

The boy is staring at Jake with abject fury.

"Hey, I said I was sorry." Jake's eyes continue to water.

"You crying, man?" asks the boy, zeroing in on a potential weakness.

"No, I just have allergies. I don't know. It might be the disinfectant they use here."

How many times have his clients outlined this very scenario to him? The new fish always picks on the guy least likely to be able to defend himself. It's a way of making a point to the other prisoners.

"Allergies, huh?" The boy wags his chin dubiously.

Jake puts his hands over his face and sneezes again. "I guess nobody in here has a Kleenex, right?"

The kid starts to close in on him. The other prisoners form a semicircle around them. Another ritual: when somebody's going to catch a beat-down in a holding pen, other prisoners crowd around so the guards can't see it.

All right. Stay cool. Don't let him know you're scared.

"Look, I didn't sneeze on you on purpose," Jake says.

The boy looks down at his shirt like it's stained beyond repair. His nose twitches. He's not interested in evasions. He wants to prove he's a man and he wants to do it by spilling Jake's blood on the cell floor.

The two of them are less than three feet apart.

"You know, I ain't afraid to put a hurtin' on you, man," says the boy. "There's a bodega guy in my neighborhood who's been in a coma two years 'cause of me. And his son's my best friend. So don't be thinkin' I ain't got the heart."

Jake tries to hold himself very still. He can feel chains of tension wrapping themselves around his spine. He tells himself the kid can't hurt him that badly with his hands cuffed. But then he remembers all the holding pen injuries he's heard about. Detached retinas, skull fractures, noses with the ends bitten off.

In the old days, he might not have been afraid to go head-to-head with this kid. He had his share of brutal fights in the neighborhood. But something has come between him and the way he used to be. Maybe it's success, or age, or love of family. But time has made him vulnerable.

All of a sudden, he sees himself being carried out of here on a stretcher. His eyes swell and water once more.

"Look, guy, I don't want to fight you," he tells the boy as he tries to wipe the tears away.

"Why, you afraid of me, man? You scared, faggot? You crying 'cause you scared?"

The boy starts swinging his cuffed hands around, like he's holding a heavy club.

"No, I'm not scared."

"Then come on, man. Let's do this right now."

The other men in the semicircle move back to avoid the boy's swinging arms. The cell light catches rust around the sharp edges of the cuffs. The kid means to do serious damage, even if it means just cutting Jake across the eyes.

"Stop with this foolishness." A voice from the perimeter.

Jake doesn't dare turn his eyes to see who it is for fear the Puerto Rican boy will lunge at his face with the rusty cuffs.

"Don't you know this man's a lawyer?"

There's no mistaking the voice this time; it's the emaciated black guy Jake was talking to before. In effect, he's just signed for Jake's hospital bed. Now that everyone in the cell knows he's an attorney, they'll all want to kill him. Lawyers are the pointy-nosed white men who send them upstate.

"You really a lawyer?" the Puerto Rican kid asks, feigning left and then right with his head.

"Yeah." Jake raises his cuffed hands protectively and sneezes twice.

"Well back off a sec, man, I wanna ask you somethin'."

Jake keeps his hands up. "What?"

"If somebody was like a juvenile and then they got like arrested and charged as an adult, would all them other cases count against him?"

Jake takes a moment to size up the situation. The more he counsels this punk, the better his chances of getting out of here with the end of his nose still attached.

"No, the cases wouldn't be added up. It's like two separate systems. Family Court and Criminal Court. If they wanted to charge you as an adult before, they could have done it. Otherwise your juvenile records are sealed."

"Damn!" The boy spits on the floor. "I told that fuckin' lawyer not to plead me out."

Sage nods and a general burble of agreement from the village elders in the semicircle. Jake is aware that the atmosphere is changing. But he still can't quite believe he's out of danger.

"It may not be too late," he says. "You might want to withdraw your plea. Especially if you think the witnesses against you won't show up."

"Yeah, yeah." The boy gets a faraway look and lowers his hands. "That *maricon* don't have the nerve."

"So why sell out?" Jake asks. "Be a man about it. Stand your ground."

A hammy old bit of Legal Aid posturing, but the crowd loves it.

"That's what I like to hear!" says the emaciated guy. 'Stand your ground.' If I'd a had a lawyer like that, I wouldn't have done no stretch in Greenhaven."

"Hey, you got a card, chief?" asks the husky one with the earring.

Instead of a semicircle, the men have fallen into a kind of informal line.

"Step off, man." The Puerto Rican kid turns on them with his hands raised combatively. "I was talking to him first."

Jake is about to tell them that he doesn't practice that kind of law anymore, but why blow a good thing?

"I wanna talk about my parole violation," says a voice from the back of the line.

"One at a time," Jake calls out.

He sneezes three times in a row. The Puerto Rican boy reaches into his pocket and pulls out a wad of Kleenex.

"Here, man. Blow your fuckin' nose already."

51

Dana has been waiting since quarter past seven.

That's what time Jake was supposed to meet her here at the restaurant called Marmalade on Duane Street. The waiter brings over another hard roll and asks if she'd like another glass of chardonnay.

"Maybe you'd like to buy a bottle," he says. "We're charging you six-fifty a glass."

"Uh, I don't know." She looks at her watch. Ten to nine. "I don't want to end up drinking the whole thing myself. Do you sell it by the half bottle?"

His actorish smile says he's more suited for light comedy than heavy drama. "Maybe I could get you a carafe of the house white."

"That would be very nice. Thank you."

It doesn't make sense, really. In more than twenty years of marriage, she can count on her fingers the number of times that Jake's been more than a half hour late. It's one of the most exasperating things about him. She's always rushing breathlessly up the stairs while he sits drumming his fingers on a tabletop. "Malcolm X wouldn't even talk to somebody who didn't wear a watch," he likes to say.

"But you're a Jew," she usually answers.

The waiter brings her another glass of wine as she sees Roberta

Futterman and her husband, Jeffrey, settling in at a table across the restaurant. Parents of one of Alex's school friends. White Jews, Jake calls them. They're always off to Cape Cod or Canyon Ranch. They even look like Presbyterians with their dry smiles and their perfect teeth. The one time Roberta came over to the old apartment on West End Avenue to pick up their son Graham when he was twelve she made a point of sniffing and saying it was too bad Dana didn't have somebody to help her keep the place clean.

Dana hopes they don't see her and come over to ask why she's sitting alone.

She hates doing things alone. She's never even been to the movies by herself. It's not that she's one of those women who can't handle problems or thinks she's nothing without a man. But somehow she doesn't feel complete unless she's part of a unit, a family. Maybe that's why she struggled so hard to keep her mother alive after the doctors said it was a lost cause. Just to hold on to that feeling of being part of something bigger. That sense of not being alone.

So where is Jake anyway? She's called the office at least twelve times today, but wasn't even able to get Deborah. Just a voice mail recording. She wishes she could take back some of the messages she left. They're too precise a record of the arc of her emotions —romantic in the morning, hopeful at noon, anxious by three, cranky by five, desperate and defiant by six: "All right! I'm just going to sit there and wait for you."

Why hasn't he called? Again she has the uncomfortable feeling that she doesn't know him as well as she used to.

52

Step Number Eight: We made a list of all the people we had harmed, and became willing to make amends to them.

After a day or two of searching and talking to old friends, John G. finally finds his ex-wife, Margo, coming out of a bar called the Holiday on St. Marks Place.

The past is the present and the present is the past. At first, he almost doesn't recognize her. Back when they were married, Margo was a fresh-faced Irish girl with apple cheeks, yellow hair, and pistonlike legs. But now she's thin and ghostly with white-painted fingernails. Her hair is dyed platinum and chopped at odd, vicious angles. And a voice at the back of John G.'s mind says, *She's sick.*

"Hey, babe," she says casually, as if she'd been expecting him all along.

"Hey."

"Come on, let's blow." The geeky-looking guy who came out of the bar with her tries to take her arm.

He has poodled-up platinum hair himself, razor-slim hips, and a black Misfits T-shirt. Pete Barnett from the old neighborhood. John heard his ex-wife started hanging around with him and doing heroin after they broke up.

"Lemme alone, will you, ya skank." Margo shrugs him off. "I'm trying to talk to my husband."

Pete pouts and rubs his chin against his shoulder, like a cat licking a wound.

Margo gives John a tired smile. "You look like hell, babe."

"And you look . . ." John's face goes on maneuvers, as he tries to think what to say. "You look the way you look."

Even this late in the game, he can't bring himself to lie to her.

"How you been?" she asks, hands on hips.

The long chase is over. Her two front teeth are missing. Something has been decided.

"I've been . . . I don't know. I've been doing a lot, I guess." He's not sure how else to explain the last few weeks. "I've been going to a lot of meetings lately. You know. NA."

"The holy rollers." She shares a smirk with Pete.

When he saw her teeth missing, John thought she might have stopped doing drugs, like he has. Now he knows she hasn't.

"No, no, it's good. It's good. I'm learning a lotta good things in there." John G. puts up his hands defensively. "Like I was looking at the—whaddycallem—the commandments. I mean, the steps. And there was one of them, it says, 'You should try to make amendments to—' "

"Yeah, yeah, 'We made a list of all persons we had harmed, and became willing to make amends.' " She recites the words quickly and nonchalantly, as if she's been to enough meetings in her time. "You're leaving out that the next step says you shouldn't bother doing it, if it would hurt somebody."

"Yeah, I guess that's right." He touches his beard, wishing he'd shaved and washed before seeing her tonight.

"So is that why you came looking for me? So you could make amends?"

"I was thinking maybe we could make them to each other." He starts to reach for her wrist but he sees a red welt on it. "I mean, all this time, we been blaming each other for what happened. Maybe it wasn't anybody's fault."

"You gonna tell me it's God's will? You back into all that Catholic shit too?" She looks like she's about to hit him.

"No, no. I'm just saying we both thought Shar would be okay. Right? I mean, all this time I been thinking I could've saved her, or maybe you could've if things had been different, but maybe that's not right . . ."

Margo turns her head away from him and looks out at the street. Her jawline is shiny where the bone is pressed against the skin.

"So maybe you know, we could kinda forgive each other," he says.

"Well, it's kind of late for all that." She coughs. "See, I'm feeling kinda sick these days. I got the HIV virus, you know."

Sunlight fading. The train plunging down. John's legs go weak.

"Jesus, what happened?"

"I got it from stupid here."

She glances over at Pete, sitting on a fire hydrant, screwing up his mouth bashfully. For some reason, he doesn't appear as sick as Margo.

"Jesus. Jesus. Jesus."

"Jesus didn't have much to do with how he got it," she says, keeping a beady unforgiving stare on Pete. "More like rusty needles and leaky rubbers."

Somehow the nearness to death has given her wit. He doesn't recall her being like that before. Her face used to be softer and rounder. Now it's all hard angles, sunken eyes, and high cheekbones.

John G. looks at the cracked sidewalk. The peddlers selling old porn magazines and incense sticks on the blankets nearby. Pete sitting on the hydrant, scratching his arms. The toast-colored lights and the fire escapes on the buildings across the street. Trying to find something that will give him purchase on the moment.

"I'm sorry I didn't come see you before," he says.

"Yeah, well . . ." She gets distracted by the sound of a siren blocks away. "You didn't know."

Though a part of him is thinking she somehow got the disease that was intended for him.

"Still, I could've kept in touch . . ."

They should've stuck together. That's what he wants to say.

They should've held on to each other. Stopped each other from falling after the baby was gone. Instead of floating away helplessly, like bodies separated in space.

"I kind of needed to try some new things," she says, running her fingers over a thin patch of her spiky hair.

"You still think about Shar?"

"Only about once a minute." She pushes her lips together and moves them up and down, erasing whatever else she was going to say.

"She was something, wasn't she?"

A flicker of a smile at the edge of her mouth. The beginning of a memory—the baby lying on the bed between them? The first tricycle ride? Nothing she wants to share, though.

"You think we made her happy when she was around?" he asks.

She starts to meet his eyes, but the effort's too much. "Yeah, I guess, we did." She tries to make her voice sound dead. "She seemed like a happy little girl. But I guess all little girls seem happy."

"You think she liked us?"

"She probably thought we were all right."

He wants to reach out and take her in his arms. He needs the connection with her. But somehow she's not ready to give it to him.

"I miss her, you know," he says. "I miss everything. Remember how we were going to buy a house out in Woodlawn and start trying to have another kid? We almost had it. We almost had the dream."

" 'Almost' doesn't mean a fucking thing, John. Don't let anybody tell you otherwise."

The harshness in her voice makes him step back. He's starting to feel sorry that he sought her out.

Pete gets up from the fire hydrant and starts to wander off toward First Avenue, looking for his next fix. Margo follows him with her dying-sun eyes. A part of John wishes he were going with them to shoot up and let the chips fall where they may. But the rest of him wants to stay on this square of sidewalk.

"There's just one other thing I wanted to ask you," he says, trying to get her to linger another moment.

"What is it?"

"You think God was punishing us?"

Her features move apart and then come together. "How do you mean?"

"Like you said before. He's supposed to have a reason for everything he does. You know? You went to Catholic school like I did. Don't you wonder? Why would he give us our little girl and then take her away and then make you so sick? You think it's his punishment for something we might've did?"

"John, look at me." She shivers in the fall night and holds up her frail alabaster white arms in surrender. The red-and-purple blotches by her elbows and armpits look like stigmata to him.

"What?" He can barely look at her this way.

"Why would God have to punish us? We're doing a pretty good job on our own."

She turns in her torn green Converse sneakers and walks down the block, leaving him with sole responsibility for carrying on their daughter's memory.

53

After ten hours, Jake is taken out of the holding cell without explanation and driven over to the Fifth Precinct for a lineup. The four other men include a rail-thin junkie in denims, a porky guy in a Rangers hockey jersey, a balding man in a striped muscle shirt, and an eighteen-year-old kid with long greasy hair and a runny nose. Perfect, thinks Jake, we could be quintuplets. The cops give each of them a card with a number on it. Jake gets number three and stands in the middle of the raised platform. He happens to look over to the left and see the duty sergeant instructing the two men next to him to hold their cards so their index fingers are pointing at Jake.

"Hey, sergeant, cut the shit," he says. "You forget I'm an attorney?"

Jake is tired and confused, but he's still a long way from giving up and letting the process roll over him. The sergeant leaves the room and bright lights snap on. Jake sees only harsh whiteness and feels the burning sensation on his retinas. From beyond the lights, he's dimly aware of venetian blinds being turned so someone in the next room can view the lineup.

"Recognize any of them?" he hears the sergeant ask. Someone's left the intercom on so he can hear some of the conversation in the other room.

There's a low mumble in response but Jake can't pick out any of the words. He'd half expected to hear Philip's voice indicting him, but this is someone else.

"Number two, step forward," the sergeant orders.

The porky guy in the hockey shirt steps up to the light with a sleepy bored look. His nonchalant stance suggests he'd just as soon be here as anywhere else.

"All right, step back. Number three, come forward."

Jake steps into the light, squinting and trying to pick out a familiar silhouette behind the blinds. But all he can see is someone short standing beside the sergeant.

"Yeah, that's the guy," a hoarse, weary voice says. "I'da known him anywhere."

54

By ten o'clock, the restaurant crowd has started to thin out. Dana takes her credit card back from the waiter, signs the bill, and starts to rise.

"Nice to see you." She waves to Roberta and Jeffrey, realizing she's had too much to drink.

On unsteady heels, she heads for the door and a night alone with her son in the big house.

55

Beam me up, Scottie."

John G. and six other people are sitting around a horizontal door, smoking crack in an abandoned tenement on Sixth Street. A squat, they call it. The front entrance is a sheet of aluminum and the only piece of furniture besides the fallen door is a burnt mattress in the kitchen.

Something about seeing Margo tonight has sent him scurrying for the pipe.

"You say something?" The bony black woman sitting cross-legged on the floor next to him is playing absently with a yellow Bic lighter.

"I said, 'Beam me up.' " John raises the pipe to his lips, anticipating.

Her eyes flash at him. "Only if you can tell me what page the Gorn is on in the *Book of Tek.*"

"Excuse me?"

"No, excuse me!"

"Look, just gimme a light, will you?"

"Only if you can tell me the page in the *Book of Tek*," she repeats with pedantic emphasis.

"Bitch, I don't know the *Book of Tek.*"

"Then you can't be getting high in my house. This is my rules. You have to cite a page before you can see Scottie."

John sighs and looks at a hunk of plaster lying on the rug. It's hardly worth the effort of coming here. After not smoking rock for a couple of weeks, he thought he'd enjoy getting high again. But he just feels edgy and irritable. Like he might go off at any minute.

"All right," he says. "Page two twenty-eight."

"What verse?"

He looks up at the bare bulb on the ceiling and makes a tired horse noise. "I don't know. Verse seventeen."

"What line?"

He stands, barely resisting the urge to throw the glass stem at her. "All right, the hell with you, you Uhura-lookin' bitch. Fuck the Gorn. I've about had it with this shit."

"Don't you be talking nasty to me," she says, pointing a filthy four-inch fingernail at him. "This is my house."

Is this why he's survived? Is this the reason he's outlived his child and will outlive the woman he loved? So he can argue with some skanked-out crack whore about the *Book of Tek?*

It's not right. It's not doing justice to their memory.

He takes the woman's wire-thin arm and checks her watch. It's half past eleven. He's been away from the Interfaith Volunteers Center for almost twelve hours. He still has a half hour to make it back for the curfew and he doesn't want to get thrown out on the street again.

He gives the woman her stem back and starts to walk out.

Beam me up Scottie. There's no intelligent life here.

56

Judge Arthur Sand has a walleye on the left, which makes it appear that he's looking at both the defendant and counsel when he's glaring down from the bench.

"Mr. Schiff," he says, looking at the empty space next to Jake. "Who are you representing here today?"

"Myself, Your Honor. I'm being arraigned here today."

It's roughly twenty-four hours since his arrest. Some get swifter justice, some get slower. Susan Hoffman gathers her papers and goes to join Jake before Judge Sand as the clerk calls the case.

"Your Honor, I'm counsel here today," she says. "I don't think it's wise for Mr. Schiff to be addressing the court at this juncture."

The judge looks flustered, as if he's already displeased with Jake for upsetting the delicate moral universe in his courtroom.

Jake looks to his right and sees Francis O'Connell, the young prosecutor from the Hakeem Turner case, bounding up to address the judge. Not a bad choice, Francis. He's been up against Jake just enough times to know some of his background and to work up a decent-sized hate-on for him. If Jake had been DA, he might have assigned Francis too.

"Your Honor, this defendant is being charged for committing an exceptionally heinous crime," Francis begins, almost rising on his toes like a ballet dancer. "We have evidence that Mr. Schiff knowingly and willingly entered an underground dwelling inhabited by homeless people, and with careful premeditation, killed one of them with a baseball bat.''

Jake is again surprised that only one murder is mentioned. Didn't they find the other body yet?

"In fact, Your Honor," Francis continues, "this office is seriously considering asking for the death penalty in this case."

The judge screws up one side of his face, as if he can't believe what he's hearing. Jake can't quite believe it either. Francis's inflated rhetoric hardly seems real—typical prosecutor's hype. He's shot it down a million times himself as a defense counsel. But then he turns and sees four reporters he knows sitting in the second row, taking notes.

Judge Sand hoists a brow high over his walleye. "Mr. Schiff, do you wish to enter a plea at this time?"

Jake starts to open his mouth, but Susan cuts him off. "Not guilty, Your Honor."

As Susan makes the standard futile noises trying to get the case dismissed, Jake stares down at his shoes, feeling every whisker that's sprouted and every inch of grime that's accumulated in the last twenty-four hours. After being in that sludgy jail-cell purgatory for so long, it's hard to adjust to everyone moving at normal speed.

"What are we going to do about bail?" the judge asks.

Francis raises and lowers himself on his toes. A tight bow tie accentuates the size of his Adam's apple. "Judge, our office is taking the position that Mr. Schiff should be remanded without bail. Given the seriousness of this crime, we think it's very likely he might try to leave this jurisdiction."

"Oh puh-leese!" says Susan. "The man's a lawyer. He has a family and a town house on the Upper West Side. He's not going anywhere."

Judge Sand's upper lip protrudes with the mention of the town house. It's hard to tell if he's impressed or jealous. "How 'bout it, Mr. O'Connell?"

"A million dollars bail," Francis says, as if he's being generous.

"I was thinking fifty thousand," Susan counters.

"Could he do five hundred thousand?" asks the judge.

Jake turns and sees Dana entering the courtroom. Somebody must have finally called her. She wears dark clothes and tinted glasses, as if she's attending a wake.

"I guess he could put up the town house as collateral," Susan is saying.

Jake swallows and feels the back of his dry throat cracking. Offering up his town house, the home he's worked all his life for, the place where his wife and son live. Isn't that a little high-handed? Then he remembers he's made similar offers without explicitly consulting his clients.

"All right, five hundred it is." The judge bangs his gavel.

Jake's mind starts whirring like an adding machine. Where's he going to come up with the ten percent cash payment the court requires? After the huge down payment and all the house repairs, he's not sure if he still has $50,000 in his account. Everything's tied up in mutual funds and Treasury bills. And then he's got a $4500 mortgage coming at him every month.

Before he has time to figure it out, the judge is signing a paper and adjourning his case for a month. Susan touches his arm and another defendant steps up to take his place. A sweet-faced black kid in an eight-ball jacket and felony sneakers.

Dana waits at the back of the courtroom. By the time Jake and Susan join her the judge has remanded the kid in the eight-ball jacket for thirty days on Rikers for holding two vials of crack.

57

After the arraignment, Jake stops by his lawyer's office for a few minutes to talk things over. Then he catches a cab home and finds his wife sitting at the breakfast nook, smoking what as far as he knows is the first cigarette of her life.

"I'm not sure whether I should curse you or throw my arms around you," she says quietly.

"Try the latter."

She gets up and hugs him tightly. He feels her fists balled up against his back.

This day has already been brutalizing. At the office, Susan told him the DA isn't giving him much play; Francis wants at least eight and a third to twenty-five years for his sentence and the revocation of his law license. They must think they have a strong case, but why? Jake wonders. The only witnesses he can think of are Philip and his cousin, and they're accomplices. So what else do they have? He rifles his mind, looking for information, but he's too tired to come up with anything.

"You're all right?" Dana says, too tense to ask for much assurance.

"I'm all right. Everything's going to be all right."

She pushes him away so she can take a good look at him. She has dark circles under her eyes and the vertical line in her brow has deepened by about a sixteenth of an inch.

"I'm going to need some help with this, Jake," she says. "I'm going to need you to explain this to me very carefully."

He lowers his eyes and goes into the living room to fix himself a drink.

"We probably have about eight to twelve weeks until trial. There'll be an indictment. Then we'll file our papers and wait to see what evidence they have in discovery. Probably there'll be a Wade hearing about the witness identification . . ."

"Forget all the legal crap."

Dana is standing at the kitchen pass-through. "What happened?" she asks in a voice as cold as the ice going into his glass.

He doesn't look at her. "I made a mistake." He fills the left side of his mouth with air and lets it out. "I'm not sure what else there is to say. I thought I was doing the right thing. But I was wrong."

"That's it?"

He still can't quite raise his eyes to meet hers. "Well, Susan asked me not to say too much."

"That's it? That's all you have to tell me? We've been married for twenty years!"

"You don't have to shout." He glances at the staircase, wondering if Alex is home.

"A reporter from the *Times* called an hour ago looking for you! Your son already knows you've been arrested. Now he's going to have to read about it in the newspaper and see it on television. And all you have to say is, 'I made a mistake'?!"

She deliberately drops the cigarette and crushes it out on the $500 area rug he bought for the hallway between the kitchen and the living room. He starts to protest, but her eyes warn him off.

"Did you do this?" she says.

He pours himself a scotch and flops down on the couch. "Dana, I . . ."

"I asked you a question, Jake. Did you do this?"

He looks across the room at her and feels the Atlantic Ocean opening between them.

"No," he says.

"Then why are they accusing you?! I've heard you say it yourself a hundred times. Almost everyone you represent is guilty."

He closes his eyes and sees that flash of light again. "Well I'm not."

"Then why are they saying you did it?"

Jake opens his eyes again. From the way her face is reddening, he can tell she's already had a drink today. "Are they making it up out of whole cloth? Are you saying you had nothing to do with what happened?"

The ice in his glass cracks and spits at him. "I was there," he says softly. "I was there when it happened."

Dana sags. "Oh my God, it is true. You killed someone. I can't believe it."

"Dana . . . "

He starts to come toward her, but she turns and locks herself away from him, bowing her head and hunching her shoulders.

"Jesus," she says. "I always knew you were this angry—"

"It's more complicated than—"

"But I didn't think you were capable—"

"I wasn't the one who—"

"How could you do this to me?!"

Her voice is like a gun going off. Everything stops for a second.

"I had my reasons." Jake puts his glass down and tries to begin again.

"But you never said anything. I thought I knew you. You've been sleeping with me for twenty years. You held our son's bare bottom in the palm of your hand. You slept at the foot of his bed when his brain was swelling and we thought he was going to die. . . ."

"I didn't do it," he says, opening his arms. "I didn't kill anyone."

"But don't you see?" She comes over and thumps him hard on the chest. "The fact that you didn't tell me before makes me doubt everything you say now. You came in this house every night for three weeks, knowing this was hanging over you, and you never said a thing to me. You lay in bed with me! You made love with me! And you never told me our lives were about to fall apart! You never even gave me a *hint*. You were a stranger. Tell me how I should feel about that!"

Her words echo through the white room and then die in the middle. Jake stares blankly at the space.

"I thought I was doing it to protect you and Alex," he says carefully, still feeling the scotch burning the back of his throat.

"You lied and hurt me more deeply than I've ever been hurt before," she answers. "It'd be easier to take if you'd just come home and told me you'd been having an affair. I feel like I've been married to a stranger for twenty years. You deliberately hid what you were from me."

"That's not true."

"What if I told you I'd been married before?" she says in cold undirected fury. "What if I told you I'd had someone else's baby?"

He's so tired he finds himself wondering if this could be true. But then he remembers the way Dana looked when she was nine months pregnant with Alex. The front of her summer dress billowing and her hands locked under her belly like she was carrying a secret garden inside. The memory of that time blazes up and then fades in his heart. He wonders if he'll ever be that happy again.

"Come on, Dana," he says.

"No, you come on." She pushes him away. "You tell me that you're trying to protect me and then you expect me to spend the rest of my life alone, waiting for you to get out of jail? What is that? What are you leaving me?"

He puts the heels of his palms up to his eyes. He's already been grappling with the possibility that he might lose his license and go to jail in the next six months. Now does he have to worry about his marriage too? A kind of blueprint for sadness unfolds in his mind.

"Dana, we can't let this break us apart. We have to stick together."

"We're going to. But that doesn't mean I have to be happy right this minute."

Though they're less than a foot apart, he still feels as if she's stepping back and looking at him in a different way.

"I need you," he says.

"I know." She doesn't cry. "I love you too, Jake. I'm just not sure I know you very well."

58

Philip and Uncle Carmine are having coffee at a brand-new Russian bagel place on Twentieth Avenue in Bensonhurst. A white Ford Bronco pulls up outside and two pasty-faced Italian kids get out with their baseball caps turned sideways and their jeans riding low on their hips. A walloping hip-hop beat from their speakers rattles the windows of the restaurant.

"Minchia," says Carmine. "It's gettin' so you can't tell our kids from theirs."

A pregnant-looking girl gets out of the Bronco and spits up in the gutter, like she has morning sickness. Then the three of them go into a Chinese takeout place across the street.

"You know, I worry about your mother being here."

"Yeah?" Philip spreads butter on his bagel and looks over at one of the beefy Russian waitresses.

"Ronnie too," says Carmine. "He's living over on Bay Ridge Parkway. He listens to all that rap music and wears all them nigger clothes. It's like I raised a yom."

"Ah, Ronnie'll be all right."

After all, the neighborhood hasn't changed that much. The outsiders have made only minor incursions so far: a Korean sweatshop here, a Russian dry cleaner there. And some of them even pay tribute to the old-timers like Carmine for using his turf.

He gives Philip a hard look. "I still haven't worked out why they let the both of you go so soon," he says.

That hair tonic smell wafts across the table.

"I told you already. We're cooperating and making a case on the Jew lawyer."

"I don't like anybody being a rat about anything." Carmine's eyes tilt back behind his glasses. "Especially not my own son."

"Hey, it's not like we're talking about you, C."

"You better not be." He looks at the gold watch lost in the thickets of his arm hair. "Funzi was supposed to talk about me to the grand jury. Look what happened to him."

They found Funzi in the weeds near Kennedy Airport with something in his mouth that didn't belong there.

"Funzi was an asshole," says Philip, thinking about the tape recorder the DA wants him to wear.

A Russian waitress with raven hair and almost translucent skin brings Carmine his cup of espresso.

"I hope Vladimir finally figured out how to make one of these things," he says, taking the cup and saucer from her. "What's the matter? You don't know how to make an espresso in Russia?"

The girl just rolls out her bottom lip.

"Next time you see him, tell him he was a little short with the last envelope," Carmine says.

She shrugs, either not understanding the threat in his voice or not caring, and walks away.

"Anyway," says Philip. "No one's going to bring you into what we're talking about with the DA. It's a murder case."

"I still don't like it."

"Hey, C. It's the only way out of this."

Steam from the espresso cup rises and condenses on Carmine's glasses.

He looks at Philip like he's not really seeing him. "Why'd you have to bring Ronnie along when you whacked these bums? Now he's on the spot for it."

Philip puts his bagel down.

"No, C. He's on the spot for what we did with Walt. Which you told me to bring him along for. Remember? 'Show him the ropes'? So why you pointing fingers now?"

Carmine puts his right hand over Philip's left hand and squeezes until it hurts.

"All I'm telling you is I'm holding you responsible for anything that happens to Ronnie," he says in a low middle-of-the-night voice. "You're my nephew. But if you cause me suffering, I'll make sure you never forget it."

Under the table, he pushes his knee hard against Philip's thigh.

"How's Nita?" He draws back his chair and stands up.

Philip hesitates, wondering if Carmine's heard about him moving out. Is this a test to see what kind of liar he is? He feels the disgrace of a man without a family.

"You know." Philip shrugs. "Women."

"Yeah, I know." Carmine chucks him under the chin. "Bring the kids around one of these days. I feel like they're growing up before I get to know them."

59

John G. is back at the Interfaith Volunteers Center. A piece of brown cardboard is stuck over a window Yankel the Jew hater punched through after he stopped taking his meds. Geraldo Rivera is on the rec room TV, running down an aisle with a microphone in his hand.

"Look at that Jew!" says Yankel, who's back on Thorazine.

"He's not a Jew," says John G. "He's Puerto Rican."

"I'm telling you he's a Jew!" says Yankel. "His real name's Jerry Rivers."

"That's his real name? Bullshit." John rocks from side to side. "Jerry Rivers was a fake name. He's always been Puerto Rican. Why would a Jew pretend to be Puerto Rican?"

Yankel smiles. "Because the P.R.'s are the ones who really run everything. The Jews are just a front."

"Maybe he's a Puerto Rican Jew," says a third guy sitting between them, a chunky, high-voiced black man who calls himself Shitskin. "Maybe his mama's a Puerto Rican and his daddy's a Jew."

"In my old nabe," says John G., "the Puerto Ricans and the Jews hated each other almost as much as the blacks and the Jews."

"So maybe he hates hisself," says Shitskin.

They all just sit there for a minute, thinking about that.

Over in the corner, a Dominican catatonic named Miguel

dances in front of the fish tank, waving his hands like he's trying to hypnotize the guppies.

"Say, man, you wanna go see Scottie?" says Shitskin.

"Nah, I just wanna chill," says John.

John stares at his fingers. He's still tempted. Since he saw Margo the other night, he's thought about getting high two or three times an hour. But he knows that if he falls again, he might not get back up.

Easy does it. One day at a time. Keep out those bad ideas.

"How's it going?" A gruff man's voice interrupts his flow.

John G. turns and the first image that registers in his mind is a black fire hydrant. He takes a second to concentrate and organize his thoughts. The side of his brain that's been having its way lately tells the rest of his mind that it's not a fire hydrant. It's a squat sloe-eyed black man wearing a gray golf cap. Possibly a new resident. Almost definitely another homeless guy, albeit without the dirty clothes and the funky street odor like a halo of flies around him.

"How you doing?" he says a little louder, making sure John is listening.

"I'm doing all right."

Just let me watch my show and leave me alone, John thinks. Bad enough he missed his last appointment at the clinic and showed up late at his NA meeting last night. Now they've got annoying friendly people at the center.

Geraldo is screaming at two fat white women on the panel. "You're both grandmothers! And you're both sleeping with your granddaughter's boyfriend! Do you expect people to feel sorry for you?!"

The grandmothers' boyfriend, a bristle-headed twenty-three-year-old mechanic, looks on sheepishly.

"Ho, that's fucked up!" says Shitskin.

John's reached a different kind of ledge in his life. On the one hand, he's not sure how to climb any higher; on the other, he's afraid he'll slip and fall into the abyss. The nights are what's hardest. He finds himself waking up and calling out Shar's name. The need to be with her and Margo, to touch them, to be lying in bed next to them is as bad as his craving for drugs.

But then he remembers Margo is dying, and that yearning will never be satisfied.

The past is the past.

"You en-joying it here?" the man in the golf cap asks, sitting down between John G. and Shitskin. His left nostril and earlobe have the same skin pigment as a white man's.

" 'S all right," John mutters, edging away from him down the couch.

A commercial comes on the television. Nobody Beats The Wiz. Two happy, adorable children getting Nintendo from their parents.

"Don't give you much to do here, do they?" asks the man in the golf cap.

"I don't mind." John G. has almost reached the edge of the couch and the armrest.

"Hey, anybody ever say you look like Myron Cohen?" Yankel asks the man.

"I'm just saying there are other kinds of places," the man in the golf cap says to John G. "Some of these volunteer centers, they give you a place to sleep and they send you to NA meetings and that's it. So where does that leave you?"

"Hey, man, I'm trying!" says John, finally having enough of this fool and figuring the only way to shut him up is to talk back. "I've been clean for like a month."

Not counting the other night.

"So what?" says the man. "Now you're maybe on a par with the rest of the world."

He gets up and walks over to the window, gesturing to the fleet of taxis, buses, and regular cars making their way up Broadway. "Most of these people are clean too," he says. "You come out of this place and say you don't do drugs anymore, you know what they're going to tell you?"

He opens his arms as if he's trying to pick up a boulder. "They're gonna tell you, 'Kiss my hairy butt sideways.' There isn't anybody who's gonna give you an award for not doing drugs. 'Cept somebody else in your program. And when they give you that little plastic me-dal-lion and a hug, how are you gonna trade that in for a steak?"

The Geraldo show has returned to the screen. A therapist in a bright red dress is introduced and she comes out, giving high fives to the young meatheads in hockey shirts in the audience. John G. watches her sit between the two grandmothers and their boyfriend, dispensing sensible advice. Soon the two women are on the floor hitting each other, the therapist is jumping out of her seat, and Geraldo is standing back from the scene, looking perfectly aghast.

"Please, please, ladies," he says. "Violence is never the answer."

"Ho, that's fucked up," says Shitskin.

"Okay, okay, okay. So what are you selling me instead of NA?" John looks at the man in the golf cap. "God or drugs?"

"Neither. I'm talking about the higher power. Of the J-O-B." He takes a card out of his wallet and tosses it onto John's lap.

The name on the card is Ted Shakur Jr. His company is called the Brooklyn Redevelopment and Reclamation Society.

"This about jobs or putting up buildings?" John asks.

"Both." Ted Shakur starts to rise. "Think about it awhile. Then give us a call. I'll tell you about it."

"What's the matter? Why can't you talk now?"

"I'm not supposed to be hanging around here. The people who run this place might think I'm trying to steal away their clients and bite into their funding." He gives a sly smile before he walks away. "There's money to be made in poverty, you know."

WINTER

60

A gray smeary day in the city. Snow coats the sidewalks and licks the curbs. Maintenance men in orange jackets spread salt on the pavement. Christmas shoppers hurry by, expelling quick balloons of cold air. Dark birds huddle on windowsills for warmth.

Jake sits in Susan Hoffman's office, surrounded by cardboard boxes full of evidence just turned over by the district attorney's office.

His life has been circumscribed by these boxes. He no longer sees his favorite buildings and landmarks, the pretzel man on the corner, or the Peruvian flute players in the subway. There's a force field between him and life's normal pleasures. He closes his eyes and he sees cardboard boxes.

Act, he tells himself. Complacency is death. This is the time to think and take charge.

"Okay, we have a month until the trial begins," she says. "So in cases like this, I usually find there are two things the defense has to do."

Jake looks up from reading the formal indictment.

"Number one." Susan holds up a finger. "We have to discredit the prosecution's witness. And number two, we need to present a believable story of our own."

"Sounds easy when you say it like that."

Susan's brow comes down like a storm cloud. "Let's go back to number one. What do we know about their lead witness, Philip Cardi?"

Jake pulls out the grand jury transcript. "He has two prior convictions and he's entered into a plea agreement with the state."

"We need to find out more if I'm going to do a thorough cross-examination. So that's one of your main assignments for the next two weeks."

"Right, teach."

Jake starts taking notes on a yellow legal pad. It relaxes him, to think about strategy. It reminds him of when he was just a lawyer and not a defendant.

He doesn't go to the office anymore. After a tense meeting with Todd Bracken and the other partners, it was determined that he would work from home until the trial is over. So as not to interfere with the final stages of the Greer, Allan merger. "Thanks for being a team player, Jake." Todd gave him a limp handshake. "We'll remember it later." Yeah, right. The only reason they don't fire him outright is because he still has Bob Berger as a loyal client and an insurance policy. Good old Bob. Keeping him out of the gutter.

"Now what about their other witnesses?" Susan leans back in her chair, a blue pen sideways in her mouth like a tango dancer's rose. "Who's James Taylor?"

"The singer?"

She checks some papers on her desk. "I'm reading the grand jury testimony of James Taylor. Are you telling me this isn't someone we know?"

"Never heard of him."

She flips back a few pages and reads. " 'Question: Where were you living at the time of this incident? Answer: In them tunnels under the park. It's easier for me to get along down there. Question: You mean, because of the disability with your arm? Answer: I mean, 'cause I don't pay any rent.' " Susan lowers the pages. "This ring any bells for you?"

Jake concentrates hard and pulls Philip's flashlight beam up from the recess in his brain. He puts himself back in the tunnel that night and sees the man with one arm hunched over a shopping cart, squinting into the light. He can even hear his voice: "Come the fuck out, man. These people want to see you."

"I think that's probably the guy who identified me in the lineup."

"He's a real problem for us," Susan warns him.

"Why? This is a guy who takes drugs and lives next to a set of railroad tracks. If I was cross-examining him, my main concern would be not taking him apart too quickly so the jury doesn't feel sorry for him."

"That may be," Susan sighs. "But he can still put you on the scene in the tunnel that night."

"So what?" Jake scratches his wrist. "Their whole case is built on the testimony of Philip, who'd be my codefendant if he hadn't cut a deal, his cousin Ronnie, and this guy Taylor, who's a dwarf on crack."

"Don't forget that baseball bat with your prints on it. That may have been what gave them the confidence to go ahead and indict."

"Yeah, yeah."

It took Jake a while to figure out how the prints got there. "Here, hold this." Philip handing him the bat with the taped handle while he tied his shoe. It's those thoughtless little Kodak moments that can ruin your life.

"I still can't even believe the DA brought this case to the grand jury. It's just because that cretin's got a hard-on for me."

"Do me a favor. Do not refer to Norman McCarthy as a cretin in public. All right?"

"Well I don't see how he puts these clowns in the witness box with a straight face," Jake says. "Why don't we make another motion to dismiss?"

Susan looks at him with wistful indulgence, as if he's a child who finally needs to hear the truth about Santa Claus. "You're missing the larger picture. Yes, it's true you can pick apart individual witnesses, and it's true you can argue the physical evidence, but what they can give the jury is an overall pattern."

"What are you talking about?"

She massages the bridge of her nose. "What they can do is demonstrate that Jacob Schiff is a man obsessed with homeless people. It's not just the newspapers getting it wrong. They have the sergeant from the precinct where you first filed a complaint about Alex being harassed. They have the minutes from the Mental Hygiene hearing at the hospital where you tried to have a homeless man committed." Her voice rises to emphasize each point. "Then they have Philip Cardi saying you came to him, asking him to help you solve the problem. They even have checks you wrote him."

"For fixing my door and my chimney!"

"And to top it all off," says Susan, keeping her voice above his, "they have this Taylor saying he saw you in the tunnel and they have your fingerprints on the baseball bat used to commit the murder."

Jake becomes very quiet. "I still think a jury might sympathize with me."

"You are an officer of the court," Susan tells him in the stentorian tones she used when she was a prosecutor. "If they believe you were involved in the commission of a major crime, they will show you no mercy."

Jake gets up and goes to look out the window. A small dark car is trying to nudge its way through the snowy intersection of Thirty-fourth Street and Fifth Avenue. From this high up, it looks like a bug trying to make its way across a vast bowl of white rice.

Hanukkah has been and gone. Christmas is coming up in a little over a week. He should be out doing last-minute shopping for his family.

"I could testify myself," he says, still looking out the window.

"Then you could get on the stand and talk about all the little child killers and drug dealers you got released as a lawyer and how you went crazy when some lawbreaker showed up on your own doorstep. That'd be good. And then you could try lying when they ask you on direct if you were there in the tunnels that night. So you could perjure yourself and lose your license even if we do manage to win this case."

"I could say I tried to stop Philip from killing the guy."

Susan shakes her head gravely. "I don't think so, pal. I haven't made up my mind whether to have you testify or not."

"It's my call, Susan." He starts tracing a tic-tac-toe board on a fogged-up part of the window.

"And I'm your lawyer." She leans over her desk with poochy eyes and a wised-up mouth. "It's your neck, but I'm trying the case. Right?"

"Right." Jake draws an X in the center square and begins filling in the rest of the board.

"So that brings me to our second point: having a story of our own to sell the jury. It would be much more convincing if there was somebody else to corroborate the fact that you tried to break up the fight, don't you think?" She peers over, not quite getting his full attention.

Jake draws a diagonal line through his three X's and then wipes away the board. He's left staring out the window again, as if he's looking at a picture of life without complications.

"So can you think of anybody like that?"

"Like what?"

"Somebody in the tunnel who could back up your version of the story."

He starts to draw another tic-tac-toe board and then thinks better of it. "Not unless Johnny Gates wants to say a few words for me."

"Who's that? The homeless guy who was bothering you in the first place?"

Jake half smiles and hangs his head. "Yeah. I don't think he's looking to do me any favors. He's dead."

"What makes you say that?" Susan pulls a file out of one of the boxes. "The police only found one body in the tunnel."

Jake blows on the windowpane and draws a zero. It isn't that he hasn't considered the possibility. But after replaying the scene in his mind, he'd concluded that either the police hadn't located the body or that Gates had gone somewhere else to die. There were no reports of him turning up anywhere else.

"All right. So maybe he's alive. So what?"

"Do you think he saw what happened?"

"I guess." Jake coughs, wondering why Susan's looking at him so intently. "But he's crazy. He's a crackhead."

"So's their witness. The one who isn't an accomplice, at any rate. They'd cancel each other out."

Jake comes back to his chair and sits down. He notices the crease isn't as sharp on his suit trousers since he started taking them to the cleaners once a month instead of once every two weeks. But with the bail bond hanging over him, plus Susan's fee, the mortgage, and Alex's school bills, he's learning to economize.

"I don't even know where to start looking for Gates," he says. "He's probably in jail or a state mental hospital, if any of them are still open. Or back out on the street. For crying out loud, he harassed my wife and attacked my son. Now he's supposed to save my neck?"

"When you have lemons, make lemonade," Susan says. "Ancient defense lawyer's maxim."

Jake finds himself actually visualizing lemons and he bites his lips in distaste. "But I don't even know where to begin looking for this guy."

"Can I make a suggestion?" Susan puts her feet up and tips back in her seat.

"What?"

"You have less than a month. Try."

61

Don't look at the cue ball, John G. tells himself. Whatever you do, don't look at the cue ball.

He's in the rec room of the Brooklyn Redevelopment and Reclamation Society, being interviewed for admission by Ted Shakur. Behind them, two other homeless men are playing pool on a green felt-top table. The room is clean almost to the point of characterlessness. There are no slogans on the walls, no bars on the windows, and the new color TV in the corner is turned off. Nevertheless, John is still having a hard time screening things out.

He keeps looking at the smooth white cue ball instead of concentrating on Ted's questions.

"Are you now drug free?" asks Ted, pinching his white left nostril and his black right nostril. Ted Palomino Nose.

"Uh, yeah. Basically. I haven't done anything except the medication."

"What kind of medication?"

The cue ball knocks a solid red ball into the upper left-corner pocket. It's funny the way that little white ball moves the others around, scattering them across the table, sending them spinning into their rightful holes.

"I said, 'What kind of med-i-ca-tion?' " Ted asks in a loud voice.

John G. realizes he must have missed the previous question

because he was distracted. He tries to bear down and control the shit storm in his mind.

"Just the Haldol the doctors prescribed," he says, showing Ted the orange bottle and trying to sound sure of himself.

Ted strokes his salt-and-pepper beard and gives John a searching look. "You know we're not supposed to be taking that many people with psychological problems. We only have room for a couple like that."

"I know, I know. But I'm getting better."

Ted still looks suspicious. "You ever try and kill yourself?" His eyes scan John's arms and wrists.

John G. takes a quick mental inventory. Has he ever really tried to kill himself? He wants to be honest. Truthfulness is the one thing he's held on to on the street.

"No, I've thought about it," he says, remembering that bleak morning on the subway platform and the times he's looked into a pair of oncoming headlights, "but I haven't actually gotten around to trying it."

He's starting to mind-trip again, despite all his best efforts. The white ball slams into the eight ball.

Sunlight fading. Shar waving from across the street.

I love you, Daddy.

She died in his arms.

John G. grips the table, trying to hold on to the present. The past is the past.

Ted is still talking to him. "So what I'm saying is if you get accepted in this program, you're gonna get your urine tested regularly. You got a problem with that?"

The white ball slams a purple striper into the side pocket and then rolls back just a little, to avoid following it down.

"No, that's all right," John G. says, struggling to focus and meet Ted's eye.

" 'Cause a lot of guys don't like another man handling their piss. They get kinda sen-si-tive about that."

For a second, John is lost in a daydream. He sees himself perched on a ledge with Ted's scarred hand reaching out to him from above. He's afraid to take it. Afraid to move. Afraid he'll fall.

Oh my daughter, forgive me, for I have sinned.

Would she forgive him? Her smiling toothless face floats in front of him, framed by yellow hair.

One side of his mind says he should cry out to her, ask her to absolve him again. But the other side tells him it's just an illusion, the light fixture hanging at a certain angle. The past is the past.

"No, I don't mind the piss tests," he says finally. "What's gone is gone. It's not like it's in you anymore, is it?"

SLAM! The yellow-striped ball rolls into the lower right-hand corner. The cue ball backs away.

"Okay," says Ted, adjusting the kente-cloth hat on his head and making a note to himself. "Now if you get accepted into this program, you're gonna be turning your life over to us. For the next few months, you're gonna sleep in this shelter, eat with other men in this shelter, and go to work with them in the morning. We get you a job with a construction crew helping build apartments for other homeless people. You get a hundred and seventy dollars a week, and sixty-five of that goes back to us to cover your rent."

Blam! The solid blue hits both sides of the lower left-corner pocket and then bounces away. The cue ball keeps rolling, though, stopping maybe an eighth of an inch before it falls in.

"You ever swing a hammer before?"

"I used to drive a train. I was a motorman."

Ted writes that down, duly impressed. Slam! Green solid in the side pocket.

"You'll learn," says Ted. "That's what we're about. Teaching you a trade. Giving you a struc-ture you can fall back on. Can you handle that?"

"I need it," John tells him. "I need it the way other people need water."

The cue ball goes flying into the lower right-hand pocket. It disappears with a gulp and starts rolling along the lower deck of the table.

John straightens up. "When do I start?"

"Well, you haven't been accepted yet." Ted makes another notation. "Though to be honest, we have a couple of slots open right now and you may qualify. I have to talk to the administration."

"I'm ready," says John.

But in truth, he's not sure he is. He just knows it's time to move off the ledge he's been on. If he stays at the Interfaith Volunteers Center he'll start having fights with Ms. Greenglass and begin using drugs again.

"I hope it works out. We'll be glad to have you." Ted Shakur stands up and offers him his hand. A big dry bear paw with scabs across the knuckles and calluses on the fingers.

John takes it gratefully and squeezes it.

62

Over the next few days, Jake and the private investigator hired by Susan, Rolando Goodman, divide up the work. Jake concentrates on trying to track down John G. while Rolando looks for information to undermine Philip Cardi's credibility.

On a brisk Tuesday morning, Jake shows up at the 241st Street Dispatch Office, looking to talk to Gates's former coworkers.

Mel Green, the supervisor, is standing there in an Everlast weight belt, stacking bootlegged videotapes of films made by various members of the Sheen family. Ernest Bayard, John G.'s old conductor, sits on a chair in the corner, staring at the trains going past the windows.

"I have to say John G. was more a family-type guy the last few years," says Mel, once Jake's introduced himself. "The rest of us didn't spend that much time with him."

"So you wouldn't know where I could start looking for him?"

"No, man. Like I say, he was mostly with his wife and little girl. And once he lost them, he just fell apart on us. I don't know where he went." Mel puts his hands on his hips and looks at Ernest in the corner. "Hey, didn't he stay with you a while?"

Ernest just sits there, with his bald head pitched into his hands, looking shell-shocked.

"What's the matter with him?" Jake asks.

"Ah, he just got promoted from conductor to motorman." Mel piles *The Mighty Ducks* and *Hot Shots* on top of *Apocalypse Now*. "He took over John G.'s old line."

"He doesn't seem too happy about it, does he?"

"Well." Mel rubs his hands together. "He's had two people jump in front of his train in the last month."

Meanwhile, Rolando Goodman, a six-foot four-inch, two-hundred-fifty-pound, half-black, half-Dominican ex–pro football player, is out in Bensonhurst. He's talking to the owner of the Crown Royale Auto Body Shop.

Jake's used Rolando a few times on old cases. His toughness has never been an issue; his thoroughness and subtlety are seriously questionable, though. He's a prideful hothead who tends to storm away when he feels people aren't giving him the respect he deserves. A real liability for an investigator.

"So you don't know this guy Crazy Phil or his cousin?" he asks.

The owner, a lardy pockmarked slab of a guy named Tony, who has hair that goes straight back like he's driving a hundred miles an hour, shakes his head. "I just told you. I don't know any Crazy Phil."

"Well, do you know a guy named Philip Cardi?" asks Rolando.

"I know a lot of guys named Phil. It's a common name in this neighborhood. Kinda like Leroy in your neighborhood."

"Leroy?" Rolando's shoulders stiffen. He's wearing an Armani suit, a Turnbull & Asser shirt, and an Hermès tie with a gold pin on it. He wanted to show these guineas how to dress. "Leroy? What's that supposed to mean?"

"Means you probably live near a lot of guys named Leroy."

"Look out that window, will you?" Rolando points to a white car in the parking lot facing Eighty-sixth Street.

"What am I looking at?"

"That's a Lexus, man. That's one of the most expensive automobiles on the market. I paid fifty thousand fucking dollars for that car. You think I drive it through a neighborhood full of Leroys?"

"How the hell should I know?"

"Rolando Goodman does not live with Leroy," he says, drawing himself up like a society matron who's been given a paper plate.

"And I don't know any Crazy Phil." Tony, the owner, staples a couple of pink invoices together.

"Good-bye," says Rolando.

He stalks out to his Lexus and drives away.

Tony, the owner, watches the exhaust float up into the white winter sky. Then he opens the door to the garage and calls out to a short young guy welding the underside of a black Impala.

"Hey, Carlo. You still got Ronnie's number? Someone was here looking for his cousin."

63

Pressure begins to mount. The trial date is now three weeks away. Money is getting tight. Under $40,000 in the bank after all the legal expenses and another big school bill is coming. Jake tries to drum up some business from home, but there are no new cases coming in. No one wants a lawyer whose problems are worse than his own. Thank God for Bob Berger throwing him enough work to keep him busy when he isn't looking for John Gates.

In the meantime, Dana has joined the search. Through a friend in the hospital records department, she hears that a woman named Greenglass called from the Interfaith Volunteers Center some months back, trying to get John G.'s file. Dana makes an appointment to see her.

"You can't believe how much I did for that man," Elaine Greenglass is saying. "Every morning for three months, I stood in front of subway entrances and supermarkets, handing out leaflets for him. Every weeknight and every other afternoon, I worked the phones."

"You were a dedicated campaign worker," Dana says, trying to sound sympathetic.

She's been sitting in Ms. Greenglass's office for a half hour, trying to figure out how to work the conversation around to John G. and his current whereabouts.

"I got that man elected mayor." Ms. Greenglass pulls out a hair and inspects it under her desk lamp. "But when he got to City Hall—nothing. Not one phone call. No job waiting for me at Department of Personnel. No position at HRA. Nothing available at Landmarks Commission or HPD. Just forgotten. All that work. Slaving!"

"That's gratitude," says Dana, pulling on her fingers and trying to hide her impatience.

Ms. Greenglass sighs as if she's just noticed the bitterness in her own voice. "You know what I realize now? They're all like that. All men. Even the ones who seem decent. They expect to be taken care of like children and then they give you nothing in return. They don't even know how to give. My ex-husband was the same way. Twenty-two years of marriage, he never once cooked a meal or changed a diaper. Not once! Every night he fell asleep in front of the television. Never once asked me to go on a vacation where I wanted to go."

She clucks her tongue and waves her hand as if none of it mattered. Her eyes are still angry, though.

"Don't you find that?" she says to Dana.

"What?"

"That they're all selfish children."

"Well." Dana puts her fingers to her lips, still looking for her opening. "I actually do get along with my husband and my son."

"You know, the men at the center here are the same way." Ms. Greenglass charges ahead, as if Dana hadn't said anything. "They use our beds, take the medication we provide, watch television, and then they just leave when a better program comes along. So you know what I say when people complain I make too much for someone working at a nonprofit?" She curls her upper lip and affects a road-show-company Mame voice. "Tough luck, baby. I got mine, go get yours."

If Ms. Greenglass were her patient, Dana would describe her as someone setting herself up for disappointment so she can feel vengeful and righteous later. But this isn't therapy. It's an attempt to locate a witness who can help her husband's case.

"I'm sure you have very valid reasons for feeling the way you do," she says.

That's right. Give her some space. Make her feel comfortable talking to you. Develop a bond of trust.

Ms. Greenglass leans back in her chair, so her curly head is framed by the green Christmas wreath hanging from the criss-crossed bars over her window.

A tall black man with a mop in his hands and a scar across his bald head appears in her doorway.

"What do you want, Flamort?" asks Ms. Greenglass.

"Bennett went out awhile to get some lunch. He said he'd call you later."

Ms. Greenglass draws back her lips and her nose seems to get sharper. "Goddamn it, who told him he could do that without my permission?!"

"I'm just passing the message," says the man with the scarred head.

"You tell him I want to see him when he gets back. This isn't any game. I'm the executive director here." Her eyes flick up at the man. "And do my office before you do his. The floor is filthy."

Actually, Dana notices, the floor is immaculate. The man bows his head and backs out of the office.

"I know they resent me here," Ms. Greenglass tells Dana with barely contained fury. "I know the staff and the consumers talk about me when I'm not around here. But I don't care. Really I don't. My ego isn't so fragile that I depend on their good opinion."

Dana lowers her eyes, sensing it's time to get on with her agenda here. "I came by today because I was trying to locate a particular client of yours."

"Consumer."

"Yes, consumer." Dana tries to smile agreeably. "I was looking for a John Gates. I believe he was staying here. Is he still around?"

Ms. Greenglass's eyes turn hard and distant. "What's your interest?"

"I'd been seeing him on an outpatient basis. And you called our hospital looking for his file awhile back."

Ms. Greenglass cocks her head to one side, like a cheetah catching the scent of gazelle in the wind. "Are you trying to steal this consumer away from us?"

"No."

"Then what do you want with him?"

Dana feels as if she's six years old again, caught in her mother's bathroom playing with the lipstick and rouge. To lie at this point would be dangerous to her professional life.

"We may need him as a witness in a criminal case my husband is involved in."

"I see. And you want me to violate our rules of confidentiality to help you?"

"I just thought we could share some information as a matter of professional courtesy," Dana says gamely.

Ms. Greenglass takes a moment to assess the situation, trying to figure the best way to position herself as the outraged victim.

"Don't you think what you're asking me is terribly inappropriate?" she says.

"I didn't think it was that big a deal. He's someone I'd seen at the hospital. If he doesn't want to talk to me, he doesn't have to. All I'm asking for is an address for him."

But Ms. Greenglass isn't interested in these finer points. She's seized the moral high ground and she's defending it with the fervor of a Masai warrior.

"Are you trying to get me in trouble?"

"No."

"Is that what you're trying to do? Are you trying to get our funding cut off? Because if you are, you can forget about it. I worked too hard to get where I am."

"Please. I think you're being a little paranoid."

"Paranoid? You're calling me paranoid?"

"No. I . . ."

"Listen, Miss whatever-your-name-is. I'm the only thing between these men and the street. I'm not going to let you march in here and expose them irresponsibly."

Dana resists the temptation to remind her that not a minute before she was calling these men selfish children.

"No, no, no." Ms. Greenglass half rises from behind her desk. "I am not going to allow my staff to cooperate with you."

In spite of her better judgment, Dana finds herself getting pissed off. It isn't just this last outburst. It's having had to sit through this whole self-pitying, self-justifying monologue without getting anything in return.

"I'm sorry you can't find it in your heart to help us," she says in the coolest voice she can muster.

"What hospital did you say you were affiliated with anyway?" asks Ms. Greenglass, reaching for a telephone. "I'm thinking someone should talk to your supervisor."

"Be my guest." Dana gets up and drops her card on the edge of Ms. Greenglass's desk. "If you're going to help me, help me. If you're not, don't. I don't see any reason for me to sit here and listen to this. I care, but not that much."

It's only when she's halfway out the door that she realizes she's just used one of Jake's lines.

She turns left and heads down a long hallway where the tall black man with the scarred bald head is mopping the floor. She steps carefully to the side he hasn't mopped yet.

"You looking for John G.?" he says, as she starts to pass.

"Yes, that's right."

He must have heard every word of the conversation while he was mopping outside the door.

"I think he went to one of them work shelters in Brooklyn," he says. "One of their outreach workers came by and talked to him a few weeks back. I think John G. went over to their program."

"You don't remember which one, do you?"

"Nah." The guy touches the scar on his head. "I'm no good with names now."

She wants to clasp his hand in gratitude, but when she looks in his eyes she just sees bottomless wells of rage and numbness. With the scar across his head and his flat voice, she wonders if he was the victim of either a savage attack or a seriously botched lobotomy.

"I appreciate your talking to me," she says slowly.

He looks down, comtemplating the soapy water in his bucket. "I appreciate a clean floor."

64

Philip is standing on the balcony above the Rockefeller Center skating rink on a frigid Thursday afternoon, waiting for his cousin Ronnie.

There's a slim young guy dressed in black performing in the middle of the ice. He leaps and turns, doing spins and double axels, and for some reason Philip can't stop looking at him. He finds himself imagining what it would be like to skate along behind the guy, mirroring his movements, putting his hands on the guy's slender hips.

Ronnie walks up. "Yo, my man Philip C. is in the house. Word up, blood. What it is."

The kid's appearance is jarring. In the week and a half since Philip last saw him, Ronnie has immersed himself even more deeply in black street culture. He's got Bob Marley smoking a spliff on his T-shirt, a black Triple F.A.T. goose-down coat over it, baggy jeans, a pair of Air Jordan sneakers, and a red-and-white striped stocking cap just like the one the Cat in the Hat wears. No wonder Carmine's worried about him.

Ronnie twists his right arm around like a pretzel, offering his cousin the latest uptown handshake.

Philip just stands there, looking at him.

"What are you calling me for?" he says. "You know we're supposed to stay clear of each other until the trial begins."

Ms. Fusco's concern. Even though they're cousins, she doesn't want it to look like her witnesses are hanging around together all the time, cooking up a story for the prosecution.

"I just wanted to give you some four-one-one," says Ronnie.

"Some what?"

"Some information, bro." He makes his right hand into a gun and points it at his crotch, like a rap star. "Tony called from the auto body shop on Eighty-sixth yesterday. He said some nigger came by asking about us."

Through his gloves, Philip feels the cold pulling back the skin under his fingernails. "Yeah, what'd he want to know?"

"I'm not sure. Tony thought he might've been working for a lawyer or something. Like an investigator."

Philip turns away and leans over the brass railing. The young man skating below starts doing leaps and vaults, like he's performing just for Philip.

"So, like, what should we do?" asks Ronnie.

"What should we do?" Philip looks back at his cousin, with his eyebrows frozen. "We should cross the fuckin' borough to avoid this guy. He probably works for Jake Schiff."

"Yeah, you think so?"

"He ask any questions about me being in prison?"

"No, why?"

"I just don't like people asking about what went on there. It was private."

The skater below does a triple spin and his blades shave the ice. Across the rink, men in dark blue uniforms are starting to erect the enormous Christmas tree.

"So I don't get it." Ronnie's chin lolls idly at the bottom of his face. "The lawyer's the one on trial here. Why's he got an investigator asking about us?"

"He's looking for dirt, that's why. *Capisce?* He's trying to put us on the spot, so we do the prison time instead of him."

"But—"

"Ronnie, look. Don't think. Just do like I say. All right?"

He quietly simmers in the snow. Why does he have to keep worrying about this? He's already made his deal with the prosecutors. Now he has to concern himself with what the defense might dig up about his past. It's not anyone's damn business.

"But what do you want me to do?" Ronnie does a nervous side-to-side hip-hop shuffle. "You want we should pop this nigger with a bat next time he shows up?"

"No."

Philip tries to calm himself by watching the skater. It's the craziest thing; he keeps picturing himself skating hand in hand with the guy. It's not a fag thing, he tells himself. It's a display of manly athletic grace, the two of them together.

"You just keep track of this yom," he tells his cousin. "And let me know if you hear about him asking any more questions. I'll take care of the rest of it."

65

So how's the case going?" asks Bob Berger, slurping down his miso soup.

"Okay, considering," says Jake.

They're sitting near the back of an upscale Japanese restaurant on East Sixty-third Street. Though it's after two o'clock, the place is crowded with businessmen and -women speaking softly with their heads inclined. The walls are covered with gray flannel to cut down on background noise, and the only soundtrack on the expensive Bose speakers is a solitary koto being plucked. This is a place where deals are made, not just talked about.

"Actually, it's going rather badly." Jake pushes his own soup away. "The judge has decided to allow in all the fingerprint evidence; most of the good people of Bensonhurst won't talk to my investigator; and meanwhile, with only two and a half weeks until the trial begins, we can't locate the one witness who might be able to help us. We're looking for him night and day, but he keeps moving around. I don't suppose you have a lot of contacts in the homeless community."

"The only bums I know personally are the kind that summer in the Hamptons."

There's no mirth in Bob's deep-set gray eyes. He clears his throat with a loud phlegmy rumble. Hrrmmm.

"How you fixed for cash?" he asks Jake as he wipes his mouth with a pink napkin.

Jake holds up his empty water glass at a passing waitress. "We're not going to the Riviera anytime soon."

He stops and tries to read Bob's expression again. But there's still nothing there. No crinkling around the eyes or tightening of the mouth. Just that hrrmmm phlegmy rumble from the back of his throat.

"So that's why I was a little concerned that you haven't sent over the Poverman contracts yet," Jake says.

"My regular girl, Ingrid, is out. This new one, Felicia, doesn't know her ass from her elbow. . . ."

"Bob." Jake puts the glass down. "Is there a problem?"

Bob clears his throat once more. God, it sounds like he has a carburetor in his larynx.

"Jakey," he says, slowly sitting up. "You know, Chet Allan and I go back a long time."

Jake hears a high-pitched bell sound ringing in his ear.

"No, I didn't know that."

Bob hocks into his handkerchief and folds it up. "Well, it was before your time," he says. "Chet helped me with some exigencies a few years back."

"Exigencies? I've never heard you use a word that long before."

"It means you do today what gets you to tomorrow."

"Actually it means situations requiring immediate attention."

"Whatever. Chet did me a favor with the attorney general's office when they were looking into some code violations I had up in East Tremont. Serious business, you know. They had a couple of fires and an old lady died when the roof fell in on her. Christ, it was awful. Newspapers calling, some *schvartze* assemblyman from up there yelling for my head. Anyway, Chetty made it all go away. So you can see how I'd owe him."

Jake is aware that the lull in conversation around them has become a valley. Bob's eyes have receded into his skull, as if they've seen enough of this life.

"So you want Chet Allan to represent you instead of me? Is that what you're saying?"

"Look, kid." Bob pulls a Cuban cigar out of his pocket even

though smoking is not allowed in the restaurant. "I'm in a tough spot. I'm not managing tenements in the Bronx anymore. I'm trying to build hospitals, corporate quarters. I'm with the fucking School Construction Board. I can't have a convicted felon negotiating for me . . ."

"I haven't been convicted of anything, Bob."

"Whatever." Bob lights the cigar and waves the first puff of smoke away. "You know what I'm talking about, kid. How would it look, the situation you're in right now? These 'respectable' people. They wouldn't understand. Think of the stories in the newspaper."

Somehow the white tabletop seems suddenly to rise toward Jake's face.

"But Bob," he says, struggling to keep an even voice, "you know I need this work. I need you as my client. Todd Bracken wants to throw me out on my ass."

"Kid, I'm sure it's just going to be a temporary thing. Just until the smoke clears."

But in fact, the smoke isn't clearing. It's thickening over the table and Jake finds himself vaguely nauseated. Without Bob and some of the other major clients he's lost in the last few weeks, he's as good as dead at Bracken, Williams.

So all the things he's done for Bob—winning the settlement disputes, breaking the tenants' union, diving Kamikaze-style on Noel Wolf, protecting him from Philip Cardi—have meant nothing. He realizes now that he misjudged Bob as badly as he misjudged Philip. This is not the gruff but benevolent father figure he'd been looking for. This is a shrewd businessman who understands when an asset has lost its usefulness. Jake is ashamed of himself for losing sight of the distinction.

"So this is just another exigency, right, Bob?" he says, trying to hide the wound in his voice.

"Everything's an exigency, kid." He looks down and sees his cigar has gone out.

"But how could you do this?" Jake asks, before he can stop himself. "I thought I was like a son to you."

Bob relights the cigar. "I don't speak to my son."

66

It's the cars that start all the trouble," says Mrs. Vogliano from the bakery.

"The cars," says Rolando Goodman, the private investigator working for Jake and Susan Hoffman.

"In this neighborhood, a girl sees a guy has a nice car and that's it. That's all she cares about. She doesn't look at his character. You know what I'm saying?"

"For sure."

Rolando looks out the window to make sure no one's touched his white Lexus, parked out on Eighteenth Avenue.

For the last week or so, he's been walking up and down the streets of Bensonhurst, stopping into every other store and shop to ask about Philip Cardi. Rolando knows people have been questioning his abilities lately and he's determined to show he's worth $500 a day as an investigator.

So finding this Mrs. Vogliano is the break he's been looking for. She's the first person he's found who'll say more than "I don't know nothing about nothing." She has a full pulpy face and a hard raspy voice.

"Now the one we're talking about, this Philip," she says, curling her lip, "he had an Alfa Romeo or something like that. His uncle gave it to him. A Christmas present, he says. Ha! They stole it right off the street, those two. And Philip drove it around until he ran it into a guardrail on the BQE. But my niece, she didn't care. She wasn't dumb, just kind of naive. She saw he had a nice car. She didn't pay any attention to any of the things people were saying about this boy.''

"What kind of things?''

"You know. That there was something wrong with him. That he had a screw loose. You understand? He went around saying he'd been to Vietnam but he'd never been out of boot camp. He had some problem with one of the other boys.''

"So, did they go out?''

"No, but they were friendly like. You know, my niece, she didn't have many friends, growing up around here.'' She leans across the counter and whispers. "She's half Puerto Rican.''

The bakery is empty, but Rolando plays along, making a big O with his mouth.

"You see, my sister Val, she married a Puerto Rican fella,'' says Mrs. Vogliano, casting a wary eye around before she brings her voice back up. "And a lot of people in this neighborhood didn't like that. They stayed away from the daughter. Understand? Like she was unclean. I'm not saying everyone here is prejudiced but some of them are.''

"I noticed,'' says Rolando.

"There you go.'' Mrs. Vogliano points toward the window and winks. "So my niece didn't have nobody to hang around with, being half Puerto Rican and all. So when this Philip Cardi was just a little nicer, it meant the world to her. And when he came around in a nice car, forget about it. It was all over. She would've gone to the moon for him. She followed him everywhere. In fact, can I tell you something?''

"What?''

Again, she looks around furtively, like she's worried the stale brioches and cannoli are listening. "I think she had a little crush on him,'' she says sotto voce.

"Is that right?''

"And then he goes and does this terrible thing to her in the warehouse.'' Mrs. Vogliano thrusts out her hands as if she's trying to give him the dilemma to solve.

"It's sick," Rolando says agreeably.

Mrs. Volgliano shakes her head and sighs. "It breaks your heart. I tell you."

"So what happened?"

She stoops her shoulders. "Who can say? She asked him a question and he didn't like it. Something she'd heard about him. The way he was. You know?"

"No, I don't know."

She cups her hand around her mouth and whispers again. "She heard he was a *maricon*. Understand? We call it a mameluke. So—how would you say?—he got upset with her."

"I got it." Rolando straightens his tie. "So your niece is still alive?"

"She works at this bar on Mulberry Street, in Little Italy. Like I was telling you."

"Would she be willing to talk to me and my client about what Philip Cardi did to her?"

"That I couldn't tell you. She has to speak for herself." Ms. Vogliano looks down at her reddened hands on top of the glass counter display case. "But it was a shame, I tell you."

"Maybe I'll stop by and see her."

"Your client a white guy?"

"Yes."

"And does he have other white people who work for him the way you do?" Parts of her face turn purple and her eyes get as small as dots on dice.

"I don't know. Maybe."

"Then maybe you ought to send one of them instead. People in this bar can be kind of particular."

67

Carmine calls Philip on the telephone.

"Some shine just called the bar downtown, asking about you," he says. "Said he was an investigator for your Jew lawyer."

"Who did he talk to?"

"Isabel."

Philip slips his fingers through the coils of the phone wire. "She tell him anything?"

"No. But he said he might come by and see her."

Silence.

"Let me just remind you about something, Philip," says his uncle. "I don't like lawyers coming around my bar, asking questions. Your problems should never become my problems."

"I know that, C."

"So keep it that way. Shit doesn't go back in a donkey."

68

The Wallaces aren't doing the Christmas party at their house this year," says Dana from the kitchen.

"At their house." Jake looks up from the piles of court papers and case folders that cover the dining room table like Indian burial mounds.

"Yes. That's what I said. At their house. You think they're doing it somewhere else without telling us?"

"Yeah, they are."

"Well that's just your paranoia." She takes a bottle of Columbia Crest chardonnay out of the refrigerator, $4 cheaper than the Kendall-Jackson she was drinking two months ago.

"No, it's not," Jake says matter-of-factly. "I ran into Dave Curtis on the street. He asked if we were coming to the Wallaces' party at Jim McMullen's."

"The restaurant on the East Side?"

"The very place."

"That can't be right." Dana pours herself a glass of wine and comes into the living room. "Kathy told me they weren't doing it at their house this year."

"Don't look so stunned. At least she didn't lie to you. Technically. They're not doing it at the house. Right?"

Dana shakes her head. "I don't get it. She's been one of my best friends since college."

"Oh, I get it."

Dana puts down her glass and does a yoga stretch with her arms. This is what their lives have become. No one has come right out and said they are now socially ostracized. It's been a more subtle kind of strangulation: unreturned phone calls, brief and awkward conversations on the street. What's worse, though, is what's happened to their marriage. All they ever talk about anymore is THE CASE. Everything else—all gestures of tenderness and intimacy—have been flattened by the weight of the impending trial, which is supposed to start in ten days. Those fleeting moments of distance between them have stretched out into weeks. Jake can't remember the last time they touched each other with any real warmth. The opposite sides of the bed have become lonely outposts.

"Alex get home?"

"Over an hour ago," Dana says. "He's upstairs listening to Gregorian chants. Can't you hear them?"

Cold moaning flutters down from the stereo. Jake finally looks up and catches her staring at him.

"You hungry?" he says.

But what he means is: I'm drowning.

Before she can answer, the phone in the kitchen rings and she runs to get it.

He goes back to reviewing documents about Abraham Collingwood. The deceased. Until recently, he's just been the VICTIM, like the anonymous coefficient in an algebra problem. Something to be worked around in a trial. But now the details of his life take on new import. Born in Bed-Stuy to a drug-addicted mother and a prison-bound father. Raised by a series of overwhelmed and underfinanced aunts and grandparents. In and out of foster homes and mental facilities from the time he was ten. One year at the School for Performing Arts, two arrests for sale of controlled substances, three-quarters of a tour in Vietnam cut short by a shrapnel injury and a rat bite. The rest of his life spent drifting aimlessly with the occasional arrest for assault or robbery and a couple of trips to Rikers until he finally came to rest underground. Not a bad guy when you added it up. Just a bad case of wrong-place-at-the-wrong-time-itis.

Jake knows he should be thinking of ways to taint his character and drain the jury's reservoir of sympathy. But for some reason, he's finding he doesn't have the heart for it. He's defended worse people in his time. Much worse.

Dana finishes her phone call and comes back into the dining room.

"Dana." Jake puts down the case folder and stands up. "I think we have to consider the possibility that I . . ."

He looks at her, expecting her to finish the sentence for him. But they're not connected that way anymore.

"We have to consider the possibility that I may not win this case," he says slowly.

"I don't want to hear that."

Her vehemence surprises him, like a bright light in a dark room.

"Well, I think we have to start planning around the idea that I might go to prison," he says, trying to sound stoic. "I want to make sure you and Alex are going to be taken care of. You know most of the money is—"

"Don't talk like that."

"I'm just trying—"

"You're just trying to make yourself sick."

A flicker of familiar feeling.

She takes off her glasses and starts fussing with her hair. "I don't know why you're giving up all of a sudden. I thought Rolando just tracked down the girl from the warehouse for you. Aren't you going to see her tomorrow?"

"Yeah, but she's probably not going to talk to me."

"And what about that old case you were going to cite to keep the fingerprint evidence out?"

"Ah, Susan says it's probably not going to fly with this judge."

The judge at his trial is going to be a former defense lawyer named Henry Frankenthaler. Thaler the Brawler, they called him when Jake was at Legal Aid. In court, Henry liked to stand and bluster in oratory that would make Cicero blush. But behind the scenes, he was always the first lawyer to sell out his client and take whatever deal the prosecutor was offering. For that reason, other attorneys hated to work with him in cases involving multiple defendants; by the time you got to court, Henry had already arranged for his guy to testify against all the others. When you'd ask him about it later, he'd simply sniff and act like the fault was yours for not getting to the slops quickly enough. "He who hesitates is lunch." It doesn't bode well for Jake's case.

"Well, would you like to hear some good news?" says Dana, sitting down.

"Sure. Something. Anything."

"I think I just got the name of the shelter where John Gates is staying."

Almost automatically, Jake stands up and moves toward the phone in the kitchen. "Oh my God, hon, that's great."

All of a sudden, he feels like a shaken can of soda. Everything's rising. He makes himself stop to kiss her on top of the head before he trots into the kitchen.

"I gotta get a hold of Susan and Rolando so we can make arrangements to see him right away . . . ."

"Ah." She clears her throat. "Maybe that's not such a good idea."

He pauses in the kitchen doorway. "Why not?"

"The last time you saw him, you brought two guys with baseball bats. He may not feel that comfortable talking to you."

He comes back into the dining room, carrying the cellular phone. "Dana, I tried to save Gates and his friend. How long's it going to be until you believe that?"

"It's not important what I believe, Jake. It's important that we get out of this."

"I didn't do it."

"That's what you keep telling me."

He puts the phone down and looks at that fourth chair at the table. Again, there's that space between them. Jake wishes there were a child there who could bring the two of them together in a hug. But Alex is busy with his homework and his dreary monks' chanting. Maybe it's not just garden variety my-dad's-an-asshole contempt Jake's been experiencing these last few weeks. Maybe the case really is getting to Alex. But Jake still isn't sure what he should say to his son.

"All right." He turns back to Dana. "So if I'm not going to do it, who is going to talk to Gates?"

"I was thinking I would," she says, straightening an unruly stack of documents. "I was the one who found him."

"Forget about it. No fucking way. You're not going there yourself. The guy's violently psychotic."

"Actually he never got a diagnosis. I suspect it was probably schizoaffective disorder made worse by drug abuse, but it shouldn't be a problem if he isn't getting high anymore."

"Don't even think about it. It's too dangerous. You're not going."

"I am going," she says, clearing a space on the tabletop so she can put dinner plates down. "It's a shelter, Jake. There'll be plenty of other people around."

"You don't know what these guys are like."

"I *do* know what they're like. I work with them every day. You can't pull rank on me anymore, Jake."

He starts to argue with her, but a dull throbbing pain in his chest stops him. He pauses for a few seconds, with his hand over his heart, waiting for it to pass. These last few weeks have been more than hard; they've put twenty years on him. He's noticed new aches in his joints and new shades of gray in his hair. Anxiety is turning him into an old man just in time for his prison term.

"It's my war," he says, trying to keep up a game face.

"You can't do it alone."

"I've always done it alone."

"No, you haven't. You've done it with me!" She smacks a stack of papers. "It's been you and me for twenty years. We made it through law school together, we made it through childbirth, we made it through Alex being in and out of the hospital for six months."

"This is different."

"Bullshit!"

He almost jumps, hearing her curse like that.

"All of a sudden, I'm supposed to be the little woman, stay at home, keep the fires burning?" she says.

From upstairs, the chanting monks have grown quieter, as if they'd just realized the gravity of what they were singing about.

"Look, it's not about ego," Jake says, peering at her from behind a tall pile of grand jury transcripts. "It's not about you or me being in control. It's about my case. Okay? My future."

"NO!" She sucks in her cheeks defiantly. "This isn't just about you. It's about us. That's the mistake you've been making all along. You've been thinking everything is just your decision. And it's not. It's about *our* future. About the life we've made together. About our family. It's not just your problem or my problem. It's our problem. I'm mated to you for life, Jake. And I will not accept this family being torn apart. I just will not accept that."

She starts pushing more of the papers down toward the far end of the table, so there's more open space between them. "Maybe if you'd talked to me about this all along, we wouldn't be in this trouble," she says. "He was my patient, remember. I might know something about talking to him that you don't."

Jake is silent for a minute. He has a vision of himself as an exhausted marathon runner, collapsing in heat prostration before the finish line. He sees Dana with her thin arms and a number on her back, trying in vain to drag him the rest of the way.

"You asked me if I was still in this with you. And I am." She stands up and goes to get dinner ready. "I'm going to fight this no matter what happened in those tunnels. You and Alex are my life."

"So I guess you're going," he says, studying a whorl in the table's wood.

"I guess I'm going."

69

A bleak winter morning. Ice envelops the streets and sidewalks like a skin. A rusty yellow Ford van pulls up in front of an old tenement insulted by age and graffiti on West 133rd Street. John G. gets out and takes a long look at the building.

"Recognize this place?" says Ted Shakur, climbing out after him.

"It's a crack house, right?"

A couple of junkies stumble up from the basement steps, lugging lead pipes and pieces of copper wiring, and squint into the sun like West Harlem vampires.

"You been in this one before?"

"I'm not sure." John G. holding a hot-chocolate thermos against his chest. "But I been in a lot of other ones just like it."

"Well, today's gonna be different," says Ted. "Today you're gonna do to this house what we're trying to do to you. You're gonna knock it down and build it up."

They join the five other guys in the work crew who've already entered the building.

Inside, the halls are dusty and the stairway makes no promises. The banister is wobbly and parts of several treads are missing. On the top floor, the walls are covered with several generations of wild style spray painting. Half the apartments are padlocked and spike-nailed shut with signs on the doors that say WARNING: DO

NOT ENTER. TRESPASSERS WILL BE PROSECUTED. Of the ones that are unlocked, most are filthy and unkempt, and the floors are severely burned in places. Crackheads falling asleep with lit matches, thinks John G. A trick he's done a few times himself.

Ted hands him a sledgehammer and taps a drywall between two bedrooms.

"This has gotta come down," he says.

"Okay."

"But be careful. Just looking at it, I can tell there's a lot of de-bris inside."

"I'm not scared of debris." John G. studies a dark spot where it looks as if the wall has been sweating.

"Well, you should be," says Ted. "Don't pick up anything you can't see with your eyes. Use a shovel. Otherwise, you're liable to get stuck with some old junkies' needle."

John G. looks at the hammer in his hands. Something about being in this place makes him blue. The nearness of death again. He doesn't want it anymore. But he's not sure if he's ready to go back and join the working people of the world either. He wonders how much those junkies are getting for the copper they stripped off the basement pipes.

"Well, go ahead, hit it," says Ted, bringing him back to reality. "Put some rhythm into it."

John G. tests the weight of the hammer in his palm. It doesn't seem strong enough to do the job. He swings it once and hears a dull crunch. The wall is unimpressed. He swings it a second time and hits a wooden strut solidly. The vibrating hammer hurts the joints in his hand.

"Give it one more shot."

Using both hands, John hits the wall a third time. A little piece of light appears.

"There you go." Ted pats him on the butt and walks away. "Just make sure you don't bring the whole thing down on top of your head."

By midafternoon, John G. has found that rhythm. He takes down four walls and two doorways. He'd forgotten how much he liked working. The regularity, the satisfying ache in his muscles, the feeling of seeing a thing through to the end. It reminds him of making the last stop of the day at 241st Street.

But in another way, he's just going through the motions. Why should he get to live and get better? The light in his mind turns green. Shar waves. He's as hollow inside as the wall he's destroying.

"Yo, John G.!" He hears Ted calling to him from downstairs.

He ignores the voice and keeps hammering at a rotted baseboard.

"Yo, John G.!" Ted is coming up the stairs. "Someone's here to see you!"

He puts the hammer down and feels an anxious twinge in the back of his neck. He suddenly flashes on the men with baseball bats who attacked him that night in the tunnel. How have they found him again?

But then he looks through the scrim of brown dust and sees a familiar blonde woman standing next to Ted in the doorway. Snow melts on her fur collar and he notices how thin and lovely her legs look even though she's wearing boots, instead of high heels.

"This your pa-role officer?" asks Ted, looking up since he's a couple of inches shorter than the woman.

"No." John G. glances at her and then turns back to the hole he's been making. "This is somebody else."

Ms. Schiff shivers with embarrassment and tries to manage a smile.

"Well then, you don't have to talk to her."

WHAP! He snaps the cheap wainscoting in two. "It's all right," he says.

"Okay, take five minutes." Ted starts to go back downstairs. "But let me know if it's gonna be any longer. I need the extra man today."

70

Jake walks into a bar called Alpha on Mulberry Street, blind from the white snow and bright sun outside. In the brief seconds before his eyes adjust to the light indoors, he's aware of someone moving around behind the counter.

"Miss Perrara?" he says.

"Yeah?" A heavy middle-aged woman's voice, sodden with booze and disappointment.

"I think my associate Mr. Goodman mentioned I'd be coming by to see you today."

Gradually, she comes into focus. The damp rag in her hand. Her slumped shoulders. The hennaed curly hair around her head. And that face.

Rolando said that Philip beat her literally within an inch of her life in that warehouse twenty years ago, but Jake hadn't really prepared himself to see what was left. Isabel Perrara's left eye is about a quarter-inch higher than her right eye and doesn't open all the way. Her mouth is crooked too and a thin white scar runs along the length of her jawline. The right side of her face has a smooth angular cheekbone, hinting that she might have once been attractive. But that has nothing to do with the left side, which is pale and puffy with the texture of curdled butter.

"What do you want from me?" she asks.

"I wanted to talk to you about Philip Cardi."

She looks down the length of the zinc-topped bar. It's three in the afternoon and the place is empty, except for two withered old men sitting at a table in the corner, talking quietly and drinking scotch. Everything is painted black—the tables, the chairs, and the walls. There are mirrors on the ceiling and Boyz II Men on the stereo. It's one of those borderline places that could be SoHo chic or totally mobbed up.

"Who told you I knew him?" she asks.

"I heard it around the old neighborhood."

The aunt, Mrs. Vogliano, made Rolando promise he wouldn't give her up. She'd said Philip picked up her niece Isabel off Eighty-sixth Street and then drove her to a warehouse near the Brooklyn Navy Yard, where he broke six bones in her face. She needed to use her fingers to chew her food for years afterwards. Charges were filed and then mysteriously dropped. The aunt intimated that some uncle of Philip's, a mob capo from Staten Island, had bought the family off and given the girl a job at a bar he owned in Little Italy.

So here she is twenty years later. Barely able to see straight. She takes her rag and starts to swab out the inside of a highball glass.

"I don't have anything to say to you."

Jake takes a deep breath. "I know it's hard to talk about these things. But I need your help."

If he can get her to testify, he can show that Philip lied to the prosecutors in his plea agreement by not mentioning all his previous crimes. It won't just undermine his credibility; it will establish once and for all what a crazy sonovabitch he is.

"I know what Philip did to you," he says. "I know how he hurt you."

"I'm not interested in talking."

She moves down the bar and picks up another glass. The cheap silver charms on her necklace make a tinkling sound. He's going to have to work to get through to her. This is someone who's spent the last two decades giving up on life.

"Look, Miss Perrara," he says, following her down the bar. "I'm a lawyer. I've been around a little. I know there are different ways to hurt people. You can hurt them on the outside by breaking their bones. Or you can hurt them on the inside by treating them badly and making them think there's nothing they can do about it.''

She stops polishing her glass and looks at him skeptically. "Yeah? So what are you gonna do for me?"

"I'm not saying I can fix your body. But maybe there's some other way I can help."

He realizes he may be misleading her by making himself sound like a personal injury lawyer. But what the hell. He's desperate to get her to tell her story. An exigency. That's what Bob Berger would call it.

She steps back for a second to turn down the stereo. Yes! She's going to talk to him.

He's so happy he could almost buy the old guys in the corner a round. But then she tilts back her asymmetrical chin and half closes her one good eye. "Philip!" she calls out.

A door opens next to the icebox behind the counter and Philip walks out like a bull entering a ring. He stands next to Miss Perrara and gives Jake a murderous look. And in Jake's head, that train sound begins to rumble again.

71

You may wanna be careful walking around this room." John G. turns and paces away from Dana, not meeting her eyes. "Some of the floors are kinda old and burned in places. You take a wrong step, you might end up falling through the boards and breaking your neck."

She watches the little circling motions he's making with the hammer in his right hand and wonders if he's trying to give her a warning.

"I had a hard time finding you," she says. "They gave me the address of three other work sites at your shelter. I had to keep calling them back from pay phones on the corner."

"Maybe you're not supposed to find me."

He stares at the hole he's been making and his tongue pushes hard against the left side of his mouth.

"You seem much better," she says. "I guess you're taking your medication again."

"What the hell do you want from me?"

She hears the whine of a buzz saw from downstairs and the sounds of men arguing.

Tread lightly, she reminds herself. She takes a step toward him and the floorboard creaks under her boot.

"Well," she says. "I actually need your help. My husband is involved in a criminal case and—"

"Fuck you."

"Excuse me?"

"I said, 'Fuck you.' You got that?" His green eyes glare through the dust. "You were supposed to help me."

"I realize our treatment plan never quite got off the ground . . ."

"FUCK YOU TWICE!" he shouts. "You tried to have me put away."

She sees the hammer in his hand is shaking. She takes another step, and this time the floorboard actually seems to bend a little.

"I understand you have reasons to be angry."

"I have reasons?" He slaps the head of the hammer into his left palm. "Oh, thank you very much."

She holds her head up. "I just wanted to see if you remembered anything that happened that night you saw my husband and those other men in the tunnels."

"Jesus Christ, lady! I don't want to remember! I just want to do my little job and take my medication. All right? Let's make a deal. I'll leave you alone and you leave me alone."

If only he'd made that offer four months ago. He reaches under his grime-smeared sweatshirt and scratches himself.

"Why d'you wanna talk about this anyway?" he asks.

"My husband's been charged with killing your friend."

"Yeah, well, life's full of tough breaks, isn't it?" He turns back to the wall and starts banging on some white trim.

"Is that what happened?" she asks.

"Why do you wanna know?"

The look he gives her freezes the breath in her chest. She realizes she's afraid to hear the answer.

"I want to know if you saw my husband kill that man."

"What's it worth to you?"

"What's it worth?"

"Yeah, what would you pay me to say he didn't kill Abraham?"

"Just tell me, goddamn it!"

Her voice sounds raw and unfamiliar to her.

"What's the matter?" he asks. "He didn't tell you?"

She starts to back off. She's shown him too much of what's churning inside her.

"It would be better to hear it from somebody else."

The back of her head tightens. She takes another step back and a small piece of floorboard drops away.

"You must have some marriage." John G. tosses the hammer from hand to hand.

It's enough. He's just playing with her. She starts fixing her scarf and buttoning up her overcoat. Trying to figure out what she's going to do with the rest of her life. It was foolish to come here today. Jake is going to prison and her heart is going to break. Nothing can change that.

"I'm sorry to have disturbed you," she says.

" 'C'mon Philip, gimme the bat.' "

He's looking down at that hole in the floor.

"What?"

"He said, 'Give it up,' and then he tried to get between Abraham and the other guy."

"And this is my husband you're talking about?" Don't sound too eager, Dana cautions herself. Don't put words in his mouth.

"Well, the guy I always see you with."

"And you saw him say this and try to stop that other man from killing your friend?"

She has to resist the urge to run over and throw her arms around his neck.

"Yeah," he sighs. "I guess you can tell the judge that's what I saw."

"But can you tell the judge that yourself?"

All of a sudden, the flow of their dialogue stops.

"You want me to go into a courtroom and testify?"

"Is there a problem with that?"

"You gotta be kidding." He draws back as if he'd just touched a live wire.

"No, I need you to do that . . ."

"Okay, I think I've heard about enough. I've gotta work now. All right? So I'll see you. Good luck and everything."

He turns back to the wall and starts banging it with his sledgehammer.

"You have to tell the judge what you saw . . ."

"You gotta go, you gotta go." He keeps pounding without looking at her.

"Because otherwise my husband could go to jail . . ."

"Gotta go, gotta go." His banging drowning out her rising anxious voice. "Can't stay, can't stay."

"And that would be a tragic mistake . . ."

"Can't stay! Gotta go, gotta go!"

The wall is starting to come apart and he's stuck on the same phrases like a needle on an old phonograph record. "Can't stay! Gotta go!" And her nervousness is just making him talk faster and bang the wall harder. Has she pushed him too far? "Can't stay! Gotta go!"

A huge chunk of wall falls away and light streams in from the next room.

"Mr. Gates, please calm down!" she half shrieks.

The echo of her voice hushes both of them for a moment. She hears tiny timbers crackling and snapping under her feet.

"Why can't you just let me be?" he says. "You want me to help you, I can't even help myself." He wiggles one of his loose lower molars with his tongue.

"I just want you to say what happened."

"Oh yeah, sure, right, that'll be a breeze." He sputters. "Talking to a bunch of lawyers and a judge." He raises his hand. " 'I stipulate the defendant has to stop taking drugs. I stipulate the defendant has to turn over his assets. I stipulate the defendant has to give up his freedom. I stipulate the defendant has to go back to a shelter.' "

"I understand if you're reluctant."

"Reluctant?" He almost starts laughing. "Lady, these people are going to rip my fucking head off."

"My husband's lawyer wouldn't let them do that to you."

"Oh yeah, right." There's not much bite left in his voice. "Look, I'm sorry, I just can't handle any more pressure right now," he says, rattling the pills in his pocket. "I wouldn't be much of a witness anyway."

"What makes you say that?"

"Because look at me. Who's gonna believe me? I'm not a person anymore."

She takes a moment to look him over. He's certainly more

presentable than he was that first day he came into her office. His beard is shaved and his hair is shorter, though it's thin and graying in places. Understandable for the life he's been leading.

"I'm looking at you. You look great."

Oh, the shame! Trying to manipulate a mental patient by flirting. He half smiles to accept the compliment and then shakes his head, rejecting it.

"Nah. You're good," he says. "But you're not that good."

"But I mean it." She takes another step toward him. "You're a hundred times better than the last time I saw you. Seriously. You're working. The people at the shelter say you have your own room and you're earning money. In a few months, they say, you might even be able to go out on your own."

"But none of it counts."

"Why not?"

"It just doesn't. I'm faking it."

"Faking what? You're alive."

"Yeah, I'm alive, but I'm one of those people who might as well be dead. You know? I had my chance to be happy," he says. "I had Margo and I had Shar and I lost both of them. God doesn't give you two more chances like that."

"I just don't know how you can be so certain about that."

She senses that he wants to testify, he wants to do the right thing. But something's holding him back.

"No, it's no good." He shakes his head convulsively, denying everything. "I've fallen too far. I've done too much bad shit. I'm not a person anymore. God won't forgive me."

"Forgive you for what?"

"You wouldn't understand."

Dana feels as if she's trying to pry open a sleeping man's eyelids. But how's she going to do it? He could go either way.

She needs to give him a reason to help her out.

"Listen, can I tell you something?" She arches her neck and touches her throat with her fingers, trying to figure out how to begin.

"What?"

She flips through her mental files, trying to come up with

something that will have meaning for him. Don't lose him. Don't let him slip away. But she's just a nice Catholic girl from Connecticut. What's she going to tell a man who's been living on the street, smoking crack, and eating out of garbage cans for so long?

She lunges at a memory, hoping it will jar him.

"You just made me think of this thing that happened when I started at the hospital," she says quickly. "My supervisor suggested I go on a few runs with the ambulance crew."

"Yeah? So?" John bangs the hammer against his left leg.

Keep going. Don't lose him.

"So we went on a run to a fire in Chelsea and there was this one body that looked like part of the wreckage. You just looked at it and you felt sick. But then we realized it was still breathing. So the technician bent down and said, 'Are you a man or a woman?' Because it makes a difference in how they treat them. And this thing that didn't have any eyelids anymore just looked up and said, 'I'm a man. Can't you tell? I'm still a man.' "

"So what's that got to do with me?" asks John G., half curious but trying not to show it.

"That if he could still somehow hang on and say he was a man after what he'd been through, so could you."

Pause. Did she get through to him?

"Easy for you to say." He swings his hammer at a beam of light coming through the sooty window.

"Well, think about it."

He puts the hammer down and faces her. All at once, Dana knows she's reached him. Maybe he found something in the story or maybe he was just looking for an excuse to say yes. But then his eyes meet hers and for a second, she has the uncanny and uncomfortable feeling that he's about to ask her for something she doesn't want to give.

She starts to panic, wondering how far she'll have to go to save her family. But then he drops his eyes and looks away, like the shy boy who used to stare at her in geometry class.

"Yeah, I'll think about it," he says. "Maybe you ought to tell me what day they want me in court. Just in case."

"Thank you." She reaches out and touches his hand.

He quivers a little and there's a loud crash from downstairs as if part of the building's foundations have just collapsed.

"By the way." John G. turns back to finish off the wall. "Did that guy in the fire live?"

Dana hesitates only for a moment before she decides to tell him the truth. "No," she says. "He didn't."

72

I said, what the hell are you doing here?" Philip looks around the Alpha Bar.

"Just asking some questions."

Jake glances over his shoulder. The two old men who'd been sitting in the corner are gone. The scotch left in one of their glasses undulates slightly.

"Why don't you leave decent people alone and mind your own business?" Philip's face tightens like a fist.

"I have a court case I'm working on," Jake says evenly. "I have some information I'd like to get from Miss Perrara."

"And she doesn't want to talk to you."

"I didn't hear her say that."

"You hear me saying it, don't you?" Philip raises his right hand as if he's about to give Jake a slap.

The charms on Perrara's necklace make that tinkling sound again. Jake looks over at her and suddenly things start to seem more involved. Philip isn't just talking. He broke six bones in this poor woman's face. He crushed a man's skull with a baseball bat. He forced a crowbar up another man's anus. This is a human being who gets something out of hurting other people.

"If you got a problem with me, you keep it that way," Philip says, leaning over the bar and pointing a finger at Jake. "Don't go bringing other people into it. Or else the people you're close to might get brought into it."

"You threatening my family, Philip?"

"It's not a threat. It's a prediction. Shit happens."

Smart. Stopping just short of an actual threat.

"I still think Miss Perrara can make up her own mind whether she wants to talk to me." Jake puts his business card down on the bar counter.

Instead of looking at it, though, Isabel Perrara turns to Philip and puts an arm around him. The torturer and the tortured. What do you expect? She owes him her job.

Philip smiles and fingers the charms on her necklace. "So now you got your answer," he says.

73

I really don't understand this case," says Judge Henry Franken-thaler, looking from Jake and his lawyers to the two young prose-cutors. "I mean, what do we have here? One nut testifying against another."

They're sitting in his chambers during a break from another tedious buy-and-bust case a week before Jake's trial is supposed to begin. There's a spectacular color photo spread of the Brooklyn Bridge hanging above Frankenthaler's grayish Brylcreemed head, which used to be covered with unkempt curly brown defense lawyer's hair.

Just to his left is a black-and-white picture of Henry in a tux, a swarthy bear laughing and shaking hands with the governor and the county chairman who helped him get nominated for the bench. In the background, there's an orchestra and women in long dresses on the dance floor, looking impatient. A networking dinner. A schmoozefest. The pretext was probably a wedding or a bar mitzvah, but the real event was going on at some side table or banquette, where favors were being traded, posteriors were being kissed, and careers were being made and broken. This was the type of meal that could change your life; a move-'em-in, move-'em-out defense lawyer like Henry could rise to the office of distinguished jurist over hors d'oeuvres. The kind of event, in other words, where Jake will no longer be welcome once this case is done.

He's already tried to get Susan to put it on the record that Philip threatened him in Little Italy the other day, but the prosecutors shot it down, saying that he'd come to the bar to question the witness and no direct intimidation was involved.

"I mean, we're just talking here, right?" says the judge, looking at Francis X. O'Connell and Joan Fusco, the two ADAs.

"Of course," says Francis, ever eager to please a man in a black robe.

"I don't understand why the DA even brought this case," says Frankenthaler. "You have the word of two accomplices, this Cardi and his cousin, and then you got this character Taylor who's been in and out of jail all his life and is currently living in a railway tunnel. It's cockamamy. That's the only word I can think of."

"The grand jury didn't think so," pouts Ms. Fusco.

"I could get a grand jury to indict my dog if I was DA," says the judge.

Jake feels a surge of hope. Maybe this case will get dismissed after all. But then he remembers that Henry used to bluster on in court this way before dashing out into the hall to cut some pathetic deal for his client.

Sure enough, Frankenthaler turns toward Susan like a cobra sizing up a chubby mongoose.

"And Miss Hoffman," he says "I must say I'm somewhat disappointed in you. The best witness you can put forward is this John Gates? I see from the record he's been on Rikers for a drug charge as well as being arrested recently and hospitalized for his hallucinations."

"Isolated episodes," says Susan, keeping an even tone and graciously not pointing out she'd beaten Henry with far weaker cases when she was a prosecutor. "In any event, he's no less reliable than their witness. We're prepared to present expert testimony from the head of the psychiatric department of NYU Hospital that Mr. Gates is capable of remembering what happened that night."

"And we have an expert of our own who will disagree," says Francis.

"Fine. So it's dueling fruitcakes." The judge, exasperated, looks down at the case file. "How's a jury going to make a qualitative judgment about the credibility of their testimony? I don't want to turn my courtroom into cloud-cuckoo-land."

"With all due respect, Your Honor," Ms. Fusco interrupts. "How many cases have you tried where it was one drug dealer testifying against another? I think juries are sophisticated enough to understand that choirboys are rarely present at the commission of a major crime."

The judge nods and sighs. "Point taken," he says. "It's a crime committed in a railway tunnel. Who else is going to see it except someone who lives underground?"

"Exactly, exactly," says Ms. Fusco, with a trace of a Belt Parkway accent pushing through her overbite.

Jake's stomach clenches. This is what his life has become. Gloom, accusations, and the taste of ashes in his mouth. There's no solace in knowing the DA recently decided not to seek the death penalty against him. He still has a vision of himself stumbling out the front gate of some prison after twenty years and seeing Dana, worn out and frayed: her hair gray, her face lined, her mouth hard and bitter from waiting for him. He sees Alex, grown and unrecognizable, with children of his own about to reach their teens. Grandchildren who'll never acknowledge him. A lonely and bleak old age stretching out before him.

"Tell you what I'm going to do," says the judge. "I always tell my wife I like to get to the movies in time for the previews because they're often more interesting than the film that follows. So I'd like to arrange for a preview here. Just to avoid a circus."

Jake notices that since ascending to the bench Henry has started speaking even more often in sculpted, portentous tones instead of the peppery banter of a defense lawyer. More Park Avenue and less West Islip. The judge presses a button and has one of the exhausted-looking young men who clerk for him bring in his calendar.

"I want to bring both of these gentlemen in for a Wade hearing," Frankenthaler says. "Make sure both of them are able to identify the defendant. I have a spot open on my calendar for Friday. And then we can start the actual trial on Monday as scheduled."

Jake hears a rustle of nylon and sees Ms. Fusco whispering nervously to Francis.

"Your Honor," says Francis. "We seem to have temporarily lost track of our witness, Mr. Taylor. We might need the weekend to get in touch with him. He moves around a lot."

"Then I suggest you find him a fixed abode," says Franken-thaler, going high church again. "Otherwise I'll be forced to reconsider Miss Hoffman's motion to dismiss." He shifts his eyes to look at Susan. "And I expect you to have your witness here too. There are two sides to this. Have both of them take their medication, and may the best prescription win."

74

I don't like this business with you threatening people," Ms. Fusco tells Philip.

They're sitting in a $15-an-hour room at a motel near the Bronx Zoo. The walls are thin and the mattress on the double bed is light and spongy.

"Who threatened anyone?" says Philip, sitting at the foot of the bed. "Jake came into a bar to talk to a friend of mine. I was there. I told him to mind his manners. My friend didn't want to talk to him. End of story."

"I still don't like it." Ms. Fusco stands across the room, wearing a preppy herringbone jacket and nibbling on one of her bloody cuticles. He notices her hair is in a ponytail today.

"I want you to stay away from the Schiffs."

"Hey." Philip shoots his arm out. "If they have a problem, it won't be with me."

"And another thing," says Ms. Fusco. "The DA wants to know when he's going to see some production out of you investigating your uncle."

"Jesus Christ, one thing at a time." Philip holds up his hands, like she has him against the ropes. "I thought we were going to finish this case against Jake before we started concentrating on my uncle."

Another delaying tactic. Philip figures that Carmine is almost seventy. If he can drag his feet and draw things out long enough, Carmine will be dead by the time the investigation wraps up and they turn in the court papers. He'll die never knowing his nephew was an informant.

"What do you want me to do?" Philip asks Ms. Fusco. "Start wearing a wire right away and asking him, 'Do you remember?' all the time? You think my uncle's an idiot?"

She studies his face for a moment, not quite satisfied.

"All right, let's get back to the Schiff case," she says. But her eyes are still fixed on a point somewhere behind him. "The trial begins on Monday. We don't want any mistakes from here on in."

"I'm not making any mistakes."

She takes the rubber band off her ponytail. "And we want to make sure we're all clear on your plea agreement. You've told us about everything you've done before. Right? We're not going to learn about any other crimes you've committed."

"Absolutely not."

He's not going to tell her about Isabel now. That would bring the whole roof down. The prosecutors would come around the Alpha Bar asking questions, and then Carmine would get nervous, and before you knew it Philip would be admiring the view from inside the trunk of a Chrysler.

Ms. Fusco shakes out her hair. "You're also aware that any discrepancies between your grand jury testimony and your trial testimony will lead to us revoking your plea agreement, right?"

"Sure. You don't have to keep telling me."

She pulls back the musty green drapes and looks out at the parking lot. "We just want to make sure you're not jerking us off."

From the next room, he can hear bedsprings squeaking and the mechanical groaning of a thoroughly professional Fordham Road prostitute doing her job.

"I don't jerk anybody off unless they want me to," Philip says.

Ms. Fusco lets out a deep breath. For a moment, Philip thinks she's going to come over and slap him.

Instead, there's a knock at the door and she goes over to open it. The pudgy Hispanic detective who'd been sitting in the red Chevy outside comes in wearing a porkpie hat and a mustard sports jacket. The Irish wooden Indian is nowhere in sight today. Maybe he had a fight with Ms. Fusco, Philip thinks.

She says something to the new detective in rapid-fire Spanish. He mutters an answer and gives Philip a sidelong glance that puts a chill in his belly. Then he heads back out to the parking lot.

"Did he say something about me being American?" Philip asks.

"No, why?"

"I thought I heard him say the word 'American.' "

"No, that wasn't the word he used." She pulls back the drapes and watches the detective walking back through the snow to his car.

"Well, what did he say then?"

"It's not important." She puts her nails up to her mouth again but then thinks better of biting them.

"Come on, tell me."

"It was nothing."

Something inside him begins to vibrate. From the next room, the bedsprings are getting louder.

"If it's nothing, you can tell me."

"All right. He called you a *maricon*. Are you happy?" she says with harsh impatience.

"What?"

"I told him I was a little nervous being alone in the room with you and he said I shouldn't worry about it because you were a *maricon*."

"He called me a *maricon*? He called me a faggot? You know what happens to people who call me that?"

"No. What?"

The bedsprings in the next room sound like they're about to snap.

"Never mind." Philip catches himself. "Why the hell did he say a thing like that?"

"He talked to your old cell mate from prison."

Philip's arm flings out involuntarily again. He has a sudden urge to walk across the room and hurt her.

"Look, it's not any big deal," she says. "I have a brother who's like that and he's terrific."

"What are you saying? I'm not gay."

He stares at a dark spot on the rug, trying hard to control himself.

"Hey, if that's the way you feel, no problem." She puts her hands in the pockets of her skirt.

"You think I'm gay?"

She straightens her shoulders. "It's none of my business."

"But is that what you think?"

She licks her lips and stares at her shoes. "I just know that sometimes if you're not honest with yourself things can come out in funny ways."

"What are you saying to me?"

"Oh come on, Philip, look at yourself. You assault a gay man with a crowbar, you cut off another man's nipple . . . God knows how you get along with women . . . You're an intelligent person. Haven't you ever asked yourself what that's all about?"

The bedsprings stop squeaking.

Philip just looks at her. Is it possible she's right? The light coming through the drapes changes. For years, he's been telling himself that what he did with Diego in prison didn't count; you were only a faggot if you sucked a prick on the outside. But maybe there was more to it than that. Maybe he is that way. Maybe that's why he's gone through life with a fist cocked back over his shoulder. Maybe that's why he smacked his wife. Maybe that's why he beat the living crap out of Isabel that day in the warehouse when she teased him and called him a *maricon*—just because he couldn't perform with her. Maybe that's why he feels so torn and angry sometimes when he looks at other men's bodies. Maybe that's why he has to work so hard to prove he's a man.

But then he thinks about what his uncle and the rest of the Bath Avenue crew would say. No, it's unacceptable. He'll kill someone else before he admits that's what he's about.

"Listen," he says to Ms. Fusco. "If you're not sure about me, come sit down on this bed. I'll show you."

"Oh Philip." She brings her hand up to the side of her face. "Just forget I said anything."

75

Alex Schiff and his friend Paul Goldman are having lunch at a hamburger place across the street from their private school on the Upper West Side. Greek cooks work over the grill like men digging a grave. Frankie Valli sings "Sherry Baby" on the radio. Smoke and humidity fill the room.

"I just got my tongue pierced. You wanna see?" Paul opens his mouth.

Alex ignores him and stares straight into the vat of pickles in the middle of the table. Life sucks.

And now that his father is about to go to trial for murder, it sucks even more.

His grades have been going down the drain for weeks. He can't concentrate in class anymore. And he constantly has the feeling people are looking at him.

Until just lately, he hadn't even thought of his father as just a guy. He was a dark powerful force to be resisted, like the Shadow King in an *X-Men* comic or the disco revival. An embarrassment. An object of ridicule. And maybe once in awhile someone he loved. It was only in ninth grade that Alex stopped to consider that his parents might have had lives of their own before he was born and might still conceivably have sex. But the idea of his father frightened and vulnerable, an ordinary man in trouble, is more than he can get his mind around.

A slightly older white kid wearing a Snoop Doggy Dogg T-shirt under a purple warm-up jacket and a Cat in the Hat striped cap sidles into the booth next to him.

"Excuse me," he says.

"Hey, we're already sitting here." Paul opens his mouth, revealing the lump of metal on his tongue.

"Now I'm sitting here too," says Philip's cousin Ronnie. He looks at Jake's son. "You're Alex, right?"

"Yeah. What about it?"

Ronnie studies the menu for a second and then sets it aside. "I got a message for your father," he says. "Don't go where you don't belong."

"What's that supposed to mean?"

"He'll know." Ronnie gets up and looks down at Paul, whose mouth is hanging open.

"Damn, boy!" he says. "You got a fuckin' paper clip on your tongue!"

76

Jake arrives home just before midnight that night and heads straight up to his son's room.

"How you doing?"

Alex is lying on his bed with the headphones on, Kurt Cobain screaming wordless adolescent fury into his brain.

"You got any more messages for me from the knuckleheads?"

Alex shrugs. If the visit from Philip's cousin Ronnie bothered him that much, he hasn't let on about it yet.

"You mind if I turn this down a sec?" Jake asks.

The boy's eyes remain motionless. His mouth twists slightly. A heavy secondhand feeling lingers in the air, like all the oxygen in the room has been through his lungs twice already.

"I'm sorry you had to get involved with all this crap." Jake turns down the volume a little and sits at the foot of the bed.

No response.

"You know, starting on Friday, things could be kind of different around here."

Alex still doesn't say anything. Kurt Cobain is just murmuring at the moment. At least Jake has a shot at his attention.

"Once this hearing is done, I could be in a lot of trouble. There's going to be a lot of talk about filing motions and revoking bail and making sacrifices to pay for lawyers' bills."

Alex rolls his eyes a little, as if to say, Tell me something I don't already know.

Jake puts a hand on his son's leg and then takes it away as if spikes had just shot out of it. "I suppose where this is all leading is . . ." He pauses to put his thoughts in order. "Is to talk about the possibility that I might be going to jail."

The air doesn't just seem heavy anymore; it feels leaden. Alex's mouth goes tight. Nirvana's music grows quieter on the headphones. Jake's stomach feels as if it's just filled up with cold water.

"You've thought about that, I'm sure."

"Yeah," the boy says, sounding tentative and surly.

"Well, I just wanted to tell you—I'm sorry."

Nirvana's music explodes again into raging guitars and feedback. Jake realizes he had it backwards before. Alex isn't so much listening to Kurt Cobain; it's more like the earphones are somehow broadcasting the angry soundtrack in his mind.

"Is there something you want to say to me about that?" Jake asks.

His son's mouth stays closed and defiant. At least he's not wearing that nose ring anymore.

"If my dad was going to jail, I know I'd have something to say about it."

Still no response from Alex.

"I would've said: 'Bout time."

Not even a half smile. The black Nike on Alex's left foot jiggles, keeping time with the frantic music.

"I hope I've been a better father to you than that," Jake says, doleful but still striving for connection. "Remember about the bananas?"

"What?" Caught off-guard, the boy seems mildly interested and then irritated.

"I was just thinking how when you were little you wouldn't eat a banana until I came over and took all those little fibers off the side. You used to call them the strings. Remember?"

"Sort of." Alex sits up, just a little. The headphones slip and the music shrieks into his neck instead of his ears.

Jake moves a little and sees he was sitting on an empty packet of Bambú rolling papers.

"So?" says Alex, trying to distract his father from the discovery.

"I was just thinking about all the things we used to do together, just you and me when your mother wasn't around. Like the first time I took you to a baseball game. Remember? You were all nervous because you didn't think you'd be able to follow what was going on."

Alex's eyes get far away. "There was a fight."

"Yeah, I think Gooden threw at somebody's head or something and they all came piling out of the dugouts." Jake shakes his head. "Baseball players trying to punch each other. It's like ballet dancers trying to drink beer."

"No, I meant in the stands," Alex says. "There was a fight in the stands. Two guys in the next section started hitting each other and coming up the aisle toward us. You grabbed me and pulled me out to the hotdog stand."

"I was probably just trying to protect you."

"Yeah, but I wanted to watch."

"I buy you a hotdog at least?"

"And a Mets cap."

"Well, that's not bad for an afternoon, is it?"

"I guess you were trying to look out for me," Alex says grudgingly.

"I feel bad I didn't do more of that," Jake says. "Spend time, I mean. Just you and me."

"It was all right."

Jake can't tell if Alex means that he was a good father or that the time they spent together seemed quite sufficient to him.

He picks up his son's Bambú packet. "You know, back in the nineteen sixties, people thought you could get high smoking banana peels."

"That's stupid."

Jake raises his left eyebrow. "It is, isn't it."

The Nirvana song ends and Alex rolls onto his side.

"Your mother thinks you're smoking too much pot and that's why you're having trouble in school."

The boy looks up at the ceiling and his whole body tenses with rage.

"It's not fair," he says. "It's not even true."

Jake cocks his head to one side more indulgently than he would with a client telling a similar lie. "The truth is, most people would understand it if you started getting into bad habits. 'Oh, no wonder he dropped out and started doing drugs, his father went to jail.' "

"Fuck you."

Jake looks at his son for a long time.

Alex casts his eyes down, not quite ready to deal with the consequences of what he's said. "I just don't like it when you try to psychoanalyze me," he says in a low, sullen voice. "No one else knows what's going on in my head. You can't tell me how to feel."

"That's true. But I'm asking if you want to put yourself into a position where you're relying on other people's pity."

" 'You're the little man in the house now, Timmy, it's up to you to look after your ma,' " Alex says, imitating some virtuous square-jawed family man from prime time TV. " 'I'm not gonna be around much anymore.' "

"So I can't kick your ass if you fuck up," his father interrupts. "I have to rely on you to do the right thing."

"And what do you know about that, Dad?" His son looks up, his brown eyes challenging him. "You're the one who's going to jail. Right? I haven't killed anybody."

"And neither have I. Jesus Christ! You'd think I could get a little understanding out of my own family."

His throat aches and his voice sounds harsh. Somehow he'd assumed this would be easier. But why should it be? Everything in his life's experience tells him that nothing ever comes easily between fathers and sons.

"Look," he says, trying to sound conciliatory. "I know this has probably been tough on you. I don't know if people talk about it at school . . ."

"They do."

Silence like a wound opens up between them. A mournful cello sighs through the headphones, replacing the abrasive guitars.

"All my friends know what's going on," Alex says after a few seconds. "They're all like, 'Man, I'm really glad it's not my father.' And I start to laugh along and then I think: Wait, it *is* my father. So now I'm different from them. And it's not the way I want to be different. I mean, there are ways I want to be different, but this isn't one of them. It's not fair.''

"I know.''

"So why'd you kill him? That's what everyone wants to know. They ask me if you talk about what it's like to kill somebody when you're home.''

"It wasn't like that.'' Jake stares at his son, wishing he could reach over and touch the boy. "Now is not the time to get into all of it. Maybe one day when it's over.''

"Yeah, right.''

The cello in the headphones fades, as the guitar and drums launch one final desperate volley. Kurt Cobain stares down from a poster across the room that says I HATE MYSELF AND WANT TO DIE.

"All I can say is I tried to do what I thought was right for you and your mother.''

"Gimme a break.''

The boy hoists the headphones back over his ears. Jake wonders if he'll have another chance at making things right between them. The thought that he won't moves the ache from his throat down into his chest.

"I love you,'' he tells his son.

But Alex is lost in his own private universe and the words can't penetrate the cyclone of sound in his ears.

Jake goes back to his office downstairs to look at his papers and law books, headachy and as frayed inside as Kurt Cobain's voice, hoping against hope to find something other than the words of a deranged man that will help him stay out of prison for the rest of his days.

77

Hey, c'mere a second!"

When John G. comes out of his Brooklyn work shelter on Wednesday morning, two days before he's supposed to testify, there's a red Dodge van parked across the street.

"I wanna ask you something." The driver waves him over.

John doesn't recognize the man until he comes right up to the driver's side window. Then he sees a brand-new aluminum baseball bat lying flat across the passenger seat.

"How's your memory?" says Philip Cardi.

John G. is still trying to process the threat in his mind when he shows up at the employment office an hour and a half later. His interviewer, Mrs. D'Alessandro, sits behind her worn battleship of a desk, eating an egg salad sandwich on wax paper.

"I'm sorry I kept you waiting," she says, half rising to shake his hand. "But I've hardly had a chance for lunch today."

Her fingers feel moist and soggy.

"It's all right," says John, sitting down and trying to find a way to get comfortable. "I wasn't going anywhere."

His left arm starts to itch. He doesn't want to be here today, but Ted Shakur insisted it was part of his Lifesmanship Training Course. He has to learn how to reintegrate himself into society by working on the "fun-da-mentals," as Ted calls them. Going to job interviews, opening bank accounts, getting himself a telephone.

But the whole time, he keeps hearing the words: Jesus fucking Christ I'm not ready for this. His mind's been in an uproar since he agreed to testify for Mr. Schiff. And now he has this threat to contend with. How's your memory? Jesus fucking Christ.

"So what kinda work are you looking for?" asks Mrs. D'Alessandro, glancing down at the résumé John's given her.

"Anything."

"Anything?"

She looks up, alarmed. Is he sounding too desperate? Be relaxed, Ted told him. Wear a clean shirt. Shave. Be yourself. But what if the real you isn't a clean shirt and a close shave? What if the real you is a bum going through garbage cans for crack money?

"Well, maybe you can narrow it down for me a little," Mrs. D'Alessandro says in a voice like honey and thumbtacks. "What kinda work are you interested in doing?"

Outside, Eighteenth Street traffic is clogged. Trucks blare their horns and foul the air with black smoke. A cop with a loudspeaker keeps telling everyone to move.

"I just meant, I was willing to do anything," John G. says, fidgeting as the itch moves up his arm. "I could drive a van. I could do construction. I could handle rubbish removal . . ."

He tries to remember the rest of what Ted told him to say, but the words won't come. He's aware only of the truck horns and the egg salad dribbling onto the wax paper. *How's your memory?*

"Well, how were you previously employed?" asks Mrs. D'Alessandro.

"I was with the TA. I drove a train."

"Yeah, but what have you been doing for the past year?" She puts on a pair of black-rimmed glasses and frowns at his résumé. "The Shaker Realty Company. What's that?"

It's a lie. That's what it is. Ted told him that any employer with brains would wonder what he'd been up to lately. And he hasn't picked up references, smoking jumbos and pissing in the gutters the last few months. "Sometimes it's necessary to just stretch the truth a little," Ted told him.

But now John finds he can't get right with that. The itch has moved to the center of his chest.

Mrs. D'Alessandro takes off her glasses. "I never heard of this Shaker group. What'd you do for them?"

Come on, Ted told him. Everybody lies. It's the way of the world. It's dog-eat-dog in the offices, just like it is on the streets.

But John still can't adjust. Something inside him has been rigged to go off when he lies. Maybe it's what the nuns taught him or maybe it's the fact that telling the truth is the only thing that's anchored him for most of his life. But right now the itching in his chest is unbearable and he begins to claw at his heart.

"You all right?" says Mrs. D'Alessandro. "You're lookin' kinda pale."

He's not all right, though. Why does everyone expect so much from him? He isn't prepared to go back to a world of car insurance and bank accounts and having two forms of ID on you at all times. And he's certainly in no shape to stand up to threats. It's too much responsibility. They want him to testify in court and he can barely order a Happy Meal at McDonald's.

"I'm sorry," he says, getting up quickly to leave. "I think I made a mistake."

It's ten after six when he gets back to the Brooklyn Redevelopment and Reclamation Society. The sun is like a flickering candle, casting guttering light into dusk over the Bed-Stuy rooftops and water towers.

He walks into the community room and sits down, berating himself. What's the matter with him? Doesn't he want to be back in the world again?

Shaniqua, the ten-year-old daughter of an ex-junkie named Harold, is watching *It's a Wonderful Life* on the TV. Jimmy Stewart, computer colorized against a snowdrift, unshaven and weeping. Fuck it. Fuck it. That's not Jimmy Stewart, that's him cursing. They're going to throw him out of the damn program. Why does he keep fucking up?

Jimmy Stewart is imagining what the world would be like if he'd never been born. All the love and joy that would've been missed. John G. drums his fingers on the armrests. Maybe he doesn't belong back in the world. Index, pinky, ring finger, middle. Maybe if he could've seen his way to leaving the world a little earlier his daughter would still be alive. Thumb, forefinger, middle finger, pinky. The nervous tattoo. Louder and louder until it sounds like rain on the roof.

"I can't hear the movie," Harold's daughter says, turning to look at him, her pigtails swinging.

"Okay. Okay. Okay-okay-okay-okay."

He gets up, goes back to his room, and sits on the windowsill. Snowflakes are falling on the street outside, but they're slower and lighter than the ones on TV. With a sudden updraft they start to fly back up toward the darkening sky. Snowing in reverse. Those flakes must be high.

How's your memory?

Across the street, he can see a group of boys in hooded sweatshirts standing under the yellow-and-red canopy of a Yemenite bodega, like a bunch of urban monks. Maybe not sellers, but steerers for sure. They can tell him where he can see Scottie.

He gets his thin denim jacket off the back of a chair and puts it on. Then he takes it off. Then he puts it on again. Then he takes it off.

Then he balls it up and throws it across the room.

He can't decide.

If he gets high, he knows what will happen. He'll be what he's always been. A failure. The lowest of the low. Maybe he'll even hit the street again and start living like a dog. It's not a happy alternative, but at least it's a life he knows.

If he doesn't get high, what does he have to look forward to? Hard work. Uncertainty. In two days, he'll be called to the witness stand and asked to account for all his sins and misdeeds. And then he'll walk out onto the street and find that red Dodge van waiting for him. His bowels gurgle and the walls turn puke yellow.

"Yo, J.G., my man, what's going on in there?" He hears Ted Shakur knocking on his door. "How'd the interview go?"

"Just lemme be, will ya? Lemme be already."

He picks up the jacket and puts it on again. Motherfucker. Somewhere out there is a vial that understands his problems, that can ease his pain and cure his craving.

"Hey, c'mon, G., open up." Ted raps on the door again. "I wanna know what happened. Is something wrong?"

"Lemme be! Lemme be!" John punches the cinder-block wall.

The pain throbs from the knuckles all the way up to his jaw-bone. Tears well up in his eyes, and cursing shitfuckpissmother-fuckercocksucker, he tears off the jacket and throws it across the room again, inside out. Then he runs over to pick it up.

This is not a play he wants to be in. He wants relief. He wants to hear the blood rushing in his veins and the big beat of his heart. He wants to get high as badly as he wanted his mother to buy him an ice cream cone one summer day driving up Sunrise Highway. It wasn't the coldness in his mouth that he craved; it was the warm feeling inside, knowing she'd given him something.

He wants that feeling again, even though part of him knows it's gone forever. No teenaged crack dealer in a hooded sweatshirt is going to give it back to him, that's for sure.

"Seriously, G., I hope you're not thinking of getting high," Ted says through the door. "We've come too far for that."

"TED-just-let-me-be."

The sound of his own voice bounces off the hard walls. It sounds familiar but different, that staccato exhausted tone. It takes him a moment to place it. It's the way his mother would talk to him when she'd locked herself in the bathroom.

He starts stomping around in a furious circle, his mind roiling with bad intentions. Is he going to get high or isn't he? He stops and looks over at the cross on the wall, as if an answer is forthcoming. But nothing. He flings himself down on the sill next to the window.

"Aw forget it, man, I'm done talking." Ted sighs in exaspera-tion. "If you gonna stay clean, do it 'cause *you* want to."

His footsteps fade down the hall.

John just sits there for a minute, looking over at the clock by his bed. Three and a half hours until curfew. He rubs some fog off the window and peers out, trying to see if those boys in the hooded sweatshirts are still outside the bodega. But all he sees is snow. Relentless snow, coming down in thick blurry clots. It covers everything in a white blanket. The streets, the sidewalks, the cars, the tenements, the vacant lots, the boarded-up storefronts, the garbage and decay, the exhaustion and poverty of the neighborhood. It's all just snow and stillness now. He could be looking out at the Upper East Side or Pearl Street in Patchogue. Winter has rendered it all the same.

How's your memory?

He tries to remember the last time he took Shar sledding in Van Cortlandt Park. It was a December morning and he used a red milk crate to send her rocketing down, but none of the other details will come. He can't hear her laugh or see her expression. The size of her hands, the hat she wore, the red snow boots—it's all lost to him. Her memory is getting buried by the snow.

All of a sudden, he's not even sure she said, "I love you, Daddy," just before she died in his arms. Maybe he just imagined it.

He's beginning to forget her, losing her for a second time, and he finds himself weeping.

There's another knock at his door and then footsteps leading away. Down the hall, somebody is listening to WCBS-FM, the oldies station. Ray Charles's voice echoes from somewhere far away. "I can't stop loving you. I've made up my mind. To live in memories of the lonesome time."

But time won't stand still and the snow keeps falling. John G. puts on his jacket and heads out the door again.

78

Johnny Gates is in the wind."

It's quarter past nine. The words jump through the phone wire, into Jake's ear and press down on his heart.

"What are you talking about?" he asks Susan.

"He walked out of his program tonight."

In the background, Nine Inch Nails is jackhammering and yowling in Alex's room, like a band chained to a radiator in hell.

"Does anybody know where he went?"

Dana turns up her palms and mouths, "What's going on?" from across the bedroom.

"He just bolted," Susan says as static wells up on the phone line. "Apparently there was some kind of problem with a job interview . . ."

"Great."

Just when he thinks he's adjusted to anxiety as a constant condition, Jake feels several internal organs shrinking.

"What?" Dana pantomimes urgently.

"If I were you, I'd get Rolando and saddle my horse so you could go looking for him," says Susan. "The judge wants to see this guy the day after tomorrow."

"Couldn't we get the hearing postponed?"

"Henry's getting pretty fed up with this thing. He's got reporters calling his chambers all hours of the day and Albany looking over his shoulder. He wants it off his calendar ASAP."

Jake looks down at his arms and sees he actually has goose bumps though the temperature in the room can be no less than seventy-two.

"Susan, level with me," he says. "If we don't find this guy, what kind of case do we have?"

Another wave of static comes through the phone line, as if Susan just walked past a refrigerator.

"Let me put it this way," she says. "I wouldn't buy any tickets for next season's opera."

79

For more than an hour Jake and Rolando drive around the snowy streets of Bed-Stuy with a coil of tension heating up inside Jake. His whole future depends on keeping a dedicated crackhead from getting high over the day and a half. It's over, he tells himself. Your whole life is over.

They finally find John G. at quarter to midnight, standing behind a Dumpster on Marcy Avenue, flaring a lighter at a green-stemmed pipe.

"How's the shit?" says Rolando, getting out of his white Lexus first.

"It's just Italian baby laxative givin' me wicked cramps." John G. drops the pipe and tries to look innocent. "You guys cops?"

"Friends," says Jake.

Gates looks at him hard and grimaces in recognition.

"The fuck do *you* want?"

"I was a little concerned about you."

"Yeah, right. You're concerned. Get outta my face. Last time I saw you, you were with a couple of guys carrying baseball bats. That's how concerned you are."

Snowflakes melt as they touch Jake's face. "I thought my wife talked to you and we were straight about this," he says. "I was trying to stop them."

"All right, so we're straight. What do you want, a medal?"

"No, I just want you to be in court the day after tomorrow."

John G. makes a hissing sound and cold smoke streams out of his mouth. He looks over at a cigarette billboard ad across the street: a happy black couple under a waterfall.

"Yeah, well, I've been having some second thoughts about that."

"Why? What happened?"

"I don't know. Just a lot of heavy shit, man. I'm dealing with a lot of heavy shit. Maybe I'll be there. Maybe I won't."

"You better be there." Rolando stares him down.

"Oh yeah?"

Gates balls up his right fist and then realizes hitting Rolando would be like hitting a Coke machine.

"Is it because you've been getting high again?" asks Jake.

John G. turns on him, hands on hips, hair caked with snow. "Hey, buddy, let me tell you something. Drugs are the only thing I got. I am a drug addict. That's all I've ever been and that's all I'll ever be. Even if I'm not putting a needle in my arm or pipe in my mouth right this second, the thought is still in my mind." He taps the side of his head. "And if I decide I'm gonna get high to deal with the pressures in my life, there's not a fuckin' thing you can do about it."

The coldness of the street gets into Jake's bones. He feels fingers closing around his throat. This is how it's going to end. On a street like the one he grew up on. Done in by another man like his father who can't control his own impulses. Maybe he never really escaped from Brooklyn and this whole life he's had has been an illusion.

"Please, don't do this," he says, giving it one last try. "If you don't testify for me, I'm going to go to prison and lose everything."

"Hey, don't lay all that on me. It's not my responsibility."

"It *is* your responsibility!"

"Well, I CAN'T FUCKING HANDLE IT, ALL RIGHT!" John G.'s shout is muffled by the falling wall of snow.

Jake and Rolando look at each other, unsure how to calm him down.

"Jesus fucking Christ," Gates mutters in a quieter voice. "I can't take all this pressure. I swear I can't. I was watching that movie before, *It's a Wonderful Life,* you know? They oughta do it again and call it *It's a Shitty Life.*"

"I'm going to lose my son," Jake says.

"Who cares? I lost my daughter."

"I know," says Jake, weighing his words carefully. "So you know how scared I am."

For a moment, he feels like an old B-52 pilot who's just opened the bay doors and dropped the bomb. He has no idea if he's hit the target.

"Okay-okay-okay," says Gates, rubbing his raw bare hands together. "So now I heard the big speech."

"What do you want me to do, beg?"

"Nah, begging should be against the law." John G. stoops his shoulders and walks away. "Maybe I'll see you in court, Counselor. Maybe I won't."

80

Philip and his Uncle Carmine are sitting in a corner of the bar called Alpha on Mulberry Street, watching Isabel Perrara wipe down the counter.

"I still can't believe that with a wife and two children at home you make love with that woman." Carmine takes off his glasses and starts to clean them with a handkerchief.

"It's complicated," says Philip.

He's not about to explain it to his uncle.

"I'd rather put my dick in a garbage disposal," says Carmine.

Frank Sinatra sings "All or Nothing at All" on the stereo. Carmine's choice. Philip taps his foot agreeably, but inside his mouth he's gritting his teeth.

"So this preliminary hearing is tomorrow, huh?" says Carmine, who's wearing a suit and tie today. "What's going to happen?"

"Ah, this bum I was telling you about is supposed to testify for the defense."

"And you're not worrying about it?"

Philip sees Carmine glaring at him sternly. Asterisks of flesh have formed at the corners of his eyes.

"Number one, I don't think he's going to show up," Philip says quickly. "And number two, if he does, he may have some problems with his memory. I had a little talk with him, you know. I reminded him how things are when you're a drug addict and a head case."

Carmine puts his glasses back on. "But what if he does testify? Is that going to put you behind the eight ball?"

There it is again, Carmine's paranoia. The thing is, he has reason to be paranoid. He *is* surrounded by enemies.

"Well if he puts me behind the eight ball, I'll deal with it. It's my problem."

"Just remember: your problems aren't my problems," says Carmine.

"I understand."

"So don't think about rolling over on your padrone."

Philip's face closes up. "Why you keep bringing that up, C.? You going patz on me?"

"You're spending an awful lot of time with that girl prosecutor for the one case about the lawyer."

"It's a big case, C. They don't lock up a Jew every day."

"Sure they're not fitting you for a wire?"

The song ends. Isabel is looking at the two of them from behind the counter, some twenty feet away. Her face is half in shadow.

"What do you got under your shirt?" says Carmine.

"Chest hair. What do you think?"

"Stand up a second."

"Come on, C. Don't do this to me."

Philip looks over at Isabel, expecting sympathy. She remains in the shadow with glowing liquor bottles behind her.

"Why don't you take that shirt off?" says Carmine.

That hair tonic smell again. Philip's belly hurts. It feels like he has fingers inside his intestines.

"Come on, C. You're not serious."

"I'm serious as cancer. Take it off. What're you waiting for?"

Philip's hands are shaking and his throat feels dry. Slowly he begins to unbutton the black Charivari shirt he's wearing. His gut hangs over his belt just a little.

"All right?"

"Take the whole thing off," says Carmine.

Reluctantly Philip takes his arms out of the sleeves and drapes the shirt over the back of the chair. He feels both Carmine and

Isabel studying him. The humiliation makes him shiver. Somehow somebody is going to pay for this.

It's a good thing he hasn't started wearing the tape recorder just yet.

"All right, put it back on, I've seen enough," says Carmine without apologizing. "Good luck with your case tomorrow."

81

Good day, Mr. Gates," says Susan Hoffman.

"Good day."

Well, at least he showed up, thinks Jake. Up until quarter to eleven this morning, even that wasn't a sure thing. It's a Wade hearing to insure that the witnesses have made proper identifications. But just before Rolando dragged John G. in by the elbow, Judge Frankenthaler was pacing around behind the bench like some huffy old pigeon on a dirty windowsill, threatening to bar the witness and cite Susan for contempt.

"Could you tell the court your full name?" she says.

"John David Gates." He tugs on the lapel of a gray thrift-shop jacket that's a size too big for him.

"And how were you previously employed, Mr. Gates?"

"I was a train operator for the New York City Transit Authority for seven years."

That's good. Jake taps out a nervous Morse code on his yellow legal pad. Establish that he was once a solid citizen. A taxpayer. When a jury is brought in at the trial, they need to see that Gates was once the type of person they entrusted their lives to as they rode the subway every morning.

"Could you briefly describe your service record while working for the Transit Authority?" Susan crosses from the podium on the left side of the courtroom to the defense table on the right.

She leans over Jake's shoulder to pick up a file and her jacket brushes his right ear, giving him a small static shock.

With some effort, Gates raises his eyes toward the ceiling.

"I was employee of the month three or four times," he says in a voice made slow and flat by Haldol. "I had the fewest number of customer complaints for three of the years I was on my line. And for most of the time I was employed, I had an almost perfect attendance record."

When he finishes, Jake notices there is a crack in the ceiling where Gates has been looking. Francis X. O'Connell and Joan Fusco are scribbling notes to each other at the prosecution's table. Something that John G. is saying is setting off bells for them. They seem excited, pumped, hyped, ready for action. Jake feels vaguely ill.

"Did there come a time, Mr. Gates, when you stopped working for the Transit Authority?" Susan has returned to the podium.

"Yes."

"Can you tell us why that was?" She stands stock-still with her right knee slightly bent and her high-heel pointed toe down, like a dancer about to waltz across the ballroom.

"I was experiencing a severe depression because of the death of my daughter."

Fine, thinks Jake. Fine. She's eliciting information at the exact right pace. He wouldn't have done it any differently if he was counsel. Susan was the correct choice. He looks back at Dana, sitting in the second row of the gallery, and without quite winking he tries to tell her with his eyes that everything is going to be okay.

"Can you describe the circumstances of your daughter's death?" Susan asks.

"Objection." Francis is on his feet, buttoning his jacket.

Judge Frankenthaler looks at him in a daze, as if he's been awakened from a rich confusing dream.

"It's really straying far afield to talk about what happened to various members of Mr. Gates's family or parts of his family background," Francis says. "I don't see any relevance. He's not even the defendant in this case. Mr. Schiff is."

He points a bony accusing finger at Jake.

Susan walks in a half circle toward the judge. "It goes to the witness's state of mind at the time of this incident. That's the whole point of this hearing: to make sure he's capable of making an ID."

"All right, all right, but I don't need to hear a whole Homeric recitation of ship names," says Frankenthaler, already sounding fed up.

Great, thinks Jake. If he's pissed off now, how's he going to feel once the trial begins?

"That's my point exactly, Judge," says Francis, trying to seize the advantage. "Even in a preliminary hearing, there has to be some limit to the scope of the questions. Otherwise, we'll be here until next week discussing Mr. Gates's views about the 1969 Mets."

"I was a Brooklyn Dodgers fan myself," the judge grumbles.

"The jury still needs some foundation for understanding Mr. Gates's condition," Susan insists.

"All right, let me think about it," says the judge, shooing both of them away with the back of his hand. "Move on to something else in the meantime."

Susan crosses back to the podium, her blazer and dour black skirt making a quiet seething sound as they brush against each other.

"Mr. Gates," she says, "shortly after your daughter died and you left the Transit Authority, did there come a time when you became homeless?"

"Yes," Gates murmurs.

"NO!" Jake scrawls on his legal pad. "GOING TOO FAST! STRESS CITIZENSHIP!

"And at around that time, did you start experiencing problems?"

"Yeah . . . maybe a little bit before that."

"Can you describe those problems?"

Gates mumbles.

"Could you repeat that?"

"I was confused," he says. "I couldn't understand how things got the way they were."

"OY!!!" Jake writes on the legal pad. There's nothing intrinsically wrong with what Susan is doing. When you have a witness with a troubled history—whether it's with the legal system or the mental health system—you try to bring it out and cast it in the best light before the other side has a chance to ask about it. The problem is that Gates has a number of other strong points Susan could be talking about first: his family life, his work record, his determination to elevate himself after a childhood of abandonment and foster homes. Somewhere there's a backbone in there. Otherwise he'd be dead by now.

Jake looks at his lawyer with a bitten lower lip and a raised left eyebrow. Susan asks the judge to excuse her and then comes over to see what Jake has written.

She purses her lips and her brow folds over as she reads. Then she leans over and whispers in his ear: "Remember. I'm the one trying this case."

Having uttered the very same words five or six thousand times, Jake sees no way to argue. He slumps just a little in his seat as she goes back to the podium.

"Did there come a time, Mr. Gates, when you started seeing a city psychiatrist?"

"Right after I left the MTA."

"Did that doctor prescribe medication for your condition?"

"Yes." Gates reaches for a glass of water.

"What was that medication?"

"Haldol."

"And while you were taking Haldol, were you more or less lucid and able to make rational decisions?"

"Yes." Gates raises the glass to his lips and Jake sees the water shaking a little.

"Would it be fair to say you were aware of everything going on around you?"

"Yes."

"Objection." Francis stands. "She's leading him around by the nose with these questions."

"Sit down, Mr. O'Connell." The judge doesn't look up. "This is just a hearing."

Susan nods at John G., trying to keep him focused. "Do you have trouble recalling things that happened to you while you were taking Haldol?"

"No, I don't."

Jake looks over at the prosecutor's table, expecting another objection. But Francis and Joan Fusco are busy passing papers to each other.

"In fact, you're on Haldol right now," says Susan. "Is that correct?"

"Yeah."

The water glass goes down. Jake is relieved to see there's no other obvious shaking. The last thing he needs is for his lead witness to have some kind of breakdown on the stand.

Susan studies her notes for a moment before she starts the next line of questioning.

"Did there come a time, Mr. Gates, when you stopped taking your medication?"

There is a very long pause. Gates stares at her. Jake hears a crystal snap near his ear.

"Could you repeat the question?" Gates says.

"Sure," says Susan, trying not to sound thrown. "Did you stop taking Haldol at some point?"

John G.'s mouth fakes to the left, twitches to the right, and then hangs open for a second. "Yeah. Yeah. I did stop taking it for a while."

"And can you tell us why that was?"

Gates reaches for the water glass again. This time the shaking is much more pronounced. It's as if he suddenly developed Parkinson's disease. His right hand seems terrified of his mouth.

"I thought I was dying," he says. "I was raped at a men's shelter in Brooklyn and thought I'd been given the HIV virus."

The shaking is so uncontrollable now that droplets of water are appearing on the front of Gates's white dress shirt. Come on, Jake finds himself muttering through clenched teeth. Keep it together, man. A couple of months before, he was trying to put this guy in the loony bin. Now his whole future depends on John G. maintaining his tenuous grip on sanity.

"And so after that incident, you stopped taking your medication?"

"I didn't see any point," he says abruptly, as if Susan was the one he was angry at all along. "I didn't have anything to live for. My baby was dead. I didn't give a fuck."

With the rise and fall of his voice, the courtroom is silent again. The only sound is Gates slamming down the water glass on the railing of the stand. Jake's stomach groans as he leans forward to see if it's cracked. The judge thumbs his lower lip as if he's considering asking Gates if he wants to pause. But he doesn't. Gates just sits there, watching his left fist open and close.

"During this time, Mr. Gates, once you stopped taking your medication, did your behavior begin to deteriorate?"

Susan is on truly dangerous ground. But there's no way to avoid it.

"I was out on the street, living like an animal," Gates answers in a low, wounded voice. "What do you want me to say?"

A loose cannon. No matter how often you go over the testimony with some witnesses, you have no idea what they're going to say on the stand.

"Did there come a time when you became violent?"

"There were things going on in my mind that I couldn't control."

Jake turns around and sees Dana looking pale and shaken. He has the terrifying sensation of being on a roller coaster that's just broken free from the rails.

"And it was around this time that you first met Mr. Schiff and his family. Right?"

"His wife over there, she was my social worker." John G. stares at Dana, as if he'd like to lunge at her. "She was going to help me put things back together."

"But you never reached that point in your therapeutic relationship. Right?"

"I went off on her."

They're in free fall. Jake closes his eyes and waits for the crash.

"You began behaving erratically? Is that correct? You showed up at Mr. and Mrs. Schiff's house and acted in a threatening way."

"That's what they tell me." He gives Susan a surly glare.

"Did you menace Mr. Schiff's son with a box cutter?"

He blinks three times and lists to the right a little. "It's possible."

"And did you confront the whole family on the street, yelling that you were going to kill them?"

Gates just looks at her and blinks twice. There's no way around this knotty part of the case. So Susan might as well get right to it. She has to establish that Jake had reason to fear Gates and therefore it was understandable that he would act to protect his family. Yet she then has to come back and show that John G. is credible when he says Jake tried to stop the assault in the tunnel.

"I wasn't in my right mind," says Gates carefully, looking down at the brown oak railing in front of him.

A wave of heat hits Jake as if the temperature in the room had just risen a dozen degrees.

"So did there come a time when you began taking your medication again?"

"Yes." Gates puts his hands out straight and rests them on the railing, trying to steady himself.

Francis drops a pen loudly on his table, to register incredulity and perhaps to distract the witness.

"When?" Susan leans forward so far that Jake worries she's about to go crashing down with the podium.

"When Abraham made me start taking it. Like right before the thing we're going to talk about."

"Objection," Francis says.

"Sustained," the judge drones. "Let's get a move on, Miss Hoffman. The Renaissance is coming and soon we'll all be painting."

"Okay." Susan takes a deep breath like a marathon runner trying to pace herself for the second half of a race. "To the best of your recollection, were you back on your medication the night of September fifth?"

Gates rubs his right eye, then his left. "Yeah, I was."

Susan clears her throat. "So do you have any recollection of the events that took place on the night of September fifth?"

John G. stares out into empty space, as if he's grappling with some incorporeal presence in the courtroom.

"Yeah," he says finally. "I think I can recollect some things."

Francis starts to stand and object, but then waves his hand as if to say, Ah, never mind.

"On the night of September fifth, where were you living?"

"In the tunnel with Abraham."

"You're referring to the Amtrak train tunnel under Riverside Park. Is that correct?"

"Yes, it is."

"Did there come a time during the course of the evening of September fifth, when you saw my client, Mr. Schiff, in the tunnel under the park?"

Gates shifts his gaze over to Jake. Their eyes meet for just a second, but it's still jarring. This man doesn't like him, Jake realizes. Doesn't care about him. It's only by force of circumstances that he's the one who could end up saving Jake's neck.

This is it, thinks Jake. This is where John G. is going to lose it once and for all.

"I seen him a bunch of times," says Gates slowly, still looking at Jake.

He stops and seems ready to leave it at that. Susan looks down nervously, trying to come up with another question to prompt him.

"But only once in the tunnel," Gates says suddenly, his timing throwing everyone off.

"I see," says Susan, trying to fall into his rhythm. "Can you tell us who was with Mr. Schiff that night you saw him in the tunnel?"

Again there's a long pause, this one even more nerve fraying than the last. Listening to this testimony is like watching a drunk lurch around in the dark. Gates looks blank. Jake could swear he's about to say he didn't see anyone with him that night.

"I think there were." Gates puts a hand in front of his mouth and rests his nose on his knuckles. "I think there were a couple of other guys with him."

The stenographer, who wears patent leather high heels and a tumbleweed of black hair, throws up her hands in exasperation.

"Could you speak up?" Susan asks.

"There were some other guys with him," says John G., raising his voice just a little. "Two of them."

"I see. Can you describe them?"

Gates looks thoughtful and then startled, like he's suddenly realized one of the men was Abraham Lincoln. "One of them was bigger than the other," he says.

"Can you say more?"

"Hmm." He looks around the courtroom, as if he's making sure Philip isn't there. "Well, uh, I guess the bigger one, he was older. He had, like, light-colored hair, you know. I didn't get that good a look at him. Actually. Huh." He seems to lose his place for a second. "He was kind of solid like."

Jake looks at the judge. He's massaging his temples. Is he buying this or getting ready to throw it out? It's hard to tell. The vagueness of the description might actually work in Jake's favor, as it shows the witness wasn't overly coached. On the other hand, there seems to be a thickening cloud of ozone forming around the witness stand, as Gates grows more tentative in his answers.

"The other guy was smaller," he's telling the judge and Susan. "I don't remember much about him. Except he had a baseball bat. I remember the baseball bat."

He touches his midsection where he got walloped and then jerks his head back. He doesn't seem assured that Philip isn't there. Instead, he stares at a bald moustachioed attorney named Howard Jaffee sitting in the back row, as if he's a potential conduit to Cardi.

"Can you describe what happened that night?" Even Susan's sounding tense. "What did the men say to you and Mr. Collingwood?"

"Jeez." Gates's eyes open wide and his jaw goes slack. Where to begin? "I remember Mr. Schiff over there, he told me to leave his family alone."

"And then what happened?"

"They attacked both of us with the baseball bats. They hit Abraham over the head with the bat. Then there was a spark and that was it."

"Right. But what was said before that?"

"I just told you, he said, 'Leave my family alone,' " Gates says, turning testy.

"But what did the other men say?" Susan asks, with carefully measured patience.

"How the hell should I know?"

The judge's fingers stop their massaging. He looks directly at Susan, as if he's about to ask whether this should be declared a hostile witness.

Gates begins to list to the left. "There were words," he says in a flatter voice.

"What kind of words?" says Susan, struggling to get back on track.

"They . . . He . . ." He stops, grimaces, and looks up. He seems surprised to find himself in the witness box. "They had words with each other."

Jake is no longer watching from the analytical lawyer's perspective. His heart is on a bungee cord.

"It's hard for me to think of it all . . . It was dark down there . . ."

"To the best of your recollection," Susan says evenly.

Gates's mouth goes one way. His eyes go the other. "I dunno. I dunno."

He's still struggling with that invisible presence.

"Mr. Gates. Please. Try."

"They said something, then Abraham said something." He appears as much annoyed with himself as with Susan. "Then they jumped us with the bats and there was the spark. That was it."

This won't work. "What about Philip blinking the flashlight?!" Jake scrawls on his legal pad. If he mentions that in subsequent testimony, it will seem like an inconsistency. But it's too late. Susan is too busy trying to bail out the sinking boat of this testimony to look his way.

"Was Mr. Schiff one of the people who attacked you?"

Gates looks over warily, as if he's never seen Jake before. He starts to say something that sounds like "yeah," but then catches himself.

"He didn't have a bat," he says. "The others had them. He didn't."

An unexpected moment of relief. Jake rubs his aching eyes. At least Gates doesn't have him leading the charge. But only one wheel of the plane is down on the runway. The fact that Jake was standing there still makes him party to the assault and the homicide.

"Mr. Gates," says Susan, taking a long beat, "do you recall if Mr. Schiff actually tried to prevent the attack?"

A large bubble of saliva forms between Gates's lips. It lingers for a moment and then breaks. "Yeah, okay," he says unconvincingly, as if making a deal with his invisible adversary. "He tried to stop it."

"Do you recall his exact words?" Susan tries to strengthen his resolve.

"What?"

"Do you recall the exact words or gestures he made to halt the attack?"

John G. stares at her as if she were an eighteen-wheeler bearing down on him. His lips move but no words come out.

"Mr. Gates?"

He reaches for his water glass, but his palsied shaking is too much. The water is leaping over the sides and splashing over the rail before him. He's having some kind of breakdown right here on the stand.

"Would you like me to repeat the question?"

Gates's whole body is shivering and his lips appear blue.

He mutters something that sounds like "I don't even wanna be here."

Jake is looking hard at him from counsel's table twenty feet away, but he can't get Gates's attention. His chest tightens and his left arm goes numb. Is he about to have a heart attack right here in the courtroom?

"Mr. Gates? Could you please answer the question?"

A harsh noon sun slants through a window high on the courtroom wall. Gates turns and blinks into the white light, as if reconsidering something. He still doesn't answer.

A clerk drops some papers into the judge's basket. A phone rings in the background.

"Anything else, Ms. Hoffman?" asks the judge.

"Not unless you got any good ideas," says Susan.

"So on a scale of one to terrible, how do you think we did?" Jake asks, trying to catch his breath and get the feeling back in his arm in the hallway afterward.

"Almost completely terrible."

For the first time, Susan is starting to look depressed. Dark circles ring her eyes and her lips look dry and ragged.

"If I were Francis, I might even skip the cross-examination," she says. "He's already made it to the barn. The judge sees Gates is a space cadet. All Francis has to do is put his homeless guy, Taylor, up on the stand and have him avoid saying he's Gandhi."

"You think he'll leave it at that?" Jake asks.

A knowing, wary smile cracks the dry lips. "No way. I've worked with guys like Francis all my life. Everything's win, win, win and football metaphors with them. It's not enough for them to make it into the end zone. He's gotta spike the ball and do the dance."

"Good," says Jake. "Then we stand a chance."

Francis begins his questioning coolly. He asks Gates about his history of arrests, drug taking, and sessions with psychiatrists. He even breaks out the transcript of the Mental Hygiene hearing and the police complaint Jake swore out against him. Oddly, the more hostile questions are, the more focused and aware Gates seems.

"Why do you think he would call you a menace?" Francis asks.

"Maybe he didn't really know me," Gates says with the beginnings of a sweet smile.

This kind of comeback doesn't sit well with Francis. He somehow decides Gates isn't respecting him, so he steps up the attack.

"Isn't it true that when you were living on the street, you went around telling people you were being pursued by parasites and flesh-eating ghouls?" Francis asks, studying a new sheath of papers.

"Just parasites."

The judge laughs out loud. Francis grows rigid and tight lipped.

"Didn't you almost cause a major subway collision because you thought you saw someone standing on the tracks?"

"That was before I started taking my medication."

"Well, Mr. Gates," Francis says. "You've already testified under oath that you've been a crack addict, a mental patient, and a person who's experienced hallucinations when you fail to take your medication. Why should we believe your account of what went on in the tunnel the night of September fifth?"

"Because I'm telling the truth."

"I see." Francis turns away, running his tongue over his upper lip. "Did it ever occur to you that you might not know what the truth is?"

Gates gives the judge a quizzical look as if to say, This is all getting too metaphysical. "Could you repeat the question?"

"How would you know what the truth is?" says Francis, spreading out his hands and making it as simple as possible.

Gates just stares at Francis's hands and doesn't speak for a long while. A side door squeaks. Jake looks at the empty jury box and then glances back at Dana, thinking you can never tell what's going to happen in a courtroom.

"I never lie," Gates says.

"Never?"

"I've eaten out of the garbage, I've slept on the street, I've robbed old ladies to get money for drugs. But I don't lie."

"I see." Francis smiles thinly. "So did you take money for your daughter's shoes and use that to buy drugs too?"

"No, I never did that."

"But did you continue to take drugs after she was born?"

"Yeah," Gates says sheepishly. "But not that many then. Just some speed to stay awake when I was doing double shifts and maybe a joint once in a while."

Francis is pacing back and forth in front of him, lost in a kind of vicious rhythm. Jake recognizes it as the state he'd work himself into while he was trying to destroy a witness with hammer and tongs.

"So I guess you'd just steal grocery money to buy drugs and that wasn't lying," says Francis.

"No. I always told my wife when I was stealing it."

The judge gets a laugh out of that, taking it as a Willie Sutton kind of line. For Gates, though, it's just a matter of simple conviction. Francis's posture grows ever more tense and resentful.

"Mr. Gates," he says, drawing himself up with sneering disgust. "Would you have described yourself as a good father while your daughter was alive?"

Gates seems depressed by the question. "Yes. I guess so."

"Even though you were taking drugs from the time she was born?"

"Yeah."

Francis hitches up his pants and throws a half sneer at Jake. Watch me now, sucker. "Tell me, Mr. Gates, is it not a fact that you told city staff psychiatrists that you blamed yourself for her death?"

Gates stares down at his knees. "I felt that way for a long time."

"And do you still feel that way?"

"I guess."

Jake hunches his shoulders and glances back at Dana. She shrugs. She'd always suspected that was part of what was bothering John G., but he'd never told her so outright. Francis's notes must be from a shrink who interviewed Gates right after he left the MTA. Damn, Jake thinks. Francis did his homework on this witness.

"Can you tell us why? Why you blame yourself?"

Gates's mouth twitches the way it did when Susan was questioning him. "It's . . . it's kind of hard to explain. I don't know if it makes sense."

"Why don't you give it a try?" Francis smiles as if he's doing John G. a favor.

Jake leans forward in his seat. Where is Francis going with this? Is he going to try to impugn the witness by blaming him for his own daughter's death? It's a risky strategy that might backfire with this judge.

"I was working all these double shifts," Gates begins slowly. "Because we were gonna move and needed the money. I started doing a lot of speed so I could stay up all the time. Also—you know, I'm trying to be honest here—I still kinda liked getting high . . ." He stops and puts a hand over his chest.

"Go on."

Francis seems pleased with the way the witness is rambling. There's a destination, though, and he's leading Gates there.

John G. blinks to rouse himself. "So my wife," he says, "she was getting all stressed because she was the only one with the baby most of the time and she was still working a few days a week at the DMV. And instead of day care, she ended up leaving Shar with her sister Jo once in a while. Because it was family."

"Her sister was a junkie. Is that correct?"

"Yeah."

"She was present with you at the time of your daughter's death. Isn't that right?"

Gates closes his eyes and then opens them, as if there's something he doesn't want to see in front of him. "Yeah."

"For which you blame yourself. Correct?"

Long pause. "I blame myself."

He sits in the witness box, with his head thrown forward and his shoulders shaking slightly.

The judge looks at Francis sideways, as if to say, All right, you've made your point.

The accident, Jake thinks. We should have thought more about the accident. Rolando had only discovered the truth about it within the last few days. Gates and his wife left their daughter at her sister Jo's apartment in the Kingsbridge section of the Bronx. They must have known it was a bit of a risk, but they were both working, and in the later reports the Child Welfare people agreed the sister was a good soul within the narrow parameters of junkiedom. What happened wasn't really anyone's fault.

They were just crossing the street at dusk, that was all. Going from one side of Bailey Avenue to the other, where her daddy was waiting for her after work. The light was green and then it turned red. The little girl let go of her aunt's hand and went running to her father. And a Pechter Fields bakery truck going forty miles an hour knocked her down. That was all. Just an everyday accident. The little girl insisted on getting up and trying to walk again before she collapsed again. She died from internal injuries at North Central Bronx Hospital. The aunt killed herself with a drug overdose three months later.

Up on the stand, Gates is absolutely coming apart. The shaking shoulders have given way to crying. His fingers wriggle on the railing. And his face turns bright red.

"See what happened was, the light was green before it turned red," he says, trying to continue. "And I keep thinking maybe if I'd just gone then and crossed the street, I could've gotten her. But instead I just stood on the corner. 'Cause I was watching her and thinking how lucky I was. She was so beautiful. My life was so beautiful . . . And then it was over. I had her in my arms and then she slipped away."

Tears are streaming down his face. Jake looks back and sees Dana is crying too. Maybe they should just ask for a recess before the witness completely self-destructs.

But Francis has come up with a unique way of finishing the job without pissing off the judge. Instead of using dynamite, he's decided to smother the witness in velvet.

"So," he says gently, "looking back, from your current medicated vantage point, how realistic is it that you could have saved your daughter?"

"I don't know." Gates sniffs.

"Well, it was an accident. Right?"

"I don't know. I keep thinking maybe if I did one thing differently that day, she wouldn't have died. Like if I hadn't stayed at work to make a phone call. Or if I'd run my train closer to schedule. Or if I hadn't shaved that morning. I would've been standing there on the corner a little earlier and then I would've been the one to cross the street first. And she wouldn't have had to come running to me like that. And I would've taken her by the hand and we would've gone on with our lives the way they were."

"So you still feel it's your fault your daughter is dead. Right?"

"Sometimes I think about getting in front of a train or a car myself," Gates says, wiping his face with a Kleenex and fighting hard to get control of himself.

"But you know that's not going to make a difference. Right?"

"It's how I feel."

"But you know there's a report from the police and Child Welfare saying no one was at fault. Don't you?"

"Doesn't matter," Gates says, drawing himself up rigidly. "It's still the way I feel."

"So sometimes the way you feel is more important than the reality of a situation. Is that correct?"

"Sometimes," Gates says before Susan can object.

"Then why should this court believe you when you say you know what happened the night of September fifth in the tunnel under Riverside Park? You don't seem to have a very firm grip on reality, do you?"

The fingers stop wriggling on the railing. The jaw sets. Gates takes a deep breath, as if he's reaching down deep inside himself for something he's never been able to find. Then he looks Francis right in the eye.

"I know what happened," he says in the steadiest voice Jake has ever heard him use. "I saw that man"—pointing to Jake— "step between my friend and the guy with the bat. I heard him say, 'All right, guys, let's leave.' And then I saw them knock him down and hit him when he tried to take the bat."

There's dead quiet, except for footsteps outside and the echo of a door closing down the marble hallway.

After all these years trying cases, Jake is amazed the cliché still holds: the sound of truth is unmistakable in a courtroom. It's like hearing a gunshot for the first time. You may not be able to describe it exactly, but you know it when you hear it.

Francis whirls on the judge. "I move that his answer be stricken as unresponsive."

"You opened the door and invited him in, Mr. O'Connell." Frankenthaler shrugs. "It's too late to pull back the hors d'oeuvres tray."

"Isn't this burst of recovered memory rather convenient?" Francis asks Gates, his voice dripping with acid sarcasm.

"You can try tearing me down or pulling me apart." Gates raises his chin, as if he's daring Francis to take a swing at it. "You can't take any more from me than what's already taken. I'm still a man. I know what I saw."

For a split second, he looks past Francis and past Jake at the defense table to Dana in the front row. Something seems to pass between them, but it's gone by the time Jake turns around to look at her.

"Any further questions?" the judge asks Francis before looking down to sign some papers.

"No. That will be all." He nods to the stand. "Thank you, Mr. Gates."

82

Two days later, Philip Cardi goes to see his attorney, Jim Dunning.

He finds his lawyer pacing back and forth in a cramped, windowless lower Broadway office, a filterless Camel burned down to the nub in his right hand. A poster on the wall shows a huge finger pointing and says SOMEONE TALKED!

"You know how there are times when people say, 'Relax, don't worry, things will work out okay'?" says Dunning, dragging hard on his butt. "Well, this is not one of those times. Okay? This is a time for concern. This may even be a time to be anxious. In fact, if you considered getting an ulcer before, this may be the time to develop one."

"Why?" says Philip, trying to settle into an uncomfortably narrow seat with a maroon vinyl cushion. "What's going on?"

"Is this me talking? Or is this them talking?"

"Whoever. What are they saying?"

"You know. They're pissed. They're asking for a dismissal on recommendation for the case against Schiff. Apparently their bum blew our bum out of the water at the Wade hearing. Our guy Taylor couldn't even make a positive ID of Schiff. He showed up in court high on angel dust."

"So why is that my problem?" asks Philip, noticing his left armrest is loose.

"Philip, they're talking about throwing out the case and starting over with you as the defendant." Dunning stubs out his cigarette. "They don't just want to throw the book at you, they wanna throw the whole friggin' library."

"How can this happen? I was their lead witness." Philip sags to his right and the other armrest breaks.

"Well, you're not anymore. They're probably going to charge you the day after tomorrow."

Philip finds himself gasping for air. The walls and ceilings of the room seem to move a little closer. SOMEONE TALKED! A hundred years before, sweltering immigrant hordes had suffocated and rotted from disease in tight airless rooms in this neighborhood; today he's the one dying.

"So what kind of case do they have?" Philip asks.

The lawyer sits down at his desk and looks at the file, the fingers of his right hand splayed across his ruddy forehead. The posture of the professional man about to deliver bad news.

"They've already got this homeless guy Gates saying you did it. And I understand from Francis that your cousin Ronnie isn't exactly steady on our side."

"Figures," Philip grumbles. Ronnie has a line of drool where his spine should be. He'll go whatever way the wind is blowing.

"But what's really going to kill us is they're probably going to get Schiff to testify against you." Dunning takes off his wire-rimmed glasses and rubs his eye sockets. "And I have to say, he's going to make a very powerful witness."

"But—"

"They're pissed off, Philip," his lawyer interrupts. "They think you screwed them. The girl in particular, Fusco. She's very upset. With the way you misled them. This is them talking. It's not me."

Philip starts cracking his knuckles. "What's gonna happen?"

"Looking at it objectively, your situation is not good." The lawyer frowns and puts his glasses back on. "The DA's not interested in taking a plea from you since you've apparently lied to them already. Schiff's people have the name of a girl who they say you almost killed in a warehouse about twenty years ago. That's a crime you didn't tell them about, which effectively scotches your plea agreement."

"They say anything about my uncle?"

"No. So you might still have a little leverage there if you agree to testify against him immediately. But you're still looking at serious time for this murder in the tunnel. Just a bit less time if you roll over on Carmine. Francis's best offer is still eight and a third to twenty-five."

Philip becomes very still.

"I can't do prison time," he says.

"I understand how you feel. Maybe we can knock this down to manslaughter. It sounds like there was provocation."

"You don't understand. I cannot do prison time." Philip's eyes remain steady. "I will slit my own throat before I spend another day locked up."

"Why? What's the big deal? You already have a record. You've been away before. You must know people inside."

Philip doesn't say anything for a minute. He has the look of a truck driver who's seen too many white lines go under his wheels.

"I did a stretch when I was younger," he says quietly. "And some things happened to me in there."

"Yeah, like what?"

"Things I don't like to talk about."

Philip crosses his legs and folds his arms in front of his chest. He can't go back. Going back means he'd have to become what he can't accept.

"So what are my options?" he asks his lawyer.

"Options? What options?" Dunning looks down at his desk as if all the papers had suddenly changed places on him. "I just told you. They have three strong witnesses against you, physical evidence, and an office full of prosecutors who think you made them look like assholes. Pack your bags, my friend. You're going."

SOMEONE TALKED! The finger on the poster is pointing right at Philip.

"There's gotta be another way." He pulls on his ear.

"Philip, I have to be honest with you. You've lied to them and now they're going to get you for it. As long as they can pin this tunnel murder on you, they're going to put you away for as long as they can. You have to start preparing yourself."

A curdling rage turns inward and a burning compressed gas

forces its way up through Philip's stomach into his chest. It's not indigestion from the heavy lunch uptown. It's sickness. Sickness of the soul. Sickness of life. He sees himself on an opera stage, a tragic figure in whiteface, being dragged down to the bowels of hell by faceless demons. He's always secretly thought of himself as too large a presence for the mundane world he moved around in—the tar roofs, the long drives on the Long Island Expressway, the humiliating dinners with Uncle Carmine on Todt Hill—but even that world is about to end. A black despair begins to poison his very being.

No. He won't allow it. He won't allow things to be done to him again. He looks at the wall over his lawyer's head. Law degrees, courtroom sketches, and just over to the left, a group of citations from the USMC. United States Marine Corps. All this time, he'd been thinking his lawyer was just some drunken hack. But there they are: the Purple Heart and the oak-leaf cluster, the Bronze Star. Symbols of courage and valor. The values men lived and died for.

Nothing in life is achieved without risk, Philip reminds himself. He's done courageous things before to get out of trouble. Now he looks inside himself, trying to find that nerve again.

"What if those witnesses didn't testify?" he asks. "What if Schiff decided he wasn't going to cooperate? Think we'd stand a chance?"

"I don't see how that's in Schiff's interest. Then he'd still be the one on the spot."

"Well, he might change his mind." Philip turns up his palms. "People are funny that way."

83

At three-thirty that afternoon, Philip Cardi shows up at the Schiffs' house in his red Dodge van. He parks on the south side of West Seventy-sixth Street and gets out carrying a blue toolbox. It's a bitterly cold afternoon three days before New Year's. The air hurts. Philip goes up the steps to the town house and tries the key that Jake gave him on the front gate. But the locks have been changed. He curses and looks up at the pink-and-gray smoke sky.

A garbage truck rumbles by and a blonde woman in thigh-high suede boots teeters past walking a dachshund. Philip opens his toolbox and takes out a small pick set in a black vinyl case. He unzips it and finds the right file for a Medeco lock. While he's inserting it, one of the neighbors, an old man with an egg-shaped head and thick glasses, comes out to watch him. Though it's the middle of the afternoon, the man wears a flannel bathrobe.

"How's it going?" Philip says.

"I wasn't sure who you were at first." The old man points to the window he was watching from. "But I think I've seen you before."

"Yeah, I was doing some work on their chimney." Philip smiles. "You're right to be careful, though. There's a bad element in this neighborhood."

The old man goes back in his house just as Philip breaks the lock.

• • •

Jake, Dana, and Alex come home at quarter to five with the groceries.

"Now the thing I want to do first is attack the living room," says Dana, hanging up her shearling coat and reaching for the light switch. "We've been letting this house go all to hell because we thought we had this trial coming up. But we don't have that excuse anymore."

She flips on the light. Philip Cardi is sitting on the new George Smith couch with a copy of *Atlantic Monthly* on his lap and his feet up on the glass coffee table.

"Let's take a ride," he says.

Twenty minutes later, Jake is behind the wheel of Philip's Dodge van, driving the four of them across the Brooklyn Bridge.

A portion of his mind is still refusing to accept the reality of what's happened. Their lives are supposed to be going back to normal. They should be turning around and heading home. They've got no business riding in vans with men holding .357 Magnums. They're supposed to be having dinner at Café fucking Luxembourg tomorrow night.

Philip hums "The 59th Street Bridge Song." "Do, do, do, do, feelin' groovy . . ."

Jake glances off to the right, looking for the Statue of Liberty around the bend in the frozen river. Brooklyn approaches. The giant cargo loaders towering like dinosaurs over the piers. The Jehovah's Witnesses' Watchtower building. The old disused warehouses so ugly they're beautiful. A fading dusk light touches all of them, infusing this part of the city with a kind of bittersweet glory.

Jake tells himself he won't let this life slip away so easily. He's worked too hard, looked forward to too much.

A silver Integra starts to pass him on the left and he turns the wheel just slightly toward it. Maybe an accident is the way to get out of this.

"Counselor, look at me," Philip says from the backseat.

"What?"

Jake's eyes move up to the rearview mirror. He sees Philip grab Alex by the hair and jam a gun into his right ear.

"If you do that again," Philip says calmly. "Everybody in this car dies."

Jake straightens the wheel and listens to the hum of treads under the van. All of a sudden, he understands how John G. lost his mind.

By nightfall, they've reached Bensonhurst. Thirty years melt away before Jake's eyes. There are the same low-slung pale brick houses, the little bakery shops and espresso cafés, the social clubs on Eighteenth Avenue with the plaster saints in the windows and armadillo-skinned guys in dark clothes pacing around outside. It's still like a little Italian village, except with satellite dishes now, and he remembers how frightened and lonely he was growing up a skinny Jewish boy in nearby Gravesend. How bigger kids in gangs would rough him up after grade school and steal his baseball cards. How his father would beat him and embarrass him in neighborhood joints like Randazzo's. He'd sworn he'd never come back unless he really had to.

But as he glances out the driver's side window and sees two big-waisted guys in short thin jackets hauling a massive refrigerator off the back of a truck, he's reminded that there's something else about this place: its toughness, its harsh vitality, its sheer in-your-faceness. This is part of the real New York. The men and women who live here aren't a bunch of wan aerobicized Manhattanites, but people ripe and sweaty from the life struggle. Not just the Italians, but the new immigrants too: the Chinese, the Koreans, and the Russians. The streets here are bordered by real blood and muscle. And in some way, he knows growing up around this neighborhood made him strong enough to leave it.

"All right, pull up in front of the surgical supply store," says Philip. "But don't park near the hydrant. The last thing I need is a fucking ticket."

Jake stops the van in front of the store on Sixty-fourth Street. The prosthetic arms and legs in the window are arranged exactly the way he remembers them from the mid-sixties. All of a sudden, he feels like a small boy trembling before his father's rage again, trying to work up the nerve to protect his mother.

Philip pushes Alex out first and presses the gun into the empty-eyed Grateful Dead skull on the back of the boy's T-shirt. Then Jake helps Dana step down to the curb. He's never thought of her as particularly stylish or clothes conscious, but she looks completely out of place here with her beige ribbed Bloomingdale's sweater and her understated makeup. Welcome to Brooklyn.

The blood has drained from her face, but the corners of her eyes have turned deep red. The last time he saw her look like that was when Alex fell into an encephalitic coma for two days all those years ago. He remembers how he prayed and promised God he'd be a good man if he made his son well again. He wonders if he's being punished for not keeping up his end of the bargain.

A hard winter wind strafes his face and the sky offers no stars. Act, he tells himself. Don't do nothing. A man cannot go too far to protect his own family.

Philip leads them into the building through a glass door and an older woman wearing a blue cloth coat, a thick mask of salmon-colored makeup, and a brilliant corona of dyed black hair nods as she lets them in through the second door in the foyer.

"How you doing, Mrs. Tonetti?" Philip says, pushing the rest of them past her.

From upstairs, Louis Prima's voice floats down like a memory of another time.

Philip shoves Alex up to the second-floor landing and stands there waiting for Jake and Dana to catch up with them.

"I just wanna remind you," he says in a low voice. "If either of you try to run, I will shoot your son. If you try to grab my weapon, I'll kill all three of you." He looks over at Jake. "We understand each other?"

"Yeah."

There are two green-painted doors on the landing. Behind one of them is silence. Behind the other is the sound of an old movie on television. Jake hears pounding in his ears and realizes it's his heart beating the way it did that night he went up the stairs to face his father with the broken Piel's bottle.

"You don't love me," an actress is saying. "You don't even know what love is."

Philip opens the door on the right, revealing a small overfurnished living room with cream-colored walls and a wine red carpet. There's the same kind of smoked mirror above the couch that Jake's father once punched in the old apartment. An old woman in a black dress sits in a wheelchair right next to the four-foot-wide Sony color TV.

She turns and says something angry to Philip in Italian.

He ignores her and roughly pushes Alex and Dana into the room.

"Hey, watch it." Jake tries to step between them.

Philip shrugs and slams him over the head with the gun butt.

Jake falls to the carpet and blood clouds his vision. When he tries to stand, he finds he can't. There's terrible pressure on the right side of his head as if part of his skull's been crushed in.

The old woman in the wheelchair begins to shriek. Jake lifts his head to look at her and Philip kicks him in the face with a work boot. Blood and mucus explode on the laces and Jake begins to throw up.

"Let me let you in on a little secret, Jake." Philip looks down at him. "Gravesend ain't Bensonhurst. We used to kick the shit out of you faggots from Avenue X all the time."

The woman in the wheelchair begins to wave her meaty white arms and squawk like a great angry bird.

"All right, Ma, don't worry, all right?!" Philip shouts back at her. "Just go in the back bedroom and watch your program. I'll clean it up."

Jake senses Dana kneeling beside him, stroking the back of his neck.

"Get over on that fucking couch and shut up," says Philip, pointing the gun at her.

The old woman wheels herself out of the room. Dana goes over and sits on a blue-and-yellow striped couch next to Alex. Her mascara is starting to run. The Grateful Dead logo drips down the front of his T-shirt. Philip grabs Jake by the scruff of the neck and hauls him to his feet.

"What are you, a tough guy?" he says. "You think you're tough?"

He knees Jake in the nuts and carbonates his scrotum. "There, that's tough."

Jake's eyes water and bile rises in his throat again. He turns to his wife and child on the sofa. They look pallid and shaken, like a pair of passengers on a plummeting airplane. Dana rocks back and forth, her arms wrapped tightly around herself. Alex bangs his knees together.

"All right," says Philip. "Everybody into the bathroom. The party's over."

He sticks the gun into Jake's left ear and makes the three of them march out of the living room and down a short hallway.

The bathroom is completely pink. Pink tiled walls, a pink linoleum floor, even pink toilet paper and pink soap. Jake sees an enema bag with a long white hose sitting on the back of the toilet and a quiver goes through his stomach.

"You and you." Philip turns to Dana and Alex. "Go stand in the bathtub."

They look at each other and then at Jake, as if expecting him to somehow explain what's going on.

"Just do it!" Philip shouts. He takes the gun out of Jake's ear and points it at them.

Dana and Alex step carefully into the tub, ducking their heads to avoid knocking down the spring-loaded curtain rod.

Philip turns and locks the bathroom door. In a terrible moment of clarity, Jake understands what's about to happen.

"Don't do this, Philip. It's a mistake."

"Shut the fuck up, Counselor. You're not talking to some spic car thief about a plea bargain. I only got one way out of this and you know what it is."

There's whiskey on his breath, but he isn't just drunk, Jake realizes. Philip's thought about this. He intends to kill all of them and wash the blood out in the tub. Then maybe he'll take the remains and burn them in a Dumpster under the Manhattan Bridge. No bodies, no witnesses, no mess. All it takes is a stone cold heart.

"All right, get down on your knees in front of that toilet," Philip says, jamming the gun into the back of Jake's neck. "You're gonna show your family how to die like a man."

Jake starts going to his knees slowly with the right side of his head still throbbing. For the last half hour, he's been waiting for some brilliant strategy to occur to him. But since veering into the Integra on the bridge, he hasn't had a hint of inspiration.

"What do you need, an invitation to kneel?" Philip pushes the back of Jake's head.

Jake starts to shove him back, but then Philip kicks him in the back of the head, causing him to bang his nose on the porcelain rim.

"You fuckin' educated people can't do anything right, can you?" he says, putting the gun to Jake's head again. "You need somebody to do all your dirty work, don't you. You can't even fight your own wars or fix your own house. It's a wonder you can piss standing up without any help. Am I right?"

He glances back at Alex shivering next to his mother in the bathtub. "What do you think of that, junior, huh?"

Alex says nothing.

"You wanna come over here and suck my prick? Maybe I'd let your old man live a little while longer."

Alex mumbles something indecipherable.

"Fuckin' kids are useless," Philip sighs. "Don't you teach this one any respect?"

Tears sting Jake's eyes as he kneels before the toilet with the barrel of the gun burrowing into the base of his skull. He no longer feels confident that he will be alive in thirty seconds.

"Think of something pleasant," says Philip.

A Kotex commercial plays on the TV down the hall. Jake turns to look at Dana and Alex. It's too soon to die. He wants to see Alex grow up and decide his father's not such an idiot. He wants to grow old with Dana and enjoy afternoon movies and sunsets. He wants to tell both of them that he's sorry, that he loves them, that he didn't mean for their lives to end in the same kind of cramped airless apartment he tried so hard to escape.

From the corner of his eye, he sees Alex reach up with both hands for the shower curtain rod.

At first the image makes no sense; Alex doesn't do things like this. He's been shielded from violence all his life. His parents have always told him to run away from trouble on the street, to avoid eye contact with strangers. But here he is, almost in slow motion, pulling the rod down from its place between the two walls.

Philip starts to turn with the gun in his hand.

Alex swings the rod, arms fully extended the way Jake taught him to swing a baseball bat.

Philip turns the rest of the way and faces him with the gun barrel raised.

There's a collision of steel and cartilage.

Alex has smashed the middle of Philip's face with the stainless-steel rod. Blood sprays in an arc to the left and Philip turns to follow it, hands up to his broken nose. The gun flies the other way and lands on the linoleum floor.

Everything stops for a second.

It's as if the room has tilted and all the contents have shifted. None of them have adjusted to their new place yet.

But then Philip screams out and tries to reach for his gun. Jake dives on him and pins him against the bathroom wall. He punches Philip twice in the mouth and draws blood. Then he head-butts him. But Philip is still struggling hard. He pulls Jake's hair with his left hand while his right hand fumbles around for the gun.

Alex comes over to help. He grabs Philip by the throat. Then Dana grabs the gun off the floor and holds it on Philip, trying to keep him at bay.

But the sight of her with his gun is too much for Philip. With Jake and Alex holding on to him, he manages to stand and knock the .357 out of her hand. Then he punches her in the windpipe.

She reels away, gagging.

Hatred seizes Jake's heart. He tackles Philip and forces his head down into the toilet. Alex stands back for a moment, aghast at what his father's doing. But then he sees Jake needs help. He moves behind Philip, grabs him by the ankles, and tries tipping him face-first into the toilet bowl like a wheelbarrow.

Philip's right hand scurries around the floor, like a spastic spider, still trying to find the lost gun.

Outside, Philip's mother is ramming the bathroom door with her wheelchair and screaming again in Italian.

Philip's hand finds the gun. His index finger starts to curl around the trigger and his palm closes on the handle.

Jake gives a small terrified yell. If Philip gets control of the weapon, he will surely kill them on the spot. But then Dana comes over. His gentle loving wife. Who's cared for people all her life. She leans down and bites into Philip's wrist with all her might. He yowls into the bubbling bloody water and his fingers splay out. The gun hits the linoleum.

Philip's arms bulge, and veins and arteries boil out from his neck. His entire body jerks violently. The closeness to death has tripled his strength. Jake isn't sure how much longer they can hold him down.

Philip's mother is pounding the door with her fists and screaming out her son's name, like she knows she's about to lose him.

Her face contorted in fury, Dana stops biting Philip's wrist and comes around behind him to dig her nails into the back of his neck. Alex drives his elbow into Philip's spine. Jake holds the bucking head under the water. Die, fucker, die. It takes all three of them just to hold their own against Philip's wild thrashing. All this time, Jake's thought it's been his job alone to protect the family. Gradually Philip's shoulders start to sag. His neck muscles relax. Bit by bit the struggle is subsiding and strength is beginning to ebb away.

Philip shudders and gurgles. And then all at once, it's over. There's just a body with its head in the toilet.

The three of them back away, looking at what they've done. Everything is still. The only sound is the water running in the toilet tank. Jake feels his wife and son watching him, like they've never really seen him before. He senses their presence differently too. Something has changed between them and will never be quite the same. But slowly and cautiously, they move together again.

SPRING

84

A solitary man wearing a green Parks Department uniform on a windy April afternoon.

He stands by the entrance to a playground with a rake in his hands.

Through the gate, children are laughing, crawling in and out of the mouth of a steel hippo, and going around brightly colored pretzel-shaped slides. A yellow-haired girl in green overalls, about the age his daughter would have been, goes running across the asphalt, her hands flapping helplessly in the wind, into the arms of a black woman in a gray hat.

An elderly lady, her face creased and mapped with blue and green veins, sits by herself on a swing, as if she's been waiting years for someone to push her.

Grief, John Gates has realized, is not a song with a beginning, middle, and end, but an endless symphony playing infinite variations on the same theme. One part fades and another starts. But somehow the sun keeps moving across the sky and trains keep running underground.

He pulls the rake through the grass and sees a cache of empty red-and-yellow-topped crack vials by a flower bed. The daffodils and tulips are starting to bloom. The apple and cherry trees are bursting to life along the cracked old concrete walkways. Crocuses are pushing their heads out among the discarded cigarette butts and used condoms.

God is not merciful, he thinks.

God is not cruel.

God is not forgiving.

God is not vengeful.

God is not fair.

God is not unfair.

God just is.

Like a heart beating or a tidal wave or a summer afternoon or terminal cancer or a child laughing.

He looks across the river and sees the sun glinting off the Jersey shoreline, turning the buildings gold. A cool breeze ruffles his thin and graying hair. A dark-haired child stands ten feet away, watching him with a trembling lip. A little girl in pigtails, a purple dinosaur T-shirt, and pink sweatpants.

"What's the matter, honey. You lost?"

Her trembling lower lip threatens to pull the rest of her face down into tears. "I want my mommy."

He puts down his rake. "You want me to help you find her?"

She turns her body, shying away, not sure what she wants with him.

"It's all right. I won't hurt you."

He holds out his right hand. She looks at his face again, trying to find something past the scars and the hollow eyes. The grass shivers and the sun moves a shadow, changing the field's color. The past is the past. Somehow she connects with his sadness. She slowly takes John's hand and lets him lead her back into the playground. Inside, the other kids are screaming, scraping knees, flinging each other to the ground and picking each other up with brutal disregard and ill-considered tenderness.

God just is, he thinks. God just is.

ABOUT THE AUTHOR

Peter Blauner is author of the novels *Casino Moon* and *Slow Motion Riot,* which won the 1992 Edgar Allan Poe award for best first novel of the year. His books have been translated into twelve languages. He lives in Brooklyn with his wife, Peg Tyre, and their two sons.

CPSIA information can be obtained at www.ICGtesting.com

263332BV00012B/4/P